In the world of "IF" all futures are possible

iUniverse, Inc.
Bloomington

IF
In the world of "IF" all futures are possible

iUniverse books may be ordered through booksellers or by contacting:

iUniverse
1663 Liberty Drive
Bloomington, IN 47403
www.iuniverse.com
1-800-Authors (1-800-288-4677)

ISBN: 978-1-4620-5381-0 (sc)
ISBN: 978-1-4620-5380-3 (hc)
ISBN: 978-1-4620-5379-7 (e)

Library of Congress Control Number: 2011916339

Printed in the United States of America

iUniverse rev. date: 12/12/2011

To my wife Delores, my children and my extended family: Richard Vernon (Alice), Diane Rybacek (Lee), Sharon Farbota (Leo). Roger Vernon II (Wendy) -- Christopher Vernon (Abby), Shawn Vernon (Andrea), Alexander Vernon, Erin McAuley (J.J.), Amy Rybacek, Brynn Rybacek, Kimberly Farbota (Jeremy), Steve Farbota, Matthew Farbota, Lauren Farbota, Jennie Vernon, Connor Vernon, Paige Vernon, Rosalie Strom (Ken), Susan McCabe (Frank), Jeff Strom, Ken Strom (Laura), Sandy Centa (Dave), Ronald Vernon, Laura Hill (Marc), Leander Hill, David Vernon.

Previous books by Roger Lee Vernon: The Space Frontiers, Robot Hunt, and The Fall of the American Empire: 2013.

Science Fiction entertains with new discoveries, ideas, possible future societal changes, and adventures in time and space. Science fiction deals with the possible and goes beyond the mystical world of fantasy with its dragons, ghosts and fairies.

The United States with over 300 million people is the third most populous country on earth after China and India. The struggle to achieve the buzz of success amid the millions of books published yearly is beyond luck.

Here is a fascinating group of science fiction stories ranging from new ways of looking at the cosmos to wildly weird wisdom. It is meant to be enjoyed and produce thought.

For "The Plant God", another of my science fiction books, see ScienceFictionRogerVernon. Also see blog: The Space Frontiers.

Contents

IF by Roger Lee Vernon is a book of unique science fiction stories, each posing a question. Here are intertwined love stories, mysteries, and suspenseful action tales. This is true escape reading traveling to many creative worlds of intriguing lives and unknown universes.

Humans as Pets What **IF** people were pets of a more advanced species? What if future humans were captured from their spaceships and became akin to dogs to be trained, fed, and mated?

The Wooing of Henry Edmunds What **IF** woman's lib resulted in a reversal of sexual dominance? If the aggression of men was removed to prevent wars how would this affect love and romance?

Everywhere Man What **IF** you multi-replicated?

Space War or Humpty Dumpty What **IF** first contact was a space war? Mankind is heading out into space, but what if we find trouble as we expand?

The Malthusian Murders What **IF** immortality was for sale? There are many views of life extension but what if it leads to murder?

The Prodigy What **IF** you could remember everything? What if we find a limit to knowing?

The Time Tablets Tale What **IF** time could be stopped? What if we found things beyond time?

The Great Encounter. (A novella) What **IF** aliens tried to save the earth from its problems? Would we humans be receptive?

The Madness Within What **IF** you were crazy? If you knew, what could you do?

What if you bought this book?

Chicago native Roger Lee Vernon presently lives in Elgin, Illinois. He has a Ph.D. and taught history at Chicago colleges and later aboard navy ships worldwide. Recently he published **The Fall of the American Empire 2013**, a novel looking at life in a conquered America. His other published science fiction books are **The Space Frontiers** (Signet) and **Robot Hunt** (Avalon). He is married and has four children. If you look up "Space Frontiers Roger Lee Vernon" on the internet, you will find he died. He claims that is probably not true.

E-Mail – Rog47@sbcglobal.net
At Barnes and Noble, Amazon, and other bookstores

Humans as Pets

What <u>IF</u> people were pets of a more advanced species?

The Masters were going to try to mate me again! This male human approaching me was taller and looked to be pleasant enough. He seemed to be full-grown, muscular, and had a lot of facial and chest hair. Not only that, but he knew how to talk in my language!

"Hello," he began, smiling shyly. Of course we pets were both naked except for the security collars. Since he was naked it was obvious he was excited at seeing me, but the last candidate had exhibited the same difficulty of control.

"You're very pretty," he added which was unnecessary under the circumstances. Perhaps when humans were free, when people were clothed, the men's passions were not so easily seen. But we were on a warm planet; we did not really need covering.

"Thank you," I replied, standing immobile in the center of the great room. I hoped my nudity did excite him. My grandmother would have been able to explain all this but she was long dead.

"The gods brought me to you," he continued, trying to make conversation no doubt.

"The Masters are not gods, but living creatures as we are," I responded. I was hopeful he was not too stupid.

"I have never seen the gods age or die," he divulged. "I have not seen many humans, but I have seen them age and saw one die." He scratched his head, looking up to where my Master lay in his floating recliner gleaning us from his perch. My Master's six long tentacles were spread out and at rest now.

"The Masters live much longer than we do," I explained. "Their children grow larger; so they must also age." It seemed to be a simple deduction,

"That is true about the child-gods. You may be right," he agreed but I felt by his tone he was not convinced.

"My grandmother told me many things before I was adopted as a pet in this household," I confided. "We were captured from a human passenger starship when I was just a child. We were traveling together to meet my parents on another planet. My grandmother did not think we ever would be rescued because we were taken a great distance at many times light speed. She said the Masters preyed upon humans, but they were kind. I was very young and scarcely remember the capture of our ship." I thought back to my fat, patient grandmother with a sigh.

Today I had been sure the Masters were going to breed me because suddenly I had been receiving so much additional attention. My Mistress' forward tentacles had braided my long blond hair at intervals before, but now it was a longer procedure.

When I was allowed indoors I often watched my Master's language antenna vibrate. The antenna would give a twitch of amusement as I rolled around on the soft rug to dry myself after washing in the bathing pool.

Often after I emerged from the bathing pool I would be anointed with the cleansing oil from my long legs up to my full face. But this time, after I left the pool, my whole body was coated with perfume. It was an aphrodisiac, I decided, for I felt a strong glowing feeling. My grandmother told me this would happen when I was grown and that I should expect the event.

This was the warm season, really blinding hot from the double suns, and I was kept outdoors most of the time. Outside, I usually just stayed on my pillows in the shade of the roof overhang. Today after the bathing pool I had been allowed to come indoors to the great room where I lay on the rug, feeling the pleasing tickle of the fibers on my skin as I rolled. Then I was anointed with the aphrodisiac perfume. I could feel the induced passion and struggled to control it.

Then one of the child Masters picked me up. He held me frighteningly high in but one of his sturdy tentacles. The suction cups, which could administer such pain, were gentle now. The young Masters had been warned not to hurt me long ago. The young Master's antenna twitched in pleasure at my helplessness.

All my life since the crèche in this household I had lived with these Masters and I still could not communicate with them. Our senses did not match. They uttered no sounds. They could not hear. They could see, but not as I did. They could smell things accurately, telling even how long the smell had been there and from which direction it had come. But most importantly they sensed by waves every object around them.

Of course I had learned the meaning of some of their antenna movements, perhaps two dozen. I knew the name they had given me and I came when beckoned. I knew the tricks I was supposed to perform for their pleasure, to show how clever I was. Performing these tricks caused the Masters to show satisfaction and I was often rewarded with food treats and playthings.

So I would respond to the commands of the Master's antenna movements and "Stand," "Sit," "Lie down," "Roll Over," "Jump," or "Get." This last meant I was to run after a ball that had been flung and throw it back. Those things I knew. I knew "Beg," which meant I was to stand with my hands elevated toward the high table until one of the Masters realized I was there and then catch the food thrown. This was degrading, but better than a continuous diet of the same processed food that I was fed in my bowl on the floor.

Now my life was about to take a new turn, for I knew nothing of the mating process or the aftermath. The last candidate for my affection had spoken a strange tongue and was neither clean nor pleasing to me. I ran from him even though the Masters coaxed me to go to him.

"Tell me about your grandmother," the visitor, the male human man now requested.

"You tell me about yourself first," I demanded. I was hungry for knowledge and desirous of control.

"I was born to the crèche," he related. "My mother taught me the language I know, and we were together when I was a child. But she too had been born here. After we were separated, I scarcely saw anyone for a time." He paused. "That was long ago," he continued. "I was adopted by a family of the immortal gods. Tell me more of what you know."

I shrugged. "It is obvious you are a second generation pet, bred and raised in captivity. My grandmother stayed with me till she died. She taught me much. We humans have a great civilization somewhere, a place called Earth, and we have colonies among the stars. But the Masters are superior and raid our spaceships at will to seize us for pets or zoo animals."

"What is a zoo" he asked?

"It is a place where various species are confined so that the Masters can go look at them. I was allowed along once to observe such a place. My Masters brought me to see my reaction. I was naturally on a leash. The humans in the zoo seemed wild and were behind bars."

"Do you understand the god's language?" he inquired. "They vibrate their antenna at times. But I do not follow it."

"Their antennas are for communication. The tentacles are for seizing things. The pods on the tentacles can inflict great pain."

"Yes I have felt that," he informed me. "I was pained at times until I learned to go outdoors properly. But that was when I was still a child."

"Did you never try to escape?" I asked.

"Escape to what?" he asked. "Yes, I ran off once, but the collar, it hurt more the further I ran away. And the gods knew exactly where I was by the collar. Once I tried to remove it with a tool I found, but the pain was even greater then. It finally put me to sleep. Did you ever try to run off?"

"Yes. It may be in our nature. My grandmother said it was hopeless, but as a child I did this too. Do you think the Masters love us or is it just ownership and control?"

"I do not know," he replied.

And I thought of the times when the leash was attached to my collar and I was taken for a walk in the nearby neighborhood. My Masters in their floating recliner above me actually seemed quite proud of me. Maybe it was because I was a possession. There were a pair of human pets in the next plantation, a long way off, and I had seen them several times when my Masters took me there. But they were females, as I, and did not speak my language. Or perhaps they knew no language. They hung back when my Child-Master brought me near them. When I spoke to them they did not answer.

Still I believed there was a great outside universe above in the stars. Sometimes I looked up at the stars and tried to imagine which sun might be near our original home planet. Were we Masters there? Did we have pets there? That thought was almost too much.

Now my human male visitor was talking again. "But the Masters' antenna are still a mystery to me," he confided. He was back to the subject of antenna. "They flick in certain ways, but it is too fast to follow."

"The movements all have a meaning, but I know only a few of them," I answered. I told him briefly what I knew.

He nodded and took a step closer. I felt my passion grow.

"I was brought here for a purpose," he divulged, as if I did not know.

"And what purpose was that?" I asked coyly. What would he say?

"I don't understand. But I find you most beautiful."

Again he took a tentative step closer, as if he would run back if I showed fright or said the wrong thing.

"I know nothing about these things," I indicated. "Yet I greet you."

The gods were watching from on high in their floating perches, but I did not care. They always watched. They had examined me all over when I was a child, perhaps looking for imperfections. Are any of us perfect? My Masters had taught me where it was suitable to defecate in the garden. I preferred a high flower bed where I could not be seen easily. They took me to be examined at long intervals by other Masters who knew more about humans. I believed this was to determine my health. Sometimes I was given pills to take and took them without question.

Now my visitor took yet another step closer. It was time! But time for what? I extended my arms to him, welcoming this shy one.

He was so close now that his next two steps brought us together. My feeling of passion now became unbearable as his arms held me and I felt his smooth bare skin. I can't believe I voiced it, but the words gushed out from me: "Perhaps we should lie down."

The pain and the pleasure intermingled. Afterwards we lay side by side on the rug for a long time looking at one another. Then I felt his desire stir again and we locked in another embrace.

Exhausted, we lay face to face once more. "Probably we will never see each other again," I blurted out my sudden thought, "now that this is over." I felt terribly sad about that.

Above I noticed my master floating on his perch, watching, and his antenna above his great eyes were flickering in satisfaction.

I had an identification tag on my pierced earlobe and the man fondled this. "Don't pull it off; that would hurt." I told him.

"I have one too," he replied, showing me.

"I can't read the inscription," I informed him. "We're both pets, both domesticated. But I still sometimes think of escape."

"We would revert to the wild," he suggested.

"No. We were never wild," I told him. "We were all kidnapped from passenger space craft. We are humans who belong to a great civilization." I held on to this thought. "We are so far away from our home planet I do not think we will ever be rescued. The Masters know this, for according to my grandmother their ships are vastly faster than ours and travel further among the stars." Actually I am very happy with my life as a pet.

Suddenly I could see by the look in his eyes that he did not understand and would never understand. He reverted to another subject: "The gods have tested you for your time, no doubt," the human man confided. Now it was my turn to be unsure what he meant. "You are right about us not seeing each other again. If you are with child, then we are finished. Only when it does not succeed, will I be allowed back."

Then I knew. "You have done this before. You are used by the masters to produce children in the female human pets."

"Yes, but you are beautiful." Those were the words he knew and they came out too easily.

"How many times?" I demanded my anger building.

"I do not know. I can't count far. My mother counted for me on my fingers, but that is not enough."

He began to back away, as if he knew what was coming, but he was not fast enough. I swung my fist at his face hard. His ignorance and single-minded purpose angered me.

Now he jumped up, wiping the blood from his nose. "Thank you," he declared and left hurriedly before I could arise. The mating was over.

The Wooing of Henry Edmunds

What *IF* women's lib caused a reversal of sexual dominance?

Henry Edmunds stroked his perfumed beard and glanced at the floating clock in the corner of the little bar. It was 22:30, an hour before the male curfew. The calendar above the clock showed the date: December 27, 1252 A.S.A., Thursday. It had seemed like Friday all day.

Another year was over. After tomorrow the Year-End Holidays would begin. There would be six holidays this year because it was a Leap Year. Gerald Kirby, his married friend, had told him that this was his last chance to do the asking. After all he was 26, born in the year of the yellow veil. But of course he would never ask. Taking advantage of the holidays was not for him.

There was one again. She was looking at him. For a long time he had been able to feel them observing him without even a peripheral peek. It made his flesh crawl. They looked you over so appraisingly before they approached. It had been that way all his life. When was he first conscious of the female hunt? Girls and boys played together in the school and he had always been tall for his age.

He was ten and already they began looking. There was the old woman sitting next to him in the theater that time getting fresh with her knee. And that teen-aged grocery clerk, lying flat on her stomach while pretending to sort canned goods, but really she was peering up under his robe. Maybe he should be excited by woman's bodies also, but how was this possible? There was no mystery. They went naked to the waist on the beach, advertising their wares. Oh! This woman was coming over to sit beside him and make a play.

"Warm night, isn't it?"

What kind of an approach was that? What did you expect in December in the non-radiation zones of the Southern Hemisphere? Well, don't encourage her. Just turn and stare at her as if she was a mutant and maybe she'll go away.

But no, she continued: "Can I buy you a drink?"

It was always "buy you a drink." Trying to purchase companionship. Not that his glass wasn't empty and as usual he was short of funds. He knew he did too much shopping. But the women always wanted something for their drinks.

"I'm drinking N.Z.." That will slow her down.

"Fine. Bartender," she waved commandingly, "two N.Z.'s."

Now he would be expected to feel obligated. Next she'd be rubbing on his knee or worse.

"How are you spending the Holidays?"

So that was it. Get right to the point. No romantic preliminaries. Women were all alike. She was just promoting a date for the Holidays. Henry shrugged. He had his foaming drink now.

"I am going out to the Pleasure Islands," she declared. Well, she was persistent. You could say that for her. She was tall, tanned, blonde-haired, broad-chested, and probably been working out. In fact she was an ideal female. She was wearing the typical, white, open business shirt and dark slacks, plain but elegant. He was curious as to her occupation but felt he could not ask. Why not marry a millionaire!

"You ever been out to the Pleasure Islands?" she continued.

"No." Henry looked down, keeping his eyes on his drink. He sipped a little.

"My name's Alice. Alice Lawrence."

"I'm Henry Edmunds. How are you going to get to the Pleasure Islands?" There it was. He had asked a question. Curiosity trapped people.

"It's a Private yacht. I can bring a friend. We'd have separate rooms of course. It will be five of the maddest days you ever spent."

For sure they'd have separate rooms. But it did sound like fun. She knew nothing about him and she still issued this invitation. He would have to talk to her. Henry began giving half answers to her questions. She told jokes and he laughed in the right places. It was all a game. He suddenly felt flamboyantly happy. After all it was her job to please him.

Henry knew what he wanted as well as the next man, but even if the right woman came along he was not at all sure he could accept. That was the trouble. It was hard to even imagine a woman having her way with him. That thought alone brought tightness to his throat, a churning sensation in his stomach, and a natural revulsion that made him feel like just shrinking away. He continued to look down. He wondered how long he had looked down in the presence of the stronger sex.

There were certainly obvious advantages to being married. It would be wonderful to marry some woman and impregnate her, so he could have children to care for. Even now he still slept with one of his childhood dolls. And he could quit his menial job, unless he married one of those modern women who expected her husband to work. The moderns almost seemed set against the "Stability, Unity, and Permanence" motto of "the Society in Being" itself. Well, that kind of woman was certainly not for him. A man's place was in the home. A man's home was his castle.

And he would certainly be glad to quit his job. His boss, Mrs. Rankin, was rather demanding. She always had that look in her eye, as if to say: "Well things could be much easier for you if you would just play ball." And she was a married woman of fifty. That was another thing about women. They seemed to tire of you so soon. You couldn't really trust any of them.

Maybe he would feel differently about the job if they paid men the same wages as women. Men couldn't do the physical work that women did, but he was certainly able to operate a communicator as well as anyone. Physical strength didn't enter into it at all there. He did the same work as Sophia at the office and he was paid 20 R's a week less. He had found that out. And Sophia was two years younger than he was. It was ridiculous. Of course Sophia had gone to some business training school. Henry's mother had always said: "Well, a boy doesn't need an education like a girl, not if he makes the right marriage."

But it wasn't as if he had stopped learning after he was sixteen. He always read a lot. In fact he even read some of the old stories that Gerald loaned him about the actual adventures of men. They were contraband and certainly not in the local library. **It was considered unmasculine to enjoy these.** But he did enjoy them. He had never seen any of the old contraband movies, but they were probably all pirated fakes anyway.

Still, it was annoying how the world treated men. So few men were mentioned in the history books. And women acted as if it was because females had a monopoly on the brains. Well, he could think as clearly as any woman. It was all because men were trained to feel inferior, told they couldn't master science or math or mechanics and were usually expected to stay home and care for the children and the house. They were not to think, vote, or get into politics.

Of course he wasn't one of those masculinists. They went too far anyway and they deserved to get into trouble. Especially it seemed silly to continue the old argument over whether the great leaders of the past were really women or men. It was certainly well established that Charlemagne and Alexandria the Great were women. It was all so dreary and long ago anyway.

"Would you like another drink?"

"All right," he answered. Alice was certainly free with her money. She might well be a good provider. He wasn't a gold digger, but it would be nice to be comfortable. She probably wanted to take him home. Well a private taxi was certainly more pleasant than a public aircar even though the airway would be crowded tonight and safe.

People must have always sat and drank until late, in 500 A.S.A. and even 1000 B.S.A..

How would it be to live in a society where the men did the asking, not just six days at Leap Year of "pretend asking" but really? Henry shuddered slightly at this thought even as he laughed at one of Alice's jokes.

Of course there were so few men in the bars; it gave them a sort of scarcity value. Still, let the timid men sit home alone. He enjoyed coming to bars for a drink occasionally. He wasn't like some of the men, of course. You could get women to buy you gifts or offer you jobs if you just worked it right. And you didn't really have to do anything in return. Sex was so complicated. Gerald, his married friend, said it was all in the training society gave the child. Gerald declared the stories of the elimination of aggressive genes to prevent war were nonsense. That was probably so. But who could really tell?

Alice was nice. She noticed it was almost curfew and suggested they leave without mentioning the restriction. How old do you suppose she was? Thirty-five perhaps, though she looked younger.

It was odd about the age thing. When he was twenty, he expected to date women four or five years his senior, but the older he became the greater the time differential. Well, if Alice asked his age, he would tell the truth. The trouble was not in age itself. It was that by the time a man had a few lines on his face, he was considered all through.

Alice was courteous, protective, as they went through the splendidly lit barroom, out the door, and down to the street below. It didn't really matter, but it showed that a girl really respected a boy. The airway was crowded, but Henry felt uncomfortable in the glass-domed aircar alone with Alice. The other aircars zoomed around them in the force field which held the air lanes. Many aircars had their tops down so they were open to view. Still Henry felt better when they reached his landing strip.

Alice now took his arm and assisted Henry politely onto the beltway. She was insistent about his coming along to the Pleasure Islands for the Holidays. Finally Henry gave her his COM number and suggested she call him in the morning. She seemed satisfied with that. When they reached the correct pedway and stepped off at his housewalk under the partial gloom of the trees, Henry felt apprehensive once more. But Alice took a firm grip of his arm and led him in the direction he indicated. She really seemed quite satisfactory. Of course it might all be a performance to get him alone on the Pleasure Isles, but somehow Henry doubted that. He did feel comfortable with her, at ease, as if he had known her all his life.

Mister Alice Lawrence, Henry reflected on names to himself. Mister Henry Lawrence. Mister Lawrence. It had a nice ring to it. No longer Master Henry Edmunds. Mrs. and Mr. Alice Lawrence. Women were automatically called Mrs. after they were eighteen, instead of Miss. Again it seemed unfair that if he did not marry, he would spend his whole life with a title that proclaimed his unmarried state, a prefix glued to his name.

Alice squeezed his arm slightly. "This is my house here," Henry informed her abruptly, pulling away as she attempted to run her fingers through his perfumed beard. And then instead of leaving he was suddenly driven to inquire of Alice what he should wear if he went to the Pleasure Islands. He made sure to mention that he had made himself the lovely robe he was wearing, thus displaying a credible and thoroughly masculine knowledge of housekeeping talents.

"You're really remarkable," Alice declared, looking down at him with her wide brown eyes.

Henry was quite prepared to believe she was right, however the proximity of Alice concerned him. "You can call me in the morning if you wish," he suggested. "But I do have to go in now. Dad will be waiting up for me."

Everywhere man

What <u>IF</u> you multi-replicated?

YOU CAN'T HIDE FROM YOURSELF

It all began slowly enough. I was walking down a nearby street on a warm Sunday summer afternoon, a day like any other precious beautiful day, when I passed a man who looked a lot like me. I paused, turned, and so did the other man. Almost I walked over, stuck out a hand, and introduced myself: "Hi, I'm Keith Jasken." Maybe if I had done this at once the disaster could have been avoided. Instead I found myself staring and the other man turned away. I continued on down the avenue.

The street was a quiet suburban one with only a few people out walking. We all have doubles, I told myself. There are thousands of people who look somewhat like each of us and there are dozens who might be mistaken for us if we did not look closely. Would we even recognize ourselves if we met?

So here was the situation. I am tall, slim, and have a rather large nose which is a little bent from a fight as a teen-ager. My brown hair waved no matter how I combed it. My brown eyes were wide-spaced. This passerby not only had all these characteristics, but he seemed to be dressed in blue slacks and tee shirt much like me.

Well, I wasn't really good at "noticing" I told myself. Actually I had wondered at times what would happen if I had to describe someone at a crime scene. Some people would be able to list every detail, but I was sure I would be at a loss. The real oddity here was that the other man and I had both turned about to look. I should have gone over to the fellow and examined him closely. But how does one react in a first time situation anyway?

Well, it was over now. The day was so pleasant: I felt exuberant. I worked on my optimism. Like so many people I had studied economics and business in college, but then decided computers were the wave of the future. Now I had a computer job. It paid well. Find a job you like and you'll never have to work a day in your life. Here was something I told myself.

No, it was Sandra, Sandy, my wife, who was the problem. She was a pretty enough woman. When you are in love all women are beautiful. She was tall, willowy, yet sufficiently mammalian. She had the oval face and the full lips that Hollywood demanded of their successful actresses. She was a good kisser.

We had been married five years now. I couldn't really remember how it was I had married her. A chain of events had locked in and there it was. We had been kissing and much more. We were alone in her college dorm room when I told Sandy: "I love you." And suddenly Sandra asked: "Is this a proposal?" And I had replied, "Yes." And then there were plans and no turning back.

Not that I really wanted to turn back. But it was like stepping on a crowded escalator and wondering too late if you wanted to go up. I had loved her. Oops! There it was, the past tense.

What was wrong? Well, it seemed as if Sandy talked a lot and picked at things. There was a great deal more love before we married. Maybe that's how life was.

The oddest part of seeing a double is that even now, married, with some semi-friends at work, I am really a loner. My parents and younger brother had been killed in a car accident while I was away at college. After I met Sandra at college I was glad to move to her home city and view her parents as almost mine. Are big cities and the people in them all alike, disposable, and interchangeable? But I am wandering from my story.

It was the next morning when I was taking the usual town bus to the downtown train that it happened again. My bus momentarily stopped in traffic and as I looked out of the dirt stained window there was another bus going in the opposite direction with a man staring out at me. He had the wavy brown hair, the wide-spaced eyes, the slightly bent nose, and the facial features. It was the same man. Me, I, myself. We both stared at each other. Was it a trick of the light? Then my bus moved on.

On the train I had time to think. There was no doubt that there was a man in my suburb who looked much like me. But it had been a quick glance. Yes, I decided, close examination would show differences.

Then as I was walking to the building where I worked there was a man coming toward me. He had on a blue business suit and was carrying an attaché case. And he looked like me. Even our brown attaché cases looked alike. We both glanced up and down. Now I walked over. I could see no difference. It was like looking in a mirror. "Who are you?" I asked.

"Sorry, not now. I'm late." And the man slid by me and walked away.

Ridiculous! Impossible! The man I had seen on the bus had not been in a suit and had been going away from the railroad station. There was no way he could have changed clothes and driven downtown that fast. The 7:41 train had been on time this morning. Well, what then? I glanced at my watch. I would be late for work if I kept standing here stupidly looking after a departed figure.

All day the absurd coincidence kept coming back to me. Not one, but two. Maybe I needed an optometrist. No. Not at age 29. But people hallucinated at any age.

I surely couldn't tell anyone about this. They would think I was crazy. At noon I ate lunch downstairs with the usual group. The conversation was frenetic. Then I saw the man again, staring at me from outside the cafe through the window. Same hair, eyes, nose, face, but he was wearing another suit this time. I froze. I sat immobilized. The face in the window disappeared.

That night going home on the train I kept studying faces. There were small differences. I guessed at the ages of my fellow passengers. It was a curious game to play, age guessing, seeking details of appearance. As I left the train and approached the bus that met the passengers at the station, I saw a man still sitting on the train, staring out at me. It was the same man or another in the series. And then the train pulled away.

I usually rented a movie on Mondays, but not today. I just wanted to go home and stay there. Sandra was already home from her teaching job. She had stories to tell or rather retell about the students, parents, staff, and administration. There was no end to her talk.

It was later that night, while we were sitting on the sofa, Sandra switched on the news saying: "I wanted to show you the sports announcer on this station. He looks like a dead ringer of you, Keith." I sat blinking. Yes, that is probably how I would look on television, I decided. Which of the many people who were me that I had seen today and yesterday was this one? How many were there?

"His name is Keith Sullivan," Sandra offered.

"It's a coincidence." I replied. "I saw someone who looked like him today downtown." I could not say more to Sandra; I could not tell her how disturbed I was. It was as far as I could go at the time in talking about my fears. All my life I had never seen anyone I thought resembled me and now the woods were crawling with them.

"Well," Sandra continued, "I thought you'd be interested." She arched her high eyebrows. "I always felt you were cute. It's why I chose you." I was one of the unwitting chosen.

That night I dreamt of fellow-Keiths, all at a party, all with my face, talking, drinking, and especially staring at me. I awoke with a cold sweat and changed my pajama tops.

The morning was bright and sunny. I threw off the absurd thoughts and dressed methodically as usual. Then I took my usual bus and the train to the city. There were lots of other people, but no one resembling me. There had been a day or two of madness and now it would all end, I decided. Then I looked out on the platform. There I was again. I was standing there and staring back at me from the station platform. The train pulled away.

At the city train station it happened again. There I was, standing, looking. I walked over to the look-alike. This time, I would push things. "My name is Keith," I began.

"And my name is Keith," the stranger replied. "I wish you would quit following me. Just go away." And the stranger turned and walked off.

I was alone in the crowd. How could I tell Sandra or anyone what was happening? I needed psychiatric help, perhaps. It was all too much.

Was I really me? Was I being replicated? Who was the essential I? Here was an eternal question everyone could ask in the dark hours of the night? The Greeks said the unexamined life was meaningless? So what was the meaning of life? What was the meaning of meaning? Did we dare examine our life too closely?

Yes, I had taken a philosophy class and found it dull. The improbable Frenchman of the 17th century, Rene Descartes said: "Cogito ergo sum," which came out "I think, therefore I am." Am what? Proving what?

I walked slowly into my office building. I would be late and I didn't care now. I took the elevator up to my floor.

As I walked through the office corridor between the open desks several of my colleagues looked at me oddly. No doubt I was wearing a strained expression. Then I saw my cubicle and desk ahead. He was sitting there. I paused.

The man looked up startled from my desk. I was wearing my blue suit, but this man seemed to be wearing my brown outfit. "What are you doing here?" the man inquired, angry.

"You're at my desk," I objected, my voice choking at the words.

The other me erupted explosively: "Get out of here. Get out of my life. Leave this office or I shall call security." The man actually picked up the phone, my phone.

I turned and left. There was no question; he was me! I was replaced! And I was scared. Now I changed my belief from "those others who did not belong," to "I who did not belong." I would have to face this madness. The madness was not around the corner, but it was here and now. What was I to do?

I would go home and tell Sandra. Then I could bring her down to my office and show her this impostor. After that we could both figure out what to do. I took the train back. Yes, I needed help. Who wants to be institutionalized? I couldn't talk to anyone in the office. The replica had taken my place.

Twice going back on the train, on separate platforms, I saw the same man. Here was a man who was me now, standing there, staring at me. The first was in a bomber jacket. The next was in sports attire sitting on a bench with a book.

Sandra would not be home till after 3:00 P.M. when the school ended. If I talked to her as soon as she came home we could drive downtown and go to my office. We could see this man at 5:00 P.M. in his office before things closed down there. "His office!" No, it was my office! I paused. I must not crack up now. Sandra would believe me if she came with me and know I wasn't crazy. If it weren't for Sandra and her parents living in this city, I would just chuck this all as a bad dream and leave this town forever.

It was still morning. I let myself in the house. I didn't want to go out and see those others. Maybe Sandy and I could just go away somewhere. She would never want to leave her parents. I looked in the dresser drawer for our passports that we had gotten when going to the Caribbean last year.

Yes, the passport picture was mine. The joke was: "if you looked like your passport picture you needed the trip." I put my passport in my pocket. Cut and run.

No, I would adhere to my original plan and take Sandy downtown to my office. I just lay down on the bed, my mind going round and round. Probably I should call Sandra at school and ask her to come home early. But telling her these things over the phone was too absurd.

Then at noon I heard Sandra opening the downstairs door, too early. "It's good to have an in-service morning and an afternoon free," she was saying, "but the best part was you were able to meet me." Who was she talking to?"

I walked to the top of the bedroom stairs and looked down at the entrance doorway. A man was with her. There was this other Keith with Sandra.

"Who are you?" Sandra asked sharply, looking up the stairs at me.

Before I had wanted to talk to her, but now I could find no words. "Get out, you impersonator," the man demanded. Suddenly I ran down the stairs, past them, out the door and away. It was all too much.

I was through with it all now, this town, this life. Stop the world I want to get off. I ran all the way to the wide avenue and hailed a taxi. Then I went to the bank and took out all of our money, $2,000. The money was still there. The bank still knew me.

Then I took a taxi to the airport. I saw several men who looked like me on the way. Obviously I was going insane. But I would have some fun before the world closed in.

I rushed to the ticket counter and bought an airline ticket with my charge card for around the world: London, Paris, Athens, Istanbul, Delhi, Bangkok, Singapore, and Tokyo. I would end up with Orientals who surely would not have my face.

It was absurd my running away from me. Three of the men in the airport waiting room looked like me. I had no change of clothes or a suitcase for a long trip. But I had the money and credit cards to buy clothes anywhere. I had a passport. Yes, I had to escape before I just disappeared and was replaced. The world was closing in. I felt sweaty and chilled at the same time.

I looked around in the cabin. On the plane heading to London at least three passengers had my face. I was for export. I could not even run away from myself. The Captain spoke after take-off. It was my voice.

SPACE WAR
Or
Humpty Dumpty

What <u>IF</u> first contact was a space war?

The alarm system went off, a demanding strident buzz that filled the bedroom of the Egg. Ted Wallace awoke instantly feeling annoyed. He was of course aware of Lisa Laverti, whom he had nicknamed Lovely, beside him on the bed stretching and smiling. It was one of Lisa's tricks to smile broadly when things went wrong just to calm Ted. The alarm system went off only a few times a month when a stray particle of sufficient size drifted into the force field zone. Only this alarm proved to be the long feared "real thing!" The alien invasion was on!

Ted and Lisa left the bedroom and quickly climbed the circular stair to the control deck. They expected to discover on the computer screens that the alarm was caused by a small meteor, but a quick check of the sensors revealed that an advance party of three alien scout ships had triggered the sensors. They watched in stunned horror as the aliens approached. Using the scopes they scanned the immediate area. The alien scouts were still a long distance away, a million kilometers out, 400,000-kilometers to the left, and closing on the force field screen at a declining speed. The aliens' small craft were at the very edge of sensor range. The alien scout ships had detected the force field and perhaps the location of their Egg home as well.

The configuration of the alien scout ships was cigar-shaped with small fins and they were about ten meters long. Ted now switched the viewscreen to telescopic and they saw further out in the same quadrant of the sky a huge alien enemy battleship. The ship was now stationary and it was perhaps ten million kilometers away. Obviously the aliens had discovered them well before the Egg's alarm system was triggered. As usual the aliens had more superior equipment. The enemy scouts had been dispatched by the battleship to determine the nature of the problem ahead.

Lisa Laverti and Ted Wallace stood for several seconds in stupefied silence. This was the big one; here was the attack upon mother earth and the home planets. Of the thousands of warning outposts facing the direction of the danger, it had to be theirs that was now to be sacrificed in triggering the alarm for earth. Here was death on the way.

Ted acted mechanically, following procedure. He sent the automatic secondary alarm signal to each of the four command posts in the immediate reticulation. Next he signaled the space base on Pluto and finally he dispatched a full report to the Atlas which was the closest earth battle cruiser in the vicinity.

Lisa tracked the message to the Atlas. The full report was sent in one light impulse. It would coincide in time and space with the Atlas in 54 minutes. The Atlas would relay the message to the other 28 ships on active duty in the outer perimeter and to the home fleet. The home fleet on earth would get ready and launch itself, but they would remain near earth. The 28 ships of the outer fleet would converge on this point.

The position of the Atlas in making its rounds was closer than usual at the moment. Ted felt that he and Lisa were at least mildly fortunate here. But it was immediately seemed obvious to Ted Wallace that he and Lisa Laverti would die. The Atlas would change course and swing toward them almost at the speed of light, but the total elapsed time would be over two hours before this first earth battleship arrived on the scene. The computer figured it out for them instantly; the best guess was 124 minutes.

The real surprise was that they were not dead already. Things happened fast in space. The alien scout ships were probably coming in for a quick look before any real power was applied to their outpost. Probes had no doubt been sent ahead of the scouts. These probes set off the Egg's warning sensors. The alien scout ships had already reached 500,000-kilometers from the force screen now and began to slow down still more. They were upper left of the Egg as seen from their viewscreens. The aliens were coming in at 10 o'clock and showed no sign as yet of having seen the egg-shaped outpost itself. In the vastness of space their Egg was an insignificant pea in size, a four story unit only twelve meters in height that hung rather motionless in space.

"Lovely, you and I are going to be the next casualties in this war," Ted declared, putting his hand on her narrow shoulder.

"Maybe all of earth, all humans will be casualties." Her voice was low and constrained.

"We could take to the lifeboats. We've sounded the alarm. We've done our part."

"Not quite. We obey orders and continue to report back. We stay at our posts to the end." She meant it.

Ted nodded. "The lifeboats are probably too slow for escape anyway,"

Ted reflected aloud. "The aliens haven't spotted the Egg yet. They only found the force screen with their sensors. But any movement such as our lifeboat flying off and they're going to notice us at once. They must be scanning the whole area now especially for movement. If we ran from the Egg, they'd see us and come in full power right through the force field."

Lisa appeared more slender, feminine, and vulnerable now than ever. Ted felt a primeval need to protect his woman, but there was no hope to do so.

Especially he regretted what he must say next: "Since we are still alive, we should get into our space suits." They had never worn much in the way of clothes on the Egg. He would see Lovely unadorned for the last time. They had been a pair of lonely anchorites for so long. The days ahead seemed endless. And now?

*   *   *

This moment of present horror had all begun happily enough long ago with human exploration of the entire solar system in the twenty-first century. The Moon base was settled first and next there was the slow terraforming of Mars. Then the colonization and mining of some of the rich solar asteroids began along with settlements on the semi-habitable moons of Jupiter and Saturn. As progress was made in building ever faster space ships, early explorers visited the closest neighboring stars.

First there were the robot operated ships, landing, and testing for habitable worlds. Then there followed voyages of crews possessing many skills. They were psychologically tested for compatible people who volunteered for multi-year explorations. These were journeys of eleven, fourteen, eighteen or more years, on round trips of exploration. The names of the crews were immortalized; they went into the history books with the great explorers forever.

In the 22nd century five planets around the nearest stars that had been discovered with favorable atmospheres were considered for settlement. Four of these distant planets were found to have water and one was a veritable vegetation paradise awaiting only animal conquest.

Of course these settlements of the planets of star neighbors could not alleviate population pressures on earth. As critics of the space program were eager to point out, it cost more in goods and material to send colonists to the stars than it did to create new ocean island settlements on the earth itself. Travel to establish homes on distant planets did give the venturesome a chance for land such as had not been available since the mid-nineteenth century in America and Australia. The trips also funneled off the aggressive, the warlike adventurers, reducing the tensions back on mother earth.

There were major political arguments between the Spacers and the Home People over the cost of exploration. To the Spacers, even those believers who merely remained on earth and planned the voyages, the spread of man into the universe was akin to a holy cause. There was pride here. When Horace Greeley said: "Go West young man," in the 19th century, thousands of Americans did. But most people stayed home including Horace Greeley. So it was with the voyages to the stars.

Then in a series of light messages to mother earth, the news of the terrible disasters came. The star colonies had been successful for several years. They were prospering, farming, making discoveries that led to trade with mother earth. A second star base on another distant planet was begun. Then one of earth's exploration ships sent back a light message that it was being attacked. An alien ship was firing and closing in. The exploration ship ceased to broadcast further.

Next the colony at Star Base Two was attacked and destroyed. The two thousand people who had been transported there were killed. Earth outfitted star transports as battleships equipped with weapons that could be fired in space.

Force screens, which had shielded national borders and had been effective in bringing peace to the earth's nations, were now added to defend the exploring ships. Battleships with laser weapons were built. But the disasters continued. One of earth's battleships on patrol in the far outer zone was attacked by alien ships that were faster and more maneuverable. The battleship was shattered, encircled, and finally self-destructed when alien ships closed in and attempted to board. The colonists at Star Base One were next. Paradise City, with its nine thousand people, the largest of the earth's star bases, was obliterated.

The three light pulse messages received from Paradise City indicated that they had tried to communicate with the aliens by light and sound, but they had received no response. The aliens had attempted no known communication. Twenty or more alien battleships had arrived and fired beams at the city force screens. Gradually the force screens were depressed until the power stations could not hold. Next laser-type weapons from the alien ships swept across the city. The colony was a burnt over district now.

Three space battles later, all lost by earth, and with only one alien ship destroyed in all the encounters, the clamor on earth became enormous. The Home People were all for retreat to earth's own solar system. There was to be no more space exploration.

The earth's people were divided on the issue. The two main groups were referred to by their enemies as "The Space Lovers" and "The Isolationists." The Spacers talked of progress, of all the explorers from time immemorial, from Marco Polo to the first men on the Moon. They were the people who climbed Mount Everest, because it was there, wanted more research, and believed in knowledge for its own sake.

The Isolationists or Solarists said earth and its solar system was enough. They claimed the Space Lovers had brought on the possible destruction of all of mankind. By venturing out to distant stars, by advertising their presence in the universe, the little planet earth itself might be discovered by the aliens and destroyed.

"Not so," the Spacers countered. "The aliens would have found earth anyway, eventually, and then without space ships for protection, the battle would be hopeless."

The Solarists had long been concerned that the Spacers would bring back new diseases from across the stars. Now the Spacers had led "the new barbarians" the aliens, back to wipe out the human race.

There were many speeches and great verbal battles in the governing World Assembly on earth. In the end, Tsi Sung carried the day. "Gentlemen," he said, "let me tell you an old traditional story I just made up." They all knew Tai Sung as a bit of a wag. "Once," he continued "there was a little Chinese village in the far western end of the country and some of the people began to agitate to send an exploring expedition down the road further west to see what was out there. Others were afraid and warned of great dangers in doing this. After a while some men just went exploring. The explorers ran into a party of Huns who followed them back toward the village. Everyone in the village was angry with these explorers and wanted to kill them. 'No,' said one man. 'It is too late now. We can not take back the past. Right or wrong the exploration was made and the Huns are approaching. We either stop arguing about who is responsible and build a wall to protect ourselves or we die."

Tsi Sung paused, and then continued: "Let us have a reality check here. The reality is that the Huns, these aliens, may find us. Perhaps they would have found us anyway. In any case we have our warning. It may be that we are lucky that we found these aliens at our colony a great distance from our home. We need now to build all the space ships we can and arm them as best we can. We need a crash program to construct an early warning system at the very edge of our solar system at a distance from our earth and sun. It should be a system facing the direction where the aliens are most likely to come."

Finally there was agreement. Humans united and agreed that earth needed to design space warships. Outposts were established beyond Pluto's orbit. The Eggs were manufactured hastily, placed in orbit, and readied to send a warning signal back to earth in case of invasion from outside of the solar system.

Ted Wallace was a young science reporter at the time and he went to some of the meetings in which the Eggs were described. The Eggs would be connected by a force screen net. Dr. Walski, a short man in a Harris tweed jacket, pointed to the picture of the Eggs on the screen. He spoke briefly: "In the mid-21st century we finally found the answer to nuclear weapons with force shields around our major cities. These Eggs apply that technology. We will have a rectilinear net as an early warning system facing where we expect an alien invasion. Force screens will connect all the Eggs. Each Egg will be about 10 light minutes from the next. They will warn earth of an invasion."

One reporter raised his hand: "Dr. Walski, some say we should be working on a method of communication with the aliens instead."

Dr. Walski replied from the stage: "We can't expect these aliens to look like us or to communicate as we do. They did not evolve on earth. We have been sending light and sound signals out for over a century without a response. Some scientists even felt we were alone in the universe.

Now we have found out the hard way that we are not alone. To try to communicate now could lead invaders directly to us."

Ted Wallace had leaned over to the reporter sitting next to him. "I am going to volunteer for these Eggs when they do get them afloat. This is where the action is, to save the human race."

Now eight years had passed without further incident. The Eggs has long been in place. The full potential of earth's manufacturing power was unleashed to build a fleet of space ships and Egg outposts facing the direction in which the aliens had been encountered in the far away star systems. The Eggs were connected by force screens and patrolled by battleships.

Many cities on earth were under constant force screen protection, but the security afforded by the force screens had lasted only a brief time against the alien warships on the star base colonies. Not only that but the joint earth command had considerable doubt if they could really build a space battleship that could deal with the aliens on equal terms. Still a planet facing a space ship approaching at almost the speed of light and firing missiles would have no chance at all. The colonies of earth around distant stars had been turned to burnt rubble. The enemy merely came in and destroyed the sitting ducks. Earth must not offer such a target. The Eggs were an early warning system, a trip wire to let the earth know of the arrival of an alien battle fleet.

Of course it was impossible to keep the earth's entire battle fleet airborne all the time. The hope was that the early warning system would give earth a chance to launch its battle fleet.

*   *   *

Ted and Lisa were one of the many man-woman teams who had been deemed psychologically compatible and signed up for a typical nine-year hitch in space. They had eleven months on their post and one month back on earth each year. After nine years they would be retired with full pension for life as recompense for their service. The maintenance jobs on the outpost were routine and took only about two hours a day. The rest of the time the couple spent reading, watching taped television broadcasts, exercising, and sending messages by light impulse to the other nearby outposts. Ted more and more just came to enjoy Lisa's company. This coupling, one compatible male and female, was a combination that had been tried in the early exploration of the home planets. It certainly reduced boredom. The ménages in the sky were attacked by some moralists; but they worked.

Lisa Laverti complained at first that Ted, by nicknaming her "Lovely," reduced her to a mere sex object and was Ted's way of making her second in command on the Egg. Still they were compatible, enjoyed Ping-Pong, cards, electronic games, and the same music. Lisa not only talked well: she listened better. At her insistence they both enrolled in some post-graduate college courses through the ship computer.

Ted had come to think of his assignment as a long, super honeymoon. They were only allowed a ration of two alcoholic drinks a day, since they were supposed to remain alert, but Ted felt the Egg was so fully automatic that humans were scarcely necessary.

* * *

Now their outpost was the focus of the alien attack upon earth and its solar system. They had become the point couple for earth's survival.

"It might be just an exploration party," Lisa suggested hopefully.

She had hardly expressed this wish when they spotted a second alien battleship further out, barely visible at the maximum magnification of their telescopic viewscreens. There were other vague images beyond. It was probably an entire alien fleet.

They had suited up by this time, donned the full panoply of gear, oxygen pods, launchers, communications, and magnetic boots. The space suits, in spite of all the new materials, the reduction of weight and the increases in flexibility, felt ungainly after months of walking around with little or no clothing. They had the suiting process down to two minutes flat. The see-through helmets had been designed so that the spacers could identify each other easily if there was a group. It was not necessary now, with only two people, but Ted was always pleased he could still see Lovely's face through the helmet visor.

Only four minutes had passed since the warning light signals had been dispatched. Still Ted felt amazed that he was still alive. In space nothing might happen for years, but then one mistake and you were dead. That's what the training program had instilled into their very natures.

Lisa guessed at Ted's thoughts. "Why is it taking them so long?" she inquired, not really wanting an answer. Perhaps she hoped to just get it over with.

Ted decided he was a dead man now; nothing really mattered from here on. He would die regardless of what he did. The lifeboats in the Egg were really only for emergency escape, to ride in until the backup Battleship reached them in case of major equipment failure. When the alien fleet got moving again, the Egg would be destroyed. Even when the Atlas did arrive, it too would be destroyed.

"The alien scouts are reporting back to their battle cruisers," Ted hazarded a guess. "Oh, here they come again."

The alien scout ships were moving once more. Lisa talked of the slow, deliberate alien progress. "They've moved in to about 200,000 kilometers from the force screen now. Now it's 100,000 kilometers. Now 50,000 from the force screen, and now they have slowed down again. They are drifting in. Now they are at 30,000 kilometers, 20,000, 10,000, and 5,000. Do you think they have spotted the Egg? It's pretty small in all this space."

"It's hard to say. They've come to a halt again," Ted declared. "I almost feel sympathy for the aliens in those three scout ships. They are the point people, expendable, just as we are."

"Don't feel for them," Lisa returned. "They're attacking, we're defending. And they aren't people."

Ted gave a deep sigh and then wished he had not done so. He must keep his own fears from Lisa. "Now the scout ships are moving again. A thousand kilometers from the force screen. They are slowing more and drifting in. They are a long way from the Egg, but close to the force screen."

The humans on the Egg felt the alien probe again; a probe such as this had set off the alarm system originally. This was stronger pressure and sent a shock wave into the computer which registered a "3" on the energy scale. Three percent of the available energy in the entire system went into repulsing that probe. "100" was the artificial point at which the force shield would cut off to let space objects through that were too great to contain. That way a large meteorite would not blow the entire system, but pass through safely, hopefully deflected from the Egg itself.

Maybe they will just go away," Lisa suggested, forcing a little smile that Ted could see through her space suit visor.

"They're reporting back again. This is no field trip. Not with those battleships back there. Still it has been nine minutes. Why are they so deliberate? They may think it's a trap."

"In two hours the Atlas will be here."

Ted only nodded. Let her hope. Before he put on his helmet he had gulped a tranquilizer while Lovely's head was turned. He did not want to show his fears.

The nearest alien scout, at nine o'clock, or "left out" as they said, began moving again. From the command deck they could see fully half of the sky, all the sky facing in the direction where the aliens were expected to come. And this was the direction from which the aliens had come. 'Right out', 'left out', 'down out', 'up out', and 'center out', were gross approximations for viewing ahead through the command deck's triple windows.

"Shall I inform all points that we have seen a second battleship and suspect a whole fleet further away beyond viewscreen range?" Lisa inquired.

"Yes. Prepare all the messages and get them set on automatic so you can dispatch them all with one push of the button. We may want to add something. The aliens are only about ten kilometers from the force screen, but the screen itself is invisible. They are 400,000 kilometers away 'out left' of our Egg and haven't seen us yet, apparently. Otherwise they would center their ships on us directly. I don't think they're sneaking up on us from the side." It was best to keep Lisa occupied, Ted decided.

"O.K. Since we are being probed, but nothing more is happening, would it be a good idea to bring Al or Gerry over here to help?"

"Help do what? You know the problem. If Al or Gerry took off from their Eggs in the slow lifeboats, the aliens would just seize them before they arrived here to help. The lifeboats are all so slow they would get here after the Atlas." Ted felt a little annoyed that Lisa would suggest that one of the other men come. He and Lovely would die, but they would die together. There was something sacred about it, almost.

Al and Gerry were two of the male halves of couples they talked to most in the nearest Eggs. They were ten light minutes away, a part of a reticulation that covered this whole quadrant of the sky.

Ted felt their only chance was the Atlas and this alien fleet wasn't even going to wait that long.

Still fourteen minutes had elapsed. The enemy scouts were continuing to drift in toward the force field. Then they felt the probe again. It registered a "4" this time.

"You know," Lisa declared, "with the distances involved, the aliens really arrived quite close to our Egg. If they had come upon the force screen further out, ten million kilometers away maybe, we would not have known what made contact."

"Yes. And they wouldn't have been as likely to find us easily as they are now," Ted replied. "Their battleships have sensors. The aliens felt a force field ahead and stopped way out. They sent the scout ships ahead to have a look. It was only then that our sensors picked them up."

"They don't know earth is our home planet or even if we have a base here," Lisa observed. "They won't know this is the humans they defeated so easily before. As far as we know, no earth people have ever been taken prisoner and we humans have sure never seen any of them. They will be cautious because they don't know what they're dealing with."

"I hope they stay cautious and slow. Only I don't believe it will last. You know what they did to our star colonies."

"Well," Lisa persisted after a moment, "if they had just hit the force field ten million kilometers from us, we still would have picked up the probe and they might never have found our Egg."

"They would have eventually just pushed through the screen with their battleships. And we would have had to direct the Atlas to investigate what broke through the force field. Then we wouldn't be sure. Now we know. From the point of view of earth it is better this way because now we know the aliens are coming. From our personal point of view, however, we are going to be on the front line very shortly."

"We could send a message to the other outposts and ask everyone to turn off the force screen," Lisa suggested her voice carried the undertone of really knowing it shouldn't be done. To close down the whole warning system was probably not even possible now.

"Our job now is to hold here as long as possible. It's like the Greek battle of Thermopylae. We are the Spartans this time. We are the outpost of earth." Ted sighed again in spite of his determination not to give any sign of discouragement. "We are weaponless, useless. I don't know if the time we are buying will be wisely spent by earth, but we swore to hold this post at all costs and, well, that's you and me."

Yes," Lisa replied, and there was no reading the single word.

Now there was an impact. The alien scout ship had landed, if you could call it that, right on the force field itself. The other two scouts landed next. The alien scouts must have found it unusual to just discover an invisible force field out here in space. They began simultaneous probes and the readings jumped to "7" and then moved up to "11."

"What are they up to?" Lisa asked. "Probing, trying to break through." She answered her own question.

The closest scout ship pulled away a little and then returned to hit the force field. It was not going full tilt, and it still got an "18." If a battleship did that it would sail right through.

"Sixteen minutes," Lisa announced. "The aliens are taking their time. Maybe when you have this much power they do not need to be in a rush. Only there is something peculiar about how slow they are."

"Maybe they don't want to risk a big battleship. But the aliens who wiped out the star colonies are not going to be held back for long by this energy net."

The Egg had now fully served its purpose and the two humans aboard knew they should be dead already.

"Our little Egg is not moving relative to anything and will be difficult to see," Lisa began to prattle on in this vein and Ted let her go without replying.

Then the Scouts pulled back. "Look, they're retreating," Lisa asserted.

Ted grunted. He didn't believe it.

Next they both saw the cluster on the horizon. "There is a group of small scouts coming, diverging, moving in toward the force field, but spreading out widely. There is going to be an exploration in depth by expendable craft. The scouts are pawns in this galactic chess game. "

"And so are we," Lisa added.

"The closest scout ship will be 200,000 kilometers out left when it reaches the screen." Ted announced. "I have counted eighteen craft that I can see clearly, but there could be hundreds more, further away, three, four, five million kilometers away. The scouts are not visible at a distance of much over a million kilometers even when they are moving."

"The probes are beginning again." Lisa advised. "And now it has been twenty minutes."

Ted grunted again. "The probes are still all reading at the "3" level, so this is an effort to see where the power center is. Since the probes are all what we call 'Out Left,' it will not be easy to trace the Egg that way."

Abruptly their computer transmitter picked up a light beam communication and translated it back into English. The poised, masculine voice of the computer, designed to instill confidence, gave Ted and Lisa the message: "Al/Marie, N746PT, acknowledge message received and we have retransmitted the messages to every Egg and the earth base. You have seen three alien scout ships, one battleship, perhaps more. Al can come via lifeboat if needed. Fill in details. Good luck. Out."

The outposts were almost ten light minutes away so it had taken twenty minutes for their message to arrive and be returned. If they sent another message it would again be a twenty-minute round trip. A few seconds later they heard from Gerry/Lill and Burt/Maxine. As always George/Hazel were last. Gerry also offered to come over by lifeboat.

The closest scout was approaching them now, a little erratically as it searched. The scout was still 150,000 kilometers away and continually probing. Another ten minutes passed. "It's been half an hour," Lisa declared plaintively.

Then the nearest alien scout paused and abruptly stopped. The Egg had been located. Three nearby scouts began to move in toward the Egg while the other scouts pulled back to the alien battleship. The three small ships came in, 100,000 kilometers, 50,000, 10,000, 1,000. They reduced speed and began to drift in, taking positions, Up Left, Down Left, and Center.

"It's only a matter of time now," Ted advised. "You can send your next message out to everybody and add that we have been discovered."

Lisa sent the message off to the other outposts, the space base on Pluto, and the Battleship Atlas. They hoped the Atlas was on the way.

The alien scout ships drifted in slowly until they finally stood only a few hundred meters away from the Egg resting right on the force screen. Another probe was attempted from all three points.

"Maybe they're trying to communicate?" Lisa Laverti suggested hopefully.

At that moment the three scouts lashed out with nose weapons directly at the Egg. The force field resistance needle jumped to "19." The blasts ceased. Again there was a pause.

"Does that answer your question?" Ted growled. "They're reporting back to the battleships for further orders."

The alien scouts began moving again. One scout ship dropped a large barrel affair almost over their heads which seemed to attach itself to the force field of the Egg and just hang there. The scouts moved off rapidly. Ted reacted at once. He closed the metal hatch over the triple viewplates.

The blast of the explosion went right off the scale. Most of the shock must have been carried off into space, but the impact registered at over 100 on the computer. Ted and Lisa were thrown to the floor of the control room. Ted could smell the burning wiring and see the smoke. He pushed a button to raise the air filters to high and the compartment cleared. Trouble lights were on all over the boards, but there was no drastic damage.

Ted opened the hatch over the viewplates again to view the scout ships at distance now. They were probably not aware they had hurt the Egg at all. The force screen had cut off automatically at 100 and then come back on instantly after the blast passed through.

Ted looked around. The control room floor had a jagged crack clear across. One view screen on the top right would not function. But the hull was still intact and the problems inside were solvable short term anyway.

The three alien scouts continued to observe. "We were supposed to wake up and react in some way, but we did nothing," Ted declared. "In fact we can do nothing. Only they don't know that."

"Maybe that is just as well and they will go away," Lisa hoped again.

"No chance," Ted told her.

The scouts converged once more, firing blinding light beams from their nose guns. The beams were deflected. Then as the alien ships came in to a distance of a few hundred meters the quality of the attack beams changed.

"The needle," Lisa indicated, looking at the dial and the power being used up. The deflectors were using up energy at "15," then "20," and then "25."

"They are too small. Their guns don't have the power to break through," Ted decided.

"It's been forty-five minutes," Lisa observed.

"And the Atlas won't even have our message yet," Ted responded.

Several more minutes passed. The aliens had power even in these scout ships, but they tried everything too long. Ted could not understand it. There was something odd here. After a few more minutes the scout ships abruptly broke off their attack and scattered as if on cue.

The leading battleship now came closer to the Egg, accelerating rapidly. One moment it had been about ten million-kilometers away and then it was roaring in toward them in an elliptical orbit. The battleship was also cigar-shaped, but a thousand meters long. It rushed down in a curve that took it just twenty kilometers from the Egg, firing at them as it passed. The needle went to "72" and stayed there for two seconds while the Egg's force screen deflected the beam.

The alien battleship had almost broken through their force screen power at twenty kilometers distance while traveling extremely fast. The battleship was far away now, just hanging there motionless. It was apparently examining the Egg.

"The battleship will be back," Ted asserted. "When it hits us again with more power it will go right through the force screen and into the Egg itself. Only I've seen statistics that the force screen can be made to resist to 160 near the source of its power. The 100 cut off is so passing meteorites will go through the net and not destroy us."

They had never expected to have time for these alterations in strategy. The Egg outpost was a "point" as in the nomenclature of old military tactics even before the World Wars of the twentieth century. Ted and Lisa were equivalent to "points" sent ahead to spot the enemy. They were the bell of the alarm for earth and its billions of people. The function of an alarm system was to warn in times of emergency and to indicate the direction from which the enemy was coming. They had served that purpose in full and yet, somehow, they momentarily remained alive.

Ted talked to the computer. He concluded with questions: "How badly damaged are we? Can we go to manual override and put full power into our shields?"

"Working," the computer replied in its well modulated all too human sounding voice. It always began that way, even though the next words came almost at once: "The explosion did no damage to the power floor. The command deck control floor is structurally damaged, but there are no air leaks. If manual override is utilized, power could be exerted overhead to 160 and perhaps beyond. Would suggest decision making be given to the computer. The force screen is being held fifty meters out from the front hull. This could be dropped back closer before the system was turned off to save blowing out."

Ted disliked giving away autonomy, but the computer had been informed of the problem and it could react in microseconds. Ted talked the matter over with Lisa and then he agreed that the computer could run the show.

"Working," the computer voice came through again. "Cutting lights to dim and all basic services except life support. Food supply is closed down. If you need a glass of water, get it now. All power is going into the force shields. If the control room floor is destroyed by having the force field pushed back through here, you should go to the power floor and take direct control from there. At that point I will have ceased to exist, since I am fixed to the control room floor. Out."

The computer contemplated its own demise with apparent ease. The lights dimmed: the air circulation slowed down to a trickle: even the music ended abruptly. Ted felt his throat dry at the mention of water, but he wasn't going to take off his helmet for even a moment. Lovely sighed deeply. It was like death already.

The Egg outpost had four floors with a circular stair for climbing through the portholes that separated the top floors. There was a pole that could be used for climbing up and down to the other floors. Climbing a pole was not difficult in the near weightlessness of space.

The top deck or command floor could be curtained off into three fair-sized rooms by the use of moveable curtains. This deck was almost one-quarter of the Egg and measured fifteen meters in diameter. It was over two meters high at the sides and three meters in the middle. The command deck came with panels, telescopic viewscreens, and it was curved outward to give the crew a look at the universe. The triple windows had a unique view and the metal hull could be closed around the viewscreen in emergencies.

The second floor, just below the command deck, was the living floor of the Egg. Floor and ceiling tracks could hold moveable walls at all kinds of angles. The crew of two, if they grew tired of one interior design, could rearrange room sizes as well as furniture. Right now this floor contained five rooms. The bedroom was a square, five meters on a side, right in the middle of the circular floor.

The rest of the living floor was partitioned off into four somewhat trapezoidal rooms. These outer cubicles were the kitchen, shower room, a lounge, and a recreation room. The kitchen was electronic, connected to the computer. The lounge and recreation rooms contained not only books, but also 3D interactive television, video, communication, audio equipment, a bar, and a changing variety of electronic and exercise games. One needed active workouts that kept you moving while you were in space.

The third level of the Egg was for storage. It held a year's supply of frozen food, water for drinking and showering with recycling equipment neither occupant liked to think about. Finally there were the two small lifeboats, each capable of holding two people. This floor had port doors that swung open wide to admit visitors in anchoring lifeboats. The bottom floor was the power chamber, containing two large energy boxes, Unit A and the backup Unit B, which now was also in use."

"It's been almost an hour," Lisa intoned.

"I don't know why they are taking so long," Ted grunted and shook his head. "Why don't the aliens just get their job over with? I guess I am determined not to hope anymore. A whole alien fleet is out there. It is like cat and mouse. Only what kind of a sneak attack is this? The aliens have made no effort to communicate. Perhaps we should try a light signal. Maybe contact could be established yet. But any signaling would change the status quo. The only thing holding up a further attack is probably the alien concern that this is a trap. If we appear scared, the attack might begin at once. And it will be over at once too." Ted talked himself out of taking any action.

Then the Egg rocked again. Scout ships once more were firing at the force field, out at great distances, the sensor readings indicated they were more than one hundred million kilometers away, and banging on the force screen with vibrations and shock waves that ran from "2" to build ups to "26." The alien fleet was trying to see how far out the force field was. But from where the aliens had made contact, near the middle of the system, the enemy could go out a long ways, before they found a path around. Of course if the aliens explored outward far enough they would encounter other Eggs.

After a few minutes of rocking, the alien battleship was back for another dive and attack, slower, and closer in. The blast was for six seconds, surging up to "148" on the dials, which was near the capacity of the system even on maximum overload. The next attack would probably double in intensity again and they would be shot right out of the sky.

"If we hadn't gone to computer control and override, that would have gotten us," Ted indicated evenly.

"The Atlas will have our message now and be on the way," Lisa replied.

"And in an hour it will be here," Ted growled. Lisa would just not stop telling him what time it was.

"Look, here come two of them," Lisa Laverti indicated. There were two alien battleships approaching now, obliquely, a hundred thousand kilometers off, slowing, coming in cautiously. At 50,000 kilometers both vessels stopped and fired a blast through their nose guns that focused right on the Egg. The force shields gave readings of 20, 40, and then 60.

The beams ceased and the alien battleships moved slowly forward until they reached a range of 20,000 kilometers. Now a differing beam came from the nose guns, emitting very little light but more powerful. The numbers moved more rapidly on the dial from 30 to 60 to 90. The beams went off again and the ships came down methodically to the 10,000-kilometer range. The indicator on the Egg showed strikes applying pressure in increasing strength of 55, 110, and 167 this time. The lights dimmed further in the command room on the Egg, but the force screen held.

"You had better leave the control floor," the computer voice cut in.

"Acknowledged," Ted replied to the computer. Then he added to Lovely, "If the next surge goes up at the same ratio, they will wrap our power screen around our necks and crush our eggshell."

Ted placed a gloved hand on Lisa's metal clad arm and led her back to the stairs to the bedroom below. Standing here at the porthole on the floor below, they could still watch the screen on the deck above.

The aliens were coming in closer. This was it! The enemy battleships were at 5,000 kilometers, hovering. The beams came on slower than before, and the force field built up almost leisurely, but it was continuous: 50, 80, 110, 140, and 170. The computer voice came on and seemed strained: "The force field is bending back. Ten meters, five, two. Status. All power utilized. Closing ports."

"Acknowledged," Ted replied. The ports closed. Then the next surge hit.

"Distance zero. Transferring control to the power deck," the computer voice had become a squeal.

Ted's last view of the control deck was of the hull collapsing inward, the windows shattering, the screens going out, and the ceiling descending toward the floor. He pushed the button to automatically close the hatch between the floors. Even as the hatch snapped into place they heard the "whoosh" above them as the hull went and with it all the deck equipment vanished into space. They had lost the control deck, the computer, the viewscreens, their communications with the outside, and their ability to coordinate any defense.

Then they watched in something close to despair, as the ceiling above their bedroom seemed to round out and pull away from them. One of the metal pillars parted. In a moment the disaster was going to reach their bedroom, a private place no longer.

"Quick," Ted demanded, and he pushed Lisa for the chute to the next level. It was just a circular opening with a pole and with the near weightlessness they pulled themselves down rapidly.

"The whole Egg is going," Ted moaned. Even as he clamored down he looked back one last time to see the rounded ceiling of the bedroom flatten and descend toward him. Down on the storage floor, Lisa closed the round port. It too snapped into position.

"Lovely turn your magnetics full on," Ted asked.

Ted watched approvingly as she pressed the wrist control button and her boot magnetics came on, holding her securely to the metal floor. Then he turned on his own boots. They would be held tightly, but walking would be harder. "Let's try and launch a lifeboat and see what happens to it," Ted suggested. "If it gets away, we could try escaping in the other one."

Ted reached in to the open lifeboat to set the controls on manual, toward the Sun, full speed take off, in thirty seconds. He jumped back out of the way, and hit the switch to open the launch doors. The doors opened at once, the length of the wall. There was another "whoosh" as every bit of air was pulled from this level. Ted and Lisa swayed on their magnetic boots but remained upright. Even as the lifeboat took off, Ted saw the ceiling above crack. The lights flickered, but came back on. The force shield had quit for good.

The lifeboat sped away and through the open launch doors Ted saw an alien scout ship fly after the lifeboat, rapidly overtaking it. They were not firing. "That's one reason they have been fooling around. They may have thought it was all a trap at first, but now they want some prisoners." With its power off, the Egg could be destroyed in seconds.

"Maybe we can try to get away in the other lifeboat while they are stopping that one," Lisa suggested"

"I see four or five more alien scout ships out there, and they are all faster than the lifeboat," Ted replied as he looked through the open launch doors.

"Watch it Ted," Lisa yelled. An alien scout ship was turning directly for the hanger doors which still stood wide open. Ted pressed the button to shut the doors. The alien ship was a hundred meters out as the doors began to close slowly. The hanger doors were not functioning well anymore. There was a crunch and a soundless rupturing of metal. The alien ship was stuck more than half way into the Egg and covered a third of the room.

"Get below," Ted shouted. Lisa stepped through the last port and pulled herself down the chute pole to the power floor below, the bottom floor of the Egg. The whole cone end of the alien scout ship came open as Ted paused to look.

Ted Wallace was the first human to see the aliens. A space suited head emerged from the scout ship, a huge head, almost a meter in diameter. Then an enormous creature began pulling itself meter by meter out of the small scout ship. The alien moved slowly, cautiously, in what it may have regarded as a suicide mission.

"It's more than twice our size," Ted gasped into his space suit microphone. "These creatures are giants."

"Or we are small," Lisa responded.

The alien's front two feet came down and heavily hit the metal floor. The form fitting suit indicated huge claws at the end of the toes. Humans classify everything and thus turn the foreign into the familiar. Ted immediately likened what he saw to a great cat. Now the final shock came when the single rear leg emerged, just one huge central leg, or perhaps it was an extremely curved tail. Ted dropped his head through the hatch and Lisa pushed the switch to close the hatch door.

"It's like a three-legged cat, one leg in the rear. And it is five meters long, bigger than both of us together. Those alien scout ships must be powerful. These creatures take up half of one of their scout ships. Yet they fly quite fast, carry weapons, and can even transport a barrel of explosives as we have seen. What a report we will have, if we can get back to give it."

"Listen! Hear it on the floor above?" Lisa asked. There was no noise in space, but the vibrations above were being carried down through the walls to the floor on which they stood. The creature was banging about.

"It's been more than ninety minutes now, Ted. The Atlas will be on the way."

"We might have done better if we had just flung ourselves into space with out suits on," Ted suggested. "The aliens would have gone after the Egg and its force screen, but we would have been such small objects to scan, they might not have found us as we drifted. Our four hour air supply might have lasted till the Atlas came. We can't even get out from this level. No doors, no windows. How do we hold off those things for another forty minutes?" Ted laughed a little hysterically. "The creature is ripping the doors off all the cabinets up there. That's the vibration you feel. In a moment it will try to get at us and then" Ted did not finish.

There was an extra hard blow from above on the floor. The creature had discovered the escape hatch to this lowest level. "He's trying to smash the hatch door."

The hatch door abruptly glowed red and simply dissolved. The edges cooled in a moment in space. A huge paw sheathed in metal armor came through the hatch, feeling below, as a cat might, for mice, slowly, carefully. Now was the time to have a laser pistol or any kind of a weapon. Lisa screamed. Both humans backed up to the huge rectangular Power Unit A that extended from the floor to almost the ceiling. This unit was still supplying light to this bottom grim room on the Egg.

The alien claw continued to fumble about for a moment and then retreated. Again a minute passed. Now a wider circle five meters in diameter began to be inscribed by a weapon from above. When the segment was cut, it was lifted out of the way like opening a tin can. The humans could both see the creature above now, staring down through the hole at them with an eye that was semi-circular across its entire large head. It had one elongated continuous eye emitting a band of flickering light across the upper face. The eye was exposed to their view through a visor plate.

The alien held the weapon he had been using in one of its paws. It sat on its curled rear leg on the floor above. For several seconds it held that position. Then the creature bent its head and descended through the hole it had created in the ceiling. It sat for the moment in the center of the floor in front of them. The weapon was pointed at them menacingly and seemed to say: "Don't move." But there was something odd. The alien had descended so very slowly, really too deliberately. The creature's head and one front paw were near them now. Lisa screamed again, involuntarily. She probably did not even know she was doing it, Ted reflected.

"Lovely," Ted demanded forcefully, "we've got to try. Crouch down here behind this power unit and get the back cover off. See if you can pull some live wires out to stun that thing. It appears to be moving very slowly. It's our only chance. I will use my launcher to try to distract it by flying over behind Power Unit B on the other side of the room. If I aim myself at slow, maybe I can go right past the alien to the other side. The alien has a gun of some kind, but I think it wants us alive. I don't think it can reach behind these units. They are too big."

"O.K., but be careful with the launcher. It's not for indoor use." She laughed nervously, and started unbolting the cover at the back of power Unit A.

Ted watched for his chance. "O.K., here I go." Ted leaned forward and pushed his wrist button. The launcher carried him right past the alien to the other side of the room. He bumped the wall with outstretched hands and landed upright on his mag boots. The shock was punishing, but he recovered in an instant and stepped behind power Unit B.

Ted did not believe the alien could reach into the narrow space behind the power units. But if the creature fired at them their suits would open and they would die. Perhaps that was better than being captured. If Lisa could use the power with two live wires and shock the creature then maybe they had a chance.

The alien creature had taken its time getting situated on the floor of the power chamber. There was not much room for it to move in between the two huge power units. Now it turned ever so slowly to look at Ted. Then the floor above vibrated. From where he stood, looking up through the hole in the ceiling, Ted could see something forcing the hangar doors open on the floor above. The creature waited patiently and then Ted saw the hangar doors snap. The big doors were bent inward and crushed now. Another enemy scout ship had docked by affixing itself to the side of the Egg. The pilot of this craft was another space suited alien, the size of the first. This alien slowly moved from his small ship into the floor above.

Lisa might actually use live wires to shock one of the brutes. But she could never kill two. The creature on their own level moved slowly to the side of Unit B and its face looked directly at Ted, who was back behind the Unit. The creature tried to reach in a paw, and just as Ted had hoped, the alien's huge space-suited paw would not fit. The second alien creature was beginning to slowly climb down. Ted thought suddenly of old movies with zombies walking slowly. The aliens were in a different time phase than the humans, moving slowly. Then the alien on their floor raised its gun to point at Ted.

Ted felt there was nothing to do now except use his launcher and try to reach the other side of the room again. He bent forward, pushed the wrist button, and shot out across the center of the room. Using a launcher in a narrow space was neither simple nor safe, only nothing seemed to matter now. As Ted flew across the room this time, he kicked out at the paw of the second alien descending. He spun, hitting the wall. For a moment the breath left him. Then Ted stood up again.

The second alien had come down in a heap as if the blow actually hurt. But then the creature sat up, the only position the alien could take in the low ceiling of this room. Ted was against the side of the wall between the power units. Both aliens stretched out long arms toward him. The aliens seemed deliberately ponderous, as if they were acting in slow motion. Ted cut the power in his mag boots to minimum and ran back to Lisa's side.

Both aliens made a grab for him and missed. It was hard to believe they could be so ridiculously slow. Ted even felt that one of the aliens he was watching was startled at his speed. But then what must a hyperactive fly think when a huge man aims a hand at him and misses completely? It was no trick at all in running between their languorous paws.

"You're back. Thank God," Lisa shouted. "I've got the wires ready. Four meters length on each side and enough juice to kill an elephant. Be careful of the ends. The way they missed you just now, I think you could run out and get them."

Ted turned his magnetic boots back to 20% power; there was no point to stumbling and falling on the dangerous wires. Carefully he grasped the wires by the insulation noting that Lisa had peeled back the open end a full ten centimeters with the wire cutters in her suit's tool kit. For an instant Ted watched his target, which was still lumbering toward him, so very slowly, one paw extended out. Ted left the shelter behind the power unit to lean forward and touch a wire to either side of the armor-suited paw. The sparks flew. The creature did a jump that carried it slowly to the ceiling and then it crumbled back to the floor. The other alien, further back, moved no closer, but began to raise its gun.

The electrical wires were not going to reach that far! Ted ran back behind the power unit. The alien's weapon was not on low anymore; the blast shook the power unit and dissolved a four square meter chunk in a puff of smoke. Ted touched his wires together for an instant and there were no sparks. They were dead.

But the alien was so slow. The creature was looking at the effect of its blast now. There was no time to make another hook up from Power Unit

B across the room. The creature could continue blasting until it had them. Ted leaned forward, checked his launcher button on the wrist control, which was still on low, and aimed just past the alien head first. As he flew across the room he kicked at the gun.

To his intense surprise, instead of Ted's own suit ripping, which he had feared, the huge claw of the alien seemed to shatter and the gun went spinning away. Ted bounced off the opposite wall and landed upright on his mag boots. He rushed back for the gun and picked it up with one sweep.

The alien also started to reach for the weapon, and then paused. The alien must have realized it was too late and backed away in abject terror. It sat on its rear leg and spread out its front paws wide to the side baring its chest. It seemed an obvious gesture of surrender. Ted had no idea as to how to use the huge, but strangely lightweight weapon. Still he pointed it menacingly. Ted noted that one of the alien's paws had been injured, but the amazing suit had resealed instantly.

Now the alien creature began to emit flickers of light from its single curved eye. Perhaps it communicated that way. How, Ted wondered, did you establish contact with a being that communicated by light flashes from its eye? What did it all mean? The language of the eyes!

Ted and Lisa were still alive, but the situation was impossible. He would have to hold the alien at bay till the Atlas arrived, and then the Atlas would have to take on a whole enemy fleet.

In the last space battle between aliens and humans, earth had lost four battleships and then somehow by accident or chance destroyed one enemy ship. The alien ships had then retreated, taking their one blasted battleship along. The remaining earth ships had felt themselves lucky to run and escape.

But at hand to claw combat it might be a different matter. The aliens were so ponderously slow, apparently existing in another time plane entirely. How long could he and Lisa continue this stalemate? The one huge alien sat there in an attitude of surrender while its companion was probably dead beside it on the floor?

"Lovely," Ted shouted, "we have one wild chance. I'm afraid to try to fire this gun. I know nothing about it. This creature won't give me a chance to practice. There is a dial and a button on the side of this gun, but if I show my ignorance this alien may come back after me. Run over to Power Unit B and see if you can pull some live wires from there and get up behind this creature and do it in. It worked before."

"I'll try." Lisa darted past the alien. The creature appeared to be looking up and away from Ted now, its eyes still flashing. Perhaps it was transmitting a message to its home ship.

"Ted," Lisa called, "this panel still has juice."

"Our best chance is speed," Ted declared. "They react slowly and perhaps think slowly. That's probably why they took so long to close in on the Egg. They don't care about communicating with us at all. To them, we're just a smaller, lower form of life to be destroyed. Their technology is way ahead of ours. But they are slow."

After a bit Lisa called: "I'm ready."

"Be careful when you come up behind it. We don't know about that rear leg." The creature still faced Ted and Lisa was coming from the back. Then the alien began to turn toward her, slowly, sensing something. Ted dared not try to shoot his unknown weapon with Lisa nearby.

Now there was a bump and something locked on to the remainder of the crumbled Egg. The alien creature lost its balance and pitched over. Lisa ran in with the wires like a matador to touch the alien's rear paw from each side. The shock of electrical power ran through the creature and it collapsed.

The Egg gave another bump and began to accelerate. Lisa momentarily lost her balance and almost fell on the wires. "Watch it," Ted called uselessly. But Lisa recovered and put the wires down carefully, moving away from them. "Where are they towing us?" she asked.

"Let me climb up on this wall and look," Ted replied.

"Be careful of the edges of that hole," Lisa warned. "Don't puncture your suit."

Gingerly Ted grabbed the edge of one surface in the hole of the ceiling and pulled his head up to look through the torn hangar doors of the Egg's supply deck. He could see nothing except space. And then they turned.

"We're being pulled into the alien battleship!"

And there it was. Ted saw the enemy battleship; a port door much larger than the Egg was opening. He watched fascinated as they came in slowly to a gigantic chamber with muted blue light. Ted could not see how the Egg had been grappled or conveyed, but now the power was cut and the Egg was deposited inside. He heard the doors of the space ship closing behind them. They were prisoners.

Ted let go and floated to the floor of the power room beside Lisa. He quickly examined the alien weapon he held. It was twice the size of an earthly laser pistol, but very light. It gave Ted the feeling of playing with a giant toy. The weapon had a nozzle and a barrel where a claw could hold it. On the side of the gun's handle there was a dial and a button in the middle. Ted pointed the gun at the ceiling and pressed the button. A yellow light shot up at the ceiling and glanced off. He held the button down and turned the dial. Now the intensity of the beam increased and the ceiling metal sheered off and vanished. That was full power.

"I will carry this in the kit on my back so they can't see it," he told Lisa. "Let's go out and meet our hosts. We might as well get this over with."

"Ted, in just over fifteen minutes the Atlas will be here. Maybe we can hide in one of the storage lockers on the Egg." Lisa was still hoping.

"When the Atlas does come, it is going to be outnumbered and shooting with all its got at this alien ship we are on or any enemy ship it sees. Come on."

Ted pulled himself up to the storage level and gave Lisa a hand. Then they looked in shock at the vast almost empty room before them on the alien craft. Here they had been deposited along with the remains of the Egg. Along the side was a lot of red machinery which was beyond understanding at a glance. At the opposite end of the chamber was a door and creatures were emerging from a corridor.

It was difficult to take it all in. Ted and Lisa saw the aliens as akin to great cats. The three aliens at the other end of the room, not wearing space suits, were if anything larger than the monsters that the humans had encountered in the Egg. They were all over five meters in height. Their long back leg or curled tail pushed them along and the front two legs were at mid-body. The first impression was that of huge size, then tawny ocellated fur, a head with round, open mouth, edentate perhaps, and possessing a prognathous lower jaw. There was no sign of a nose or ears and the eyes were a continuous semi-circular cluster at the top of the head, flashing constantly, in motion, changing colors.

What Ted took to be the leader of the three aliens was approaching the Egg very slowly at the other end of this huge room. This creature held, as a rider on its upper back, an entity not unlike a huge dragonfly, a meter in wingspread, a neuropterous insect with eight bent, spindly legs, perching on the cat's furry back. Ted wondered briefly which was the dominant species?

Ted helped Lisa descend to the floor of the alien battleship. "Put your arms to the side in surrender as the alien did aboard our Egg," Ted suggested.

The creatures advanced again. "Their weapons are better than ours," Ted continued, "or at least they were at the time of the last space battle and I don't think we've improved much. Their ships are faster and more maneuverable. But the creatures themselves are slow. Perhaps time is different for them."

The leading alien now sat down in position some ten meters away, holding one of their big weapons in a front paw, resting as the others had done on his rear leg. The multiple eyes flashed at them, effulgent gleams of various intensities, a potpourri of color.

Ted waved his arms just a little. "He's trying to communicate. What can we do? What an opportunity. I think they were slow demolishing the Egg because they wanted prisoners. But also they move very slowly."

"It's no good, Ted," Lisa protested. "They destroyed the star colonies. When they find we can't flash our eyes, they'll think we're just dumb and kill us. We can't communicate; we're worthless to them."

"They look formidable, Lisa, but they're not strong. In my spacesuit, I knocked into the top of the paw of the one and hurt it. I took his gun right away from him. If they raise their guns, I'll turn on my backpack launcher and try to bowl them over. If it works we'll go right down that passage ahead. O.K.?"

"We might as well try. I'm ready to follow. The longer they flash their eyes and waste time the better."

Regardless of success before with the two aliens in the Egg, if Ted had not psyched himself up into believing he was going to die anyway, he probably would not have even suggested attacking these creatures. A grasshopper doing battle with a squirrel was not much more ludicrous.

Abruptly the light flashing eyes seemed to change. The front creature's toothless mouth opened even further and rounder, and then a tractile, long thin tongue emerged, flickering at them. It was a round purple tongue two meters in length.

"Do you think the dragonflies are pets or enjoy a symbiotic relationship?" Lisa asked.

"That tongue may be a secondary method of communication," Ted suggested. "We can't perform that feat either. Watch out, the gun! Come on." The last was spoken rapidly.

The leading alien began to raise its weapon. The gun came up so slowly that Ted thought for a moment how they would have laughed at that draw in the old west. Ted leaned forward, pushed on his wrist control, and his rocket launcher shot him right across the room into the creature. Even after what had occurred before, Ted was not prepared for this. The middle creature reared up and Ted caught it squarely in the soft chest. The huge insect on its upper back was thrown against the ceiling and burst on impact. What the humans took to be the leader of the aliens fell backward into the other two creatures. Ted and Lisa, moving fast, continued past them right down the corridor ahead.

The corridor was fifty meters long with side passageways that were narrower. Ahead the hallway opened into a great circular room, thirty meters in diameter, dome-roofed with a convex floor. Many corridors, like spokes of a wheel, converged on this room. A dozen aliens were accumbent on pillows, couchant, watching screen controls. To Ted this view produced all the more the appearance of big cats. Overhead, on perches, two of the huge dragonflies sat motionless. Ted landed with a jar on his magnetic boots. He pulled the alien gun he had captured from his backpack, set at full power now, and fired almost instantly into the ship controls, the screens, the cat-like creatures, and the dragonflies alike. Smoke and flames erupted from the panels. A dozen aliens began coming down an opposite corridor toward him.

To Ted's surprise, Lisa pushed her launcher into full power and headed right down the corridor at the oncoming aliens. She yelled: "Destroy their control room. I'll see what I can do to hold them off."

The huge beasts were light for their size, slow, clumsy and weak. Lisa knocked the approaching pack in all directions and she ceased being volitant only after she had compressed a mangle of bodies in the corridor. Yet more aliens continued to come in and to push. Lisa lost her footing and fell. An alien raised a huge paw atop her. Lisa screamed and then slammed both hands down. The paw seemed to crack and was withdrawn.

Ted watched the instruments shatter as he fired the alien gun. The control panels were dissolving, bursting into flames, masses of equipment comminuted, while the creatures ran from him in stark terror. In trying to escape from the room, three of the alien cats ran down the corridor toward Lisa. Lisa was trapped, unable to move in the press of bodies. Ted dared not fire in that direction.

Then he heard the buzzing. Three dragonflies were approaching down each of two separate corridors. Each of the dragonflies was carrying a gun in their long black pencil-thick legs. The guns were held by pinchers in the dragonflies' feet below their bodies.

Ted knew it was just seconds before the dragonflies fired. He pressed his launcher on full and shot down the left corridor and swept under the dragonflies. They turned, very slowly, quite gracefully and dropped to three levels, one below the other. They aimed their weapons. Ted saw the huge door ahead of him closing and he turned sideways in flight and went through. In the room beyond he tried to turn and catch himself with the magnetic boots on the metal wall at the end. He did not make it.

The crash was a hard one. He felt his right arm go snap and the gun spun away. He landed upright but dazed, his right arm broken and useless. He could not even see the gun he had been carrying. Ted turned to watch the door that had closed behind him being vaporized by the dragonflies' weapons outside. He looked about in desperation now, but there was no other exit from this room. His arm was very painful and his part of the struggle was all over.

He was trapped.

Then the ship began to weave back and forth. This room, Ted's prison, tore open. The whole alien ship yawed and partly exploded. Ted found himself in space, thrashing around in debris.

Only later, when Ted and Lisa had both been picked up by the Atlas and after the rest of the alien fleet had retreated from the scene, did they learn the full story. In the last battle between the aliens and earth ships, the only occasion when one alien ship had been damaged, pictures had been taken. It was believed that the alien ships had a weakness down under their center guns, if they could be hit there.

When the Atlas came on the scene at full speed the officers saw one of the alien battleships wallowing, out of control, and not firing. The crew of the Atlas did not know this activity was due to Ted and Lisa. The Atlas had instantly tried the often-rehearsed only successful strategy of the last battle, moving down under the alien ship's guns and firing. The Atlas had blown a huge hole in the alien battleship. Ted had been thrown out of the hole in the ship into space. Lisa and a number of the alien crew had followed as the air was sucked into space from all the open compartments of the enemy ship. Ted and Lisa survived because they were still wearing space suits.

The remainder of the alien fleet had immediately retreated, as they had done before when they had a battleship blasted. Only this time the damaged vessel was left behind. Now the Atlas was towing the remains of the alien ship to port with some prisoners of both alien species safely secured on board in airtight compartments. For the moment the incursion was over.

Perhaps earth scientists could learn to decipher the language of the eyes. It seemed that earth had a chance again.

The Malthusian Murders

What _IF_ immortality was for sale?

This is a report on the confession of Bob Fond:

No! I never would have begun the adventure if I had known the denouement, but then how many of life's doorways would we leave unopened if we knew what was beyond? I moved into an action drama not realizing the end result.

My private seaplane flew in from the north, circled the tiny Caribbean Island once, very low, and I took some pictures as if I were a tourist. I was able to survey the adjacent ship harbor where three large yachts came into view. Two yachts were anchored at the pier, and one was just pulling out to sea. There were two other seaplanes in the landing basin below.

Then I told my pilot to land. The spray of the pontoons made a pretty scene in the water of the smooth inlet all the way to the plane dock.

It was annoying when my own jet was refused permission to land here. There was no airstrip and the tiny island accepted only seaplanes. So I had to rent what amounted to an air taxi. A charter ship would have taken a full day's trip each way from Antigua.

There were two burly men waiting on the dock to greet me, looking very tough in their striped tee shirts. On the beach at the base of the cliff a back up team of three men watched carefully.

"Hi, I'm Bob Fond here for an appointment with Dr. Cutter," I told them. My mood was not improved when the guards insisted on padding me down. There was not much room for a weapon in my tight fitting pants and gray short sleeve shirt. Only after these monkeys frisked me was I allowed to use the outdoor elevator that took people up the sheer cliff from the beach. The cliffside elevator was a nice touch; but I was thinking that it was probably all a scam anyway in spite of what I had been told. It could be an elaborate con game. Still, Steve Blazer of Argo International had recommended it. Steve was a man to be trusted.

At the top of the cliff I was led to an enormous home, something in the area of 20,000 square feet I guessed. The walkway up to the house further up a hill twisted and passed through gardens, beside an Olympic outdoor pool. There were two tennis courts next to a walkway leading to a patio and a wrap around veranda before the main entrance.

I was ushered into a small waiting room. All doctors like waiting rooms.

I sat facing a wall full of framed University degrees, medical associations to which the doctor belonged, academic societies, and awards won.

Then a nurse showed me into the paneled reception room where Dr. Cutter was waiting for me and we finally stood face to face. I had a feeling this was all staged. But after all the phone calls with information denied, probably from fear of taping, I at last met the great man.

What a name, I had reflected a number of times. It was a pity Dr. Cutter was not a surgeon instead of a research scientist. Joe Cutter did not look especially young, handsome, or even distinguished, considering what he was selling.

I am 47 years old and I guessed the doctor was ten years younger. I'm balding just a little, working on staying slim, and nothing here would help that. I'm still tall, strong, and hoped I was in the prime of life. It would be nice to stay that way awhile. It was exactly why I was here.

Dr. Cutter was a slightly built man, with short blond hair, very tanned, and was dressed not in medical clothes, but quite casually, in an open brown shirt and shorts. Ever since I had entered the business world, a quarter of a century ago, I had habitually looked at other men I met and thought to myself: 'I could lick him.' Now I could think it again. Was that sort of thinking simply business dominance or a flaw in my own character? I wondered. Twenty years ago I had taken up karate, working up to black belt with the same determination I showed in business. Of course there are degrees of black belts. I was only a first degree.

"I call this place the Island of Dreams. And I welcome you, Mr. Fond," Dr. Cutter declared.

"Thank you. It appears the dreams have done well by you."

Dr. Cutter just smiled and led the way back through some French doors onto the open veranda where we had a remarkable view of the harbor, the palm trees below, and the lushness of the tropics. Joe Cutter waved me into a colorful deckchair.

"Would you like a drink?"

"No. Not right now. You said on the phone that you could only tell me about your procedure in person."

"That is true. But before we talk, I want you to sign a waiver in which you promise to tell no one what I will reveal to you without my permission." Joe Cutter produced a sheet of paper.

"You didn't tell me that I'd need my attorney." I laughed and took the paper. I had seen enough contracts to feel I was almost a lawyer.

"It's a legal document, but as nearly free of jargon as I can get it." Joe Cutter had a ruddy open face and a wide smile that he turned on now.

It was a single page, essentially stating that certain things were going to be revealed and I was to promise never to tell anyone. If I did talk, I might be sued and damages obtained. If I wished to tell someone about this conversation, I must obtain Dr. Cutter's permission each separate time in advance. How binding the document was, that I did not know. But it was obvious since I had traveled three thousand miles from California to get information, that unless I signed this paper I might as well go home. Besides, I am not in the news business. There seemed to be no harm as long as I did not talk. I signed and dated the document, returning it to Dr. Cutter.

"Thank you. It is just a formality, but I do ask for strict confidentiality. I do not want the multitude, the great unwashed out there, knocking on my door and begging. Now tell me exactly what brings you here?"

"I hear you have the fountain of youth."

"No, rather a product designed to arrest the further ravages of time and freeze your age where you are now. Why do you want it?"

"That should be obvious. Because there is so little time. Sometimes I have thought I would like the words: 'There was not enough time' on my tombstone."

"It would be even better if there were no tombstone necessary for a long while," Dr. Cutter interjected. "But go on."

"I am a businessman. I suppose I enjoy the power that I have acquired and would like to hold on to it. If that makes me a bad guy, so be it. I have a younger brother who is a physicist at a University. He has less time than I do, he says."

"He will have to come out here himself. If you wish to tell him about the program, you will need permission even for a brother. But, what is true is that the most brilliant men may get a Ph.D. at twenty-five and then they have till they are forty to do their best work. The problem is universal for all of us short-lived humans. Movie starlets, prizefighters, football stars, and many others have even less time to achieve success."

"Life is short, nasty, and brutish."

"Now you are a philosopher too," Dr. Cutter asserted. "That is a quote from Hobbes. You asked me to come to the point, and I will. The cause of aging is to be found right in the DNA. We each have in our own cells what amounts to a computer tape that dictates how fast we age and ultimately when we will die. Some people die of accidents before their tape runs out. Some people die of diseases that can't be controlled by the technology available at the time they are living. Some drink or eat to excess. But the rest of the people all eventually die anyway. That has been true so far. I have a product, pills and a treatment, which stops the aging process."

"An anti-aging pill," I suggested.

"You could call it that. After the American laws of 2015 everyone has heard of telomerase. Life extension is illegal on the mainland of most developed countries now. The population explosion worldwide has caused that. The facts are easy. In 1650 A.D. there were a half billion people on the entire earth. In 1850 populations doubled to one billion people. Only in the 20th century did the numbers go up to two, three, four, five, and over six billion. Thomas Malthus warned of excess population in the 18th century. Now there are many new Malthusians."

"When news about immortality pills leaked out in the media there was consternation," I agreed.

Dr. Cutter laughed. "Yes Bob Fond" and Dr. Cutter looked right into my eyes, "if everyone became immortal and had one extra child, the population could double again at once. That would be the ultimate Malthusian dilemma." He paused. "That is why I bought my own independent island."

"Go on," I urged. And what followed is the most tedious part of my confession:

"Why do we age at all?" Dr. Cutter asked. "Leonard Hayflick, who wrote **How and Why we Age,** explained the problem better than anyone. He studied the replication of cells. As early as 1961 he found that after dividing 50 times, human cells would simply stop or die. This final entropy was called the 'Hayflick limit.' The cells had gotten old. The older the human being the cells were taken from the fewer times the cells divided before they stopped."

"Then in the 1990's it was discovered that telomeres, small bits at the end of DNA sequences which cap the chromosomes, are shortened with each cell division. The telomere is akin to a molecular clock, programming the cell, telling it when to stop dividing. The next step was telomere stimulators and enhancers, which allowed cells to continue dividing and thus prolong middle age. The ends of the cells could be enhanced so they provided more telomeres and hence divided longer."

I smiled. "I read the magazines and newspapers. The answer for immortality was discovered, but not for the masses."

"Besides," Dr. Cutter continued, "the process is expensive. Should we deny people who do not have the money? And then the religious organizations got into the act. 'We were playing God,' they said. Pressure was applied to all governments. In the end it was outlawed for everyone. Perhaps certain members of Congress, entrepreneurs, stars of the media with enough money, have found ways. I believe there are other clinics like mine out there, but we do not communicate with each other since it is internationally illegal."

"Who would invade your island? The United Nations?" I scoffed, chuckling. "This is the inverse of genocide. The whole effort to prevent the advancement of science amuses me."

Dr. Cutter went on: "My program acts upon the DNA, the cellular structure of the body itself. Diseases and accidents will still kill you, but you will not age appreciably under my supervision. You will not become older. You can still get sick, catch a cold, get the flu, and even die of other diseases if you don't seek medical attention. And that is up to you. But you will remain as healthy and youthful as you are now with my program. You will in effect freeze at this age."

"How long have you had this?" I asked.

"Five years. I experimented three years before developing this formula."

"But then it became illegal," I interjected.

"True. But for the last five years I have been selling my wares. The price is high; but you are a very rich man." And again Joe Cutter gave his most engaging smile.

I asked directly: "Is five years long enough to be sure? A lot of people in their middle years don't seem to age at all in five years. People are a long-lived species to test upon."

"That is true. It is why fruit flies and mice have been used in certain experiments. But I have examined the cells, including my own. The proof will be in the pudding. But this does come with a money back guarantee."

"And what is your price?"

"There is an initial charge of ten million dollars. You must return here for the pills each three months afterwards and there is a charge of one million dollars a year after that."

I stared in disbelief. This was a bit thicker than I expected. My net worth is around five hundred million and raising ten million was not a problem. But if this were a con game; it was a lot of money to lose. I had expected a price somewhere in the hundred thousands.

"The money back guarantee is simple," Joe Cutter continued. "If at any time, and that means any time, you wish to quit permanently and forever you will receive a full refund of all the money you put in."

"With interest," I asked.

Cutter smiled. "No. I'm afraid not. If you leave the program and the program has not failed, you get back only what you put in. There is one exception. If the program fails, you will, under the contract, be entitled to receive your money back in full with ten per cent annual interest compounded. I don't expect the program to fail. If, for instance, you have a heart attack or stroke, your heirs will receive the money and interest."

"But I am not allowed to tell my heirs!"

"Without my permission, you may tell no one. You have permission to tell one attorney only that you have what amounts to a life insurance program stored in your safe or bank vault. You will be given a document, which states that in effect. It is guaranteed. The policy does not apply to accidents, suicide, or preventable diseases. That is the deal and you can take it or leave it. And I do not expect to have to pay out. The program works."

"Tell me about the health guarantees," I inquired,

"If I accept you into this program, you may go to your private doctor on the outside and be checked. You must not tell him about the program you are in. You can get the usual base-line medical tests showing your over-all health. If there is aging proven in the future, in one year, five years, ten years, or forever, you are entitled to your money back with interest. If you attempt to climb Mount Everest and are killed, you get nothing. If you pick up some disease and do not seek medical attention, you get nothing."

"I belong to a 'life extension' clinic right now," I interjected.

"They do not offer what I do, but they are a good idea. Prevention is always better than cures."

"What side effects do these pills have? Do they make you sick?"

Dr. Cutter laughed: "No. The initial reaction to the first pill is usually a feeling of tranquility and well-being. This feeling intensifies sometimes as you take more pills. After you pay your deposit you will be put through a series of tests that will take two or three days before receiving the first pill. You will be expected to return each three months forever, for an hour of tests. If you don't return, you lose your money and everything."

"Why can't I take the pills along, a year's supply at a time?" I knew the answer to that, but I had to ask.

"For the same reason that you will swallow the pill in front of me each time. I do not want these pills to leave here and be analyzed. This is one reason I have set up on a private island as independent as a little nation. I do not intend to submit to the tests of any government, nor do I intend to share this formula with the multitude."

I smiled in agreement: "This is for the classes, not the masses or the asses. So we're both elitists. How many people do you have in your program now?"

"Thirty. I intend to expand to no more than fifty."

"That is still quite a bit of money," I said, thinking. Thirty people at ten million dollars each initially would be three hundred million. Then at a million a year each thereafter, that would be thirty million each year. Joe Cutter could afford his island and his mansion atop the cliff. The money Dr. Cutter received would all be tax free out here, unless the doctor had to pay one of the neighboring island nations for protection.

"Why is the number of your patients increasing so slowly when you offer immortality?" I inquired.

"The high price and," he shrugged. "I can't advertise. This is illegal. Word of mouth among the elite is slow."

"How many people have begun and then dropped out of the program?"

"None. One person has been killed in an accident."

"No refunds on that."

"I'm afraid not." Joe Cutter smiled again, his disarming open grin.

"Have you considered that perhaps the greatest men of our age should be given immortality rather than the wealthiest?" I asked. "Should some men be invited to partake of immortality?"

"That is a question I have never been asked before. You are an unusual person. But I am not in the philanthropy business. On the other hand you could finance such a person yourself. You have the money to do it. You mentioned a brother who is a physicist. What is greatness, Bob Fond? Define a great man for me. How would you choose?"

I did not reply. Instead I asked another question: "What is the longest anyone has been on your pills?"

"Six years. That would be me."

"How old are you?" I asked Dr. Cutter. We are all more aware of our own age than any other fact.

"I'm forty-three, now," the Doctor replied. "I started taking the pills when I was thirty-seven. I was quite lucky. I think thirty-five is the optimum age for people to begin the pills. I intend to try to stay close to that age forever."

Joe Cutter did not look forty-three. How do you tell? Now my personal question was: should I buy into this program? The money was not a problem, if the treatment really worked. But I had grown up poor and made my money in the software end of the Internet business, which was not as easy as it sounds. I respect money. Andrew Carnegie, the steel magnate, had given away two hundred million dollars. Only Carnegie never gave to beggars. Carnegie believed everything in life was educational. You taught beggars to continue begging by giving to them. I never gave to beggars either.

"How long do I have to think it over?"

"As long as you like. Have lunch. Have a swim down there in my pool. Swimsuits are available in the cabanas. If you want longer than today, I will ask you to leave and return when you have decided."

"Do you give group rates?" I was stalling now.

"You mean a wife?"

"I am currently long divorced. This is one place where I think the radicals have it right. I do not intend to marry again and get taken. But I do have a young lady friend whom I might be interested in preserving the youth of, if this seemed to work for me. I also have a son who is twenty and a daughter eighteen, both in college."

Dr. Cutter sighed. "And your lady friend's age?"

"Cynthia is twenty-four." I did not call her by her nickname, 'Sin'.

"Let them all age a little," Dr. Cutter advised. "Then it will be worth more to them. Until people are about twenty-five there is still a growth cycle which we must not interfere with."

"So in essence the people you want most are those in that broad middle ground of life from twenty-five to fifty-five, where we notice aging the least and therefore could be most easily fooled the longest."

"That is true on the age parameters. But I am not fooling anyone. The choice is yours. This does work. You can stop the program in one month, one year, or five years from now."

"And I get my money back without interest." I waved my arm to cut him off. "How long has my friend Steve Blazier been in the program?"

"He had my permission to tell you about the program, after I checked on your background."

"And you checked my ability to pay."

"That is true. If you want to ask Steve Blazier that question and he wishes to answer, then he may."

"Can I be put in touch with others who believe this has worked for them?"

"I'm afraid not."

"Suppose, Dr. Cutter, you yourself die in an accident, what happens?"

The doctor came right back with an answer: "My assistant, Dr. Mel Greer will carry on for me if I have an accident. He is on the island and you will meet him."

"I think I'll borrow a suit and take that swim. I would like a little while to think."

"Sure."

I swam and thought. It had all gone well, maybe too well. 'We're all in sales' had been one of my early mottoes. The first thing we sell is ourselves. Did I want to live forever? Maybe this wasn't forever. I could quit anytime. Would people wonder in five years or ten if I didn't seem to age? No it would take longer than that. This was illegal. But only Dr. Cutter was liable for breaking the law, not the patients. I had done some research of my own. And in ten years or twenty the times could change. Well suppose the laws became even more stringent? If there was DNA testing for instance to discover people who had taken the 'forever pill' then I could always pack my money and buy my own island.

What would it be like to live for eons? One could take it one day at a time. Oddly, the only times I remembered being bored was as a young child.

I thought of Cynthia, my current 'Sin.'

Previously I had married foolishly, too soon while I was still in college, and it had not lasted. My life with Helen, Hell I thought of it now, had seemed splendid at first. She was beautiful and we did well for several years. We had two children whom I loved dearly and still see every other weekend. I had made a lot of money. Then one day Helen announced that we needed separate bedrooms and no more sex. She declared she was fulfilled, had served her purpose as a woman, had two children, one of each gender, and she wished now to spend the next twenty years raising them. Perhaps after that we could try sex again.

At the time I could scarcely believe what I heard from Helen. We talked, we argued to no avail. I asked and she said there was no one else. I termed this result "the Black Widow spider" complex. After the female black widow spider had sex, she ate the male. The male was no longer needed. I felt I had children enough; but I did not feel sexually fulfilled for a lifetime. I suggested counseling or therapy. No. Helen said she knew what she wanted and did not need any advice from therapists or psychiatrists. Someone said once you really did not know a woman till you met her in divorce court. Yet I was still friends with Helen, even now.

I moved out, gave her the house, and supported her in the manner she had become accustomed to. Fortunately my business had begun to take off and I could afford it. I next lived with a series of women. Cynthia (Sin) was not after my money. She had finished college and had a good job in the advertising business. She was interested in psychology and philosophy. Sin was young, but perhaps, if my own aging slowed down we could be even closer in the future. Right now I sometimes I felt as if I were dating a daughter. Someday something beyond living together might happen with Sin, but not now.

Dr. Cutter had said that especially I must promise not to tell my children or Cynthia. That was an easy promise to make. I would feel foolish telling them that I was seeking immortality.

For immortals how many affairs might there be? Would a person eventually understand their own life and themselves? Why was I driven to make more money when I had enough? Did I want to be a billionaire? No. It was probably just power. Making money had become a way of life. For better or worse, there it was.

I finished the swim and made the decision. Yes, I would enter the program. I had done twenty laps of the huge Olympic pool easily. The swim test could be taken annually to see if my health was holding up.

There were medical forms to be filled out, tests to be taken, questions asked. Did I smoke? No. Had I taken hard drugs that might have done things to my chromosomes? No. How much did I drink? I lied a little.

Dr. Cutter's clinic had equipment that rivaled the world's best hospitals. There was twilight sleep during some tests and injections. Then I was told I had been accepted into the program. For some people the program did not work well. I *was assured it would be successful in my case.*

Now it was my turn. It was a matter of selling stock fund options, at not the best time, and transferring ten million dollars electronically to a neutral Swiss bank.

Then there were further injections and not one pill but a series. I was in the program.

Dr. Mel Greer, whom I met during the testing, was tall, stoop shouldered, and shadowy, certainly an assistant, staying in the background. The nurse, Betty Hines, was young, quiet, and could not be opened up for conversation. She may have been more than a nurse to Dr. Cutter.

I returned three times to the island clinic, after three, six, and nine months, right on schedule.

I asked permission to tell my brother George. "Bob, how will your brother George come up with the required fee as an Associate Professor?" Dr. Cutter inquired of me.

"I would finance him," I replied simply, though George was proud and this was not a simple matter. Dr. Cutter had agreed George could be told.

But George, who was 39 years old, said he would think about it and I heard no more on the matter from my brother. George thought about things for years. George promised to tell no one.

*   *   *

And then the frightening events began. Steve Blazier, who had invited me into the program, saw me at a business dinner and while we were talking casually Steve said: "It's important I meet with you, Bob. I don't want to say more now. I'd like to arrange lunch at the outside terrace of the Raven." Why outdoors, I wondered, but I agreed.

Steve Blazier was about fifty, of medium height, but solidly built. He had a flattened nose from a youthful altercation.

There was a third man who joined us for the lunch at the Raven. Jerry Walters was CEO of Conrath and on the board of directors of a dozen companies. I did not know Jerry Walters well. He was sixty, perhaps. Jerry always wore gray suits. He was a nervous, thin man with a hatchet face and a beak nose. Jerry looked ashen now, the color of his suit.

Steve came to the point as soon as we were served our food. "I'm sorry to have to tell you this, Bob, since I invited you into the program. Jerry, here, invited me in. He was my contact. It's like a chain letter, only with just one link we each know about."

Jerry looked about anxiously then he opened up: "Really, we have promised and even signed a paper to the effect that we would not do what we are doing now." His voice seemed to rasp.

"That's true," I agreed, "but I sure won't give you away. You seem worried."

"Really," Jerry went on, "I've been in the program five years. I'll he sixty-five this year. At sixty, Dr. Cutter said I was entering the program late, but I was in good health and he finally accepted me. I am not about to retire. I own so much of my company; the Board of Directors can't and won't dump me. But really that's not why we're here. I got Steve in and he got you in. Harold Flowers in London got me in. You've heard of him?"

I nodded. "Only from the newspapers and TV stations he owns. I never met him. Go on."

"It was an auto accident. Harold and his wife were both killed. They were both in the program."

"They were your contacts. It could be unnerving," I suggested, trying to be soothing, trying to relieve the obvious tension I felt at the table.

"Harold told me last week when he was in L.A. that his contact was Brett Ryan. Really."

I knew Ryan well. He had inexplicably jumped to his death from his penthouse in New York City a few weeks ago. Ryan's business seemed solid. There was no suicide note. But there was apparently no one else in the penthouse at the time. It was still under investigation. I nodded again. "I knew Ryan and his family," I divulged.

"Harold told me that if anything happened to him, I really better watch out for myself." Jerry Walters spit out all the words at once, anxious to get this over.

I felt a cold chill. "Is Dr. Cutter rolling up his network because the program doesn't work?" I asked. "There will be no refunds to any of the people who died."

"We all mostly knew only one person, the one we recommended into the link," Steve Blazier suggested. "Yet I feel good. I felt the program was working."

"Are they all men except Harold and his wife?" I asked.

"I really recommended someone else," Jerry Walters offered. "Henry Winslow."

I gasped in disbelief. "He was killed two weeks ago in a hunting accident. So the chain can have more than one link. But if someone cut the links to the chain, how do we know how many others who were in the program died?" I wondered out loud.

"Have you recommended anyone?" Steve asked of me.

"My brother George. He'll think it over for years. He isn't in. I received permission to ask him, but he's very indecisive."

"Maybe he's safe," Steve concluded.

I shifted uncomfortably, toying with my salad. Suddenly I wasn't hungry. "I also felt the program was working," I related.

"We all did," Jerry declared. "Really, my medical tests have been so much the same each year that my doctors are surprised. It may be really just a placebo effect, where you feel good because you have been told you will feel good. But no, I think the program is really a success. Only there is the money. Maybe Dr. Cutter has enough money and wants to get out."

Jerry Walters thought for a while and then let the rest of what he was feeling out: "Really, Bob touched on another element we should examine also. My wife died before I could get her into the program. She was only fifty-four. It was a sudden stroke. She died before I found out about the program. Really, I am sure my wife's death had nothing to do with these recent deaths, all in the last month. You can swear people to secrecy, but how far does that go? Sometimes secrets get out because one person is told, who really only tells one other person and so on. Casey who ran the CIA during the Reagan years defined secrecy. He said: 'A secret is something you know and tell no one else.' I am telling you what I know. And I'm really scared."

I reviewed in my mind all the names mentioned. Then I suggested: "Where do we start? Some of these people may have asked others into the program that we don't even know of. These deaths go beyond coincidence. We could get a private agency to investigate if other men of great wealth have died in the last month. We would not have to mention Dr. Cutter, the program, or his island. We could discretely inquire of relatives of those who have died if they had heard anything from the deceased before their deaths. The attorneys of the dead men would have investigated their wills and safe deposit boxes. They will have found Dr. Cutter's documents indicating there was an insurance policy. Questions will be asked."

"But," Steve interrupted, "the guarantee we received, which looks a lot like an innocuous insurance policy, declares there is no payoff at all in the case of accident or suicide."

"Yes," I agreed, "only the sum of money is such that lawyers would certainly investigate. I wonder what the lawyers may have discovered."

"We really know little of this chain of people who are part of this program," Jerry observed. "Really, Dr. Cutter said he had thirty-five participants when I was in for my annual checkup last month."

"We do have some places to start," Steve indicated. "I will look into the detective agency approach. Jerry, maybe you can contact some of Harold's relatives. This is Tuesday. Maybe we can meet back here at noon Friday?"

"I am going to New York tomorrow," I told them, "but I will return Friday. I would like to talk to Brett Ryan's sister, Peg, about her brother's death. I know Peg fairly well. She's married to Hollister Aimes."

Steve gulped. "You haven't heard. Aimes was killed just yesterday in a boating accident."

We looked at each other. It must be that Aimes had been in the program.

We all agreed to meet for lunch at the same place Friday. I walked away feeling a bit dazed.

It was absurd in a way. Three middle aged rich men seeking immortality and meeting to discuss murder. Perhaps their own murder.

In New York I arrived just after Hollister Aimes funeral. Peg was a willowy woman, distraught over losing her brother and then her husband. Her face was red and puffy and she had not bothered to hide the tears with make-up. Her pent-house over Central Park was plush, lavish, right out of "House Beautiful." There were several people in the place. There were introductions. I had been here before. After I offered the usual condolences, I found a way to get Peg to a quiet corner and ask her if she knew of a program her husband had been in.

Yes, she knew. Her husband and brother both had been in the program. They had told her to say nothing. She was scheduled to go into the program herself next month. Now she was afraid. Peg said that I should talk to General Jackson Turner. He was against the program and had warned her husband.

"Warned him how?" I asked.

"Oh, Jack is all right," Peg insisted. "He's an old friend."

"Yes, but what was his warning?"

"Jack is a member of the 'Right to Death Society' and a little peculiar on this subject, so you won't want to get him started. But he is not involved in this. He would do nothing to hurt me."

I thought about this statement. Nothing to hurt her? What of her husband and her brother? Would he hurt them? And then right on cue the doorbell rang and the General was announced.

General Jackson Turner, retired, was tall, gray-haired, but quite tanned and carried himself severely erect. He was wearing a dark business suit. General Turner seemed startled when Peg introduced me: "This is an old friend, Bob Fond." It was as if the general knew my name, but could not quite place me. He gave Peg a hug that could pass for sorrow over the recent twin funerals, or something else. There was body chemistry here, at least on the General's part. I suddenly felt like an outsider with these two.

In a moment the General opened the conversational gambit further when he declared: "I'm so glad Peg that you did not become a part of this illegal conspiracy." So the General knew of the program.

The General's comment seemed designed to draw me into the net and I accepted the bait. "People have always yearned for longer lives, General," I declared. "That seems natural enough to me. Five years from now, or ten, further questions may be asked about life extension, but we seem to be dealing with murder here." There! I put the situation as mildly as I could, but I wanted a response.

The General gritted his large teeth: "I took retirement three years ago at 52. There were no further promotions in store for me because the whole country has gone lax again after the Terrorist Wars. The military has been cut. People who have not earned it want to live forever, not just five or ten years longer. Congress, the majority at least, has passed laws. It is illegal."

"But you got your star," Peg interrupted.

"Yes, one-star. A retirement gift after five years of being passed up for promotion by lesser men. They were glad to get rid of me. I was a nuisance."

I felt the general wanted more stars, but it went beyond that. Even at his pay scale, he could not afford ten million dollars for Dr. Cutter's clinic. I had talked of murder and the word had been ignored in the conversation so far,

"How do you earn immortality, General?" I asked, reverting back to the earlier conversational thread.

"Actually there is no way. No one but God deserves that. The Bible says three score and ten. It is all a matter of allotted time."

"There are men in the past that have lived to be a hundred," I informed him. "They were always a small minority, of course. Perhaps we should change the allotment of time."

"You make fun of me, sir," the General flushed.

I wanted to say how easy that would be, but instead I raised the pressure: "Are you planning on suicide at age seventy, General?"

Jackson Turner's face went livid. "Have you ever been in the military sir? Have you served your country? Why should you be chosen for immortality only because you have plenty of money? A missile up your ass would solve the question of immortality pills."

"Now Jack, really, please." Peg remonstrated, but she also squeezed the general's arm. I wondered who had told the General I was in the program.

"General, if my country was under attack, I would join, if I could, even at my age."

"Maybe. Man is the dominant creature on this planet because he did not worry about endangering other species. Man domesticated animals, not the other way around. Man attained supremacy not by standing around like cows waiting to be milked."

I had heard enough. Peg continued to hold the General's arm, for support or, well I just did not know.

"I had better go," I declared. "I have a late night flight back to California and I better get ready." Actually I had decided to move the flight ahead, get out of New York right away and return to an environment I knew where I might feel more secure.

*   *   *

Paying extra always helps especially on first class flights and I got out of New York quickly. Back at my own home, it was time to tell my live-in long-term girl friend, Cynthia, all that had happened. We stood in the oversized kitchen, sipping a light wine. Cynthia's big blue eyes went wide in astonishment. She twisted and played with her long blonde hair as always.

"What will you do," she inquired simply?

"I don't know. Tomorrow is Friday. I'll go back to the Raven Restaurant at noon and meet Steve Blazier and Jerry Walters and see what they have found. If they haven't hired a detective agency and started to investigate then I intend to."

Cynthia nodded. "Come to bed. Tomorrow will be a better day. But I worry about you. If you are doing this because of our age difference, you shouldn't."

"No. When you are a bit older, I can involve you as well. But right now I just don't know what is happening. Well, tomorrow better be a better day."

* * *

The next day I arrived early on purpose and walked through the Raven restaurant to the wide outside patio overlooking the city. Had I been followed? Was I being watched? Was scanning and listening equipment trained on me? As they say: 'Just because you're paranoid doesn't mean they aren't after you!' I found a table where I could survey the entire area. It was nearly noon now.

Time dragged its feet. Somehow the minutes passed. I ordered just a coke and waited and waited. No one showed. Steve Blazier was always punctual. Jerry Walters would not be a half-hour late. There were no messages of calls when I asked the headwaiter. My cell phone had no messages either. Then it was half past twelve. No one was coming. I was alone!

I ate and left the restaurant walking quickly, sending for my attendant parked car. I decided to go up to Steve Blazier's home and see what was going on there. There would be no warning calls ahead; I would just drive out and see what was happening,

There are many coastal roads in California along the high cliffs. I had never really thought before about the four-mile stretch of unpaved road leading to Steve Blazier's home. He lived in a mansion he called "Mountain View". Only now as I entered this lonely side road was I aware of being followed. There was a big black van on my tail and it was not even pretending or hanging back.

What to do? I had one advantage. I had been to Steve's parties and driven this road several times. But here I was in an open sport car, with a huge van closing fast now. It attempted to ram my bumper from behind.

Then, when I sped up, taking the turns a bit too fast, the van swung to the left lane and there was contact. They were attempting to push me off the road. To my right there was this vast drop. Then for a moment both our vehicles passed between rocky cliffs on each edge of the road and both sides of my car showered with sparks. I was being crushed between the van and the smooth rocks. In a moment the rocky cliff would end on the right and then the van could push me off the precipice. I hit the brakes hard, nosing into the rocks on the right just before the wall ended and the sheer drop began again. The van swung wide ahead and then in the open space went off the road and over the cliff. It all happened in seconds.

In the movies when these things happened there was always an explosion and fire. Here the van just rolled over and over. The occupants should be killed or badly injured. My right fenders, both front and rear, were gone, torn to shreds. And my right front tire had blown. The wheel felt loose. I walked the final mile to Steve Blazier's house. His house was deserted. The front door was strangely unlocked, but there were no servants, no secretary, no one to question. It was a fool's errand, a wild people chase in the worst sense.

I have never considered myself to be especially brave or daring. Maybe the General's words had aroused me. Certainly the attempt to kill me was real. I felt totally angry now. I called a taxi and took it back to the nearest town that had a rental car agency. Then I called Cynthia at work. I told her about the events of the morning.

"Cynthia," I told her, "I want you to leave work. Get a hotel room under another name. Stay out of sight. Tell no one where you are going. From time to time use a public phone and call our home phone and listen for my message on the answering machine. I'm going out to the island clinic and confront Dr. Cutter. I want some answers. If you haven't heard from me in two days, you have to assume they got to me too. Then you should pull the money from our joint account and leave town. Wait a month or more. I don't think they are after you, but they may assume I told you and try to get you too. I want you to be safe."

"Go to the police," Cynthia pleaded. "This is interstate. The FBI could intervene."

"What I did to try for immortality was also mildly illegal under current law. I feel like I am on my own. I have to do this." We talked further, but I was adamant.

I flew to Miami and then rented a seaplane. It was already late and the plane would not leave till Saturday morning. I stayed overnight at a hotel under an assumed name and paid cash so there was no way to trace me.

Now I was returning to the island of dreams, but under very different circumstances. The pilot, well paid, noticed my tension. There were no other planes at the island this time and only one yacht in the inlet harbor. I was not met at the dock at all, but three men in their striped shirts waited for me to come to them.

"You have no appointment here," one of the men called to me. "Get back in your plane and get out of here."

"I am a patient of Dr. Cutter. I want to see him."

The men waited till I reached the dock shed and then swarmed all over me. "You were told, now go back."

In the movies the hero knows karate and defeats them all. I landed one good kick, but this struggle was soon over.

Then Dr. Cutter appeared. "Stop," he ordered. "Frisk him and then let him in."

They padded me all over, even more carefully and intrusively than before. "He's clean," one of the men announced.

Again I was alone with Dr. Joe Cutter on the veranda.

"What brings you here?" he inquired his voice not quite normal. "Your next appointment is in a month."

"I think you owe me ten million dollars and an explanation."

Dr. Cutter was pale. "It wasn't you then, who has been causing trouble. My assistant, Dr. Mel Greer, took his yacht and went to Miami for supplies a month ago. He disappeared in Miami."

"Maybe he sold out," I suggested. "Or maybe he is behind a whole series of murders."

"Hardly. They found his body yesterday. He had been tortured and dumped in the ocean. He probably did talk and told all he knew. Two of my bodyguard assistants were shot by long range snipers yesterday while they waited on the dock. My employees are afraid to go far out on the dock now. My patients are being wiped out one by one. I have followed all this on the internet. Some of my patients did not come in for scheduled appointments. When something happens to high profile people it is easy to follow. I don't know who is killing my patients or why." Dr. Cutter's words came in short bursts, not necessarily following rationally. "I am packing and going to close down. I did my part of the bargain. I owe no one anything. My patients are all being targeted."

"Shouldn't they all have been warned? How many are left?"

"I don't know. A fellow in Bombay I talked to on the phone last night is still O.K."

"They will probably trace the call and get him too," I ventured.

"Something may happen to me," Dr. Cutter exclaimed his voice rising. "I suppose I owe you something. You thought this was me doing this, and you had the guts to come out here. Here, take this disk. This is a copy of my notes and the program. I have made several disk copies of the formula. They may get to me. I would like you to have one copy as insurance." The disk was in a little plastic case enclosed by a plastic zip-lock bag. I took it and put it in my pocket. It could contain something or nothing.

Suddenly I believed Dr. Cutter. "When are you leaving?" I asked him. And then I added: "No refunds on any of the murdered people."

"I didn't murder anybody," he replied, angry.

"You are the one pulling out. The program stops and I get nothing. Is that the way it ends?"

"I can transfer your ten million to your bank today," Dr. Cutter replied. "You can watch me do it." He shook his head again. "It takes a while to pack things. I was never good at that. I have so much research. Will you stay here tonight?"

He wanted company. Maybe he was afraid or wanted a chance to kill me. "No," I countered. "It's still early afternoon. I do believe you. But I see no reason to stay. Do you know a General Jackson Turner?"

"Yes, he has made threats. Tell me what you know."

"No. You tell me more first," I demanded.

"I am in the middle of some computer things," Joe Cutter asserted.

"Take a swim in the pool and relax a little. Sorry my guards roughed you up. Perhaps I can finish packing and get out today too."

I decided that his guards could shoot me anytime. But if that were Dr. Cutter's intention, it would be all over already. Why give me a disk unless it was real? Or it could all be a scam. I didn't really trust anybody now. "I want to know more," I told him. "An hour then?"

"All right," Cutter agreed.

I went down to the pool area and changed to one of the swimsuits hanging on hooks in the cabanas. Then luckily, as it turned out, I laid my clothes out at the pool edge with the disk from Dr. Cutter in my pants pocket. I swam my twenty laps. It felt good.

Cynthia was right, I decided. I should go to the FBI. I had broken the law trying for immortality, but murder was a bit worse. If I told what I knew, I ought to be able to make a deal. I probably needed to sell some stocks anyway and then leave the country for a while afterwards. I could change my name and identity if necessary. My assistants could manage my corporations. And there were plenty of places to visit in the world. In a few years the governmental policies against immortality could all change.

I was right at the side of the pool beside my clothes when I saw the plane coming in slowly. Then the missile was fired low, heading for Dr. Cutter's house of dreams. "A missile up your ass," General Turner had said.

I grabbed for my clothes and the disk and dived under water. The explosion took out the house and the firestorm rolled right over the pool for an instant. The water felt warmer as I surfaced.

The house was in flames. My pilot in the rented seaplane down at the landing dock made an effort to take off and then there was the rattle of a gun from the attacking plane. My seaplane started to climb and then nosed over, dead in the water.

There was more gunfire beyond my view now. Then the invading plane circled and left. I watched till it was a dot on the horizon, then climbed out of the water and checked that the disk was still safe in its plastic bag. Next I wrung out my wet clothes. The house was still burning brightly. I would not have any more conversations with Dr. Cutter. His aides, nurse, and guards were all finished I was sure. I climbed a ridge and looked at the boat harbor. Dr. Cutter's yacht had been shattered by gunfire and sunk. There was still a small speedboat tied to a dock at the other end of the shore. The speedboat was under the trees and hard to see from the air no doubt.

I looked around a little and then took the speedboat in toward Miami. On the boat I spread out my wet clothes to dry in the sun. There was a compass but I was still not sure I was headed in the right direction. The water began to get choppy for the small boat. Then I was stopped by a coast guard ship looking for smugglers.

It was time to tell all and let the coast guard investigate. I was returned to Miami to await special agents. I later turned the disk over to the Justice Department.

How many connections General Jackson Turner has, I do not know. General Turner and his organization were going to need them all.

* * *

This concludes the confession and statement of Bob Fond. He will be a witness in the case against General Jackson Turner. The illegal immortality formula on the disk has been turned over to the investigating authorities.

The Justice Department wanted to close down the "Right to Death Movement" and here was an opportunity.

Bob Fond made a copy of the disk for himself before he turned it in. Someday there would be a new house of dreams and a fresh start to immortality.

The Prodigy

What <u>IF</u> you remembered everything?

Is there such a thing as
remembering too much?

"Henry … Henry Bryce … Come here!" A shrill voice spoke the magic words and a small, skinny boy scampered and skipped into what was curiously called the living room. He was smiling in anticipation. Mrs. Bryce, Henry's mother, was a slender woman with deep-set eyes, a pinched face, and a sharp nose. She beamed at the two elderly ladies who were her guests today and had to pay the price for their tea and cookies now.

Henry knew what his mother's smirk meant and he beamed, brushing back his straight black hair, and then clasping his little palms behind him. Next he spread his feet far apart until he felt securely balanced for a long siege and began reciting poetry.

In between poems Mrs. Bryce interjected that these were poems Henry's father had read to him only once. The elderly guests exclaimed in disbelief. It was easy to exclaim, for they really didn't believe it.

The poetry was mixed as it poured from the boy's lips. Some words he pronounced poorly and he never stopped for punctuation. The tumbling words were amusing, so the one old guest nudged the other, but they dared not laugh. The titles were run into the verse and since Henry started the next rendition immediately after finishing one offering, there was considerable confusion.

The elderly guests listened with apparent pleasure for several minutes. But as time passed and Henry gave no sign of slowing down, the eyes of the visitors began to wander. It took the proud mother some minutes longer to grow restless, but at length she turned to the reciter and declared quietly: "That will be enough now dear."

The boy broke off almost at once, but an unhappy expression crossed his earnest face. "I never get to finish," he grumbled.

His mother was a patient woman: "How much longer will it take, dear?" she asked as the visitors shuddered.

Henry looked startled at the question. Then he shrugged his narrow shoulders and declared simply: "Don know."

Mrs. Bryce waited till her son left the room before she exclaimed to the visitors: "Imagine. He won't be five until October. I'm going to try to get him into first grade and skip kindergarten."

As you guessed, this is the story of Henry Bryce. He was his mother's first and only adventure into parenting. Henry's father was a CPA, working for a large corporation, but he also had a dream of being a poet. Mr. Bryce was a quiet, rotund man, willing to let his wife rule without a struggle. Mrs. Bryce worried and fussed over Henry. She had been especially worried when he fell on his head at the age of ten months.

Henry was small, but even as a baby there was something distinctive about him. He talked before he was eight months old, repeating whole sentences he had heard. His father read him numerous stories and poems and Henry loved to recite.

There were some expensive private schools in this mid-western suburb, and after due deliberation it was arranged that Henry should attend one of these. The school authorities were sufficiently impressed when Henry reeled off the first two scenes of Shakespeare's **Hamlet** to place him in second grade at once. But for a while there was trouble.

Henry did not seem able to learn to read. At first his teacher was convinced he knew how to read already and was a genius. She was actually a bit frightened of Henry. But then one day she gave Henry a book he had never seen before. No one had read this book out loud to Henry and he could not read a word of it.

There followed a bit of a bumpy ride in school. His teacher felt it ought to be easy to teach a child of Henry's ability to read, but after she experienced some difficulty, Henry was demoted to first grade to pick up the fundamentals. Mrs. Bryce began to work with Henry at home on reading and pronunciation. She was really aggravated when in spite of her best efforts Henry made very slow progress and flunked first grade.

The principal, who was sympathetic, put it more kindly; declaring Henry was "only temporarily detained." The boy was given a push with private tutors during the summer and eventually Mrs. Bryce's day did come. Once he did learn to read Henry tackled all kinds of books from novels to dictionaries. He was double promoted three times in a row. He tackled mathematics with violent speed and repeated back everything in amazing fashion.

Henry was just twelve when he entered high school. Mrs. Bryce watched eagerly for some clue that would indicate a direction to Henry's life. The boy took French, Spanish, and German. Soon he was speaking these languages as well as the teachers at the school. Chemistry with its formulas was easy. The history instructor declared the boy knew more than she did. He seemed to know every rule in English grammar. In English composition alone he struck a snag, but luckily there was not much essay writing. Teachers did not like to read and grade such papers.

In physical education Henry was undersized and slow, but he knew every baseball and football score since the games had begun. This knowledge won him a few friends and impressed the coach enormously.

Henry worked hard and finished high school in three years, graduating first in his class at the age of fifteen. His scores on the various college entrance examinations led him to receive a full scholarship.

Mrs. Bryce cried when Henry left for the big Eastern University. The school was on the quarter system and Henry decided he would go all year round and finish in three years easily. He had a number of college credits already, having taken all the advanced placement classes his high school offered. There was something about finishing college at age eighteen that appealed to him. That would make him a genius, wouldn't it? There would be so much time then to decide what to do with the rest of his life. Perhaps he would go on at once for a Ph.D. or an M.D..

He held the thought of being a genius close when he went to sleep on cold winter nights; it kept him from feeling lonely so far from home. He was fortunate in having a comfortable two-person dorm shared with a bright boy, Bertrand Reginald Woodside Dunster III, who came from a wealthy family. Bert had twenty preparations in the bathroom, which somehow still did not cure his pimples.

It was the age of the computer and Henry Bryce had his own computer. There was a great deal of information to be learned on the internet.

But sometimes Henry was afraid. There was the time in a history class when he offered to recite the American Constitution and everyone laughed. Why? Something was wrong. But what? He comforted himself that this was one of the trials of being a genius.

His feeling of uneasiness increased during his second year in college. At length Henry came to think that he had missed something along the way. He had read hundreds of books. But perhaps his knowledge was not systematically arranged. He began reading the Encyclopedia Britannica in the University library.

It was in the spring quarter that it happened. His psychology professor, Dr. Harvey Fiske, gave him a "B" grade. Dr. Fiske was a man who gave very strange tests and never seemed to notice Henry. When, on top of that, Henry received a "C-" in English composition, all other considerations rushed from his mind. The 'minus" seemed particularly appalling. Of course some people did not like anyone who was smarter than they were. But he must find out what was wrong!

So Henry Bryce found himself at the door to the office marked: "Harvey Fiske, Psychologist".

*　　*　　*

Harvey Fiske had never intended to be a psychologist. But he was one and nothing could be done about it now. Not that Harvey Fiske ever really did anything other than lecture anyway. He thought mostly. He thought about thinking. Thinking was an interesting thing to think about. Harvey Fiske had been thinking about thinking for twelve years and now at age 41 he was at the top of his profession. He believed he had thought about thought more than any man. Or so he liked to think. Sometimes he thought words into his recorder and his secretary typed it on the computer and Harvey edited it. Later the critics, who couldn't understand it anyway, said it was a great book. But no matter, only a few bought the book. Psychology was like that.

Tangible things annoyed Harvey Fiske. What was the use of discussing something you could just look up and find out all about? Thought now was different. No one knew what caused thought or how it had all begun. Now there was something to think about. You could sink your teeth into intangibles. Harvey was a fatalist in a way. He felt there were some questions no one would ever be able to answer, for he couldn't.

Harvey Fiske was also a bit of a philosopher. In one of his books he had argued that just as it was impossible to define a word in terms of itself, so it would be forever impossible to discover the inner workings of the mind by the use of the mind. It was akin to a puzzle solving itself.

Harvey's brother had been feeble minded and Harvey was a genius. His brother's head and brain were the size of his own. And yet his brother had been unable to learn, read, speak, or think at all. About this Harvey thought also. He had known psychologists who went insane thinking about thinking. But then Harvey Fiske was not sure what insanity was either.

*   *   *

Harvey Fiske was in. This was his required office hour. Henry Bryce knocked diffidently and then at the single word: "Come," he opened the door and rushed in quickly. The office was small, containing a roll top desk and many shelves along the wall with books piled high.

Fiske was forced to devote three hours a week to consulting students who might need consulting. But he didn't encourage anyone to come. "Yes?" he inquired.

"Dr. Fiske, if it please you sir, I, well. I took an intelligence test when I entered this school. What was my score?"

"Uh." Harvey Fiske always said "Uh." Then he questioned: "Your name?" Here he betrayed his ignorance of a pupil who had been in his class for two quarters.

The psychologist asked for other information and then turned to one of his large file cabinets, extracting a manila folder. Finally he requested: "Sit down, won't you."

Henry sat. His hands gripped the edge of the chair. "Well?"

"I don't always disclose this information because sometimes due to nervousness or ill health on the day of the test, a student may do poorly and still be quite bright. In your case I find you have achieved a 178, which would rank you in the high 99th percentile. Still one number can't classify a person. There are many kinds of intelligence, musical, artistic, mechanical, personality itself, among other things that are not measured here."

Henry sighed in relief. Next he frowned. "Well then why am I having so much trouble? There's my roommate. He's considered very smart and he got an "A" in your class. But in chemistry he has to read the book over four or five times before he learns it and then he's forgotten half of what he read in a week!"

Fiske raised his eyebrows slightly. "Only half? If you're in my psychology class you should know that half is exceptional after a week. Do you remember what a forgetting curve is?"

Henry brightened at this and quickly quoted four paragraphs from each of three texts on the forgetting curve. Fiske was startled. Slowly he opened one of the volumes Henry had quoted and turned to the page. Yes, the answer had been given word for word.

"I didn't ask for memorization in any of my classes," Fiske related. "Besides, one of those definitions is a rather poor one. Why did you learn them?"

"I just read them."

"You mean you only read it once?"

Henry felt himself breaking down entirely. There was perspiration on his forehead. Dr. Fiske seemed to be questioning the very basis of his ability. Henry replied rapidly: "Yes, I read it once. Is there something wrong with that? I used to think that everybody read things over once and then remembered them. If you don't remember what's the use of reading? You don't read to forget, do you? This isn't a society with thought police yet. Is it a crime to remember what you read?"

"How much of what you read once do you remember?" Fiske asked raising one thick expressive eyebrow very high.

"All of it."

Fiske's other eyebrow leaped up and passed the first.

Henry went on: "I thought everyone did that. Or at least all really smart people. But it doesn't seem to do me much good."

Fiske considered the problem. "You are saying you remember everything you read and never forget it?"

Of course the psychologist didn't believe him. "What does a forgetting curve mean to you in your own words," he inquired?

Henry blinked his eyes, and stared straight ahead for moment. "I don't like those 'in your own words' questions," he replied after a moment. "I just quoted three sources."

"True. But now I would like to determine if you are learning things you don't really understand. Tell me, in your own words, what a forgetting curve is."

Again there was silence for a moment. At last Henry brushed the hair back on his head and looked at Dr. Fiske defiantly. Then he replied. "It is a curve showing the time elapsed as people forget what they read or heard. But it does not apply to me. I don't know any more."

"So you are mouthing verbalisms. A forgetting curve shows the rate of forgetting for normal human beings. Most of what we learn we forget in 24 hours. How long ago did you read these books?"

"Two I read last month and the one you are holding, three months ago. I am telling the truth. That should make me a genius or something."

Fiske considered the new problem. "Not necessarily. The intelligence test you were given was weighted with vocabulary, mathematical problems, and things you might have learned and remembered. What other parts of this book did you learn?"

"You still don't understand," Henry protested. "I read all three books. I know them all. I've read hundreds of books and I know them all. I am currently reading the **Encyclopedia Britannica** and have reached 'Q'. I also have started the **Oxford English Dictionary**."

Fiske opened the psychology book he was holding and began jumping from place to place, asking what came after a particular line. Henry was one hundred per cent accurate with every quote. For nearly an hour Fiske kept it up and Henry beamed with pleasure. He had not been asked to recite for such a long time.

Dr. Fiske tried another book from his shelf Henry had read. At last he confessed: "Yes, I believe you."

"Then I am a genius," Henry insisted.

Dr. Fiske felt some annoyance. "Not necessarily," he replied. "It does not seem to me that a genius is one that memorizes everything easily that comes his way. You may be a great walking reference library. But are you an original thinker? A genius, it seems to me, is a person who learns what is known and then adds to it for the good of the human race. To just learn what is known isn't advancing. We need men who will discover, invent, draw, compose, experiment, and add to the sum of our knowledge. What you can do is pretty amazing, but any good public library or computer can supply the same information."

Henry.Bryce's world seemed to crumble. "But how do you know I'm not original?" he demanded.

"I don't. But I think I would be taking orders from you, even if you are only seventeen, if you coupled originality with such wide learning."

"I'm sixteen," Henry corrected.

Fiske rummaged through his desk drawers for a moment and then handed Henry some printed pages. "These will test your originality. Go into the next room through that door and answer these questions. These are problems calling for actions. In most cases you will not have met with similar situations in life. They will test your creative ability."

Henry took the papers into a small room with only a table and chairs. He closed the door and sat down. This was surely not what he expected. The problems did not seem to have any possible answer. He hunted through his memory looking for applications. Nothing seemed to click. At last he began to make blind calculations, writing down numbers and ideas. It was akin to the English compositions that gave him so much trouble. When the topic for the compositions did not depend on his life experiences, reading, or current events in the newspapers, he had problems.

Henry looked at his watch. He had been at this for an hour and gotten nowhere. He could remember anything he read, saw on television, or was told. But Fiske was right. He wasn't a genius.

There were two doors to the little room where he sat. Henry opened the second door. There was a hallway and he made his escape, returning to his dormitory room.

Bertrand Dunster, his pimpled roommate, was in the dorm room and he had to tell someone. He blurted the whole story out to Bert Dunster who listened in open-eyed amazement and then began pacing the floor with great lanky steps: "Well?" Henry asked at last.

"Well, I believe you. Yes, yes, I believe you. I knew there was something odd about you from the beginning. That was why you never took notes in class. Well, you've got nothing to worry about. So, you're not a genius. So what? You're still a prodigy, and more. You can finish college. You may not be at the top of the class, but you'll be close. I'll help you with English compositions and you can help me. You read and remember and I'll apply things for you." Bertrand Dunster III looked up from his circular pacing, indicating he wanted agreement.

Henry nodded solemnly.

"You and I will be partners. How does that sound?"

"Good, I guess," Henry agreed.

"Is it a deal?"

"Yes."

"Listen Henry, there is a great future for you. You know everything and I'm full of ideas. Look at the quiz shows you can be on! Big firms will hire us. Law and medicine are both built upon knowing things. Big law firms will hire you to tell them things. A walking reference library, Fiske said. Well, huh, what's wrong with that? A library is a big place. A computer can give you answers, but it takes time to find things even on the internet. But we've got a whole Internet and library in one moveable package, you, Henry Bryce. You could learn thirty foreign languages and be the greatest linguist of all time. And remember, I'm your manager."

Henry was carried away by his friend's enthusiasm. "Yes, sure," he managed to say.

"Now just don't start forgetting things, that's all," Bert laughed and abruptly said goodbye and left for a class.

* * *

The funeral was small. Bertrand Dunster even took three days off from school and went to Henry Bryce's hometown. Mrs. Bryce was crying all the time. She asked Bert how it could have happened.

Bert shook his head sadly the first time, but later that night, when Henry's mother insisted, he told her. "You see Mrs. Bryce, Henry began going out with girls."

"I knew it," Mrs. Bryce snapped with conviction. "I told him not to see girls yet. Most women will ruin a great man. Some drive them to drink."

"Well, it wasn't really that," Bertrand Dunster hesitated, and then added: "You see he fell pretty hard for this one girl. Patricia something. She was a nice girl, really."

"How can you say that? Mrs. Bryce raised her voice.

"It wasn't really her fault. He just met her once. They had a pretty intense time of it though. She told Henry to call her up some time. Henry never did see her again."

"Well then why? Why should he jump from the dormitory window at school over that?"

"You see, ah, well, it's kind of hard to explain. It's just that he forgot her phone number."

THE TIME TABLETS TALE

What <u>IF</u> time could be stopped?

This story does not begin with "Once upon a time," but it should.

Terry Thomas first thoughts about the Time Tablets hit him like a tidal wave. At the time the adventure started Terry Thomas was working on his Ph.D. in chemistry at the University in Los Angles. He was sitting in his tiny carrel at the school library with the solid door closed, reading back and forth from six open books at once, cross-referencing, searching. He knew the joke about how copying from one book was plagiarism, but copying from six books was research! After hours of suppressing yawns he had put his head on his arms and taken a nap right there.

He awoke in a few minutes to make a startling discovery. There on the desk, taped to his computer, was a large printed note on a sheet of his own paper. "DON'T TAKE THE TIME TABLETS!" the words read in block letters.

Terry blinked. Then he gulped the coke on his table coming wide-awake with the caffeine and the astonishing mystery.

He stretched out his lanky legs, clenched his square jaw, adjusted his thick glasses, and looked back at the carrel door. It was still tightly shut. Terry was not a sound sleeper and the door squealed embarrassingly whenever he opened it.

How had anyone entered his carrel, written a note on his own paper, taped this note in front of him on his computer screen, and then left without his seeing or hearing them? It seemed to be a magic trick, a grand illusion.

He had no idea what the note meant, then. He did not have friends who were fiendish practical jokers. Indeed, Terry Thomas was rather withdrawn, introverted, shy, bookish, a loner, a nerd in the parlance of the times. He was tall, good-looking in spite of the thick glasses, but especially now, in graduate school, he had few friends outside of his classes. He had left the small western town of his birth and the friends he had there. Terry was one of those people who always thought wild parties and happy carousing might be fun, but he had never participated.

Did the note lead to the experiments in spite of the admonition? It seemed to be one of those 'which came first questions,' as in: "Is a chicken just an egg's way of making another egg?" Later he had forgotten this mystery only to have the problem forced upon him again in a really strange way.

*   *   *

Three years later, when he had graduated and landed the job as a chemist with the Los Angles branch of Ersatz Drugs International (EDI) and was experimenting on new products, Terry Thomas came to sampling some hallucinogens. Here again he had plenty of warnings.

Peggy Windsor, the project manager of his section, had come into his cubicle and sat down on the chair beside him one day. Peggy had left the outside door completely open with a gesture that was full of meaning; this was not a social call. But then, as if feeling it was safe to taunt him, she crossed her magnificent legs far too invitingly.

His boss was beautiful, but this conversation was all business. She told Terry bluntly: "You know these are controlled substances you are working with, Thomas."

Somehow by calling him by his last name, Peggy distanced herself from Terry even further.

Peggy went on: "Every gram must be accounted for," she continued. "Every test must be recorded. Be careful in sampling. Some doctors and pharmacists become addicts, because they believe they can play god. They feel they are so smart, that they are above natural laws. No one is."

It was difficult to take Peggy Windsor seriously as his boss, though she was probably a bit older than Terry. Not taking Peggy Windsor seriously might be a sexist attitude, Terry told himself. But she was such an obvious mammal, possessed a trim figure, such long dark hair, a perfect oval face, full red lips that teased, lovely deep blue eyes one could dive into and take a swim.

But Bob Posak, who was a chemist on the same team as Terry and occupied the very next cubicle, had quite a different view of the beauteous Peggy Windsor. Terry often ate lunch with Bob in the company cafeteria and they talked of their boss. Terry had declared Peggy was too gorgeous to be a manager.

Bob was a great bear of a man, as tall as Terry, but wide with ample belly. He had opinions and did not mind voicing them while eating heartily: "Watch out for her. She's a man killer, Terry old boy. The guy you're replacing made some mistakes and she got him. She's hard on the men under her." Bob Posak made a throat cutting gesture across his double chins. "She's all business. How do you think she got to be manager?"

"Talent," Terry suggested casually.

"Using her body. She has eyes for the Vice-President, Harry Powell. Besides she's probably five years older than you."

"Age is irrelevant," Terry replied.

"My grandmother was beautiful once," Bob declared, with his mouth full, in what he thought was a joking voice. "She's a widow and available." Bob's bulging eyes twinkled in merriment.

Still Terry Thomas persisted in his fantasies. Every time Peggy Windsor came into his cubicle her perfume seemed to linger there for hours afterwards, remaining in time after the persona left. He asked Peggy's advice often, and finally nerved himself to invite her to dinner the following Friday. Amazingly she agreed and for two days Terry walked on air.

Friday night began auspiciously enough. The restaurant and the food were perfection. The wine was fruity and audacious. Afterwards they talked across the dinner table, Terry running through his limited store of jokes. He suggested some further drinks at Nesbitts, a fancy bar nearby, as he reached clumsily to grip her hand. Then Peggy punctured his balloon with an ease that was sad indeed.

She withdrew her hand gently and offered an analysis of their situation. "I want to thank you for the dinner, Thomas," she indicated. "It was great. I don't usually go out with people in my department, but you are a very attractive man. However, Thomas, you are working for me, and I don't really date such people. I have access to personnel records. I am not only two years older than you are; I am earning $20,000 a year more."

Peggy took a deep breath and continued: "Your clothes are rumpled and you picked me up in an old car. You are not a good people-person, and while you are a very competent chemist, I don't see you rising in the company. If you want an after dinner drink at Nesbitts, we can go, and then you will escort me home please." It was hello and goodbye in one sweep.

Yes Peggy Windsor was correct. Terry could not deny this. He was not a good mixer. He was interested in his chemistry laboratory much more than any human chemistry, except that exhibited by Peggy Windsor. She had been cruel to him, but Terry did not see it that way.

When Bob Posak asked him how his "date with the Beast from the Black Lagoon" had gone, Terry was not really amused.

"We had fun. But there's no chemistry, I guess," he admitted.

"You better stick to the chemistry you know. She's bad news. Leave her alone," Bob warned. "Chemistry sometimes explodes."

It seemed to Terry that his timing for the date with Peggy had been poor. If he could make a breakthrough on his experiments, Peggy Windsor would see him in a different light. He was working with some controlled substances, but Terry Thomas was really not desirous of trying hallucinogens for the sake of a buzz. Terry was testing painkillers and the great discovery came almost as a side effect.

Everyone had known for years that certain drugs caused people to experience time differently. There was an apparent speed-up or slow-down in time caused by various drugs. In some cases this effect had produced a frightening reaction in people who had tried the drugs. Experimenters had taken some drugs which caused them to feel as if it would take forever to just walk out of the room. Time-frame perceptions had altered. Trying some of these drugs led Terry to wonder anew about that apparently immutable dimension: TIME.

The conception of time was different for various people. Could the time-bending features of the drugs be isolated and understood? Would time-altering drugs be of value in slowing down the spread of a disease?

Terry personally sampled the drugs in such minute quantities that he received little stimulation and he saw no danger in addiction. When the danger was perceived, it was too late. The breakthrough, when it did come, astonished Terry completely.

One particular formula showed promise and he had produced some tiny blue tablets. There he sat, alone in his cubicle at work, using himself as a guinea pig, swallowing the tablet, and testing a newly created designer drug. The first effect he noted was a ringing in his ears, a vacuum like sensation, as if he were leaving his body behind. The feelings intensified. This would never be a popular drug, he decided. The noisy ringing in his ears, the feeling of being alone in the universe, that is a sensation of isolation, these were unpleasant effects. He waited a moment for the effect to pass. It seemed to linger.

Perhaps there would have been nothing else, only an entry in a journal, information which another researcher later might have used to make the real discovery. Then Terry Thomas noticed his digital electric clock on the desktop. It read: "2:58, 14 seconds."

Then the "15 seconds" number came gradually into view, only much too slowly.

Terry glanced next at his wristwatch, which he always kept five minutes ahead, so he would get to work on time. It was silly, because he certainly knew the watch was exactly five minutes ahead, and so he allowed for that discrepancy. Only while the watch was five minutes later than the clock and had old-fashioned hands, the sweep second dial was also scarcely moving. The seconds appeared to be passing at maybe one-tenth normal speed.

Of course, all observers are at the center of their own universe, Terry told himself. The universe was not slowing down; it was Terry, himself.

He rubbed his eyes, arose, and walked to his door to get some air. He seemed to be walking all right, though perhaps a little unsteadily. It was akin to learning to walk all over again. The doorknob turned very hard. Was this difficulty with the door just his perception? Suddenly he was frightened. What was happening to him? He pulled on the door hard and it opened as if it were a great vault portal.

Terry looked out into the corridor. Bob Posak was the only one in close view down the hallway. Bob was heading for his own little office, his back to Terry. But Bob was moving much too leisurely, out of phase, taking a long time to put his foot down, to turn slowly in front of the door. Terry started to call out: "Bob," but even the one word did not seem to come from his lips, lost in the ringing in his ears.

Now Terry was really frightened. He gripped the doorframe for support, watching as Bob Posak laboriously, apparently in slow motion, reached for a key ring attached to his belt to open his door. Terry turned back into his room, without trying to shut the door, and sat back down at his desk.

*   *   *

What had he done to himself? He came around to a more philosophical question: What was TIME? Sure we all spend time, use time, take time, have time, and run out of time. Only analogies seemed to suffice. Time was a river, sweeping us along. At some point we entered the great river of time-life and at some point we would be washed ashore and leave the Time River. Had he slowed himself down in the river? Perhaps he had climbed right out of the river of time and was observing it from the shore.

This was perhaps why some people in the drug culture talked about drugs being a "trip," a good trip or a bad trip. Was it permanent? He had taken only a small, precisely measured amount of the new drug, a tiny tablet. Again he looked at his digital clock. It read: "2:58, 23 seconds." He estimated he had been sitting and thinking for perhaps 10 minutes, yet less than ten seconds of real-time had passed. He was apart from the time dimension.

What was real? What did it all mean? There was a ringing in his ears, a great feeling of existing in an empty void. Terry had always disliked drinking too much alcohol. Being high gave him a disjointed unpleasant feeling of not being in control, not being able to do things as he wished. That feeling was present now.

How could he determine the passage of real-time for himself, the observer? One way out was not to think of the consequences, but record everything he was thinking in his journal. He began writing. Writing was almost archaic, but he had never trusted what he might put on his computer. People might come into his cubicle on weekends or at night and steal his research. The ballpoint pen seemed to push hard, but he managed. He finished a whole page, before glancing again at the clock. It read "2:58, 33 seconds." There was no way he could have written that whole page in 10 seconds. He was indeed separate from the standard time dimension. He could copy this page as rapidly as possible later and see how long this took in real-time. If there ever were a real-time for him again! Certainly this effect must pass. The drug would wear off. All drugs wore off. He hoped.

What could he do? Was there an antidote? Perhaps he could dilute the preparation. He picked up the glass of water he had used to take the "Time Tablet" originally. And then the memory of the note on his desk so long ago at the University came back to him with a rush: "Don't take the Time Tablets."

He sat at his desk, the glass of water in his hand, shaking, thinking about the story of his life: Bright small town boy, enormous overwhelming University, big city job as a research chemist at a giant multinational company. What was success? Here was a key question everyone must answer. And now he could wonder: What was the meaning of that mystery message on his desk at the University, three years ago?

Terry was shaking, but the water in the glass did not seem to move much. He put it to his lips, and the liquid came too gradually toward him, slower than mercury in a vial. Water did not behave that way naturally. Natural laws operated only in standard time. Now he was outside of standard time. Suddenly he was afraid of choking on the drink, and he put the glass down. If the water went down his throat too gradually, he could choke. He was breathing more slowly. Were all his bodily functions decelerated?

What was happening outside? He had no window in his cubicle. Terry arose again and walked back to the open door to look out. Bob Posak was just closing his door. All that time ago Bob had started to enter the room and now he was just closing his door. Terry walked out down the corridor. Just ahead were a series of windows, which offered a view of a mall and the street below. His beautiful manager, Peggy Windsor, was also looking out of another window of the corridor, much further down. She stood almost immobile, her hand gradually rising to stroke her hair. Almost without meaning to Terry walked toward her and then paused, looking out of the window.

Then Terry saw the view outside and froze in horror. Here were people in the open mall, eight floors below, standing to talk, walking, but all moving in a kind of pantomime slow motion, deliberately, like mimes. Even a running dog was almost stagnant. The moving cars and trucks in the street were scarcely changing position.

Terry held the window-frame for support. His hands were shaking. Then the ringing in his ears seemed to quiet down. It was good to just hold on. The disorientation subsided. The effect was going to end! He was returning to real-time. As he waited, watching, the people in the mall below came back into phase, moving normally.

"Thomas, you gave me a start. You really creep up on a person. I didn't see you approach." It was Peggy talking. "How is your work coming?"

The last message was obvious. It was back to work for him. "Sorry, I just needed to get out for a moment." Without a word more he turned back and walked to his cubicle. He felt unsteady. And he could sense Peggy's eyes burning into his back, watching him return. Would she think he had been drinking because he swayed around?

Inside, Terry shut the door, which closed easily. The door and knob must have been difficult before because he was moving them in such a small amount of time. The glass of water had splashed over one end of his desk and onto the floor. He had moved it too rapidly through time. The water had seemed steady going up or down, but when real-time returned the liquid had reacted in a wide spill.

It was obvious he had made a momentous discovery. But here was a drug he better not even mention to others as yet. The effect lasted for awhile and then came to an end, as with any other drug moving through the body. Aspirin relieved a headache for three or four hours and then its effect ended. But some drugs could kill or permanently alter the body when they paid their visit.

What good would this drug do? How might it be useful? That was a key question for a pharmaceutical company such as the one for which Terry was working. Certainly in the field of time study, it would be valuable. The drug might well have anti-aging qualities, which was the center of intense effort right now by many chemical companies and had been the focus of his original intention in developing this potion.

A person might slow down their time-frame and live for a long while almost in the present, without aging. Or maybe not. Would you grow old anyway within the few minutes that elapsed while you took the Time Tablets?

Would two people who took the tablets simultaneously be in the same phase together? That was doubtful. Even fractions of a second might separate them forever in time.

Only by experimentation, could any of this be verified. He might try it upon old dogs or old mice, and see if it prolonged their life, and what the effect might be. But if the animals lived in another time, what would his view of them be?

Now that he had returned to real-time, Terry Thomas had a great desire to try the drug again himself. One of his fears had been of being trapped in time, a worry about the unknown. But the effect had ended and was probably measurable. The process seemed to have parameters, beginning and ending. In real-time, the whole experiment had lasted less than a minute. Yet he felt that he had been "away" for almost an hour.

His mind ranged back and forth, thinking about these Time Tablets. Bob Posak had not noticed Terry coming out of his cubicle. Peggy Windsor had not seen him come up and stand less than ten feet away at the window. And he had been there awhile, looking out at that strange view below. Part of Peggy's annoyance with him may have been because she did not want to be seen by anyone as wasting time, looking out of the window. She was a company woman all the way.

For the rest of the afternoon Terry just sat thinking about the use of the Time Tablets. He had a discovery! What good was it? The tablets might slow down aging, but they could never be marketed, he realized with a start. Production would never be allowed because of the way the tablets might be used. FDA approval could never be secured. There were many problem products that never had been allowed on the market, some for good reason and some for unnecessary fear.

For instance, athletes were always looking for ways to run faster in races. Many athletes had gotten into trouble for drug use. A runner who took Time Tablets could beat everyone in real-time, but no one would even see him run the race. No one would believe it had really happened. A runner who took a Time Tablet at the start of a race would appear to have covered a mile in seconds. The speed would seem such as to be an unbelievable illusion. Illusions were for magic shows not races.

If the athlete was to run four times around a quarter mile track, no one would be sure he had really gone around and passed the field four times. What would the cameras show? There would probably just be a blur.

A racehorse taking a Time Tablet could win a race. But no one would accept it. This was impossible. How big a pill would a horse need and when would you feed it to the horse? Even if you fed the horse the pill at the perfect moment, it still would not be a successful venture. From the point of view of observers, the horse would appear to vanish abruptly from view after starting and then arrive suddenly at the finish line.

But there were so many other possibilities. A spy under the influence of the drug could enter top-secret offices, if the doors were open. He could walk past guards, and steal documents.

There were so many possibilities. It was scary. No. Production would never be allowed on these pills. It was best to keep these out of the hands of secret organizations. Terry Thomas mind whirred.

People could creep up to others, kill them, and leave. Murder could be committed without a clue. Thieves could enter banks and take the money without anyone knowing. This last possibility was worth thinking about. Aside from pure research, robbery seemed to be the most likely use of the Time Tablets.

Terry Thomas was the only one with the Time Tablet formula and it better stay that way. He could make more tablets. One question in science always was: "Is this replicable?" Could the experiment be repeated with the same results? Also, what were the long-term effects? Were the tablets harmful? Would they kill him? He felt shaky and his head throbbed as if from a hangover. He better not put his body through any more until tomorrow. But there would be a next time! That he had already decided.

Animal experiments did not seem to be the answer. Yes, by a series of animal tests, he could determine if his drug would kill an animal. The animal might experience time differently, but the human viewer would not know. Animal experiments would require telling people what he intended to do. And that was out of the question. He could buy a small dog and test it in his apartment, except dogs were not allowed in his apartment.

Terry went to the washroom and looked at himself in the mirror. There were no changes in his wide face or strong chin. His brown eyes were clear. Even his freckles seemed the same.

Was he addicted already? He felt a need to repeat the experiment, but no driving compulsion to take the drug. But then everyone who took habit-forming drugs turned over first their body and then their soul to a craving. They began by saying they could handle it and ended by desperately seeking more. He needed to be careful. The greatest lies were the ones you told to yourself.

The first thing to do was to make some more Time Tablets, triple the original dose for a real experiment. He did that now. When he left work, Terry packed a dozen new Time Tablets into his attaché case, along with his journal, which contained the formula and his notes. He did not want anyone spying on him. Maybe he was becoming paranoid about the drug already. On the way out he caught a glimpse of Peggy Windsor watching him appraisingly. She was wondering about him, and that wasn't good. Would she really fire him?

Peggy Windsor wanted money and power. Perhaps money was the key to Peggy. If he had plenty of money, the age difference between them would mean nothing. It was odd how he had fastened his thoughts on this one female. She had really become the epicenter of his feelings. Her refusal of him had greatly intensified his desires. He had heard of bonding and now he felt it. There was a compulsion here, an obsession, a feeling that gripped his very being.

Terry returned to thinking of banks and money. He remembered reading how once someone asked a famous thief why he robbed banks. "Because that's where the money is," the bandit had replied.

*　　*　　*

At home that evening it was a time for thinking. He decided he would go downtown during his lunch hour and take another Time Tablet. Terry was planning no robbery as yet, just scouting around and he did a lot of agonizing about right and wrong.

It was easy to rationalize and see evil in big banks. Banks borrowed money from people at low interest rates and then loaned it back to others at higher interest rates, keeping the difference. Banks could even borrow money from people and indulge in risky ventures on land deals, and if the investments failed, the government (which was everyone in the country) bailed out the banks with public funds.

Terry's own parents had struggled to send him to the University even as they fought a rear guard action to keep a big bank from foreclosing on their house. Past events in his life made bank robbery rationalizations easier.

Terry felt uncommonly tired and went to bed very early. When his alarm erupted at 6:00 A.M., he still felt tired. He turned off the alarm and went back to sleep for an hour. Then Terry phoned his company saying that he was not feeling well and would need the day off. He had decided against trying this project on his lunch hour.

He was an experimenter, right? Therefore, he should experiment. It would be just a test. Terry took a taxi downtown and walked around. He gave his workplace, the EDI Building, a wide berth. He bought a stopwatch at a store and tried it out

After a bit he found a small cafe with wide open doors and great windows looking out on the avenue in the warm April morning. He ordered a coke. Here he could observe the passersby and the busy street.

Terry opened his case and took out a Time Tablet almost tenderly. He reflected that if he were falling in love with his own drug, he would not be the first to do so. But in the interests of science the test must be made, he told himself. He swallowed the tablet gulped his coke and set the stopwatch. Two minutes passed before the potion dissolved and he heard the first ringing sensation in his ears. The effect of the ringing was known now and not as frightening. The feeling of being out of phase, alone in the universe, still was unnerving. He recorded this all in his journal. Terry watched as the stopwatch appeared to slow down and the motion of the people in the cafe grew more lethargic. Finally the moving customers and waitresses seemed absurd, taking slow steps that took forever to complete. How would they see him if they were looking in his direction?

The tablet he had taken was three times the dose of the one he had consumed yesterday. Still the Time Tablets were tiny. He had needed to see what the effect was of a larger dose. Outside the cafe window, the moving traffic had apparently come to a halt. A piece of trash paper flying in the wind seemed stationary in the air; a man who had dropped a package looked absurd, with his parcel falling at a glacial speed even as he reached to try and catch it.

Terry Thomas sat a long time at the cafe window watching the scene outside, thinking of "TIME." Perceptions of time differ. Everyone commented on how time creeps when we perform tasks we hate and rushes by when we are having fun. We are unable to grip an instant of time, to hold on to the sands falling in the hourglass. Only now he alone of all humankind was removed from the time dimension, savoring an instant, an "augenblick," the Germans called it, the blink of an eye.

At last Terry shut the attaché case, which closed only with extreme difficulty. He arose, walking around the customers in the aisles, people who were moving so slowly they appeared to be frozen. Here was his first crime; he was not going to pay his bill for the coke drink.

The slowdown was even greater than with the original dose. Now the people were not laboriously raising and lowering their feet as they walked, moving in very slow motion, today they had completely stopped. He paused before pedestrians on the sidewalk and looked directly into their unseeing eyes. He stood facing a pretty woman, just inches away. It would be unfair to take liberties. He reached into a man's flapping, yet stationary suit coat, lifted out a wallet from the inner pocket, and then returned it. It was so easy. He danced between the fast moving traffic on the road, which appeared stationary, as he leaped about exuberantly. Yesterday these frozen objects in time had been terrifying; today he literally took it in his stride. Humans learn to adapt so quickly, he decided. A prehistoric man brought to this city and shown moving traffic for the first time would have been frightened also.

Now walking about in the city gave Terry a godlike feeling. He alone was able to do these things. He was alone in the whole universe; he alone was in complete control. Then he paused. Ahead was a bank. It possessed revolving doors, with people in the doors, entering and leaving, but unmoving. There was no way past them.

He would have to try it again and start from the inside of the bank. Besides, how much longer did he have before the effect of this tablet wore off? Tomorrow he could skip work again.

Terry Thomas paused at a fountain, watching suspended water, waves in the air, moving yet still. The water traveled in great splashes, only so slowly. The effect of the Time Tablet was certainly more pronounced than the first time. The stopwatch showed only the passage of five seconds so far. Time was passing, but so slowly on this occasion that no one could notice the apparent blur of motion as Terry went along. The whole city seemed to be wide open to his grasp.

How long he walked the streets he did not know. The stopwatch showed only eight seconds of real-time had passed. He estimated the last time he had been "under the influence" almost a minute of real-time; now only seconds had elapsed. Then at last the ringing in his ears seemed to subside, a signal he was about to return to real-time. Terry had barely time to move from a street, where he was playing his game with moving cars, over to the sidewalk and stand flat against a wall out of the way, before the time came back on with a rush. People who had not seen him standing there before jumped and felt their eyes were playing tricks.

For his part, Terry felt tired, shaky, and leaned against a building wall for support. After a few moments he hailed a taxi and went home. There was a need now to rest and to arrive at a final decision.

Back home, his answering machine red light was blinking. The messages he received were so few that he wondered why he had the machine. Peggy Windsor's voice came on: "Thomas, I'm surprised if you are sick, that I don't find you at home. I just called to see how you were doing." That was a ridiculous statement; she was checking on him.

He phoned work and asked to speak to Peggy Windsor. He told her he had slept through the phone message, still wasn't feeling well, and wouldn't be in tomorrow either. She told him to get well. It was an order.

Terry awoke in the morning with a headache that under other circumstances would have led to aspirin. Now he was going to experiment with the Time Tablets and he did not want to mix any drugs. He took the telephone off the hook for the day. Let Peggy Windsor call to check now!

After taking a taxi downtown, he bought some thin plastic gloves and put them in his attaché case. He was going to try the banks. Anything might have dissuaded him, but all seemed to work well. He bought a small coke at a vending machine, opened the bottle, and made for a large bank.

Inside the bank, he eyed the guards and people. Here teller's windows were all around a circular enclosed area. A guard was watching him. Let him watch. Terry examined the interior of the bank. There were video cameras everywhere, pointing, recording, some sweeping back and forth. The pictures would really be examined if a loss of money was discovered. If they saw a man who was in the pictures and then vanished, it might cause them to look for Terry. That must not happen. Quickly he walked back to the customer service area where there were desks, bank officers, no money, and especially no video cameras. He sat down on a plush chair around the corner.

Terry took out a Time Tablet, swallowed it, and washed the pill down with the coke. After a few minutes the familiar process of the drug effect swept over him. He set the stopwatch even as he noted the moving people seemed to slow down and then stop. Yes, stop. This time the stopwatch did not appear to move at all. He waited for the next second to come up, but nothing seemed to happen.

Here was a factor worth noting in his journal. The first time the digital clock on his cubicle desk had moved almost a minute, though he had not accurately timed the experience. The next time only eight seconds had passed altogether. On this occasion there appeared to be no movement at all. The second time, he had taken the Time Tablet he judged the difference to be due to the size of the dose. But this time the tablet was exactly the same as the second dose. So the effect was increasing.

That could be worrisome. Perhaps he should not do this many more times. He remembered the character in one of the old fairy stories, the person who received three wishes and who managed to foul up and get nothing. Well, he said to himself: "This is the third time, and it will be the charm."

Terry put on the plastic gloves, took his attaché case, and walked back to the main banking section. The moving video cameras appeared to have stopped in their surveillance swings back and forth. They would record him as a blur or less. He walked boldly up to one of the tellers, who had just finished with a client. Easing around the departing customer, Terry reached over the cage bars and helped himself to some paper money. If he did this to just one teller, the employee could get into trouble. But if all the tellers suffered a loss at once, there would be no explanation. He had to get inside the cage.

Terry walked around the circular ring of tellers. There was a closed door leading in, only about four feet high. It was locked. A stationary guard was standing nearby, but he could not see Terry. Now Terry put his attaché case on the circular ledge and clamored up over the door. He was inside. He wandered from teller to teller, taking only stacks of $50 and $100 bills, filling the attaché case. Some of the bills were loose; most were neatly banded.

It would be amusing. Every teller would be missing money, and no one would know how it happened. Some had their cash drawers closed, and he had to pull hard to open them in the fraction of a second he was living through. Some of the cash drawers were locked, and there was no way in. He gave up on those.

Terry had completed an entire circle of the tellers and the attaché case was not full. In the center of the room he noticed a safe, partly open, with an attendant standing beside it. She no doubt dispersed the cash to the tellers. Inside were stacks of $100 and $50 bills all in their wrappers. Nearby was a guard pushing a money cart. The whole scene appeared like people in a wax museum. Terry finally filled his attaché case to the top with bills and closed it.

Terry was sweating out of fear now. He climbed up on a desk near the exit door of the central cashier's cages and jumped over. Then he glanced at his stopwatch. It indicated that less than a second had passed since he pushed the "start timing" button.

There was no time for philosophy now. He walked to the bank exit. There were revolving doors, but also doors that could be pulled open. Unfortunately these exit doors were filled with people coming in and going out. His fears increased. He had to get out. Absolutely, he didn't want to be around when the fireworks broke loose here. He chose a small woman and tried to push past her. Pushing, sliding, he worked his way through the door, which just did not seem capable of opening wider.

Outside, he walked rapidly away. Two blocks off, he slowed down. Here was a park, with some benches. Terry sat down on an unoccupied bench. He took off the plastic gloves and put them in his pocket. Next he recorded all the effects in his journal. Well, the "Time Tablet Effect" could wear off anytime now. He counted the stacks of bills and loose money in the attaché case; he had over $200,000.

Terry sat idly, looking about. There was a bird, on the wing, as they say, literally, appearing to float in the air. Over there was a fly heading toward a trash basket, immobile, in mid-air. He reached up and plucked the fly from the sky. The insect was oddly resistant, as he moved it rapidly through not just space, but time. Everywhere he looked it was like a still picture of the earth.

Things could start to move anytime, now. He examined the stacks of currency. The banded labels seemed standard enough, but perhaps there would be some way of tracing them back to the bank. He put the plastic gloves back on, removed the paper wrappers over the banded stacks of bills, and found a partly empty bag in the garbage to put all the bands in. He closed the bag tightly.

Terry sat back down on the park bench. Still less than a second had passed according to the stopwatch. He was definitely at ground zero, now. No time at all was passing. His apartment was only three miles from downtown. He might as well start back. He began walking, avoiding the pedestrians, who appeared to be stationary statues on the street. He moved easily between the vehicles that seemed frozen. Here was a black dog, caught in mid-air, bounding up to a curb, and he stroked its back in passing.

He felt hungry and walked through an open door to simply take some food at a deli. He seized a sandwich from the tray a waitress was carrying. That was amusing, but when he bit into the sandwich there was a problem. He could chew, but had such difficulty swallowing that he spit it all back out. It was frightening. No he could not eat in this situation. He walked outside and discarded the sandwich.

Terry was becoming panicky about the length of time that he was in the dimensional warp. The stopwatch still remained immobile, showing less than a second had passed. At last, the high rise building where his apartment was located loomed ahead, and then the ringing in his ears began to subside. He was growing so accustomed to this ringing effect, he had almost forgotten it. He was returning to real-time. Whatever real-time was! Was time all an illusion?

Terry had the "never again" feeling of the weekend alcoholic who promises to quit every Monday. But now it seemed all right again. Yes, he had approached zero time passage, or probably had reached it. No time at all had elapsed from when the Time Tablet actually took effect until the end when real-time returned. And he had been under the influence longer each time, perhaps even geometrically longer. But the effect of the pills did wear off. And then it was over.

Abruptly he felt very shaky and extremely tired. When he got back to his apartment he slept much of the day.

*   *   *

The next day was Friday and Terry called in one more time to absent himself from work. What to do with the money was the question? He had read that to foil drug dealers, the government demanded banks report cash deposits of over $10,000. This was also a problem for bank robbers, Terry reflected. The morning newspapers were full of the mysterious, unexplained, major daylight downtown bank robbery. Authorities were saying little. And there were no clues.

He drove out to some suburban banks and deposited $8,000 in each. Establishing an account and getting blank checks took time. After a whole day he had only opened nine accounts. Again there was not enough time. And he was leaving a paper trail all over town. No one asked him where he had obtained all this money, yet! They probably believed he was a gambler or a drug dealer. Banks liked to receive money and they asked few questions.

Los Vegas might be the answer. He could fly out tonight and gamble. If he played for high stakes, he could always claim he had won big and that was the source of his money. He paid cash for the first class air ticket to Vegas and no one questioned that. He could fly right away, if he were willing to pay enough for the privilege. The Vegas hotel was delighted to accept cash in advance also. Los Vegas loved cash.

He had been to Vegas before; it was only 300 miles from Los Angles. Previously he had tried the nickel slots and the dollar crap tables as a bit of vacation fun one weekend. Now he felt exuberant. The Casinos were wide open for a wild time. He played with hundred dollar bills on roulette and craps. At first he had a winning streak, and then his luck seemed to sour. By the time he went to bed in the late night, he had lost $10,000 as easily as he had lost $100 on the other occasion of his visit to Vegas. Easy come; easy go.

In the morning Terry concluded he did not really enjoy losing money even when he had plenty. Furthermore, while Vegas deserved to be robbed, even more than the banks, there was little real cash in evidence for a "Time walker" to seize. He did not try the Time Tablets. If he brought time to a standstill for himself, here in Vegas, there still seemed little opportunity to do as he had in the banks. Vegas played with chips. All the money the attendants received at the craps and roulette wheel tables was slid down slots into safes. The cashier cages had money, but it would be difficult to get into these areas as a "Time walker." Vegas liked to hold on to its money.

Terry made some deposits in Vegas banks in the morning and then he flew back to L.A.. In L.A. Terry drove to a downtown tailor shop and bought several expensive suits paying cash.

Terry looked at new cars the next day, deciding to buy a top of the line Cadillac. It was certainly less of a trauma than his usual car buying; since he accepted the sales staff inflated price and paid cash. He negotiated in only a perfunctory manner. The dealers took cash and the salesmen tried hard not to raise their eyebrows.

He mailed his parents some checks on the banks where he had deposited funds and told them in a note he had received a big raise. He still had money left in the attaché case.

On Monday it was back to work. Peggy Windsor came by his little office, as he knew she would, to check on him. She told Terry his new suit looked very professional. "How are you feeling?" she asked.

"Fine now," he replied. And then he made the pitch he had decided upon. Peggy was standing there, in his office, the door left wide open behind her as before, her perfume already permeating the air, her enormous blue eyes upon him as he sat at his desk.

"Peggy," he began slowly, "I was ill three days last week because a favorite aunt of mine died. It upset me, and I did not want to talk about it. She left me a great fortune, Peggy. I bought some new suits and a Cadillac car yesterday. Yes, I've been thinking of what you told me about my car and clothes. I am planning on quitting this job and doing some traveling. Now that I am independently wealthy, I would like to date you as an equal." He arose, to confront her. "If that's all too fast, think it over," he added as she backed away.

Peggy Windsor flushed. Her eyebrows seemed to go up to her

hairline. Maybe she liked him better as her employee. What was she thinking? And then the flood of words burst forth: "Congratulations on your inheritance Terry. But you don't get it, do you? I want to succeed on my own. I have a degree in chemistry just as you do and an MBA in management. I enjoyed the research here, but this company gave me a major promotion as a manager. Are you just going to scrap your degree and travel the rest of your life? I like this job. I don't want a free ride." And then she turned on her heel and was gone.

Terry Thomas sat back down stunned. She had called him "Terry" for the first time. They were equals now. And she had problems, which he had never considered before.

He could put a down payment on a house and travel for a while. But he had misled Peggy, in that he didn't have enough money to travel for the rest of his life. A trip with Peggy Windsor, a honeymoon, would be terrific. But he enjoyed the research himself. He didn't want to just travel the rest of his life, running away from himself and everything. He ought to do something beyond the Time Tablets to make this life meaningful.

It was akin to the experience of people who won big on the lottery. Usually they said they were going to continue their job. But if they had a job they did not care about, they soon quit. And what did they do with the rest of their lives? Lives need a purpose.

If he had enough money, he could open his own small chemical research company and pharmaceutical drugs could be produced and sold. And he could hire Peggy to help him at an enormous salary. Would she go for it? Everything he thought about involved Peggy.

He continued to wonder about the Time Tablets. Would he age if he kept taking them? If he made a very small dose and took this, would he live forever? There was always time for that.

Robbing the bank had been easy and he had to admit it, that while the exploit was frightening, yet it was exciting fun. He walked over to the personnel office at his company and asked for a week's leave without pay to settle his aunt's estate. They agreed. Then he bought two larger attaché cases.

One more really big haul from several banks would do it. He could then fly to various other big cities and make bank deposits all over the country in amounts of $8,000. He might even start buying the stock of the company he worked for, EDI stock, in large amounts from brokers. He could force his way onto the board of directors or be made a vice-president. Those were dreams! That might take many more millions than he was likely to obtain from this or any other robbery.

Terry was still doing a lot of soul searching. In spite of all his rationalizations, robbing banks was wrong. So, he was doing wrong! The whole society was at fault in worshipping money, he told himself. It was the fault of society. His thoughts went around and around. Maybe he could even pay the banks back later if he made money. How many felt that way when they started down the wrong path?

Well he had decided to go ahead. That very afternoon he walked into a big bank, one with rows of tellers along the side and of course plenty of video cameras. Again he rounded a corner out of sight of the cameras and found a table to set down his attaché cases. He swallowed the Time Tablet and sipped the coke he carried, waiting for it to take effect.

Even as he waited, he had to admit that above all he had wanted to take this pill. It was addictive! He would have to call it quits after this time. There must be no more, regardless of how much or little he obtained. His desire to take the Time Tablet for its own sake was a bad sign.

He felt the ringing in his ears, the telltale roaring sound, only somehow different, receding instead of approaching. He snapped the stopwatch to see what it would do. The second dial seemed to be unmoving again, and then instead of "00" the "59" came into place. There was some mistake. He looked about. The people were moving, ever so slowly, but they were going backwards!

Time was in reverse for him. Terry stood, shocked. No, this would pass also. The effect of the pill would wear off. He must do what he came in to do. And he must do it quickly. A sense of urgency gripped him. No one could see him. He was out of phase, not in their time sequence at all. As long as the sound continued in his ears, he was all right. He walked back to the long row of tellers, put his attaché cases on a ledge so he could reach them inside, and climbed up over the top. He found a cart with huge stacks of bills being pushed by a guard.

Again he loaded packs of $100 and $50 bills into his cases. When he had finished, he climbed back up over the top of the teller's cage.

Something was very wrong. The people were moving backwards, but the effect was accelerating. They did not see him, but they appeared to be moving faster. He glanced at his stopwatch. Four minutes had passed, in reverse. Time was speeding up for him, even as it ran backwards.

Frightened now, Terry took both attaché cases and moved around people toward the door. They obviously could not see him. It was hard to judge their movements, since everyone appeared to be going contrary to all human movements he had ever witnessed. Running a video slowly in reverse was the closest parallel.

He had checked the exit door before he had entered this bank. One door was wide open. He waited while a man and woman appeared to back into the building, and then moving quickly around them, he left the bank. Out on the street, the cars were running backwards, the people everywhere moving in a contrary direction. And the effect was continuing to accelerate! He had to get out of this crowded downtown area before someone ran into him, in reverse. He did not know what effect that would have.

A block away he discarded the plastic gloves. The time effect was continuing to accelerate. Cars appeared to be passing at great speed, backwards. The stoplights halted the vehicles for barely enough time for him to run across streets. Ahead was a tiny park and he sat on the cement atop a little hill, away from everything, his back to a wire fence, waiting for the Time Tablet effect to cease. But instead the roaring in his ears had sped up to a constant whine. The effect was increasing rather than slowing. The people and cars were becoming a blur. After a bit the people passing seemed to diminish. It was early morning. The sun was going down or rather coming up in reverse. And then it was dark. Last night!

Terry thought about his condition. He did not feel hungry, thirsty, tired, cold, or warm. He was simply out of it, beyond everything! He was a man removed from reality, an observer watching absurdity. Perhaps he had taken the Time Tablets one time too many. He should never have tried the Time Tablets in the first place. Shakespeare said: "Why would you put an enemy in your mouth to steal away your brain." Shakespeare was talking of liquor, the drug of his day.

The stopwatch was moving backwards steadily more rapidly. Terry had a feeling of permanence this time, being caught in a forever timewarp.

Maybe he would yet return to real-time. But then it became light again. Last evening, he told himself. And he hadn't even made the walk back to his place. The hours of night had passed in what seemed to be a few minutes. The stopwatch was racing backwards with increasing velocity, a mechanism gone wild, recording his life which was out of control. He did not need to measure seconds now: hours were passing in a twinkling and still the time scale was accelerating.

People in rapid reverse wandered across the park in a blur or sat for what seemed an instant on some benches down below. The traffic was going so fast, he dared not cross any streets. Cars might pass right through him or destroy him completely without knowing. The video of his life was moving into ever more rapid reverse.

It was new uncharted ground he was entering now. Could he go right back to the beginning of time? The philosophers, cosmologists, psychologists, and physicists had all wondered and theorized about the nature of time. Now, in a most unsophisticated way, Terry Thomas saw three elements to time, three main speeds: forward, call that NORMAL, a condition that most people experienced throughout their lives, NEUTRAL, in which the individual was removed from the time continuum, the time stream, and was free to perhaps live a lifetime in an instant, a sort of Time-Stop, and finally, REVERSE, in which the people moved backward in time. There might also be fourth possibility, FAST FORWARD, though how anyone could do that Terry could only guess. There were probably gradations, enhanced speeds, or fast rewind, as the switch says on the video machine. Those were interesting thoughts but he was not connected to a video machine.

Night came on again and then in moments the next day. Time was accelerating for him. He had all this money and nothing to do with it. He put his head down on his raised knees. Darkness, light, it went on, still increasing in speed. This time it apparently was not going to end. The roaring in his ears had become a hurricane. He began to count the days backward in a kaleidoscope of day and night in a kind of desperation to clutch on to sanity: "One, two, three, four" as daylight and night interspersed.

What could he do? How could he alter time? How can anyone change the time frame they are in? The month of April had certainly receded into March by now and beyond. He felt neither heat nor cold or wet from the occasional rain. Several times it seemed to rain upward, but he did not feel wet. He was a mere observer, removed from the space-time continuum, still held to earth by the force of gravity. He was immaterial perhaps. This was all a serious mistake. He tried shouting out, but could not hear his own voice. He might not even be here. One proves one is "here" by the presence of others. Perhaps he was no longer making sense. Do the insane know they are crazy?

Terry was still miles from his apartment and it was probably January already. This was Los Angles so there was no snow.

He had moved into his apartment on the first of February. It was too late to go home and try to warn himself there. He wasn't there yet.

If he somehow warned himself, would the warning change his life and his future and thus entirely end this timeline in which he was now living? It was a wild thought, meaningless. Were there many parallel universes in which the patterns of our lives could be played out differently, if we made differing decisions?

My God, he thought, he had tried to warn himself. The note in his University carrel three years ago, that was his own note, his warning to himself. But he had not heeded that warning. What to do? He should have made the warning much stronger and more definite. He counted the blur of accelerated passing days and tried to estimate when it was now. Day and night only took a few moments, whatever moments were. It was summer again now. He was a prisoner of time. He took out a notepad and pen and marked off the days, in reverse.

It was not safe to move from this park. Terry did not want this adventure to end with his colliding with many objects moving too rapidly for him to avoid. If he died, he would return to some past to be found with an attaché case full of money, and leave only a silly mystery as his legacy.

The months of last year were rushing by in reverse as he checked off the days. Time was no longer accelerating, but there was a constant whirl of day and night passing. Every occasion when he had taken the Time Tablets he had been under the effect for longer. He had gone back at least a year, now, 13 months, 14, 15. He must be somehow existent yet. He felt damp as from repeated dew. His back against the park fence and the cement he sat upon were the only reality as he plunged further into reverse. He estimated, with the help of the check off marks he was making on his notepad, that he was back over two years now. And still it went on. The progress backward, the twinkling nights and days continued.

And then gradually the days, still moving in reverse, appeared longer. The time effect was slowing down. At first Terry felt delighted, but then as the lengthening days moved into a parody of real-time, only in reverse, that effect seemed continuous as well. He arose, unsteadily. He felt his chin. He had no beard: he was not Rip Van Winkle in reverse. What is the reverse of a beard?

He had to warn himself. And it must be more extensive than just the silly warning placed in his University carrel. But for now the University carrel was the place to locate his past self. The University was miles away, and there was nothing to do but walk. Perhaps time would come back on before he got there. He was sure it would not.

Everything was still moving backwards and he seemed out of phase He was an invisible man moving through a backward universe. Terry's mind tried to come to grips with this new reality.

Still he was carrying hope. His attaché cases were filled with money. He walked in the early morning hours only when the traffic was light downtown, watching carefully to avoid the backward moving people and rushed across streets before stop lights.

He paused at a newsstand and examined the newspapers. It was indeed three years earlier.

The crowds were smaller as night came on and he wandered by streetlights out of the downtown area. By sunset light of the oncoming day he was able to walk on side streets, heading for the University. In the afternoon he was there.

The library doors were open, but it was tricky to move in around people who from his viewpoint were entering and leaving apparently backwards. He walked up two flights of stairs; it was useless to try an elevator.

Ahead was his old carrel, the door shut. When he entered he would be in his own past. Terry felt almost a compulsion to write the exact note he had received, at least for starters. He had an assignment: to warn himself. But the previous warning had not been heeded. However, if he gave any other warning would he remove himself entirely from the time he was in? He had been thinking about this all the way back to the University. If he did something else to his past life, it would change the future and then he didn't know what would happen. For instance he could throw all his books on the floor to indicate something was wrong. There were all those stories of a man who went back in time and killed his own grandfather and of course then he disappeared in the NOW, whatever that NOW was. He had no intention of suicide. That was just a silly passing thought.

Terry pulled open the carrel door, which required all his strength. There he was! There was his earlier, younger self, asleep, his head on his arms on the desk. He took a large sheet of his own paper and wrote in great block letters: "DON'T TAKE THE TIME TABLETS!" He taped the note to the computer screen.

Now there was another decision, the most important decision of his life. Anything he did now in the way of adding to this note would change the whole of the timeline of his past and create an anomaly that might remove him entirely from time and space. He would be changing the past. Could he alter the past? He would have to change the past if he wanted to make the situation he was in different now; if he wished to stop moving backwards in time his past self must be warned. Otherwise he might move backwards forever. If he wished to escape the trap he had gotten into he would have to do something. How far back might he go now? Where would it stop? Another ten years or fifty and he would be out of touch with all the progress he knew. True, his movement backward had slowed down, but it was continuing.

He stood awhile, thinking, standing in that carrel beside himself. Yes, he was beside himself in more ways than one. He had time to consider all this. He had nothing but time now. There was no point to rushing. He had all the time in the world it seemed. No. In a bit his younger self would be awake again. He had to decide now.

And then he felt the ringing in his ears subsiding! The effect of the

Time Tablet was at last wearing off. He rushed outside the carrel and slammed the door. He picked up the attaché cases with the money and raced down the stairs and out of the University. What would happen if he discovered himself? That would certainly change the future.

That was why he had written no more on that note in the carrel. It was a cryptic note but he had literally run out of time.

Terry stood remembering silly old jokes: "The man found himself. He lost himself in his work. I ran into myself the other day and knocked myself down."

Terry Thomas was back over three years in time, but once again in real-time. Time was going forward from where he had "landed." It was obvious he would have to avoid himself and his haunts until his other persona disappeared and that would be three years hence. He sure did not want to corrupt the time line.

The Time Tablet effect had been like a statistical bell shaped curve on this occasion, first sending time gradually into reverse, then speeding up as the full effect of the pill hit him, and finally a similar gradual slow down as the effect diminished. He walked over to a washroom and threw the rest of the Time Tablets into a toilet. Flush! The experiment was over, finished, done.

Terry was sweating all over, tired, shaky. "Get a hotel room, sleep it off, and then decide what to do," he told himself out loud, glad to hear the sound of his own voice once more. He would take a plane to New York or somewhere.

Plans began to form. There were a lot of things Terry knew about that had happened in the last three years, the next three years now: sports winners, Kentucky derby winners. Even the pharmaceutical company he worked for, EDI was a case in point. EDI stock had come under severe attack, fallen enormously about two years ago, and then risen again. He had followed the fate of the company and wondered if it would survive. Those were his thoughts before applying for a job there. How did you play the securities game by selling stocks short? He would find out.

He felt guilty over the bank robberies, but if he made enough money he could pay back the banks what he had taken from them with money to spare.

As to Peggy: Unless she had lied about her age, reliving the next three years again would make him older than Peggy Windsor. Yet she would never know or believe he was older. It did not matter.

If he invested enough money, he could buy so much of EDI stock while it was way down, he could get on the Board of Directors and Peggy would be working for him! There it was. It wasn't about money. He really cared nothing about the money. It was all about Peggy Windsor.

There was a whole life opening up ahead for Terry Thomas, but it did not involve taking Time Tablets.

The first pill had been a tiny experimental dose. That pill had caused time to slow down enormously, for him. Then he had made larger pills and tripled the dose. The second pill had caused time to almost completely stop. The third pill had caused time to stop completely. That should have been another warning as to what might happen. The fourth pill had sent him back three years now. It was an exponential increase. At that rate, the next pill might send him so far back that he would be in Ancient Egypt and enslaved to build pyramids. No, but he could be in prehistoric America. In any case he would never dare to take the chance again.

The Great Encounter

What _IF_ aliens tried to save
the earth from itself?

)

"I knowed I had discovered something." - Jose Herrera

This is Jose's story as he told it to me – Jeremy West

Manuel Jose Herrera watched the streak across the Arizona sky in wonder. He was walking alone down the deserted county gravel road in the late afternoon, returning home. It seemed that what he saw was some sort of plane, but it was one he had never seen before, and it was coming all the way down to land on the desert nearby. Curiosity overcame his fear and he ran through the flowering sage and around the thick yucca plants to the ridge top. Seeing nothing below, he continued on in the effortless lope of a skinny fifteen year old, moving across the plain to the next rise. Here he stood on a wide rock his wide brown eyes scanning.

And there it was below. The most important event in human history was about to occur. Partly obscured by rising dust and a few jojoba trees was a metal cylinder, resting on its side, fifty feet long, glistening silver in the sun. There were no wings on the craft and no sign of a door.

Jose crouched behind a creosote bush and a stunted single shafted saguaro tree cactus and watched, squinting into the sun. Next a small opening in the smooth silver side slid back; it did not really seem large enough to be a door. The spaceship was a hundred feet away, and Jose looked, wondering if he should approach closer or retreat. In the Saturday morning cartoons the heroes walked into the spaceships and were made prisoners by diabolical monsters. But the heroes always escaped. Only this was for real. His mother had often warned him to beware of the difference between what happened on the television shows and the real world.

Then the little opening filled with a metallic shape and a creature emerged. "A robot," Jose muttered to himself. It was good to give it a name. The object was small, perhaps three feet high, and its body was composed of four round segments, all about the same size. The creature was just floating there, a few inches from the ground, as if it were of a series of connected steel balloons.

Jose noted that the middle two sections of the short body had now sprouted many feelers, arms or spindly legs projecting that waved about. It was like a big silver ant, he told himself, only floating upright as a man. Abruptly beams of light played about, coming from the robot and circling the desert floor. It was probably examining the sage nearby and the arid gray ground. The circular sweeps gradually grew wider, extending outward.

That was enough. In a few minutes the light rays could reach him. It was past time to leave. Manuel Jose Herrera backed up a step. He looked at the ridge top just above where he now stood; measuring the distance in case he would have to run for it. Reaching the ridge would take only a dozen steps. He wished now that he had not moved closer. There was a big clump of cholla two paces behind him that he could reach easily. Back further the green yucca on the ridge top would offer better concealment.

But even his slight movement had already been noticed. Abruptly Jose was bathed in light and transfixed. He could not move. He looked back at the visitor, certain that a narrow beam of light was emanating from what he now thought of as a space monster. The light was enveloping him. Jose felt glued to the flat rock he stood upon just as some butterflies he had seen once in the museum were pinned down.

A horrible moment passed. The visitor hovered a little distance from its ship, taking its time, examining the nearby environment with light rays that appeared to leave its body and play about among the nearby plants.

And then an example of the visitor's pure power occurred that was terrifying. A large black raven came in overhead, perhaps curious too. The raven was a hundred feet away, fairly high, floating in great sweeping circles with its wide wing span. A beam of light shot from the body of the visitor below and first held the bird motionless in mid-flight and then brought it down in one sweep, a heap of fluttering feathers. The raven gave a raucous caw as it came in and then folded its curled wings, gurgling softly as it sat just beside the space visitor. The bird was a prisoner also, not even trying to escape.

Then a voice inside his head demanded of Jose in English: "Identify yourself. Are you a human?"

This happened on the Saturday morning cartoons also. Robots from outer space often did not speak English or Spanish, but they always managed to put voices in the heads of the heroes who discovered them.

"Jose," he replied aloud, as he would on the playground at school or on a street in town if approached by a stranger. All Mexicans were Jose and he could merge into the multitude and not be traced by using that name. Only now this response would probably do no good at all. He was alone and felt naked.

Jose fingered his head with one hand. It was as if he were being examined. "Who is the smartest man you know who lives nearby?" The words again were in English, not Spanish, and inside his head.

"The Professor," Jose declared without hesitation. He pictured the old, tall, very erect man, the epitome of Anglo culture. Jose was returning just now to the tiny rural village where he lived after discussing with Professor Jeremy West's study group. He had to walk three miles home instead of taking the school bus, but it was worth it to listen to the Professor and learn. The Anglo children came too, but most of them lived in town. Dr. Jeremy West was certainly the smartest man Jose knew, well beyond his high school teachers.

"You will go at once and return to me with the Professor. You will tell no one else."

The words were there. Indeed the words were imprinted on his brain somehow and he knew he must obey them. His mother would worry that he was so late getting home. It was almost two miles back to town.

"Yes, I will go and do it," Jose answered relieved he was still alive and being allowed to leave. But that was also the way of the television cartoons.

*   *   *

I always said that Jose Herrera was the first true discoverer of the visitor from an alien world. Jose's tale deserves to be told, though he is already receding into the background after all that has happened. Most people think of me, Jeremy West, as the discoverer now, and as a consequence some regard me as a world-class traitor, though as you will see none of the events that followed were my fault.

Other people feel only that the astounding aftereffects, in which I was a central character, have made any human experience meaningless today. Yet, as the world now knows, I have no reason not to tell the whole truth in this report. The results may be extraordinary, but they did occur. This story must be told now; it is my last chance.

The media has informed the world often enough that I was 67 years old at this time and a completely unknown failure until this alien visitation thrust me onto the center of the world stage. I did not ask for the opportunity of fame. I'm past my prime, though actually my body works pretty well yet and I feel great. Two years ago I retired from an Eastern University where I taught history. My wife and I moved to this small town of Las Palmas in Arizona. For me it was really an act of self-destruction. I can see that now.

Becoming a hermit is never the answer; you cannot escape the world. I had enjoyed teaching, but the books I had written were unread; I might as well have stood on a mountaintop and fed the pages to the wind. Twice I was passed over for promotion to become head of the department. Still I enjoyed working with students more than the administration. That was my failure at the University, enjoying the teaching.

I still stand six feet tall. My face I like to regard as rugged. I have most of my hair, though it is white and tends to stand up straight when I least want it to. My nose is too big. My pictures indicate I've always been pretty ordinary in appearance.

When I came to realize my mistake in retiring, because I really enjoyed teaching, I organized some freewheeling talks every day after school with a crowd of young people from the local high school and junior college in Las Palmas. Teenagers gathered at my house. I was still teaching, but not being paid for it.

My wife, Helen, needed the dry desert air, but she had not been happy away from our children and grandchildren. There was no real solution to that problem either. Our children were too scattered. There was Don who was trying to make it in the music game in Los Angeles, and having a flock of kids, four so far in four years, all boys. There was

Betty, who had been married to three different lawyers, and had what I considered a token child with each. They were all girls. Betty now lived in Manhattan working in an advertising agency. Last there was Susan, still going to College in Florida, her fifth year in a four year program, maybe not wanting to graduate and begin life.

Well, that's the story of my life and my children.

*   *   *

I heard the doorbell and punched the "save" button on my Computer. It was Jose Herrera, a tall, very thin, brown skinned youth who was part of my student late afternoon discussion group.

Jose was all excited so that his face almost glowed. "Professor West, you must to come quick. There is a great ship that lands on the desert. He ask you come."

"Who is 'He' Jose?"

"The robot from outer space of course."

"What sort of ship?" I inquired patiently.

"It is a spaceship, Dr. West."

"Obviously. A UFO?" I grinned at Jose. I was not a believer in such things. "It sounds like a case for the police."

"No. He ask I tell no one else. He want to talk to the smartest man I know."

"And you chose me. That's flattering." My smile now faded away. Jose was serious. This was curious enough to investigate. "How far away is this?" I asked.

"Maybe two miles down the county road. I run back most a the ways." Jose was sweating even in the dry desert air.

"You're sure now you really saw something?"

"Yes. We must go now."

"O.K. I believe everybody once." I called across the house: "Helen, I'm going to take a ride with Jose."

"What is it Jerry?"

"I don't really know. I'll be back soon."

And so we were off. We got into my old red Chevy station wagon. I did not care about cars except for transport and it showed.

"The county road?" I asked.

"Yes."

We were soon out of town and bumping along on the county gravel, leaving enough dust to advertise our coming. After a minute I asked Jose to tell me everything he had seen and the teenager obliged.

"You don't smoke pot or sniff glue?" I inquired, laughing.

"No, this for really real. Top of next hill. We stop and walk."

The sun would set in maybe ten minutes. After listening to Jose's story, I decided I should have told someone exactly where we were going. Had Jose been a few years older I would have suspected a hoax, the kind of joke that college students might play. The Piltdown man discovered in the Arizona desert. Only if this were really true, wow! I had never been much afraid of anything and now I had a feeling that I was so old my life didn't matter anyway. My life was over. Still, it was stupid to take chances

We left the car, Jose leading the way, striding in front of me. "How far now?" I asked.

"Two hills. Then we see the silver ship." We climbed one ridge and were crossing the plain toward another rise.

"Look, Jose," I said, "the car raised enough dust to be seen. We will circle and creep up that ridge up ahead from the other side. You point out the ship to me from the top. If this is what you say, we ought to let others know."

"Sure. But he say, bring only one."

"He's not deciding our actions," I insisted boldly. Little did I know? But then, while we stood for a moment in the arid valley between the ridges, the robot appeared nearby, floating out from cover half way down on our side, perhaps eighty feet away.

Now I was sure we should have telephoned others and left word. I even took a step back. But we had come too far to run to the car.

I tried to classify, organize, and understand this thing. That's what people did. They took the new and considered it in terms of the familiar. The four sections of the creature were resting right on one another, all almost round in shape and silver in color. Some of the small feelers or arms that projected from the body were jointed while others waved about as happy as wands.

Then an almost translucent stream of light played about me. I jumped as the light shifted to envelop both Jose and myself.

"You are the Professor?" the voice inside my head inquired.

"Yes." The only one, I thought in amusement. In retirement yet. "I am Dr. Jeremy West; Jerry to my friends."

I decided that if I did escape with my life, I wished to be able to report from actual personal observation more than a voice in my head and a small set of floating globes that might be somebody's idea of a robot or a joke. I wanted to see the spaceship Jose had mentioned. I walked to the left of the floating being toward the top of the next ridge. I did not feel caught as Jose had reported during his encounter, but I was not thinking of running away either at the moment.

This was no hoax. The voice in my head I had never experienced before. "Who are you?" I inquired.

"What shall I say to a human? I am Xan-Tu, the messenger, Dr. Jerry West." Somehow in my head I knew how the alien's name must be spelled in English.

"Glad to meet you. What is your purpose here," I asked? I was still walking slowly, cautiously, and really stalling for time with my words as I circled. Jose had spoken of a space ship and I wanted to see it.

"I am a mere observer for the Great Ones, Jerry West."

"Who are the Great Ones? Are you from one of the planets or moons of our solar system?" I was near the robot, now, twenty feet away as I climbed the ridge. Nothing had happened as yet and the diminutive size of this alien entity made me feel more secure.

"The Great Ones are those who rule. I am from a far off sun."

That is what invaders from nearby might say, to throw us off, I thought. He was talking to me as if he regarded me as a child. I paused and turned at this point, for I had passed the visitor now. In some cultures turning your back was an insult. But how would this being know a back from a front, when I could not tell which end was which on the visitor?

"I welcome you to our planet Xan-Tu," I indicated. "Would you mind if I looked at your vessel?"

"No, please do, since that is very much on your mind. Then I have a few questions for you."

I walked on to the top of the ridge. The alien craft was there, fifty feet of spaceship, resting on its side, just as Jose had said. Now I would need to report this to the authorities. It would be a sensational story. Abruptly I wished I had brought a camera. Everyone who ever encountered a UFO must have felt that way, I decided. I walked back slowly toward the robot. My purpose was to get close enough to see more.

"What is your profession?" the question was inside my mind.

"I am retired. I was a Professor of history." How I had joked about that in the town, but somehow the humor always hurt. There are the tired and the retired, I had said. The retired are twice as tired as the tired.

"Such a profession would be highly regarded in my culture," Xan-Tu replied. "The Great Ones believe the past is instructive and necessary to understand the future."

"You have an advanced culture," I snorted in amusement.

"Jose says you are the smartest man he knows."

"Jose is generous and kind." And not vastly traveled, I reflected.

"Are you a fairly typical human, Professor?"

"Everyone is typical and no one is typical." I replied. Even at that early moment I had some reservations about giving information without receiving any in turn. I was being interviewed and I wondered for what purpose?

"I wish to have some practice conversation with you before I meet the public of your world. I would like an intelligent citizen to help and advise me. Will you take on that job?" Xan-Tu continued.

Such an advisor might be considered a traitor to the human race, I thought. But perhaps the robot was serious and had no evil intentions. Maybe this visitor was a mere onlooker, a seeker of knowledge. If he was an observer, what might come next? So I asked the question: "You are an observer. What have you been sent here to observe?"

"Your civilization. Your progress. Will you accept my offer?"

"Sure." It was no good refusing. Any being able to fly here from another world probably had all kinds of other capabilities. "How would I be paid?" Let him reflect on that.

There was only a moment's pause. The robots tentacles seemed to wave about a little faster. "I understand this has value on your planet." One of the robot's arms flipped a glinting coin into the air and it arced toward me.

I reached up and grabbed it and my hand stung. It appeared to be a solid gold piece, without any decoration. The gold piece seemed extraordinarily heavy for the size of the object.

The coin Xan-Tu had tossed to me certainly had value. I own some gold coins and this object appeared to be no larger than a one ounce gold American Eagle. But it weighed more. There was quite a discussion about that later.

"Thank you for accepting my offer." The words were there, understood inside my head in this peculiar direct communication.

I hadn't really meant to ask for money, though I had requested honorariums for speeches I had given on lecture circuits in the past. It was a crude and rude thing to ask a visitor from far away for pay. Nor had I meant to enter into the employment of an alien. Rather the question of payment had been merely a delaying action while I thought of what I should do and say next. Now, to refuse after I had asked for payment appeared to compound the problem.

I put the gold coin in my pocket. Had I contracted to work? What had been said? 'To help and advise me,' were the words. That did not sound too much like a traitor.

"I will help for a time at least," I responded.

"More payments will follow. But you must carry out my orders or we sever connections. Is that understood?"

I certainly did not want my connections severed, whatever that might mean. It seemed time for a disclaimer. "I thank you for the souvenir from your world. I didn't really mean to ask for payment. Nothing further is necessary. I will be glad to help you all I can." Nor did I ever ask for or receive any payment again. Too much has been made of my accepting a fee at the beginning of this first contact. Probably I should never have mentioned to anyone that I received the payment from Xan-Tu and the matter never would have been known.

"First question," the robot began. "How is my English? Do you understand me?"

"Your English is good and I understand you? Your voice is a little mechanical as I receive it in my head, but that may be my perception from viewing you."

"Because of my appearance? Because you see me as a machine?"

"Aren't you?"

"Synergistic perhaps. A living machine. Is this better?" The tonal quality of the voice within my head deepened and became warmer, richer, more vibrant, though it now sounded a bit like a television announcer.

I told Xan-Tu the quality seemed improved and asked, "Is this your first visit here to earth?"

"Yes it is."

"Why do you come here now? By that I mean no discourtesy. But I am told there are over 100 million suns in our galaxy alone and there are well over 100 million galaxies. Why did you choose this planet? Some men have long thought that we humans were being observed by visitors from other worlds. Some believe they have evidence that such visitations occurred in the past. I have always felt such ideas were mere paranoia given the vastness of space and time. Space travel must take a long time even at great speeds. Earth has been here for several billion years. Humans have been civilized only six thousand years. Why did you find your way here just now in the vastness of space and time?" Even as I spoke it seemed to me that robots would indeed be the most likely to be sent on long journeys.

"That is a good question," Xan-Tu replied. "Professor the answer is your people on earth have advertised."

"Advertised?"

"Yes. Yes. You have betrayed your civilized presence in the universe. You have set off universal alarm bells. I sat on the edge of your solar system and measured until I understood the length of your earth's days and years. For more than eighty of your years people have been sending out voice impressions on your radios and for more than fifty years picture and voice broadcasts have been transmitted on your televisions. The television pictures have gone out at the speed of light in concentric circles, spreading among the stars as they traveled. Do you know how many suns such a message passes in dozens of years at the speed of light? You advertised that you were developing a technological culture. You are now what we call a Stage Five Civilization."

I thought about Xan-Tu's words. Perhaps television had destroyed our world in more ways than I imagined before. My wife, Helen, I privately characterized as a vidiot, a person enslaved by the tube, looking always for excuses to watch more. I felt she was almost ready to climb inside the television and live there. I loved Helen, but I had lost her to the tube. Since I retired we had been thrust more fully upon each other. We met forty years ago. In that long ago time two young people, us, made a decision that affected middle age and now old age. How many people have done that?

How do our minds work anyway? The thought flashed upon me of a time back east before I had my cactus garden in this dry desert country. That day long ago I was out destroying dandelions on my lawn by pulling off their yellow heads and spraying the plants with weed killer. And I was thinking of how the dandelions advertised their presence amid the green grass by raising their yellow flower as a signal. It made their destruction easy.

But who determines what a weed is? Was that Xan-Tu's function? Did all civilizations finally advertise their existence in the cosmos? Was he here to weed the human garden of earth?

I was aware suddenly of Manuel Jose Herrera standing beside me with his mouth open. "Do you hear the visitor, Jose?"

The tall boy shook his head. "No. I hear only your answers."

The visitor's words were directed at me alone. It was my first inkling that Xan-Tu could aim his speech. "Can you let Jose hear your words also?"

"Certainly." Jose jumped and showed he was hearing now.

"How long was your journey in our time?" I asked. That would help indicate what star the alien came from, perhaps.

"Many of your years. I have plenty of time, Jerry West."

This was not definite enough to help. Slowly I had approached Xan-Tu until I was standing only eight feet away. I positioned myself so the setting sun was not in my eyes. In turn I forced myself to examine each segment of the robot. The four globes that made up the robot's body I decided now were not metal but possibly some flexible plastic. I could see nothing that looked like eyes, ears, a nose, a mouth, and there was certainly no hair. The robot was all smooth surfaces. Each of the four balls that made up the body was maybe eight inches in diameter. Xan-Tu was under three feet high but floating in the air.

"Did you learn English from our television broadcasts?" I asked. I took a step closer to the robot. How close would Xan-Tu allow me to come? I paused and waited a bit, deciding I had better ask permission to come closer.

"Yes," the robot replied. "I chose to learn English first because it was the most widely used language on earthly television broadcasts. But your world has many other languages. I have also learned Spanish and Russian during my journey. Chinese, Japanese, French, Portuguese, and German. Only recently have I seen a need to learn Arabic, Hindi, Polish, Italian, Dutch, Swedish, Norwegian, Turkish, and Greek as a root language, as well. Then I have found there are more than one hundred others. How many languages will I need to know to reach everyone? Latin is no longer spoken much on your television." Right here I should have had clue to the stranger's intentions. I did not reply to this.

Xan-Tu paused, and then he added: "There are many forms of communication in the outer universe and sound transmission is only one of these. Learning new languages is like breaking a code. Some programs on your various national televisions offer lessons in learning languages. Only I do suspect television language is very different from your books. It is too bad you have not reached the stage of one main language on this planet."

"Many a schoolboy would agree. Learning everything you know of us from our television must have given you some interestingly shallow insights." I decided to declare myself on this matter right away.

"Your television has many contradictions, Jerry West. I am sure I can resolve these matters by personal observation. People in your serious dramas hardly ever laugh, for instance. But on game shows, the audience seems to laugh easily and for little reason. Obviously this must be stylized pleasurable expression called forth according to custom."

"Much of the laughter on our television is canned. The director has the option of pushing the laugh button over as far as he desires. Most directors believe their jokes are very funny."

"Yes, but audiences will laugh when someone says 'Hello' on a comic program and they do not do so in dramas. That is a puzzle."

After watching American television it was a wonder the visitor wanted to come here at all. "Do you have television on your world?" I inquired.

"Once the Great Ones passed through a planet-wide communication time in the far-back. Their ancestors have moved through many stages."

While I was still reflecting upon this, the robot shifted the subject back. "The United States seems among the most open of earthly societies. Therefore, I have landed here first. But what will be the reaction of your people to my presence Jerry West?"

"That will depend upon your purpose here. You can expect some tough questioning on that score." Could the stranger be afraid?

"It is difficult to know what to expect by studying your television broadcasts," Xan-Tu continued. "Some of the programs appear very silly and many others are violent."

"Our own people often feel the same way." I took another cautious step toward the robot.

Xan-Tu's arms seemed agitated and moved around as he talked. He was definitely floating, perhaps eight inches off the ground. I still could not determine how the appendages protruded from the body.

It seemed unnecessary to be afraid of something half my size, and yet my mental caution lights were on. "Am I getting too close?" I asked. "Would you mind if I touched you?"

"Do not do something odd, please. I am fully protected and you will hurt yourself, Jerry West." It was a television speech. From five feet away I could almost reach out and touch one of the vibrating arms. If he watched our television, Xan-Tu knew of our custom of shaking hands. I reached cautiously and encountered an invisible barrier about three feet out from the robot, which gave me a jolting electric shock. I jumped and moved back.

"Are you all right, Jerry West?" Xan-Tu inquired solicitously.

"Yes, I am fine. That was my fault. Sorry."

"People must be told not to try to touch me. I have a force field around me and it repels in relationship to the challenge."

"I'm glad I did not try to challenge you with more than a touch." I gave Xan-Tu a wide smile.

"My force shield is for defense against accidents as well as promoting an envelope of stable environment without changes in temperature and humidity. Also, Professor, are you aware that when I see your exposed skin, I extrapolate that you have several billion bacteria and virus covering your whole body? All of those microorganisms are in effect waiting for you to cut yourself or even to inhale, though of course with your physiology, anything that you breathe is still outside your body."

"Our eyesight does not allow us to observe objects much smaller than one-hundredth of an inch or so without aids. We need a microscope to see the clouds of microbes in the air we breathe. I suppose it is an ancient survival factor. If our eyes were more acute, early man might have gone mad with the knowledge that he existed in a sea of tiny organisms. Since he could do nothing about it, knowledge of microbes would have distracted early man from his primary purpose, that of surviving."

"But," Xan-Tu persisted, "I would guess that your outer skin alone holds more microscopic creatures than there are humans on your planet. And the size of the cloud of creatures around you is enormous."

I laughed, wishing to leave this subject behind. "I'm sure that is true," I agreed. "Yet this is 'pure' desert air here. You should see our cities." After I said this I told myself to be quiet. Don't talk down about our earth culture anymore. I wanted the visitor to think well of men even then.

"You can't really see x-rays or heat rising either," Xan-Tu questioned.

"No. Our visual spectrum is limited to what was helpful in primitive times."

"That is no doubt true. But it is no wonder that your people are always so ill and have so many pains with all those microbes."

"What makes you say that, Xan-Tu?" I was frankly puzzled.

"Your television, Jerry. There are so many advertised remedies for headaches and other illnesses."

I laughed. "I hope you don't believe all that is said on our television. Our citizens have learned that most of our advertising is false."

"That is why I would like to read some of your books."

Perhaps, I thought, humans should have sent messages of strength into space instead of television advertising pictures of people with colds, coughs, and headaches. The sun had set a few minutes before and twilight was coming to the desert fast now. My shadow, which had seemed elongated across the arid landscape, faded. In a few minutes Xan-Tu would have further evidence of how little we humans saw in the dark.

"It is late," I suggested. "Will you spend the night at my home?" Could I transport him, I wondered?

"You have books, especially histories and encyclopedias?" the visitor inquired. "I see encyclopedias advertised on your television."

I laughed. "I have a couple thousand books. Come on."

"I understand that you must perform a function called 'sleep' when the sun goes down to meet the rhythms of this planet?" It was a question.

"It's a biological necessity for us, Xan-Tu. Some day men may develop beyond this. Two great rulers of the past had such delusions of grandeur because of their success with armies they thought they could do without sleep, Napoleon and Frederick the Great. They tested this hypothesis and did not succeed."

"All languages have curiosities," Xan-Tu confided. "In English why do you fall asleep, but wake up?"

I laughed. "Language was not invented by professors. Would you have us go down asleep and straighten up?" Then I asked: "Will your space ship be all right here?"

"Yes. It can not be seen from the road and is fully protected by a force field. I landed here in an uninhabited area to conduct tests first before making contact. But people are everywhere on your planet now so I was seen anyway."

I watched Xan-Tu gliding over the desert floor, moving around the brush, just floating or rotating as if indeed he was merely four silver balloons held together somehow. The robot's force screen no doubt protected him from the needles of the cholla plants as well. I was glad to reach my car.

"Can you get into the back of my station wagon?" I swung open the rear door.

"I believe so. Stand clear and I will cut the force shield to a minimum distance." The robot floated higher and entered the back, upright, just inches from the floor and the roof.

"I will shut the door now." I said this carefully. "We can open the door any time. You will not be a prisoner."

"Hardly. I have seen your station wagons and how much they hold on television commercials."

"Jose," I told the patient boy, "I will bring you to your home first. Please tell your family I delayed you, which was why you were so late. I'm going to drop you off and turn right around and bring Xan-Tu to my house. Say nothing of our visitor to your family. Tell no one in school tomorrow about your adventure. You will have a chance to tell everyone later. Can you really keep a secret, Jose? It's the hardest thing to ask a human to do?"

Jose nodded smiling. "I will tell no one. I can do it."

"Good. Come over to my house tomorrow after school as usual. I'll see you then." That was a safeguard. If something went wrong, Jose at least would know.

I left Jose in front of his house and drove back, wondering how upset my wife Helen would be. Everything upset Helen. She was a worrier. Above all, I wanted to do the right thing here with this alien. I felt that I was an ambassador for all earthmen.

Oddly enough, Xan-Tu sensed my concern. "You are worried Professor West. You have no need to fear anything." That statement by the robot did not add to my feeling of well-being. It just made it obvious the robot could read my every thought.

It was quite dark in spite of the streetlights in Las Palmas. I pushed the garage door opener when I was still a ways down the street and slid into the attached garage easily without anyone noticing Xan-Tu.

"Jerry? Dinner's been ready for twenty minutes," Helen called. She had heard the garage door open.

"Yes, Helen. Jose made a discovery in the desert he wanted to show me."

"It was probably much more important than being on time for dinner." She didn't mean it. Helen often spoke in negatives.

"Yes, it was. It was a ship from outer space and a robot."

"Oh sure."

"I brought the robot home for dinner." I opened the house door and ushered in Xan-Tu.

"I'm sure he will be delicious," Helen declared. Then she saw the actual visitor and screamed. It was a television response. How often now does the tube tell us how we should behave? Xan-Tu's arrival called for a scream.

"How do you do, Mrs. West," said Xan-Tu. "I do not understand that greeting, actually. But it is customary. So, 'How do you do?' You are the female of the species?"

"That's what they keep telling me," Helen replied, recovering somewhat, patting her brown tinted hair, which was disheveled as usual. Her hair always looked as if she had just received a severe electric shock. I have tried talking to Helen about her hair, but she tells me it is the style for women of her age.

Helen had become a bit too heavy with a hint of a double chin that helped only in leaving her face unlined. I loved her mightily at that moment. She was obviously trying to cope.

I wondered what Xan-Tu thought of Helen after seeing the actresses on television. "What is going on here, Jerry?" Helen demanded, adjusting her glasses to peer at us. She would be angry later, because I had not given notice of a visitor coming and she was caught wearing a housecoat.

"Mrs. West," Xan-Tu apologized, "it is my fault your husband is late for dinner. I have watched not only your comedy programs but your nature programs as well. I understand you. You are the custodian of the eggs of the human species and highly sought after by the male, though in humans this is disguised in poetry and song."

Helen just looked at Xan-Tu in disbelief. And so the evening began. "We are going to have dinner," I told Xan-Tu after a bit. "I take it you do not eat food?"

"No. I have no intake apparatus. Nor is it necessary. The remote ancestors of the Great Ones ate in the long ago, but that is now many millennia past."

When I ushered Xan-Tu into my study, I had this mental picture of our guest sitting comfortably in my great black reclining chair, reading books. But the alien did not sit. Instead he floated high over a little table, parallel to the floor. He began reading the first volume of the Encyclopedia Britannica, which I furnished him. He paused just a moment at each page and lights flashed in his upper globe. Xan-Tu waved a tentacle and the pages turned without his touching them.

"I am really savoring this Professor," the visitor asserted. "I want to get the flavor of your culture."

I left Xan-Tu and sat down to eat, giving Helen a shortened version of the episode in the desert.

"What on earth will you do with him? Is it a him?"

"I didn't get into sex. It's not up to me to do with. He is going to stay here and look at my books tonight."

"I won't sleep a wink with that thing in the house," Helen whispered to me. She always slept anyway, but that is the way she talked, a speech full of mock threats that she didn't really mean. Helen would be snoring loudly at eleven o'clock as usual so that I would need to turn on the box fan in the room as usual to cover her noise.

When I did not reply Helen added: "Just because you're a historian doesn't mean we have to have aliens visit us, Jerry."

I nodded. How was I to reply to that?

I looked in on Xan-Tu, but he seemed content with the books. I did not feel any danger, but that night I popped a sleeping pill. And so began the first day of the rest of our lives, as they say.

ll

"It was better than television." - Helen West

I usually arose at seven, but I jerked wide-awake suddenly at five that morning, dressed quietly and went downstairs to the study to observe Xan-Tu. Our guest was still floating above the small table and from the stacks of books it appeared that he had gone through the Britannica along with a two volume history of the world, an English unabridged dictionary, my French, German, and Spanish dictionaries, and a world almanac.

"Good morning, Dr. West."

"Good morning, Xan-Tu. I hope you had a pleasant night."

"Yes, I did. To change the subject, I suspected this from listening to your news broadcasts, but now that I read your world history, I fear that your planet is in deep trouble. Humanity has gotten itself into a corner."

"The planet has always been in trouble Xan-Tu. Civilizations rise and fall."

"But a nuclear war, as you call it, would return most of the surviving earth's people from a Stage Five culture to a Stage Three. Further, you have built your civilization on easy to reach resources, coal, oil, and metals near the surface. Those easy to obtain resources have been consumed. Now that you have achieved a technological stage, you can manage to reach the resources deeper beneath the surface of your planet and utilize those minerals that need much more processing. But if you blow yourselves up, your technology may take centuries or millennia to come back. And if the war is bad enough, mankind could be finished."

"Were you sent here to save us from ourselves?" This was a common enough theme of various books recently. The theme represented a surrender of mankind, unable to find a way out. "Perhaps only a deus ex machina can help us now," I observed cynically.

"That was not my purpose. 'Dues ex machina' is not a television term, Dr. West, but fortunately I read your English dictionary this morning. It is an interesting concept. The Greeks had dramas in which the characters boxed themselves in so completely during a stage play that there was no possibility of a happy ending. So in the last scene the actors simply pulled a small statue of an appropriate God across the stage in a little wagon and the God solved all their problems. The God in the machine. It was a simple machine, a simple solution, and a simple God."

It seemed to me that Xan-Tu was speaking more exactly and had improved his understanding of human conditions overnight. He was learning rapidly. Was that dangerous?

I took out my camera and asked: "May I take your picture?" Certain primitive tribes felt their life force was diminished by picture taking. Anyway, pictures were private, so it was best to ask.

"All right," Xan-Tu agreed.

All along I had the feeling that our guest might just fly away without anyone else seeing him and I would be left with an unbelievable story backed up only by young Jose.

Could I even take a picture of the robot? Well I could and the pictures were there. Xan-Tu was present in his entire splendor with many of his twenty-four differing arms, legs, feelers, or tentacles pictured. By this time I had carefully counted the robot's limbs. Some arms were multi-jointed, some had pinchers on the end, some arms came to a point, and some had furry feelers and others a pod.

The surprise was that on the picture there existed a yellowish glow around Xan-Tu ending three feet out. This was the force field, I decided.

Then I thought of my Sony Video. "Would you like to watch yourself on television?" I asked by way of inducement.

"I have, of course. I experimented while on my space ship, as you call it. I had to watch your television at a very rapid rate because I was approaching at great speed. Your television gradually gave me an understanding of your species. You must have evolved in a warmer climatic period, for you are a bundled people all covered with clothes. The clothes are not only for show, as I first thought, but also for warmth. It was only when I viewed some of your X-rated movies in the last part of my journey that I realized what you humans really looked like."

"Good Heavens."

Xan-Tu went right on. He seemed irrepressible: "At first your television shows were circumspect, the older ones that I encountered before I began my journey. They were primitive, but clever in some ways. In flight I picked up increasing numbers of broadcasts and finally you began to exhibit your lovemaking to the cosmos in all its details. Was such the human objective?"

"Not really." It was embarrassing, thinking what mankind had sent out as a message to the stars. I regarded most television programming as aimed at twelve-year old minds anyway.

I found my video camera and asked some questions as I shot pictures of Xan-Tu. When I played the video of Xan-Tu back on my television, there was no recorded sound except my voice.

"You're putting those words in my head," I declared. "The film is silent."

"Since I have no mouth or vocal cords, I must use other methods to communicate with those who can not receive me directly. However, Dr. West, if you would like a permanent message just run your tape back and I will dub in some words." And the television premier of Xan-Tu came through with the following message somehow added to the tape: "Greetings citizens of Earth. I have made a long journey to visit your planet. I come in peace as an observer. I am interested in your world and its people. I thank you all for receiving me as a guest."

It was one of those pretty speeches that said nothing. You could tell something about the owner by watching the dog. The rule could be true with robots. We make robots in our image. I felt that Xan-Tu represented an older culture. He seemed to have patience and plenty of time.

After I took the pictures I sat in my large black reclining chair and watched the robot 'read', a process that consisted of moving a tentacle, which, without touching the page below, caused the sheets to turn. Then flashing lights scanned both sides of the page. Then the next page turned. When the robot reached the end of a volume, the book closed, apparently unaided, and floated back to the shelf. The next book came out and took its rightful place, open, upon the table.

"What would you like to do today?" I asked my guest after a time.

"I have enjoyed the books, but I believe there is a faster way. I see you have a computer there on the desk. May I use it?"

I had not mentioned the computer to Xan-Tu because I wondered about this alien going on the internet. How much information should I be giving him? The internet is so full of the mundane, the bad, the good, the strange, the curiosities, that it exposed too much of human weakness.

"Sure, go ahead," I replied, still uncertain.

The computer screen began showing programs, flashing faster than I could visually follow. "This is a much more rapid way of learning," Xan-Tu related. "There are programs in many languages and on human physiology. Humans seem to be a very short lived species, Jerry West."

"The older we get the shorter the time seems to be," I observed. "Looking forward seems long; looking back seems short. In many ways we have only the moment to enjoy."

"You revere youth on your television because it lasts such a short time in your species," Xan-Tu suggested. "Dawn and sunset come so close together for you."

"Yes, but there are butterflies that flit about only a single day, and when I lived in the East, I had in my garden tiger lilies whose blossoms opened only for one day." I shrugged.

"Would it be appropriate to call a press conference for you later today? You should be introduced to the world." I was not sure how one called a press conference, but it was obvious it could be arranged.

"My immediate plan is this, Dr. West: We will return to the desert, both of us, board my ship and go to your capital at Washington D.C. There we will hold a news conference."

I nodded agreement. "You want me to come along?" It sounded exciting.

"Do you have the time?"

"Yes. I will be delighted." I was surely doing nothing important with my life right now. I reflected that so many people in America were so anxious to get on television or the news that they were willing to lie about their lives and even participate in programs that made them look foolish just to obtain some fame. Shakespeare well said: "Some are born great, some obtain greatness, and some have greatness thrust upon them."

I must confess I felt elated at the prospect of being at the center of this adventure. I was actually enormously excited, though I tried not to show it. Then I remembered Jose.

"Some high school students will come to my house before four o'clock today, Xan-Tu. That is still ten hours away. We talk about a number of things. I will meet them at the door and tell them our little sessions are ended for now. However, Jose can not be expected to remain silent for long with a secret of this magnitude."

"True. There are always the details. It is doubtless best that we leave today right after four P.M. Still this time here has worked well for me; I wanted to get the feel of your books and there is even more on the computer."

"I will get some of my things ready, then. Am I allowed to bring a suitcase?"

"Certainly."

I went back to our bedroom. Helen was still snoring softly. It was not yet 6:00 A.M. When she awoke, I would tell her what was happening. She would be upset. Helen was a very dependent woman and did not like to be left alone. I would arrange a plane flight for Helen to come to Washington and meet me there tonight. I had not asked to have her come along on the space ship. That would frighten her even more. She hated flying on airplanes; a space ship would be too much.

*   *   *

Helen was upset as I knew she would be and we argued some. She disliked any sudden changes. It struck me for perhaps the ten thousandth time that we were so different, it was a wonder our relationship had survived all these years. We had nothing in common, were totally unalike, and yet lived together and loved each other.

I have always been one of these men who were frightened by the mystique of women. Women in my classes at the University, women working for the University, women neighbors, were just female people, but women to be courted and loved had always been a bit beyond me. I don't know how I ever really managed it originally with Helen. Certainly I was glad to get that part over with and just be married.

Young people have always felt "old people" to be without passion or desire, and I must confess when I was young to having such feelings also. The "old" were people who had never known love. But I did love

Helen. Suffice it to say that if I had known what was going to happen in Washington D.C., I never would have gone.

But not knowing the future can be a blessing. I took a trip list from a file folder. It was a checklist I had compiled long ago and added to many times since. I had checklists for everything. The trip list was originally begun back in the days when we took vacations with our children. It included favorite children's toys and camping supplies. But it was still useful. Now the list included all the pills I took. When you get old, at first you think it is a vitamin deficiency. I packed my things in two leather bags rather than a suitcase. What was appropriate for a space flight?

I was concerned that Jose might have given away the secret of Xan-Tu's presence and wondered if we would get a call from reporters. At 4:00 P.M. when my student group arrived, I explained our talk sessions would be cancelled for awhile. Then I asked Jose to step into the house alone. The honest boy had kept his silence. I told Jose exactly what was happening and asked him to say nothing till that evening.

"I believe you will be a bit of a celebrity when you tell your story. Here are some pictures I took of the robot, which you may keep or give to the newspapers. They might command a high price. I have a video recording I made in this desk drawer. If anything happens to me, make sure this gets played." Jose agreed, departing reluctantly. I could see the boy wished he were going along, but he had not been invited. I was taking his great discovery away from him.

Helen drove Xan-Tu and me on the County Road to the spaceship. Darkness offered no concealment this time and at the first stop light in town a child in the back seat of the car next to us pointed to Xan-Tu in our station wagon. But the child could not get his parent's attention. Then we were out of town and bumping along on the gravel of the county road. There was not much traffic out there.

Helen protested one last time. "Can't you fly to Washington with me and meet Mr. Xan-Tu there? I'll never see you again."

"Your husband will be perfectly safe," the alien interceded and Helen was silent. I was the only one she argued with. We kissed goodbye. Xan-Tu and I crossed the intervening strip of desert together. The spaceship was still lying there on its side, out of sight of the road in the desert valley. I felt the force screens around the ship open automatically as we approached, almost as a greeting. Then a small door in the side slid up.

"Sorry, Dr. West. This entry was designed for smaller creatures than you," the visitor apologized.

Xan-Tu floated in and I stuck in my head and looked around. I thought how dark it was and lights came on. Again I saw that my very thoughts could be read. The corridor inside was only five feet high. I stooped over and eased in, holding on to some railings that ran the length of the corridor. There had to be a series of rooms, but all the doors were shut. The outer door of the spaceship closed behind us.

"Please remain right here," Xan-Tu instructed. "We will ascend soon." With these words, the robot floated off. The wall of the ship appeared translucent; I could see the desert outside. The engines came on with a soft, sweet hum and we rose swiftly with almost no feeling of acceleration. The ground simply receded, as if we were on an elevator. When we were very high, I felt a slight change in direction. There were mountains below, then fleeting glimpses of plains, and abruptly we were high over Washington, coming down slowly. The entire journey had taken only a few minutes.

The building of the Capital appeared to rise to meet us. Ahead was the grassy green park around the Washington Monument. Then I saw a pair of planes, military jets, zooming in toward us.

'Oh no, don't shoot,' I thought. 'Don't start something.' But the plane was already in action. A missile came streaking toward us and exploded perhaps fifty feet out as it hit the ship's force shield. Inside I felt no shock at all from the huge blast. Then wing guns on the plane flashed as they fired. I could see the bullets ricocheting as they hit the force field of the spaceship. Bouncing back, some bullets struck the attacking plane. A wing of the plane sheared off and the pilot ejected.

Then the pilot, his chute half opened, the plane, and even the detached wing were caught in beams that held them immobile for an instant and finally set them down quite gently on a grassy hillside. The spaceship itself came to rest nearby, sitting upright this time, its nose pointing skyward, a large silver needle in the green park.

"Now, Dr. West, we will climb down and leave by the lower door."

"The planes meant no harm," I asserted to Xan-Tu. "They were merely trying to protect our capital from terrorists." Yet it was quite a welcome, I decided.

The robot floated below and I followed. It was easy to descend to the bottom of the corridor by bending over and holding the handrail. There must have been some internally controlled antigravity devise or some form of stabilization, for the spaceship was pointed upward and the corridor should have been straight down. Yet my descent felt level. I have often thought of that part of the journey since and I have understood it less each time. At the moment I had suspended all belief as to what was happening to me.

"I will now open the outer door," Xan-Tu declared. "Won't you go first please, Jerry?"

Outside there was a surging crowd of people running toward the spaceship, pointing, mouths open. It was as if a bunch of country bumpkins were gathering in great numbers at the county fair. People gasped and shrank back as Xan-Tu emerged behind me.

There were sirens announcing the arrival of the police who did nothing more than try to hold the crowd back. Soon a cordon of police was established around the spaceship. I was a major participant, and more photographed in the next ten minutes than I had been in my entire life.

I just stood observing, wondering at first if Xan-Tu was trying for a special effect. There was the great masonry obelisk of the 555-foot high Washington Monument just a hundred yards away and the small metallic appearing shaft of the 50 foot high spaceship of Xan-Tu's standing on end. Somehow this ship had become an instant monument in this city of monumental structures.

A dozen military jets were flying overhead by now, just circling. A helicopter came in, landed on the grass fifty yards away and the men inside with their gray and blue suits began running toward us. They were probably Secret Service. Other helicopters were coming in waves also.

Then Xan-Tu was speaking inside everyone's head in the whole gathering crowd. "Citizens of earth, I will make a statement in a few minutes. In the meantime keep back away at least seventy feet from my ship in all directions. The ship is fully defended and on automatic. If you come too close, you will receive an electric shock. If you attack, you will be repulsed with force in proportion to that which you exert. I will come out of the protected perimeter now. Dr. Jerry West, who is an earthman, and I, will wait for the crowd to gather further before I make my statement."

We walked through the force shield without any trouble, I simply following Xan-Tu. We stood waiting as the numbers swelled to many hundreds and then thousands many snapping pictures frantically. Reporters were arriving and taking pictures, while television cameras were being set up with power cables running back to waiting network trucks.

Then the questions began:

"Are you from Mars?" one reporter called out.

"No," Xan-Tu replied. "Please wait with other questions."

But no one waited. I was amazed at the pushy nature of some reporters:

"Are you here in peace?"

"Where are you from?"

"What are your intentions?"

"How long was your trip?"

"What do you think of Washington D.C.?"

"How do you like American women?"

"Are you a machine?"

"Are other aliens coming?"

"What's your favorite music?"

"Is your ship a flying saucer?"

"Have you been responsible for UFO sightings?"

"Why are you here?"

"Are you from Mars?" I wish I could count the number of times Xan-Tu was asked this.

The questions rolled in. Xan-Tu stood immobile, waiting.

Some of the crowd had pressed down to ten feet from us now and began to shove nearer; the police were having difficulty holding the line.

"Please do not venture any closer," Xan-Tu requested. "We are fully protected."

I felt a force screen go up around me too. It was an odd sense of lack of pressure and I just knew it was there. The crowd drew back a bit, at Xan-Tu's words.

One of the network channels and CNN were in position and they wanted to get the word out before the other reporters were ready. The questions flew.

At last Xan-Tu spoke: "Greetings citizens of earth, I come in peace. For years our people have monitored your television broadcasts and finally it was decided to send me as an observer and emissary to visit your world. I have full power to act in accordance with the wishes of the Great Ones. Yesterday I landed in the Arizona desert and was in contact with Dr. Jerry West, here. He invited me to his home last night and we decided to fly to Washington today to hold a press conference. I represent an intergalactic confederation. This is a mere first contact and we are not here to exploit your planet. I am speaking inside your heads but also in such a way that my voice will be recorded on your video camera film."

Several of the networks were plugged in by now, recording the whole show and sending it out live.

"Why did you shoot down our plane, if you came in peace?" one reporter asked.

"I did not shoot down your plane or use any weapons. You will find on analysis that your plane fired on my ship and the bullets bounced back and hit the plane's wing. He shot himself down, something which I believe has happened before, if your old news programs are to be believed. The pilot is unharmed. Do not come closer there."

One of the reporters had thrust a mike up into the three foot zone of the force screen and gotten a shock that sent him flying. He lay stunned a moment, rubbing his hand.

"I will say again," Xan-Tu commanded, and his voice was harsher. "Please stay at least six feet away from us. Eight feet would be safer."

Everyone backed off a little again. Several limos pulled up at the parkway perimeter and some officials walked across the grass, the way being cleared by security people. The graying Secretary of State, Ted Webster, and two Senators were there to offer official greetings.

There were some minutes of ceremonial welcome to earth and to this city from the people of America.

Immediately after that the reporters began again, asking questions that made me shudder. I wanted Xan-Tu to think well of America and of humankind, but the media response to this most important news conference of all time was something less than edifying. There were many repeated questions:

"Have you come in peace?"

"How do you like earth?"

"Do you think our women are pretty?"

"Are you from Mars?"

"You learned English watching television. Which television programs do you like best?"

"What do you think of our movies?"

"What do you think of people?"

"What do you do for fun?"

"Have you done much traveling before?"

"Do you watch our commercials?"

"Are you here on a shopping trip?"

"Which parts of earth would you most like to visit?"

"Can we tour your spaceship?"

To all of which Xan-Tu gave appropriate answers. Most of the questions elicited responses that did not say much.

"How long will you stay on earth?"

"Until my mission is complete."

"What is your mission?"

"I am a mere observer at the moment."

"Will others of your kind come to earth?"

"Not right away."

"Are you the forerunner of an invasion?"

"No. I come in peace."

"How fast does your ship travel?"

"Quite fast."

A dozen military jets were flying overhead just in case, which also attracted people from far and wide. Two large tanks and an armored troop transport pulled in to the rear of the throng as a show of force.

At the edge of the crowd, merchants with carts were selling ice cream and hot dogs. Pickpockets were no doubt plying their trade. I saw what I took to be a hooker soliciting. A crowd feeds upon itself, as a magnet, a black hole, pulling those nearby into its grip. Surely if there is a crowd, something must be happening. The whole event was turning into a circus.

More limos arrived. One vehicle carried the Russian ambassador who soon reached the front of the line and extended his greetings, suggesting that Xan-Tu should visit Moscow soon. American Secretary of State Ted Webster had had enough. "I think Mr. Ambassador that we should finish this conference in some private place such as Duncan House. It is only a few blocks from here. We can put you up there in comfort and discuss our relations."

"That would be fine, Mr. Secretary," Xan-Tu agreed.

The Secret Service cleared a wide path after which Xan-Tu and I followed Ted Webster back to the longest stretch limo I had ever seen. I noted that the Russian Ambassador was smiling. I decided that Xan-Tu had sent him a private message, probably in Russian, accepting the invitation to Moscow soon.

When we reached the limo, I felt my force shield come off. Xan-Tu floated into the limo, taking up a whole seat across for himself. Before I could enter the car, Ted Webster extended a hand to shake mine, but the words that went with the shake were an attempt at understanding my position. Since I did not know what my position was, it was a little hard to answer.

"You are just a day previous in this business?" the Secretary inquired.

"That's about it?"

"You are the discoverer of our visitor?" Webster continued, still holding my hand so that I could not enter the limo just yet. The implication was that somehow I should now bow out.

"In a way. A young Mexican boy saw the spaceship land and summoned me to the scene. Xan-Tu spent last night at my house."

"We'll debrief you later."

"I do want Dr. West to stay with me for the present," Xan-Tu declared. "His wife, Helen, who does not like space flight, is coming in by regularly scheduled plane and should be met at Dulles Airport and brought out to Duncan House as well. It is important to give orders also that no one comes too close to my ship. There is a force shield around it and it is fully protected. It will repel force with at least equal force. I hope it may remain where it landed for a few days. I realize this is sacred ground I am on. I regret the intrusion."

"No problem, Mr. Ambassador. Is that the correct title?"

"That will do."

Ted Webster terminated what had been the longest handshake I ever endured. I was allowed into the limo. Usually I am calm, but now I felt jumpy, on edge. I could not wait to see what would happen and I was hoping to be a part of this action. I had been involved by chance, but for the first time in my life I was inside the car of history, traveling, looking out through the tinted windows at a reality I could scarcely believe.

Duncan House was one of the huge old homes along Pennsylvania Avenue between the Capital and the White House that the government owned and used at times to put up visiting dignitaries. It was vacant at the moment, except for live-in servants who stood in readiness for just such a call. The front entrance hall was larger than my living room back home.

Ordinarily the conference that followed might have been held after the visitor had time to freshen up, but that seemed unnecessary. Also the meeting would have been one on one. Now not only was I allowed to be present, but two Secret Service men were in the paneled study for the protection of the Secretary. What protection anyone might offer was a moot point.

It was only by courtesy of Xan-Tu that I was still a part of these events. While I did not understand my role, I was enjoying the experience.

"Dr. West," Ted Webster demanded, "I must ask that you will please say nothing of these matters until you are given an official release to do so."

"I can be just as reticent as necessary, Mr. Secretary," I replied. "However, the way the reporters hound people, I really thought of typing up statement of all I know of this matter so I can be done with it."

"Well you are not State, so we can't prevent that. I would like to read any statement you prepare first, before it goes to the press." Officialdom is officialdom and always trying to maintain its dominance even in small things. People in charge feel they know best and would like to be able to exercise control. They are the true parents and the rest of us are children, at least in their eyes.

Now the Secretary of State continued the welcoming protocol addressing Xan-Tu, and finally he asked: "Mr. Ambassador, what brings you to our small planet?"

"I am a mere observer for the Great Ones. Eventually I will report back upon my visit. Depending upon the outcome you may at some future time be asked as a planetary unit to become a part of the Confederation network. Later other steps might be undertaken depending upon our progress and the circumstances."

"Who are the Great Ones that you refer to?"

"They are my masters, the rulers of the Confederation."

"How far have you come on your journey?"

"It has been a journey of some years."

"I guess it is useless to offer you some food or drink. Is there anything we can do for you immediately? Do you need any supplies for your ship?" I saw this as a feeble attempt to get into Xan-Tu's ship.

"I would like a Computer set up with world language programs. These things I have begun in a day at Dr. West's house. I would really like this as soon as possible."

"That is one of the easiest tasks I have ever been charged with. You will find a computer set up in the library here at Duncan House. The language programs can be immediately installed. The President would like to meet with you. May we set up a time for ten tomorrow morning at the White House?"

"Fine."

There were some other perfunctory questions and then the Secretary took his departure. Xan-Tu and I were alone with the servants of Duncan House. Washington was two hours later than Arizona time and so it was after seven P.M. when we arrived at Duncan House.

I smiled: "Well, we are here. Is there anything you would like me to do?"

"Not now. But stay here. I have found you willing and helpful."

Of course Xan-Tu wanted to spend the night with the computer. I was sure it was connected to the State Department and they would be able to monitor whatever he did. I asked the household staff for some food.

Secret Service men were outside along with police and reporters. The crowd of the curious around the house was growing. The crowd stood, just waiting, perhaps hoping for some important event to transpire.

The phone had been ringing and Bill Haskins, the chief of staff at Duncan House, was just taking messages. Haskins had an interesting job. He and his wife lived in an apartment on an upper floor of Duncan House. He served as a sort of butler and major domo, his wife as a cook and maid.

When Haskins noted the phone was always busy, he asked for a twenty line phone, and managed to get this installed at once, that very night. The telephone company was trying to please. When the twenty line system was plugged in, all the lights lit up. Now Haskins inquired to whom the phone calls might be referred. Xan-Tu had asked not to be disturbed. Could our visitor be laughing at us?

I barged into the library and found Xan-Tu floating over the atlas. "All the world wants to talk to you." I waved a batch of telephone call slips. "What shall we tell people?"

"You decide, Jerry," Xan-Tu instructed. "Take only the most important calls yourself and of those calls decide to which people I should talk."

So Haskins screened the calls and I talked to only those Haskins felt were important. All manner of promoters and weirdoes had the number. Then Connie Jarson, the talk show hostess, phoned in person and to my surprise Xan-Tu agreed to appear on her show the very next night if she could fly here and do the program from a studio in Washington D.C.. Connie Jarson agreed.

Even my wife, Helen, when she arrived at the Washington airport, had been met by a group of women reporters who wanted to know the sex of the robot, what kind of a house guest he was, and other important questions such as did he use the toilet?

Helen suddenly believed it was good we had come to Washington D.C.. After all it was accepted by the television.

lll

"Xan-Tu is more a man than any of us. And I can prove it.

He's got four balls." - A comedian.

By morning peddlers were selling alien tee shirts with Xan-Tu's picture to the crowds gathered outside Duncan House. There were also pennants, buttons, and silver charms for sale. There were records, audio tapes, and video tapes of the alien's words.

Kids on skateboards were showing their talents outside on the street, as were clowns, comics, and unicycle riders. Musicians were playing and passing the hat. Pennsylvania Avenue was partly blocked off. The police were looking very officious and serious as they talked to each other on their walkie-talkies. I was glad to see it begin to drizzle.

The morning newspapers were announcing the story with headlines four inches high. Pictures of the space ship and Xan-Tu covered the front pages. **Time** and **Newsweek** were out with special editions a little later. According to the television news, the space ship had been cordoned off, but was drawing crowds that filled the park below the Washington Monument.

As I expected, when I arose at six A.M. that morning, Xan-Tu was still at the computer. "How are you doing?" I inquired.

"I have completed my elementary education as to humanity, Jerry," the alien asserted, "but there is always much more. I am glad you are up early. From the first, I felt a compatible relationship with you, which is why you were chosen. I wish now to bounce some thoughts your way and see if you agree."

"Go ahead."

"While the problem is not universal, most life forms that pass through advanced stages fast run into difficulties. My problem is often to save the dominant species from itself. If men were not aggressive, humanity would not have become the dominant type on this planet. Then having achieved mastery, the dominant form of life still has this aggression. Of course it is largely true of all life. Big fish eat little fish. Now your human aggression places you in jeopardy from yourselves. Yet you do not admit this, but obscure the problem with minor issues."

Xan-Tu continued: "In past times on Earth there were wars and great slaughters in which empires fell. But the whole human race was never in danger. As late as the 19th century wars were considered romantic. Two examples are the Crimean War (1854-1856) with its Charge of the Light Brigade and the Spanish-American War in 1898 in which more soldiers died of disease than in battle and men could still charge uphill on horseback carrying flags while bands played."

"In the World Wars, except for the air battles, which often were individual and could be considered romantic, men died by the millions for no good purpose except alleviating aggression. Nuclear weapons have made human wars on this small planet very dangerous."

"Today, your world plays with minor wars, in Korea, in Vietnam, in Afghanistan, in Iraq, any of which could turn into a great final disaster. Yet you manage to fool yourself into believing this is not so. Nuclear weapons are in the hands of so many other countries now that the situation is plainly out of control. The public and the politicians as well are deluded by peace plans that take small steps."

"You are saying what we all know, Xan-Tu," I finally interrupted, "but we find no way out."

"The United States, Russia, and China as the leading world powers, must take charge and point the way. You need a force of marshals, as in your old American west, small teams that will seek out nuclear weapons and eliminate them. The great nations need to agree and then impose their will on the other nuclear nations. There needs to be complete nuclear disarmament."

"That's pacifism and you may be able to force it, which is already a contradiction in terms, but we can't seem to do it for ourselves. The military in all countries have a built in need to stay strong. Governments want their individual independence."

"You must draw the national lines of countries where you are now. Any changes should be based on free elections within each country. Thank you for listening, Jerry." I was dismissed. I felt I had been a mere sounding board and Xan-Tu had decided upon a course of action.

I walked back to the kitchen and fixed myself some breakfast. The phones had been put on standby overnight, but when I plugged them in, the whole twenty-line system lit up. I let the lights flash and walked away, switching on the early morning television broadcasts instead. The news programs were sensationalized. Only maybe this event needed sensationalizing. When my wife Helen awoke she was most impressed to find her interview at the airport last night was carried in full. Every silly question a reporter asked was recorded. "I'm on television," Helen marveled.

Downstairs again, I saw that the State Department, at Haskin's request, had sent over a secretary in case Xan-Tu needed one, and a telephone operator had been added to the Duncan House staff. A computer message had been inserted: "Xan-Tu has asked that he not be disturbed now. Please leave your name, phone number and a brief message and he will get in touch if he is interested."

The word came through that we were to be received at the White House Rose Garden at eleven A.M. that morning, only an hour's delay. I hoped that they were not trying to impress Xan-Tu by putting him off. It wouldn't work.

Finally I began to take some phone calls aimed at me, since Xan-Tu was not returning calls. Reporters wanted to talk, often asking questions I could not answer. One reporter requested full details on the weapons systems inside the space ship.

A magazine offered me $25,000 and, when I refused that, raised the offer to $100,000 for exclusive rights to my life story. What a boring tale that would be. When I refused the second offer, the publisher reminded me rather caustically that I had better understand that my story was time related and if I did not act now, the value of my life would go down. I was amused. I had been a University Professor who had written books no one much read. Now suddenly I was a celebrity for nothing that I had done myself.

It seemed time, so I cornered the new secretary at Duncan House and dictated everything that had happened to me asking only that this be printed up and photocopied so that all the reporters would have exactly the same story.

The vice-president of the University where I had taught, one Randall

Hampden, a man who had twice passed over my name for head of the department of history, telephoned me. I don't know what he was offering now, but I refused to take the phone call. That did give me some perverse pleasure, I must admit.

By ten A.M. I was pacing back and forth around the house, gripped by a feeling of anxiety. What would happen when Xan-Tu finally understood the human race? It was a chilling thought. Were we at all worth preserving?

It was just Tuesday evening that Jose Manuel Herrara had brought me to the desert and shown me the space ship and Xan-Tu. It was Wednesday night when we had come here to Washington. Now it was Thursday morning, and I felt my whole life had changed and the direction of the human race was also in doubt.

Others were wondering the same thing, for it was right then that a limo pulled up and three men were spirited through the curious throng outside by some Secret Service guards who looked like linebackers. The three men were there to see me, privately, and Xan-Tu was not to be disturbed.

We met in the spacious living room of Duncan House.

"Dr. West, we only have a few minutes and we want to ask you some questions. I am General John Tanner. This is Admiral Clement O'Connor and Vince London here is Director of the CIA."

"Hello." We shook hands. General Tanner was a huge man who shook hands with knuckle crunching force.

"Just shake it, don't break it," I requested.

Admiral O'Connor was bald, his wide chest beribboned, and he held a coffee cup that apparently was attached to his hand, for he carried it in with him from the Limo and never did put it down.

Vince London was tall, thin, angular, sharp eyed, and a very pale creature. He almost seemed to blend into the furniture.

"Let me get right to the point," General Tanner began. "That space ship is all cordoned off. We fired a couple of tracers at it last night as an experiment and they bounced back. We tried digging under it, starting at eighty feet out. When we got down twenty feet, we tunneled toward the ship. About fifty feet away the drill struck the force shield underground and exploded. Two men were badly hurt. The force shield goes down into the ground apparently and clear around the ship underneath."

"Xan-Tu said it would repel force with equal force," I advised.

"Yes. We were warned," General Tanner agreed. "Now we've told you what we know. What do you know?"

I handed them each a photocopy of the typed statement I had prepared for the press. That was not enough. They wanted me to repeat the story and I did so from the beginning leaving out no details. Even then they asked questions, as if to trip me up.

"There will be a Congressional Committee investigating all of this, eventually," General Tanner disclosed, "but they are just beginning to set up a team and you know how they operate. It will take months for them just to get ready to begin to get started to commence to proceed." The General was being scornful.

Vince London, the head of the CIA added: "The Congressmen and media will investigate and want to know such things as why we did not foresee this and plan for it."

Something clicked in my mind. These men all had their jobs in the government, as military officers and CIA chief, but in addition they were members of the famed Quadrilateral Commission, a secret organization with its own aims to direct the government along the right path, whatever that was.

"You can't even guess where Xan-Tu came from or from which direction?" Vince London asked.

"No."

"Did you see anything but a corridor on the space ship?" Admiral O'Connor inquired.

"No. I was told where to stand and I did so."

"You don't think this is all an elaborate hoax by someone here on earth trying to impose their own agenda upon us after we swallow the whole alien from outer space story?" the CIA man asked.

"No." I reflected. "Hardly. The force shields would be an entirely new invention. The ability to talk to people individually in a great crowd without a loud speaker would again be a whole new technology. The space ship is real. It arrived here in Washington from Arizona in a matter of minutes. It achieved satellite orbit in moments and then in a few minutes had covered three thousand miles without much feeling of motion or of having traveled at all. When the ship arrived here in Washington it was fired at by one of our latest planes without effect. Then Xan-Tu helped the plane and pilot to a soft landing after the bullets from the plane ricocheted back."

"That's a very good summary," Vince London declared of this analysis. He turned to the other two. "This man should have a security check and then stay with this assignment."

"As long as the robot wants him, I guess we have no choice anyway," Admiral O'Connor concurred chuckling, and sipping a little coffee.

"So we are not dealing with a wealthy group who have developed new inventions and are ready to hold the world hostage?" General Tanner restated the situation.

"Hold the world hostage I don't know," I divulged. "But there are three new kinds of technologies right here: the force field around the ship, the speed of the ship, and the voice transmissions. There are probably more. One new technology in the hands of a conspiratorial group who wanted to put on a show for their own purposes is possible. What I have witnessed is plainly beyond that."

"We have only your word for the speed of the ship," Vince London observed. "The force field and the voice transmissions are unusual. And our plane did shoot itself down. But is there anything else?"

"Well, yes. Only I want this back. It was a gift from Xan-Tu." I took out the gold coin and handed it over.

"It's too heavy for gold," Vince London commented. "We'll run some tests and give it back to you."

"What do you think he wants?" General Tanner asked.

"I don't know."

"This could mean the end of the world, or the end of humanity. It could be the end of our freedom," Admiral O'Connor suggested.

"I've wondered what it would do to our sovereignty," I admitted.

All of the men seemed uncomfortable. They asked me to find out all I could and they departed.

*   *   *

Just before 11:00 A.M. the limousines were back and Xan-Tu and I left Duncan House for the meeting with the President. The crowds were heavier than ever outside. Suddenly one man broke from the police line, pulled out a gun, and began firing at Xan-Tu. "You are the Antichrist come to earth," he screamed.

The bullets glanced off the visitor's force screen and one struck a secret service man in the leg. The crowd ran every which way, but secret service men jumped on the gunman from so many directions it looked like a football pileup.

Xan-Tu and I were spirited off to the White House Rose Garden before something else happened.

Washington is always most interested in protocol, and since apparently Xan-Tu did not sit, it seemed fitting that the meeting was held in the Rose Garden where everyone would stand. There were perhaps twenty people present including secret service men and members of the cabinet. The President, Reed Hamilton, was his jolly, smiling self, assured, and only seeming to be bothered that he could not shake hands with the visitor.

I had voted for President Hamilton. In person he appeared shorter, but more handsome and full of life even than on the television. It seemed to me that he had what all top officials have, charisma. He was dressed in a blue pin striped suit, but he was one of those men that seemed more comfortable in less formal clothes. This was probably an effect of his bushy, curly black hair. It was said that his hair was a factor in women voting for him and his election.

When the preliminaries were over the President expressed sorrow over the shooting incident. Hamilton next asked: "How do you float?" It was a simple question, but the President seemed genuinely interested. Curiously, I had not heard that asked before.

"It is an antigravity process not unlike the force field."

"Dr. West tells us that you are a messenger. What is your message?"

"The universe lies beyond your small planet. It is time for you to cross the threshold and leave the house of your fathers. Maturity beckons."

"What do the Great Ones look like?"

"They are beyond fixed physiology."

The President paused, reflecting. From the look on his face, he had a great desire to explore this matter further and even though it might be trivial he was not going to be denied. "Do the Great Ones have multiple arms and legs as you do?"

"It is very helpful to have numerous appendages of various sizes. I note on your television the oft recurring phrase when someone is not able to do a job fast enough: 'I only have two hands.'"

"I think that may be my problem." Reed Hamilton gave his famous chuckle. The President was pacing around and never seemed to be still. "What do you want of us Xan-Tu?" Hamilton asked at last.

"To establish relations. To observe. To help."

"We need lots of help. Did the Great Ones you speak of deliberately design you to be small so you would inspire less fear?"

"No. Size is relative. We could not judge your size from your television broadcasts. You might have been the size of your ants. Ants also have legs and ways to manipulate their environment, if only their brains grew enough in relation to their bodies."

"Do the Great Ones look human?"

"You have many kinds of life on this planet. Any type of life that is capable of manipulating things and developed a large brain could attain primacy. What are the odds that intelligent life on another planet would look just as you? Humans developed in response to this planet, its size, gravity, temperature, atmosphere, and other factors."

"Well, Xan-Tu, let me ask a silly question, as reporters do: How do men appear to you? Do you see?"

"Not as you, but I can read the visual images on your television. At first, as with all alien species, you looked alike to me. Then I noticed small variations that make men and women and all people individual."

"Do you want to trade with us?"

"We are probably beyond trade. Yet the universe is vast with hundreds of millions of suns. Strange things occur."

The President appeared to think that over. Reed Hamilton was at the height of his power just then, having taken office only a few months ago. "Is there anything I can do for you?" the President asked.

"I wish to study and observe your people. Soon I will make a statement."

Rex Hamilton, the President's brother, who was a part of the inner circle and Attorney General, now spoke up: "Xan-Tu, we all welcome you to earth. We understand you are going to be broadcasting live on the Connie Jarson show tonight at nine P.M. in a special program right here in Washington. I wonder if you would favor the reporters, the foreign ambassadors, and our leaders of government by attending a buffet party tonight at six P.M. at the home of Mrs. Perkins?"

Xan-Tu accepted. Mrs. Sylvia Perkins was one of the great donors to the President's political party and also one of the most notable hostesses on the Washington scene. She had an enormous home and always invited many people to her parties. A buffet seemed proper as Xan-Tu neither ate nor sat down.

When we returned to Duncan House a direct phone call came through from the CIA for me.

"Jerry West, this is Vince London." It was the CIA Director himself. "Let me give you some confidential information, which you are not to divulge, and then I will ask you a question. When we sent in that television and phone to Duncan House, we bugged both so we could read what programs Xan-Tu was using. Maybe we shouldn't have done that, but we wanted to know. Well, the bugs stopped at once. No information is coming out. What's he up to?"

This action seemed to me to be typical CIA. "I'm not surprised," I replied. "He is able to create his own circuitry somehow. He can probably read the circuits. I am sure he could discover bugs and eliminate them almost instantly. I believe he is learning various languages."

"So why the secrecy?"

"I would guess he just doesn't want to be bugged."

Vince London sighed and said goodbye.

About then there was another guest in person at Duncan House, Joe Candlelight the Chairman of Rush Research Council. He was one of the great brains in Washington. Joe Candlelight had access to the President's ear and perhaps other parts of his anatomy. He wanted to talk to me and we met in the great living room at Duncan House. I was glad to meet him, but shocked at his appearance. How did one give advice to presidents and pretend at wisdom when you were five foot four inches tall and weighed 300 pounds. Didn't Joe Candlelight include health articles in his vast reading?

"I've looked at the transcript of your briefing to CIA," Candlelight declared, his many chins wobbling merrily. "Do you realize what this really means for the world, Jerry West?"

Candlelight was at once familiar and moving closer to me, one of these people who stood so near, you automatically backed away.

I squirmed uncomfortably. "It means a lot of things, I am sure." I did not want to feel like a student, but Joe Candlelight made everyone feel that way.

"Guessing games I was not asking you to play, actually, Jerry. What it means, if this be true and Xan-Tu represents an actual contact from off planet, is that we may be in for conquest, or imperialism, or even if this is a completely benign visit, well actually lets ask, what did the Indians think when they saw Columbus? Not a bad guy in a funny hat. What did the Japanese think when they saw Commodore Perry? What did the South Sea Islanders think when they saw Cook? Were they actually aware that their lives would never be the same again? You're a historian. Primitive people in contact with advanced civilizations tend to curl up and die. They find their myths punctured, their dreams of history evaporate, and they wither."

I nodded. "True. That happens often. Yet what we must do is rise to meet the challenge."

"Actually we are out of Xan-Tu's league," Joe Candlelight continued. "He can cut off our balls anytime and dangle them."

"I don't know as he wants our balls."

"But what does he actually want, Jerry? You don't just travel across space for years to say 'Hello'."

I nodded. "You're right. I have not gotten straight answers from him either. He can be vague if he wishes."

"Does he lie?"

"I haven't caught him in any."

"Not likely. But he's cagey. He actually says nothing of inventions or trade. Of course, why should he, Jerry? Cortez never gave the Aztecs the formula for muskets."

"I see what you're getting at."

But Joe Candlelight was all over the map: "Do you think he is in a hurry?"

It was an odd question. After so long a journey, why hurry? But as I thought over the question, I had to agree: "Maybe. He is preparing for this television broadcast tonight. Of that I am sure."

"Could you announce me, Jerry? I would like to talk to our visitor."

We walked, or rather I walked and Joe Candlelight waddled behind me, into the next room. Xan-Tu was busy over the computer, which was flashing things on the screen too fast to be read. "May we interrupt, Xan-Tu?" I asked.

"Certainly."

"This is Joe Candlelight, founder and director of the Rush Research Center. He would like to see you for just a few minutes."

"Delighted. I believe that is a more desirable greeting than 'How do you do.' Is that true?"

"Yes," Joe Candlelight agreed. "I understand you are learning languages. How is that coming?"

"Just fine."

"You told the Secretary of State that earth might actually become a part of your Confederation. How would that work?"

"You are not yet ready to be asked to join the Confederation in any sense. But some day that could happen."

"You actually make too many secrets, Xan-Tu. Give me a simple answer to just one question. Tell me exactly where you are from?"

"In our nomenclature, the Great Ones originated on the planets of Star System D427 in the first galaxy."

Joe Candlelight blinked. "And on our star charts, where is that actually?"

"Ah. You said just one question."

The fat man laughed. "You actually have me there. You are the sphinx. Do you always tell the truth?"

"In your Christian Holy Book, which I read, Pontius Pilate asked Christ the most difficult question he could think of, testing Him, before sending Him to His death. The question was: 'What is Truth?' and it is recorded Christ gave no direct answer. Let me ask you and Dr. West a question. Are the documentaries on your educational channels concerning life on your planet correct? I have watched thousands of these on the way to earth."

Candlelight spoke first: "You are wondering if you can trust the data you have assimilated. The non-political documentaries made in America I would say are largely correct, to the best of our present knowledge. Some have a bias in favor of certain causes. Even ecologists have a bias." I nodded in agreement.

"Yes. The bias I expected, but the pictures are not altered as to life here?"

"No. But often it is the strange or unusual that is filmed."

"Yes, of course. I wonder if we could meet again after my broadcast on the Connie Jarson show." Joe Candlelight understood he was dismissed and left.

In the great hallway, as he departed, Joe placed one last thought with me. "Something must be going to happen on that show tonight. Here is my private phone number. If you want to talk off the record sometime, just ring me up. Xan-Tu has become the center of a storm, a tempest of a human ferment, actually. And you are the inside man, the anointed one, as it were, Jerry West. Stay on top of this."

"I will try."

I instinctively liked Joe Candlelight in spite of his obesity, but I was having some unfitting thoughts. I have a motto: 'Never lie to yourself.' The worst lies are those we tell ourselves.

When I thought about things honestly, I realized that I was concerned Xan-Tu might replace me as his intermediary with someone else, a still smarter man, a person such as Joe Candlelight. And I very much wanted to stay on in my present position. I was having the time of my life.

*   *   *

There was one more visitor in the late afternoon, oil billionaire Wesley Aimes, a master of mergers, they called him. He had State Department clearance. Since he was a big political party contributor he could get almost anything including a pass through the guarded front door of Duncan House.

Wesley Aimes was heavy of jowl and belly, but not a forty five year old fat man as Joe Candlelight, but an eighty year old who was mildly overweight and trembled on his cane. He was accompanied by a huge bodyguard who stood silently and watched.

"I'll see if he will talk to you," I advised.

"Nonsense. We will go in." Aimes could see by the direction of my gesture that Xan-Tu was in the next room. Wesley Aimes was a man accustomed to getting his way and the power was not just in his $2000 suit which was a bit rumpled.

I had no authority to prevent this meeting. The pass was signed by the Secretary of State. Aimes and his bodyguard moved right past me and into the large library room where Xan-Tu floated before the computer. I followed hesitantly, feeling I had failed, somehow.

"Hello, I'm Wesley Aimes and I wanted very much to meet you."

Xan-Tu placed his computer on hold again and revolved about. "Did you bring in this gentleman for a purpose, Jerry?" the alien asked. I had a feeling that Xan-Tu heard everything in the house right through the walls.

"No. He found his own way in, as they say. He has a note from the Secretary of State that requests admission to Duncan House and an interview with you. It is a high level request."

Xan-Tu now addressed Wesley Aimes: "You are in the financial news. Perhaps we could talk at a buffet I am going to shortly."

"This is a private matter."

"Yes, your health perhaps. CXT Corporation is troubled because of your recent heart attack."

Aimes was taken aback only momentarily. "You have the technology to extend my life?" he asked.

"Yes. But not indefinitely in your present form."

"Indefinitely!" Aimes was disdainful. "I'll take ten years or twenty, if I can get it. What do you want? Gold? Diamonds? Land? I can get you anything the earth has to offer."

"Interesting. You would sell what you consider to be valuable parts of your planet to someone from beyond your Sun System for your own private health reasons. Have you tried losing weight and exercising? There are already too many humans. What makes you more valuable than the billions who are struggling in less developed countries? What do you offer the earth?"

"I can get you things. I am a mover. I can cut corners and act faster than governments."

"Acquisition? But what is your personal value to this planet? Are you a scientist? A teacher? What have you invented? What pictures have you painted? What job do you do?"

"Look, I get your drift. But someone has to manage things, isn't that right, or the world would go to Hell. Is there anything you want?"

"Perhaps. We might set up a Foundation with half of your money to be used to build low rent housing and then extend your life for ten years as you suggested."

"Half my money!" There was real pain in Aimes voice.

"Your life isn't worth it? But we can discuss that. Let me keep you in mind. For now, though I do not wish to be disturbed."

"Look, I don't want to offend you. But the whole world is going to want to get things from you. I'm just here first. That's one of the things I'm good at, getting there first." Aimes chuckled. "Do hear me out."

"Out is the activating word. Not now, Mr. Aimes."

"Look here," Wesley Aimes began again, and then suddenly he and his bodyguard were not there.

"What happened?" I gasped.

"I shall be polite at the buffet, Jerry West. But for now there are a few things I wish to do. Mr. Aimes and his companion are now in New York City. I returned them there. I believe that is where his corporate headquarters is."

I laughed. "I will try to do better at seeing you are not disturbed."

"And I should really have taken care of that matter myself. So I shall do so now." What Xan-Tu meant by that remark was soon obvious.

Before I left the room Xan-Tu suggested: "You have not asked anything for yourself, Jerry West."

"I don't want to be sent to New York." I laughed and left, shutting the door.

It was only a few minutes later while I was staring through the front windows at the still increasing crowd outside that Bill Haskins, the butler at Duncan House, came rushing up. "Dr. West, you are the one on the spot I am told to report to you anything unusual. Could you come with me to the hallway please?"

"Sure." I followed Haskins and watched as the well tailored butler felt along the wall.

"I bumped against this by accident. I find I can not touch the wall along here."

I felt the wall myself in surprise and found nothing. "What is the problem, Haskins?"

"You are putting your hands through, and I can not," Haskins replied. Haskins was a very matter of fact person.

"Feel along here and tell me where the force screen extends?" I requested. It was helpful to give the phenomenon a name. In a few minutes we both knew. The entire library, where Xan-Tu was running his computer including the walls and doors was covered by a force field that extended a few inches out from the wall. Apparently I was programmed to enter the screened area and felt nothing. I could thrust my hands through while Bill Haskins and presumably the rest of the world were barred from entering the library until Xan-Tu desired other company. While he was staying here at Duncan House, no one was going to walk in on the visitor unannounced again.

The other unusual element here, was that while the force screen around this part of the house felt solid to the butler and could not be penetrated, no matter how he banged his fist on it, and he tried that at my suggestion, there was no electrical shock or repulsion. Xan-Tu did not want anyone inadvertently hurt.

When I did enter Xan-Tu's now private chamber an hour later to see if the robot wanted anything, the visitor was not there. He had simply vanished. So what was happening? I sat waiting in the room, before the quiet computer, not knowing. Would he return at all? Where had he gone? How long had he been gone? Should I even be waiting here inside the room for him? It was nice to be trusted to enter, when everyone else was barred. But what was really going on?

Then Xan-Tu simply materialized in the best science fiction tradition, like the Cheshire cat in reverse, just fading into the room and there he was.

"Hello. I was just checking to see if I could do anything to help and you were gone?"

"I've been all over the earth, investigating, Jerry," the robot explained. And yet it was no explanation at all.

⫾⫾

"If you had a force shield built for two, it might be fun."

- Kinky Turner.

The buffet at Mrs. Perkin's mansion was right out of a Hollywood set. The rooms were on a grand scale and interconnected, with spiral staircases leading to overhead balconies and alcoves where guests could gather in small groups and talk privately. The buffet table was roughly as long as Xan-Tu's spaceship and held a smorgasbord of every hors d'oeuvre I had ever seen and many more that I could not identify. Waiters kept refilling the table dishes and also walking around the rooms with trays of food or drinks.

My wife, Helen, had gone out that afternoon and spent hours selecting a three hundred dollar dress in which she felt dowdy compared to the rest of the guests. Still Helen was circulating determinedly and holding wine glasses. Presently she would be a bit tipsy. I had one glass of wine, but I was certainly trying the food.

Xan-Tu was standing in the ballroom, right in the middle, and talking to all comers. I watched the scene from one of the side alcoves, hoping the people would not ask the alien too many silly questions. Then I was interrupted by a tall, comely young woman. She had on a black low cut dress, which showed skin tones that a model might have envied. She was obviously a mammal on display.

I relate the next incident only to show one aspect of Washington.

"Hello, Dr. West," she enthused. "I'm Kinky Turner. I wanted very much to talk to you. Perhaps we could go out on this balcony."

There were a number of balconies through many open French doors and I agreed out of curiosity. The night was warm and the fragrance of flowers filled the air outside. Mrs. Perkins had one of the largest gardens in Washington.

"Are you a reporter?" I asked.

"No. Should I be?" She was coquettish. "I just thought maybe Xan-Tu could be left alone for a while and we could take a walk in the garden."

"We could do that. But for what purpose?" Kinky Turner was perhaps twenty-five, about the age of some of my younger graduate students back in the good old days. I had heard the name, but I am not good at identifying celebrities. Often I wondered how people became celebrities.

She took my arm, which was very pleasant, an experience that left me tingling. It was curious how these feelings persisted even at my age.

"Purpose," she continued, "if you do not like gardens, Mrs. Perkins, who owns this house and is giving this party, and who is a good friend of mine, has a number of spare bedrooms that are not in use right now."

"If you follow the newspapers, you know I'm married."

"Yes. How married are you? Does that bother you?"

"Good Heavens. I remember your name now. You were in the newspapers, involved with that Senator. And you are direct. But why me?" Here was my curiosity again. I always wanted to know about everything. It could get me in serious trouble some day.

Kinky Turner shrugged, then brushed back her sweeping blonde hair which kept moving as if it had a life of its own, jiggling flirtatiously like its owner. "I'm a groupie, I suppose. I collect people. I can't have the robot. You are known as 'The Discoverer.'"

"Like Columbus."

"I never thought of doing it with Columbus," she admitted.

"Which historical character would you most like to do it with if you had the chance?" I asked.

She hardly hesitated. "Washington, maybe. I understand he was a bit of a ladies' man. He was suppose' to be the father of his country, but never had any children. Do you think the father of his country was impotent? He married Martha and she was a widow with children, so she wasn't sterile. Oh, and Lincoln. Honest Abe the rail splitter. Maybe Ben Franklin. He was a rounder in more ways than one. Teddy Roosevelt had a really fierce mustache."

"And in the rest of the world?"

She frowned and showed what her face would be one day. "Napoleon maybe. Alexander the Great."

"Only conquerors. And not Caesar, Attila the Hun, Genghis Kahn?" Kinky laughed.

I continued my inquiry: "No artists, scientists, writers, philosophers?"

"Artists, maybe. The rest are pretty dull. Rubens. I like his pictures in the museums. It would be fun to be a model, to be painted."

She was hardly a Ruben's model, I decided, all bones under her clothes, thin to the vanishing point, but she had lovely skin. "You would like to hang in the Louvre?" I suggested.

"It's one form of immortality."

Before I could contribute further to the conversation, Kinky continued to muse. "Do it with anybody in all of time. It's a curious idea. Shakespeare, maybe."

"Not Moses, Socrates?"

She laughed. It was her chief characteristic, a bright tinkling laugh. "The press says you make a fine companion for the robot. They are right. You are a fascinating man." She squeezed my arm. "Am I striking out?" she asked.

"I can't imagine why you want to play in my bush league," I replied.

"You might be just the kind of craggy ball player that would make me want to score in the bush or anywhere."

Students had occasionally offered themselves to me for grades and I had always refused. Why start now? "My wife is here," I told her by way of excuse.

"She won't have to know. Or I can send someone to keep her company." That rather did it. Suddenly I had a very differing idea of the Senator's indiscretion with Kinky Turner. Too often we see the man as the aggressor and do not allow for the temptation of the determined woman. I bade a permanent goodbye to Kinky Turner and returned to the party to observe Xan-Tu again. This was a mere interlude for me with Kinky Turner, but it seemed to show what could go on in Washington.

Vince London, the CIA Director, came up almost at once. Vince seemed paler than before and was pulling hard on a cigarette. "Well, Jerry West, the sorcerer's assistant. We've checked you out, you know. You pass muster as a real person."

"I'm glad."

Vince London put on what passed for a smile. "Every ambassador from every little country is inviting Xan-Tu to come see their land, and he is saying 'maybe' in multi-languages. But I really think this party is for the women. They are asking Xan-Tu every dumb question imaginable. I shudder at what he must think of the human race."

"I've had plenty of fears of that kind, Vince. But is Xan-Tu giving any answers?"

"He is saying absolutely nothing elaborately, as usual. He could outfox Machiavelli without any trouble. Do you believe he will use the Connie Jarson show to tell mankind he is taking over because we are just too stupid?"

"Connie Jarson is a woman," I said.

"Ah yes, but of a different kind than these." Vince gestured around at the party guests. "By the way," he continued, "that object you were given, we tested it at the CIA lab. It's not gold. It's no known metal. Xan-Tu told you it had value here?"

"Not gold. Well, I'm sure It will have value then. I do want it back as a souvenir. I hope they didn't destroy it."

"Destroy it. They can't get into it. It's too hard to be real, they tell me."

"What is real?" I asked. I was losing my grip on reality.

*   *   *

It was the Connie Jarson show live from Washington D.C., a new first for the capital. "And here's Connie," bellowed the announcer in his usual exclamatory style, while the audience burst into wild applause, though nothing had happened yet. Massive applause without reason was one of the curiosities of American television that had puzzled Xan-Tu.

I got to watch the entire show, peering from behind a curtain in the wings, starting with the preliminary set up as Connie Jarson, the hostess, was ensconced on stage. A small table was brought in for Xan-Tu to float over which would put him just below eye-level with the hostess as she sat behind her famous desk. The background props were set up next.

The makeup men were upset because the camera lights glared a bit off Xan-Tu's silvery body and they could not apply anything in the way of dress or make up that would soothe the coloring. No one was permitted to come close due to the visitor's personal force screen.

Connie Jarson appeared to be at her unflappable best, the hostess of "The Evening Show" for years now and always high in the ratings. She was a success partly because she had that rare ability among television personalities to open people up and then listen to their musings without interrupting. She was a tall, angular woman with a pleasant pinched face. She was wearing a silver dress tonight matching her guest's coloring. There had even been talk in the studio that perhaps she should modify her jet black upswept hair and it too could be colored silver. But that Connie felt was a cheap shot, a little too obvious. She was calm now with her broad, almost painted on smile and expansive gestures as she pointed to changes she wanted in the lighting. And then it began, the most peculiar television broadcast ever seen.

"This is a very unusual evening for me, ladies and gentlemen. It is a strange evening for all of us on earth. Ordinarily I do an opening monologue and then have four varied guests. But we have canceled everyone else tonight and are going live with Xan-Tu, a true visitor from outer space who landed just recently in Washington D.C. This program is being broadcast from our Washington studio. Now may I present Xan-Tu."

And the diminutive visitor bobbed in, floating along, finally hovering over the table, as planned, to the tune of more raucous applause and some laughter from the studio audience.

"This is not a hoax, ladies and gentlemen, but the real thing. I am glad to welcome you, Xan-Tu." The audience had been prompted and they stood up breaking into thunderous applause again. Xan-Tu, to my amazement, bowed in the middle, the two upper globes of his being bending mightily, which I felt looked grotesque.

"We have been photographing you all we could since you arrived on earth, but we never saw you do that before," Connie began in her inimitable style.

"There are many things I do that are a bit more impressive that you have never seen. You may see a few of them tonight."

Connie did her famous blink and the audience laughed a bit, albeit nervously.

"This is a really special broadcast," Connie continued smoothly.

Then Xan-Tu cut her off. One of the things everyone noted later in the postmortems, after the show was over, was that when Xan-Tu 'talked' or rather broadcast his thoughts, it cut off the voices of others on the television. You couldn't upstage him.

"Yes. This will be a special broadcast," the visitor agreed simply.

"You have had some adventures here in Washington, which we as humans must apologize for," Connie began, alluding to the recent assassination attempt or perhaps the attack on his space ship by the warplane trying to guard the capital. "We as humans seem to be trying to show how barbarous we are."

"You are a young people, only a generation into space and only three hundred generations into civilization. There is so much happening for you so fast right now, you really do not understand it yourselves or grasp its significance."

"Are you a robot?" Connie asked. It was an excellent question and had simply not been asked point blank before.

"Yes and no. I am a creation. But then we all are. I am a mixture in a way. I am allowed certain latitudes in decision making. But again all of us must follow rules. I am not a purely mechanical creature with transistors and a computer brain. We have moved beyond computers, though the parallel is there." Xan-Tu paused. He had finished with that question.

It was just there at the pause in the questions that a messenger walked out onto the stage and handed Connie Jarson a note. The teleprompter had failed, but this had not concerned her. She had the questions she was about to ask in her head. She was not one to lose her cool.

She read the note in seconds and then smiled again, her trademark wrap around, wide-angle grin. "Some technical difficulties. We will break for commercials and be right back."

"Connie, I am so glad to be here," Xan-Tu spoke in everyone's head in the studio audience and out onto the airwaves. "And to show respect to your visitor, your show will be done without commercial interruption tonight, though there may be a few pauses."

Connie laughed self-consciously. "You know Xan-Tu, that we do have great respect for you. But in America television is supported by commercials and we have to have them. We will be right back."

But on the viewing screen facing the audience they did not fade. They remained on, just sitting there. "There appears to be some problem." Connie divulged, laughing. "Well, Xan-Tu, let's wing it."

There was a buzz of conversation nearby backstage and I asked what was happening. A shirt-sleeved, heavy-set man, generously perspiring, had just walked up to our group watching from behind the curtain at the side. He spoke to us in quick sentences. "I'm Nelson Rickdow, a vice-president of the network they tell me. We've got about thirty vice-presidents so it's not as impressive as it sounds. I'm supposed to make sure this is all running smoothly, tonight. Well, it's not. We've lost control. We've totally lost control."

"What do you mean?" I asked.

"First, the cameras can't swing around. They are frozen in position and locked on. We can zoom in and out, but we can't dolly or truck. We can't even change the camera angle. And we are unable to break for commercials. But that's nothing compared to the rest of what's happening." Rickdow sighed so deeply that I was afraid he would be heard on stage.

The television company vice-president continued after a moment: "This is going out on every network in America. It's greater coverage than a Presidential press conference. It's on HBO, Showtime, Disney, all the cable channels. You can't get any other program on American television right now. The other networks are calling and complaining. It wasn't their idea to pirate this program. But their own programming is preempted and not going out. And we can't do commercials," he repeated, sorrowfully.

I shifted my attention back to the stage. "What will you tell us of your civilization and your people?" Connie Jarson was asking.

Xan-Tu considered. "Our numbering system is based on twelve, the duo-decimal system you call it. Mathematically, it is a superior system to ten. We see twelve stages in the development of intelligent life. Twelve stages of civilization. This is considered a universal truth, though there is some variation among the cultures of the universe in following this pattern. It fits the way of life of the Great Ones who live much longer lives than you. There are twelve stages of life also. You would say: Pre-natal, infancy, childhood, adolescence, young adult, maturity, and old age. But that is only seven stages. We talk of twelve. You all know that a young child is a different being than an adult. But suppose your stages of life were extended?"

Connie let that thought go. "Tell us about the twelve stages of the life of civilization." She caught on fast and knew how to zero in with questions.

"The first stage is that one which is just above animals and plants; it is tool development. Some of your apes and even your ants are near this stage right now. Many of your animals build homes or nests and even use tools a little, but that is largely instinct. When it ceases to be instinct and becomes thought, individual action, which is passed on and altered then life has reached this first stage. Your histories show many humans reached the stage of tool development perhaps fifty thousand years ago or longer."

"The second stage is that of some control of the other life on the planet, domestication of useful animals and farming plants as you call it. Again, your records show that some humans reached that stage perhaps ten to fifteen thousand years ago."

Xan-Tu paused and my own private thought here was that the domestication of animals which began perhaps 25,000 years ago and agriculture which began 10,000 years ago or so were being combined. Perhaps on Xan-Tu's planet these stages had occurred simultaneously.

Anyway Xan-Tu went on: "The third stage is the development of a written language, or some way to transmit the knowledge gained and store it fairly permanently. That generally implies close association: government, schools, and the beginning of simple cities. Some humans moved into that stage six to seven thousand years ago. You call that stage civilization."

Xan-Tu paused. "Will you hear more?" he asked. Receiving an assent he continued: "The fourth stage is one of the development of power equipment. It is variously called. Usually it is built upon the mining of metals. Manufacturing you call it, or the Industrial Revolution. Invention now proceeds apace.

It should be said that creatures may backslide at any stage, decay, collapse, or not move further forward. Each stage has its dangers that may cause the life involved to drop back down the ladder they have so painfully ascended. But the progress can also feed upon itself and become exponential. You reached the fourth stage only a little over two centuries ago. The most important thing is for men to recognize at each stage where they are and what the problems are."

"The fifth stage is that which you call technology. Knowledge is stored in computers. Transportation and communication enormously improve over the whole planet. At last you have explored your whole world, its mountains, skies, and seas. Humans reached this stage only in the twentieth century. Your seas, poles, and oceans you have not totally explored even yet."

"And then?"

"The sixth stage you are now entering. It requires some population control and either the dominance by one people or the unity of all peoples. It is the transition age in which you are ready to move out to the worlds beyond your own planet. It involves intense exploration of your own sun system."

"The first six stages are measured on your home planet. The next six are measured by your journey outward. Those I can detail to you only in general terms. You are not ready for the future and your future may not even come. It depends upon the breath of your vision."

"Please tell us what you can," Connie Jarson requested.

"Very well. The seventh level, the first outward stage, involves setting up many permanent colonies on the moons and planets of your own sun system. You begin to see your home world as a center for the future, which it is. You begin to biologically change your natures and physiology to fit on new worlds and to travel in space. You develop ships to take you to far places at great speeds. You are in communication with alien civilizations and your development proceeds apace."

"The eighth level, the second outward stage, is the exploration of nearby star systems. You produce messengers who can travel and report back. You develop ships capable of traveling continually faster. The ninth stage is setting up colonies in many parts of your own galaxy. By this time you will be a very long-lived species and developing in several directions biologically. You find out how to bend time and space."

"The tenth stage is the exploration beyond your own galaxy and communication intergalactically. The eleventh stage is colonization in other galaxies and a feeling of the unity of the universe."

And the last stage, that of maturity?

"Ah, you have not forgotten. That I may not do more than touch upon here. It is the stage of the Great Ones and communication with the universal spirit. Yet, even here, there can be growth or decay."

"Very interesting. Won't you tell us more?"

"Mankind is very tough and very fragile. Your civilization is like mankind. Your potential is enormous and your problems are enormous."

Later some columnists said this was all too deep for Connie Jarson to grasp. In any case she changed the subject: "Do you have a numbering system based on twelve because the Great Ones have twelve appendages or twelve fingers?"

"Originally the Great Ones had pods, which could be used for suction, but each pod had small tentacles on the side reaching out for grasping, two on a side, eight in all, on each pod. It was a much more satisfactory system than your hands."

"Tell us about the Great Ones."

"They have at last achieved mastery because they understand the universe."

"Well," Connie observed, "please forgive me Xan-Tu, but we have counted your appendages and find you have twenty-four, two dozen, twice twelve. We have wondered if you were created in your master's image and therefore given many appendages."

At this point backstage Nelson Rickdow, the vice-president of the network, returned again to talk to me. "My God, Professor, this program is going out worldwide. Every television station in the world is carrying this, as far as we can determine. There are simultaneous translations into dozens of languages. The translations are instantaneous as if both Xan-Tu and Connie Jarson, in a simulated female voice, were speaking in each of their languages. The audio is also going out on every radio program that we can monitor so far. And all the stations are objecting to what we are doing, as if this is our fault. There are going to be enormous lawsuits here."

He paused and then continued: "Oh my God. Look! The robot is floating higher!" the network vice-president's voice rose to a squeal that almost went off the scale.

I had not noticed. The change must have been gradual. "You're right, he is not floating eight inches above the table anymore, as he started out, but maybe twenty inches up," I agreed. "It's not that much difference."

"It's a power play," exclaimed the television vice-president in real fright now. This change seemed to unnerve him more than the worldwide nature of the broadcast. "Don't you see? We always adjust the seats of the guests so they are six inches or so below Connie. If we are having a tall guest, we adjust the seat lower. That way she is the dominant figure, behind the desk. That's the nature of power and control. The appearance of control is enhanced on television by the camera angle, and we've lost control of that too. The cameras are locked in position, they tell me. Now Connie looks smaller than the robot. See the picture on that television monitor over there."

"Well, you're right, I suppose," I shrugged. In the world of illusion, the dominant figure was king.

Another man came running up, looking distraught. "We can't get through to the New York network center any more. The telephone lines are dead, both local and long distance. When you dial you only get one message: 'We are temporarily out of service. Listen to your local television for directions.'"

"I bet that is worldwide too," I suggested. "Xan-Tu wants to be heard."

"But it's all pretty tame so far, right, Dr. West?" the network vice-president suggested uncertainly, reaching for some hope.

"So far," I asserted. "The stages he outlined suggest a universal form all intelligent life may follow as it advances.   He must consider that important." We listened.

Connie Jarson was trying for a commercial break without success. She did not know her broadcast was receiving full coverage worldwide. The network vice-president had made an administrative decision not to send a note onstage and tell her. He felt there was no point to taking a chance of shaking her up while she was on camera.

The audio in her ear no longer functioned.

"Well, I guess we continue to experience what they call technical difficulties," Connie announced. "Are you responsible for this, Xan-Tu?" Connie asked. She thought she was joking.

"Yes. There once was an early television program in America that talked about taking away control of your television sets, temporarily. That is all I am doing. Actually, I should say to the people of your planet, if you are unable to turn your home television set off, that is my fault."

Connie appeared uncertain with this answer. "Well, ladies and gentlemen, I am talking to a visitor from space, Xan-Tu. How common are planets like earth in the universe?"

"Water worlds are rare. It is a matter of temperature. In America you have managed prosperity in spite of using silly old English measurements. The absurd Fahrenheit Scale for temperatures obscures from you what you might see easier with the Celsius Scale, that temperatures are enormously varied in the universe. Still perhaps you can see, even using your Fahrenheit scale that temperatures may go to millions of degrees above zero and hundreds of degrees below freezing. Liquid water exists only between 32 degrees and 212 Fahrenheit. Below that, if any water exists on a planet, it becomes ice, and above that it becomes steam. It requires a very stable temperature and very precisely balanced climate for water worlds to exist."

"So temperatures affect life?"

"Just as your microbes increase on your bodies within certain temperature frames, so humans themselves presently operate best within very narrow temperature limits. You have developed to meet the requirements of this planet."

"Xan-Tu, if you were doing this interview, what questions would you ask?"

"That is clever," Xan-Tu admitted, appreciatively, but not answering.

"Do you have inventions that you will share with us? I understand our government has given you our computers to use and you have taped into our knowledge. What will you share with us of your knowledge?"

"I used your computer to understand your people. My very presence here is a symbol of the great possibilities for mankind. Some questions I pose will have significance only in your future. There are many discoveries to be made in space; many answers and many questions."

"Try me." Connie leaned forward at her most enchanting.

"What is faster than light?"

"Tell me?"

"You have eyes to see light and ears to hear sound. Are there senses that no earthly life possesses that could give you a clue to the nature of the universe?"

"It's a challenge. And what do you think of mankind?"

"This is the place to tell you what you must do. Connie, there is a fear gripping mankind, today, to paraphrase the Communist Manifesto. Two generations have been born worldwide with the threat of nuclear destruction hanging over their head. While treaties have been made, they have merely regulated the edges of the problem. In over a half century, you have not made any real progress in controlling nuclear weapons. There is a theory among some of your military that nuclear weapons will prevent Great Wars. That is not true. The military, East and West, have a vested interest in maintaining themselves. The spread of nuclear weapons to more countries can cause nuclear war to become inevitable and any little war could turn into a Great War. At the present state of mankind, with your aggressive natures, little wars do relieve tensions and may be necessary, but the nuclear threat must be removed. You call nuclear war the unthinkable so you refuse to think about it."

"I'm afraid people don't even like to hear about this," Connie Jarson pleaded, shifting around in her seat. She looked profoundly uncomfortable. "Of all the unmentionables on the television, this heads the list, Xan-Tu," she continued, as if personally afraid. "You can sell tampons and prophylactics and talk about hemorrhoids, but nuclear war is the most unmentionable and unthinkable, Xan-Tu." Connie suddenly gave a violent shudder.

"The great nations of earth have wars, revolutions, or major riots every generation, Connie," the visitor persisted. "Do you realize what that means? People are programmed to have wars. They need them because humans are aggressive. Even the peace protestors, who are violently parading, are having a war for peace and relieving their own tensions. When there has been no war for a while there is enormous tension among the people of your great nations. You are on the edge of catastrophe."

"What should we do?"

"There will be an immediate peace conference between the nuclear powers, thirty days from today, meeting at the United Nations. The purpose will be to scrap all nuclear weapons and delivery systems, not just some. Three delegates each from the United States, Russia, China, Great Britain, France, India, Israel, and Pakistan all the major nuclear powers, will meet and nuclear weapons will be phased out completely over the next six months with worldwide verification and inspection at each stage by non-nuclear powers: the Swiss, Swedes, and Japanese."

"It sounds simple."

"It is simple. You merely need prodding. For instance, one of the three delegates from the United States should be Joe Candlelight and one of the three from Russia should be Andrei Dakeroff."

"He's a leading dissident in Russia, now in prison," Connie Jarson exclaimed. She was knowledgeable.

"So I hear. If the announcement of the members of the delegation from each country I have named has not been made in ten days, I shall appoint the other members of the delegation also to represent those countries. This is going forward."

"That sounds like what we call an ultimatum."

"It is. And to stabilize things, sixty days from today there will be free elections held in each country in the world. Anyone wishing to run for any office may do so. Ninety days from today the two leading contenders for each office in each country will be in a run off election. If in fifty days, at least two candidates are not running for each major office in each country with a population over one million, I shall appoint my own list of opposition candidates. It is time for the best men in each country to run for office. In the United States, for instance, this often is not true. Democracy should be more than merely a choice between two unfit men. This election should serve to stabilize things on earth a bit. The candidates will have large blocs of television time at their disposal, whether anyone wants to listen or not."

"We had an American Presidential election last November," Connie protested.

"Yes, but to treat everyone fairly, you will have another."

"Can you force us to be free, Xan-Tu?"

"Freedom comes from within as well as without. However, I can see that these elections are held."

"There is something grotesque about trying to force us to be democratic."

"Perhaps. But I have formed a judgment that this is best for mankind at this stage and have acted upon it. I have formed many other judgments, but I have refrained from action at least so far."

"And after you leave, then what?"

"I shall stay awhile."

There was a sort of deep gasp by the studio audience at this statement. Then Xan-Tu went right on. "You also need world unity. There has been too much splintering nationalism: there are too many little nations on your planet right now. But the first step to free association before you can have true world unity, I believe, is to let every group on your planet do their own thing for a while until they see that larger political blocks are more prosperous. Then the smaller groups can form together in some worldwide association. This worldwide organization needs real power so there is more than the bickering of your United Nations. World organizations need to have delegates and votes in terms of population."

"To make sure there is freedom of choice," Xan-Tu continued, "three months from this date there will be further elections in each state in the United States and Puerto Rico for instance, in each state in Russia, in each of the divisions of Europe, Catalonia for example, in each state in South Africa, also in Tibet, Mongolia, Northern Ireland, Hong Kong, South Vietnam and anyplace that wishes to break away from a government and establish their own. The purpose of these elections will be a vote on whether each section will remain a part of that nation. I will not urge this; however, if other groups I have not named obtain signatures and addresses of ten per cent of the population of a contiguous area, they may have such an election also."

"Well at least you are trying to give us democracy."

"There are long democratic traditions in many parts of your world. Democracy is inefficient, but the elites and the ignorant even out in a broad enough vote. The decisions are often right. In the end though there must be a unity to your diversity."

"Well, since you are organizing our planet, what else do you think we should do?"

"The so-called great powers should compete not in military matters but in the good life they offer their people and in the exploration of space. Russian and Chinese communism are a sham. They are mixed economies with one man political rule."

"America calls itself a free enterprise society, yet your national, state and local governments have grown from eight per cent of the workers to thirty-two per cent. That is also socialism. That has produced inefficiency and yet prevented another economic depression because the government employees are paid regardless of business cycles. Your graduated income tax is an obvious sham and everyone knows it. It was designed to tax the rich and now it taxes the middle class, while the rich escape. The wealthy are now so powerful your Congress can not tax them. The wealthiest one per cent of your people has more money than the bottom ninety percent. That is out of joint. Every man who wishes a job should be guaranteed one and you have it in your power to see that this happens. There should be jobs instead of welfare. It should be one man, one job. That is the most conspicuous failure of your American system, but your politicians will not address this."

When Xan-Tu paused Connie Jarson asked almost as a relief: "Xan-Tu, you say you are a mere messenger. Have you been to other worlds on this particular journey you are taking now? That is, do you have a route?"

"Oh yes. And that is another very perceptive question."

"And will you visit more planets before you go home?"

"Yes."

"Have you ever failed, I won't say with your meddling," she laughed.

"Yes. Some creatures have destroyed themselves."

"Wow! You make it sound as if we humans ought to behave. Sorry to pry, but if you get into trouble, not here but elsewhere, is there a backup you call on, a support system?"

"You have a story in your old wild west in America, Connie, of a riot in a town and a U.S. Marshall is sent there. They ask him why only one Marshall was sent. He replies: 'There was only one riot.'"

I stood transfixed, in the wings, listening. Xan-Tu's words had a deep effect upon me. I had a sudden vision of a future where there were no poor, where men lived long and fulfilled lives. I had been born too soon, into a short lived society. The future beckoned. Men in the next generations would share, not immortality, but enormously long lives and look back on this period as incredibly primitive, as we looked back on the pyramids.

"How do you feel about women's lib?" Connie Jarson asked. It was an attempt for a change of pace.

"Worldwide or in America?" Xan-Tu asked.

Connie paused, in the grip of a new thought. "Sure universalize it, Xan-Tu."

"One could spend an evening on this, as with so many topics, Connie. There are many differing perspectives. Women should surely be equal with men. This issue should not take humans' attention away from life and death matters for your planet such as solving the nuclear problem."

"Xan-Tu, we think of you as a 'HE' because your voice is masculine," Connie suggested.

"I could see that would happen, Connie. I did have to make a choice. But your early television broadcasts I listened to did give me more masculine role models to choose from."

There was a needed pause and then Xan-Tu continued: "A hundred smaller causes, many of them justified, still take attention from the issues of life and death on your planet. Women's lib. Is one such cause. Women are different from men. There is nothing wrong with roles for each sex. Trying to escape your nature can be frustrating. On earth in the West, women's lib has often been led by those who have inherited wealth or are living on their husband's income. But in thinking of women's lib, remember that the average woman on earth is that person who carries the water back from the well on her head. She needs also to be considered."

"That said it is obvious that people have been formed by evolution. On the average men are taller, stronger, and run faster than women. The women who escaped the men trying to grab them in primitive tribes did not have children. That is your heritage. America believes in democracy yet did not allow women to vote until more than a century after your Constitution was adopted. But discussing this is not why I came on this program."

It was later in the week that Playboy featured Xan-Tu as a female in its centerfold, a totally imaginary artistic creation with enormous silver breasts.

Connie Jarson touched on the problems she was having in taking a break via commercials.

Xan-Tu spoke again: "This broadcast was meant to be a ninety minute show; however, it will end after only thirty minutes. For those who may have missed it, the program will be repeated worldwide on every channel every six hours for one entire week so that it reaches all time zones on occasions convenient for viewing. Thank you citizens of earth. Ready, Professor West?" And we both left.

∪

"One trouble is that you humans are in a great universal world, on the threshold of space, and yet your thinking is still primitive and tribal. People just don't care much about each other." - Xan-Tu.

The next day the New York stock market fell four hundred points and the other world markets were all off. The decline continued all week. It was dubbed the "Alien Crash."

Washington papers headlined: "Demands Upon Mankind" and "Xan-Tu Blasts Everyone." A New York newspaper headlined: "The Human Race Gets Its Orders." And under that the caption was the question: "What if we refuse?"

There was a savage cartoon in a California newspaper which was widely copied. It showed a robot, obviously Xan-Tu, saying in successive captions:

"I travel through space."

"I don't eat."

"I don't drink."

"I don't make love."

"I get my kicks out of interfering in other planets' business."

Psychiatrists wrote articles about the father image of Xan-Tu.

And sure enough the broadcast on the entire world's television stations in dozens of languages repeated in six hours and again in six more. It was going to continue all week as Xan-Tu said. Even television stations that turned themselves off, broadcast anyway.

The whole planet went into shock. Governments were crying in pain. Some countries accused Xan-Tu of being an American creation so the United States could take over the world. Totalitarian states were declaring that they would hold no elections on demand. People were talking more than they ever had about "rights" and "constitutions." Xan-Tu was being asked countless questions.

Mail for the alien came up in an eighteen wheel truck with letter bombs in every delivery. I suggested the mail be sorted elsewhere and only the one per cent of most interest brought to Duncan House for consideration. The President gave the order for that. A group of thirty postal clerks, with careful instructions on defusing bombs and deciding what was of most interest to the visitor, began sorting through the mail.

People with a complaint, a cause, a grievance, an invention, and beggars for a thousand causes, those with any hope of gain, all those in pain, the insane, the inane, repeated the refrain: "Help me." It was largely in vain.

General Tanner phoned to talk to me. He was very angry. "Xan-Tu wants us to jettison all our nuclear weapons. And then what does his Confederation do? They take over our planet. If anything could unite the Russians and Americans, it is a demand for universal disarmament."

"It appears to me that Xan-Tu could take over the planet by himself with his force screens," I told the General.

General Tanner growled on the phone. It was pure guttural. I thought for a minute, he was choking.

At last the General became coherent again: "If we could obtain a force shield from Xan-Tu, it would be all we needed," Tanner argued. "We could shield the entire country and no one could get through with a nuclear weapon."

"Would it mean the end of armies, General?"

"Yes, force shields could mean the end of armies." There was a long pause as the General thought of what he had just said. "Force shields could also mean that one country could blast its enemies with impunity until they surrendered."

I had a sudden vision of the Aztecs looking at Cortez' army and thinking: "We've simply got to find a way to get some muskets and horses."

"Could you try to find out how the force screens work, Jerry?" the General asked after a bit.

"I can ask, General Tanner, but I don't expect to be given any formulas."

"If we had something like that we could give up everything else and sit behind our screens. It would be purely defensive, of course."

"Of course," I repeated, trying not to sound as if I was mocking. "But would we then do what we'd really like to do in this country, just return to isolationism?" I asked. "For centuries we did our own thing, sitting safe between our two vast oceans. Guided missiles forced us to deal with the whole world for the first time."

I had a sudden picture of a single man with weapons and a force shield, able to walk at will upon a battlefield and kill, completely invincible, destroying everything.

General Tanner grunted. "See what you can find out, Jerry," he repeated.

"Sure." And I did try questioning Xan-Tu once, without success. I approached the matter in what I thought of as a clever way. As usual we were in the library at Duncan House with Xan-Tu still operating the computer. I asked: "Couldn't you just give us your force screen technology and then nuclear missiles could not get inside a country. Then we would be safe from nuclear missiles."

"It would not work, Jerry," Xan-Tu responded. "Huge force screens could affect planetary air flow. And besides, there would be nothing to prevent an enemy assembling nuclear weapons inside a country."

* * *

Xan-Tu was back at the computer and I was sure he was connected up to any data bank in the world he wanted, university, governmental, military. That afternoon I felt cooped up in Duncan House. Out on the front porch, I calculated the odds of giving the press the slip and taking a walk. One reporter called out: "It's the Professor."

And then another newsman asked: "What do you think of the new robotic look, Professor?"

I had seen pictures of the four silver circles that made up the puffy dress, described as "new for winter," that caused all the women who wore it to appear fat.

"I think one of the many fashion designers who hate women has been busy again," I declared.

They could always get a good quote from me. "I take it that indicates disapproval?" the reporter called again.

"You're not sure?" I asked and went back in.

Then I took a walk the hard way and it turned out to be the very hard way, indeed. I ordered a limo to be brought around. Naturally my limo was followed by newsmen and it turned out other people also followed. I got off downtown with the request that I be picked up at the same corner in one hour.

Then I walked rapidly through several department stores, in one door and out another, until I felt no one was following me any longer. It was good just to be out alone and walking about. It was suddenly obvious to me how the famous could enjoy the notoriety of the media and yet at the same time wish to escape and just not be bothered on occasions.

And then when I was sure I had shaken off the press, the disaster occurred. Rounding a near deserted corner, I saw a man in a dark coat coming my way. It was too warm a day for a trench coat. There was something in his face, menacing even at a distance. I turned back, but too late. Another man came around the corner behind me, following me, and I knew at once they were together. I looked across the street and there was a third man waiting on the other side, watching me. A black car came up slowly, the door already opening to snare me. Then there was a gun, the barrel looking as large as a tunnel. My heart began to pound and I was sweating all over.

"I've done nothing wrong," I pleaded.

"Come with us Professor, or you're a dead man." In the car, I was in the middle between two swarthy men, with the vehicle picking up speed.

I had committed one of the sins of modern society, not being alert while walking. My anxiety to get away from the crowds had led to this.

"Who are you?" I demanded. "I have no power or influence."

"Be quiet Professor Jerry West. We know you. You are our hostage." I had the feeling I was a dead man and tried to psych myself up to meet whatever came and to be brave. I had lived a long, full life. The last few days had given me more than fifteen minutes of fame and I had done nothing to earn the acclaim I had been receiving. What difference really did anything matter?

The car crossed the Potomac to the Virginia side of the river and came off the main highway, turning at last into a subdivision at the end of a street where there was a small house set apart.

"Inside," the man directed. "Go upstairs and sit down." I followed orders. Inside a small room, my hands were duct taped together tightly and I was told to sit on a plain wooden chair.

Another man had entered the sparsely furnished room. The voice behind me sounded harsh and cruel: "Tell us all you know about that robot."

"I know nothing more than I told the press."

"You answer questions only when we talk to you. Perhaps you want to feel some pain?"

I told my whole story again in detail, even stretching it out, because I was afraid what might come when I ceased talking.

"Can you get through the force shield and into that space ship?" I was asked.

"No."

"We will try that later tonight. The robot likes you. Will he pay off on your life by telling us how his ship flies?"

"I doubt it." I managed a glance at my watch. The government car would be coming back to pick me up soon. "Who are you working for," I asked.

"We are the Islamic Revolutionary Underground Justice. Don't turn around." The man laughed. "Yes, we are right here in Washington D.C. We are in the belly of the Great Satan now. Why did the robot not mention the Arabs when he spoke of elections? Is this another Jewish plot?"

"I have no control over what the robot says. I am sure if you followed the directions for free elections suggested, then your group too could have a vote."

He snorted. "Free elections. We are Freedom Fighters for a holy cause." I reflected for an instant that one man's freedom fighter is another man's terrorist.

Now I felt the gun poked in my ribs. The weapon came higher and pressed right into my face. I watched the finger squeeze on the trigger with dry-mouthed fascination. There was an audible empty click that filled the whole room and the man laughed again. "Do you like Russian roulette? It is the best game the Russians gave the world."

It is one thing to practice meditation, self-hypnosis, and right thinking on how unimportant life is, how little the whole world and everything in it actually matters. It is a very different entirely to see a gun that seemed the size of an oil pipeline pointed at your eye and hear an empty click that means only that more horror will follow. One immediately begins to think how to please your captors and what you really can do for them. The change of perspective is almost instantaneous.

I will not make too much of my situation. My captivity in that house had lasted for some ten minutes at that point and there are others who have suffered days, months, and years with mad jailers trying to work their will upon them in some fiendish way. But I think my point is an important one. To think that one may be tortured or die is to immediately begin to sympathize with your captors, to try to help them find solutions to their problems so you may escape.

And then my captivity ended as abruptly as it had begun. The evil looking man was raising his gun again to point it at me, when he cursed and pushed at the air. I could not understand at first what his problem was. I remember hoping that he did not become too irritated at whatever the difficulty was and shoot me right there. Then my jailor turned his back on me and began to claw the air in all directions. I twisted to look about and the other three terrorists were similarly confined, trapped by force screens in very tight spaces. The force screens were closing in on them very slowly until they could not move at all. Then Xan-Tu was there, hovering near me.

"We will wait here for the police, Jerry," the alien divulged. It was perhaps ten minutes before we heard the sirens, blaring so loudly that if the terrorists had not been held tightly by force screens they would have had plenty of time to flee.

The three men who had kidnapped me and the two others who were driving the automobile were stolid, accepting their fate, glaring their defiance. They were soldiers for a cause, unafraid. The leader who had threatened me with a gun was a different story. He tried shooting away the force screen and managed to hit himself in the shoulder, which caused him to give a great outcry. He was screaming now: "You can't do this to me. I have diplomatic immunity. You shot me."

The police released me. Xan-Tu and I went back to Duncan House in a limo.

"How did you find me Xan-Tu?" I asked.

"You were easy to trace. There are extraterrestrial senses that humans do not have. Some are as handy as your sight, Dr. West."

"Tell me, Xan-Tu. I have never pried before."

"That is true. I have a really sympathetic feeling for you. How to describe a new sense to a person who does not have it? It would be as hard as describing a color off the visible band that one could not see. I tagged you, as I do all people whom I have met. That allows me to know where they are at all times, to listen in to them if I wish, and to know them better."

Tagged in the way a captured animal was, I surmised. Tagged with a tracer and then released. It was some way of knowing, as all senses are.

"You certainly arrived promptly, Xan-Tu. When the limo failed to pick me up, I suppose there was concern."

"The limo?" It was almost as if Xan-Tu laughed. "Your limo has not yet called in that you are missing. I just knew. I waited a few minutes to see the terrorist group assemble and listen to what they wanted."

*　　*　　*

When we returned to Duncan House, the press already had the story of my kidnapping and rescue. My wife, Helen, began a persistent effort to persuade me to return to Arizona. I refused insisting that I wanted to see this adventure with Xan-Tu through to the end, regardless. It was not until much later that I came to know what 'regardless' would mean to me and mine.

About that time a delegation of religious leaders representing several denominations phoned for an appointment and had a conference with Xan-Tu. I was an observer.

Their main initial question seemed to be: "Are you a hoax?" Did they think they could get an answer that was true from a hoax?

I had come to accept Xan-Tu as real. Everyone on earth had to come to terms with that idea. These churchmen wished to reject Xan-Tu as not real.

Xan-Tu said prosaic things such as "beliefs give us certainty."

"What is this communication with the universal spirit you describe as the last stage of life?" one squat, red-faced Bishop finally asked: "Is that God? Are you the messenger of God from Outer Space?"

"If you like?" Xan-Tu seemed to sigh. "Gentlemen, you, as with all others, will have to take these mysteries one stage at a time, and not try to discover the last stages first. Above all I am not here to destroy your faith. In the past your people believed Heaven was skyward. Perhaps it still is."

But this Bishop was a bit of a philosopher. "Xan-Tu," he continued, "there are on earth many grains of sand, many kinds of rocks, many trees, many of each animal, and many people. There are in space many planets and many suns. God alone is singular and One. He is a supreme being that necessarily exists. He is the creator and yet perhaps not of our world and solar system alone. There is in the whole universe only one God. I wonder if you are His messenger. I wonder if in your travels you have encountered Him? Have you ever met God?"

"I encountered many things in my travels, even more than you might imagine. And you humans as a people must be allowed to discover truths in your own good time. About half of what your scientists believe about the universe beyond your earth is true."

"But which half is that?"

"Ah that is for you to find out."

A tall Bishop with a sharp nose began with a little flattery:

"We have read all your words and find no profanity."

"Profanity has never done much for me," Xan-Tu observed. "Perhaps it is because I never become angry."

Now this Bishop spoke with deference but came back to one of the original questions: "Are you a messenger from God?" he inquired.

"No. Nor am I here to attack the underpinnings of your faith. Faith is important to many men to see them through this life."

"Have you met God in your travels?"

"I have seen many things. Does the thought that your God might have created other life trouble you?"

"Are you here to destroy the human race?"

"There is no end to arguing theology I am sure. But no, Bishop, I am not here to destroy the human race. Many of your own human civilizations have risen and fallen. So take good care of yourselves in these modern times. Your God may not always save you, if you do not work to save yourselves."

"Well, if you will not answer that question, then talk to us about the stage of existence we are in now," another Bishop suggested.

"Let me relate to you a parable," Xan-Tu began.

All the holy men squirmed uncomfortably at these words. Xan-Tu went on: "I have read that one of your Greek philosophers taught his students that the world was supported on the back of an enormous elephant that held it up. One of the students asked: 'But what holds up the elephant?' The philosopher replied: 'The elephant is standing on the back of an enormous turtle.' Everyone nodded except the one student questioner who persisted: 'But what holds up the turtle?' The philosopher was angered. The student had questioned too much."

Xan-Tu paused and then continued: "Some of your religions explain the world as created by God. Some students ask where this God came from? And you reply: 'He always was and always will be.' A few persistent students want you to explain how this can be. But that is questioning too much."

"Some of your scientists declare the world and the present universe was formed billions of years ago in a great cosmic bang that threw the present planets and suns out into their orbits. No one is to ask your scientists what came before the Big Bang. That is questioning too much. There are, however, eternal truths. You live between two infinities of time and space. What lies before the beginning and what comes after the end? Your Einstein tried to develop a mathematical model to explain it all, but he stood on one planet with insufficient data."

"Go on," one of the Bishops was wise enough to say.

"If the religious fear science, then truth may be denied to them. You need a religion of discovery; perhaps you need a religion of outer space."

As a silent observer, I couldn't help but think that Xan-Tu always kept his ideas simple, perhaps as God did, when He spoke to man so long ago. Here were simple ideas for the unsophisticated tribesmen of ancient times and simple ideas even for the semi-cultured city dwellers of our era. Xan-Tu had read and digested unabridged dictionaries. But using obscure terminology to impress was not his way. He seldom used any vocabulary except what he called television English. The great ideas, aside from those of mathematics and physics, could all be kept simple. In my youth I devised some college lectures, replete with obscure terminology, so as to be really beyond easy understanding. The lectures sounded grand, but they were devoid of real meaning. Later I abandoned all such devices.

Xan-Tu did not talk down to people.

Slowly I tuned back in to the conversation as Xan-Tu was asking: "But why have you religious men not led a holy crusade of all religions for worldwide nuclear disarmament? Yes, you have done some things, but you have not really united with all religions to prevent the end of the human race. Your world is insane to persist on its present course. I am not saying that you should have pressed for nuclear disarmament only by America. It must be worldwide." The Bishops had no good answer.

As the long discussion continued I remembered Joe Candlelight's words and had a vision of a group of Aztec holy men interviewing Cortez and his Jesuit priests after the Spanish invaded Mexico. Only the Spanish began pressing for conversion to their religion. Would Xan-Tu press us for conversion to Confederation beliefs? I was glad when that interview ended; the whole concept bothered me. Especially troubling was Xan-Tu's labeling of our present world culture as insane.

The press was not allowed in to the conference with the Bishops, but the newspapers got their stories from the holy men later or made them up as usual. One editorial screamed: "God had only Ten Commandments and this alien has twelve steps to salvation."

*   *   *

The following morning I awoke suddenly from a dream, seeing a great truth, the real answer to the enormous questions regarding the universe. It was an understanding that opened vast doors. Then the sunlight streamed in the windows and the huge doors began to close in my head. I tried to hold it, but the truth was there no more. It was a mere bubble, a fanciful creation that burst and left me with nothing. Where does the fire go, when it goes out? The greatest stories ever told are unfolded to us in our dreams and forgotten as we wake.

When I arose and talked to people around Duncan House, I suddenly discovered I possessed a personal force screen which Xan-Tu had provided for me. It was a gift, without my asking, an invisible barrier, about three feet out, as was Xan-Tu's own shield. No one could penetrate it without my permission.

The shield was apparently controlled my me mentally, for if I allowed someone to shake hands with me or when I wished to hold my wife Helen at night, there was no problem. Otherwise people who got too close to me were repelled. My force screen was not as powerful as the robot's screen and it did not shock others if they touched it, but Xan-Tu was obviously trying to protect me from people who might hate me because I was helping him. The alien did not want me kidnapped again and perhaps killed before he could reach me this time. I did not ask what would happen when he left and of course as it turned out that was unnecessary. As I certainly saw rather intimately a bit later, even Xan-Tu could not predict all human actions and anticipate everything destructive that might happen.

I tried to play down my force screen, but the news gradually filtered out. Haskins, the butler at Duncan House was probably making his own secret reports on what was going on. Soon General Tanner insisted I come down to a great hidden military lab deep under Washington D.C. where there were miles of reinforced tunnels and places many people could wait out a nuclear attack.

When this lab had been constructed and how it had been kept so secret from our prying press, I can not imagine. Anyway the laboratory was only one part of the complex, but seemed to have all the latest human medical technology. Medical people in their uniforms of sterile white coats prodded me, trying to break through my force shield. They even used electrical currents, to no avail. Later I got to thinking that perhaps they were trying to find a way to get through to Xan-Tu. General Tanner was amazed that I could shake hands with him or reach for things at will, but if something unexpected attacked my force barrier, such objects could not penetrate. I had no trouble sitting down or passing narrowly through doors. My force shield was different in several ways from Xan-Tu's.

I rather liked the bluff, gruff, patriotic General. There are those who hate all things military, but to me General John Tanner was a man who had given over his life to his country, to its protection and security. Perhaps all his kind was now outdated and mere relics. I am sure Tanner would not mind becoming an anachronism if it would serve his country. It seemed to me that Tanner would have gladly given his life, if his country could be forever secure.

"This is a force screen without teeth," General Tanner asserted at last. "You told us there was a force shield over part of Duncan House, which Haskins the butler there could touch without being shocked. This screen too, I can not penetrate, but it does not produce an electric shock when I touch it. Xan-Tu is wearing a force shield, which if you try to penetrate it, you get a nasty electric shock. His ship is even better protected. His ship repels by slamming you back at two or three times the energy you use to try to get in."

I shrugged. "So I'm not as well protected. It is enough,"

"It's better for our test purposes to try to understand these shields. But damn it, man, how do you do it? What do you think about when I put this cane out and you let it penetrate the shield and touch you and then you don't?"

"I'm sorry General. You told me to try to let you through and then stop you from touching me. And I have done just that by merely thinking of it. And I don't know why it works. I'm not wearing anything. There is no technology that I know of." I felt Xan-Tu was monitoring all this in some way and perhaps laughing at us. Could he laugh? I had never seen him do so.

"I can't believe in witchcraft or magic," the General grumbled. "Would you mind taking off your clothes?"

They checked my clothes, but I could perform the feat naked. Indeed, they all regarded it as a feat, a trick, and it was the easiest thing I had ever done. The medics examined my body all over and found nothing. They even x-rayed me and ran me through a full body scan, an MRI. Nothing was found.

*   *   *

Several times when I walked into Xan-Tu's room in the next days, he simply was not there. I did not ask him where he had been when he returned. He was out visiting throughout the world, of that I am sure, but he did not take his spaceship as he did on formal visits just a bit later. Since there were no reports of sighting him, and the press had gone crazy on the subject of the alien, I wondered if he might have been invisibly hovering about, observing.

The power of Xan-Tu's force screen was amply demonstrated by the alien's much publicized second visit to the White House. Xan-Tu went alone that time and as it turned out I was glad not to share in the experience. Our non-human guest left Duncan House in a stretch limo and as he traveled down Pennsylvania Avenue there was an enormous explosion. The whole street had been mined down in the sewer pipes and the blast was set off as the limo passed over. The driver and two Secret Service men in the limo were killed and a number of people on the street were severely injured. Buildings for several hundred yards along the avenue lost their windows. The limo was blown to shreds, but Xan-Tu floated up out of the blast unharmed.

*　*　*

The day after this blast Xan-Tu flew to Moscow in his space ship, leaving me behind in Duncan House. The flight took only a few minutes and the alien landed in Red Square. There were many television pictures of the great military parade in honor of the visitor, the longest, largest, and most impressive display of might the Russians had ever staged. The troops and weapons went by for hours and some commentators televising the event for American audiences joked that perhaps the same military groups were coming around to be counted again, sort of reruns. The speeches and welcome were laced with statements declaring that no explosions and attempts to assassinate him would greet Xan-Tu's visit to Russia.

There were many scare headlines in the United States speculating as to what sort of deal the alien might be making with the Russians and criticism of the American government because it had not made a deal. What sort of deal our government should have concluded with Xan-Tu was left vague.

Xan-Tu stayed in Moscow for five days and then flew to Peking, landing in the great square of the Forbidden City. After three days in

China he flew to Trafalgar Square in London for three days, landing amid the pigeons. Then the visitor was off to the Champs de Mars in Paris where his space ship was parked in the shadow of the Eiffel Tower for two days. There were a lot of reporters who felt the relative numbers of days spent in each country were significant. In all the countries there were official conferences and receptions.

In France there were a great many parades and then a televised confrontation with French government officials followed that made world headlines.

"We will not be bound by treaties forced upon us," the French Premier declared.

"If you sign the treaty, you will be honor bound to follow it, and you will sign it," Xan-Tu replied. "The French word is good."

"We are an independent, free nation. You have come to our land as a visitor, not to give orders. This is our country."

And watching this back in Washington I remembered a biting country type song in the United States where the refrain ran:

This land is our land.

It ain't your land.

And if you don't get off,

We'll blow your head off.

But Xan-Tu answered the French: "Yes, and it is your world too. You French sell nuclear reactors to all who will buy without many controls on the sales. That goes beyond boundaries."

"We do not sell missiles," was the reply.

"Yes, but a terrorist nuclear devise brought into France in a van could take out your city of Paris. How would you feel about that?"

The argument went on; Xan-Tu had come up against national pride.

A French television interviewer sought to gain information ala the Connie Jarson's show, and his program was covered widely world-wide with translations. The interviewer was a man with long hair that stood straight out in all directions; he made a rather spectacular appearance himself. The most ordinary question in the interview brought a curious answer from Xan-Tu.

"Do you find your work interesting as you travel around the universe?" the interviewer asked.

"Yes. I have a built in pleasure instinct. There is of course a habit to happiness. Beyond that, for stability during long-term travel, it is essential to maintain pleasure and happiness. Many lucky humans have such built in mechanisms. It is vital to progress as humans should guess."

"Suppose we just do not attend your forced disarmament conference?" the interviewer asked.

"Then the decisions for the nuclear powers will be made without France," Xan-Tu replied.

"Ah, but we are a member of the security council of the United Nations with veto power," the interviewer put in.

"This is not the United Nations," Xan-Tu declared. "It is time that France got over its belief that it is a great nation as in the days of Louis XIV or Napoleon. You were given the Security Council position by the United States, even though France was crushed in World War Two."

The French interviewer gasped at the audacity of the alien. A truth had been uttered that others were afraid to voice.

Xan-Tu was naturally invited everywhere, to small countries as well as large, but it was my feeling that unofficially he had already been all about the world, visiting personally many countries. I was sure our guest from beyond had the power of local instantaneous travel anywhere on earth after I watched how he had sent financier Wesley Aimes back to New York City after he tired of talking to him.

In any case Xan-Tu returned to Washington again in two weeks, landing his space ship as before in the green near the Washington Monument. There was a great "Welcome back Xan-Tu Parade," a kind of spontaneous affair, after which the robot returned to Duncan House by government limousine.

A joke ran: "What did Xan-Tu say when he landed in Moscow?"

"When you've seen one human, you've seen them all."

*   *   *

I suppose I could have used the time I had with Xan-Tu to ask more questions, but I did not want to presume on what I saw as a friendship. Especially, I did not want to be a pest. We did talk privately on several occasions. Let me leave you with some of his insights.

Xan-Tu spoke to me once about concepts of real time. "Humans will shortly discover, to their fascination, the variations in real time, Jerry West. I, for instance, comprehend humans as blinking on and off with many a pause, even in your most rapid speech. What is time and what is reality?" I leave that statement of Xan-Tu's behind for what it is worth, though I did not understand it.

I was reminded of a story I read in my childhood by Mark Twain about a man who was drunk in a bar. He passed out and had a seventy-year dream between the time he fell asleep and his head hit the table. I reflected now on what Xan-Tu had said about the relativity of time.

At another point Xan-Tu amplified the matter by saying, "I had to slow down my own real time by a factor of almost four to synchronize with your time and make sense of your words and actions."

Later Xan-Tu gave me the clue I used to put together some surmises about the visitor's travels about the earth. "If I moved fast enough, Jerry, in my time frame, I could stay in the same place and yet you would not see me."

On still another occasion Xan-Tu declared to me: "You know, the greatest human invention or innovation occurred long ago and it has since become an adaptation."

"And that is?" I asked.

"Laughter. Without that you would have none of your comedy, none of your jokes. Though I must say that some of people's jokes, in many languages, are among the most difficult for an alien to comprehend."

"Or a resident," I replied.

And another time Xan-Tu spoke very kindly to me: "Professor, having looked at your planet and people, I still think your profession as historian is an exceedingly honorable one. But you must know that most of the people of your world have no sense of history. Many are too poor to think of such matters. And many simply do not understand or care. Of those who have a sense of history, the world would be better off if half of them would forget their knowledge of your world's past. Except for some scholars, many of those with some knowledge of history are often ready to use what they know to hate and destroy others. They are angry over battles lost and land lost in the past."

"I am sure that is true," I agreed. "The problem goes back to primitive tribes and desires to take over their neighbor's territory. There is the story of the old farmer whose needs were simple. He only wanted the land next to his own."

Another time I inquired: "Xan-Tu, if I am off base here, let me know, but something puzzles me."

"What is that, Jerry?"

"You have outlined stages that civilizations may pass through if they survive. But at the last stage, you have life expanding through whole galaxies. In such a case, do not the most advanced creatures come into conflict with each other?"

"There are several reasons why this does not happen. One is the simple vastness of the universe."

This was a period when Xan-Tu was still studying humanity, and waiting for the time of the disarmament conference he had called.

*　　*　　*

In a rather rare interview some reporters were allowed in to the great living room of Duncan House and one particular pushy newsman asked: "What if the delegates to the disarmament conference you have called can't agree?"

"Oh, they will agree," Xan-Tu assured him.

"Follow up. Follow up," the reporter demanded, loudly. "Suppose that the delegates do not have the authority from their governments to make decisions? Checking back with their governments could be long and frustrating."

"These delegates must be allowed to act and make decisions on the spot. They can telephone home. But if the heads of state do not trust the delegates which they send to make absolute, final decisions, then the heads of state should be the delegates."

That news conference produced some headlines and television commentary, a lot of it dealing with the visitor's pressure on mankind. Xan-Tu asked that the United Nations set aside two floors of conference rooms for the delegates. Individual bedrooms for the delegates were to be arranged just off the main conference room. Apparently the delegates were to be sequestered, as in a jury trial, and not allowed to leave until they had arrived at a decision. Actually, we did not know the half of it.

At last the day of the nuclear conference came. All the nuclear powers sent their requested three delegates each to the United Nations in New York City. There were a number of ceremonies that first day, a banquet, toasts, speeches, and of course every kind of protest imaginable outside on the streets in New York City. The whole world was literally holding its breath. At the conference, the delegates of several countries asked of Xan-Tu: "How do we know we can trust you if we scrap our nuclear weapons?"

And Xan-Tu replied: "Your nuclear weapons are as nothing to me. But if life is to continue on your small planet, you must end nuclear weapons."

The next day there was a breakfast in the great conference hall and Xan-Tu talked to the delegates. There were no press present, but a worldwide television hook-up had been established and the broadcast as before played on every television channel simultaneously in many languages, whether the stations wished to participate or not.

"My instructions to you delegates are simple," Xan-Tu explained. "Scrap all nuclear weapons and delivery systems within six months. Verify at each stage this is being done. Some nations have only a few weapons. For you it will be easier. I do not wish to spell out details, but rather have you delegates arrive at these details for yourselves."

"You have given us a broad outline to follow of no nuclear weapons and no delivery systems, all eliminated in six months with verification," one delegate complained. "So why do we need to meet at all?"

"There are many details. How will you verify disarmament and be sure? Which weapons systems will go first, second, third, and so on? What other conventional armaments should be scrapped to produce further safeguards with nuclear weapons gone?"

Before Xan-Tu was able to disclose his real shocker, what he truly had in mind for the delegates, an English representative, Sir John Hightower, adjusted his thick glasses, crossed his lanky legs, cleared his throat menacingly and demanded seriously: "If you take away nuclear weapons from the world, you leave Western Europe open to Russian attack by conventional armies. The Russians have superiority in regular weapons, more tanks, and larger armies. Is this all a Communist plot?" The Englishman was really speaking to the world audience beyond this room.

"It is not a plot at all," Xan-Tu replied.

But Hightower was determined to have a discussion. He had a classically ugly face and blinked his eyes constantly, which was distracting, but he voiced an important view: "You must know Xan-Tu that nuclear weapons have protected this planet from having a Third World War. Nuclear weapons have allowed limited wars in confined regions, Korea, Viet Nam, Afghanistan, Iraq, the former Yugoslavia, areas in Africa and the Far East. But these limited wars have sheltered the world from a major war. The small wars allowed the great powers to release their aggressions and tensions as you yourself suggested. Without the nuclear component, Western Europe will be wide open."

Hightower paused, looked the world camera in the eye, and continued, expressing his concern: "If nuclear weapons are eliminated and the Russians attack Western Europe, then if America and Britain respond to the Russian invasion, there will be a conventional World War Three with both sides scrambling to be the first to build new nuclear weapons from scratch."

The microphone in front of Hightower went dead and Xan-Tu answered: "You are covering too many questions, Sir John. Let me deal with the issues you raised so far. You are right that the small wars defused the military spirit. I would suggest some further studies of human aggression patterns and war cycles. Ending nuclear weapons does not have to end small, contained conflicts, if that is what is necessary to relieve worldwide tensions."

Now as the other delegates clamored to talk and their microphones all went dead, Xan-Tu continued: "Sir John, you can not have it both ways. If nuclear weapons prevent big wars and small ones relieve tension, it is still the case that nuclear weapons can be used by accident and mankind has been merely lucky so far. Second, terrorists can get control of your nuclear weapons. Third, the more countries that have these weapons the more dangerous the situation becomes, and nuclear knowledge is spreading. Fourth, the small wars can escalate to larger conflicts. Therefore, Sir John Hightower, your solution to preventing World War Three must not continue to be based on such a false hope as nuclear weapons. For those reasons we are not debating here, but setting a timetable to end these weapons."

"Why do you interfere in our life on earth?" still another delegate demanded angrily.

"Do you not see that the situation you are in is unstable?" Xan-Tu inquired. "Your world is not standing still. You keep making progress, including progress in armaments. Each change is technologically destabilizing. You have to find a solution to this problem."

Sir John Hightower now cleared his throat and began again: "Xan-Tu, this will just take a minute. Do not cut me off." He was letting the world know what was happening; that is that he had been cut off. "My question is: how do we humans know you won't invade our planet once our guard is down?"

"That is a phony issue, Sir. John. If I wished to destroy mankind or any particular species upon the earth, you would all be dead tomorrow. Perhaps we need an example to prove to you that I do not speak idly. Tomorrow watch for mosquitoes worldwide. But for now, enough of your diplomatic talk. You will begin to take action."

Another delegate asked pointedly: "And if we refuse?"

"You will stay in these rooms, with individual adjoining bedrooms, connected to the outside world and your governments by telephones only. You may phone all you please. The main proceedings will be broadcast on all the world's televisions, until you arrive at a conclusion. You may of course take as long as you wish. However, you may not leave this building until the treaty is completed. There is a force screen around these two floors. There is plenty of water in the water fountains here. But there is enough food on these floors for only three days. After that you may become hungry if you do not arrive at a treaty."

The delegates, long-talking diplomats who had hours of speeches prepared to deliver as filibusters, talks which were mostly protests against each other, went into shock.

"You can't do that," several protested.

"Ah, but I will do that," Xan-Tu countered.

And I, who was watching the show on the television back at Duncan House, could almost paint a mouth on the top globe of Xan-Tu and see him smile now.

"It's inhuman," someone yelled.

"Ah, but I am not human," Xan-Tu retorted. "Now I think it is time you began." Then quite suddenly, the visitor from outer space was no longer in the room.

Once long ago, some pacifist had proposed that all peace conferences be held by delegates who stood on one leg until they could arrive at a solution. Xan-Tu was not quite that cruel. I wondered if Joe Candlelight would lose weight as the talks proceeded.

I had a sudden insight, a flash of prescience as to what was happening here. It was as if we earthlings were being visited by the Enterprise and the crew of Star Trek who saw clearly what was obviously wrong.

Why would no one talk about this nuclear thing? When we were young we talked of weather and women, of baseball and beer, of schools and science. When we were older we talked of jobs and money, money and what it would buy. We were children, infants, struggling toward the light. And in one swoop Xan-Tu stepped in and saved us.

But if Xan-Tu had not come, then what would have happened? What warning would be necessary to create action?

The first day of the conference there were a lot of arguments about how to proceed, but whenever any delegate talked too long, there were protests. By the end of the first day, there was agreement that no one should talk over five minutes on any question. Xan-Tu was seeing to it that the conference was the only thing on television and the whole world was watching. People around the globe not only watched, but sent telegrams, demanding action. It was obvious the earth's people wanted to end nuclear weapons.

The next day it was discovered what Xan-Tu meant about mosquitoes. They had vanished. In some tropical places where mosquitoes once were very thick, some bodies were found. A whole species of pest had been destroyed as an example of the alien's powers. There were protests by some environmentalists that this would upset the balance of nature. Spiders and birds would be deprived of necessary food. But there were other bugs for spiders and birds to eat. I for one could not mourn the end of mosquitoes. Humans had tried dredging swamps, pouring oil on the top of waterways to reduce mosquitoes breeding places and cut down their the number. Now in a twinkling they were all gone.

A German newspaper cartoon that was widely copied showed a mosquito in a circle with a diagonal line through it. Waiting on tap for its extinction next was a man also circled. As the news of this event traveled around the planet it was apparent that Xan-Tu did not need to worry about our nuclear weapons if he wanted to destroy the human race. He was not planning an invasion.

Still Xan-Tu rumors floated everywhere. It was said that the alien was kidnapping human babies to take back with him to outer space, that he had started the AIDS epidemic to depopulate the earth before a large alien invasion arrived, that he was planning on taking all of our oil, gold, food, water, endangered animals, and so on.

The second afternoon of the disarmament conference the delegates made a great use of their telephones calling their home governments and the outline of an agreement began to appear. The third day the treaty was nearly completed. The impossible had been accomplished quickly. The conference ended the morning of the fourth day with a signing of the treaty.

Running out of food in three days does focus your perspective. These were diplomats who wanted to continue to eat. They were not going to join the starving millions. There was no hunger strike by these diplomats.

*   *   *

Already the governments of the earthly nations were concerning themselves with the coming worldwide elections. Humans kept showing they could be as barbarous as animals. I cringed at some of the news stories.

As one small example, several presidential candidates were killed in

Haiti. When Xan-Tu ordered the Haitian army to collect and lock up all weapons on the island, there were protests from that small country that their rights were being violated. The government of Haiti declared that aliens led by Xan-Tu would invade their island if they surrendered their weapons. Xan-Tu talked directly on Haitian television and told the people there: "If the major powers must comply with my requests to discard their nuclear weapons, why do you think you need to keep your rifles, pistols, and machine guns?"

Even after the Haitian army was forced to search and round up weapons, people who desired to run for office were hacked to death by machetes. There is always a way to kill. It looked like a stalemate.

Again Xan-Tu appeared on Haitian television. "Your land is the poorest country in the Americas. You cannot allow evil men to continue to kill any possible leadership. If this happens again an example will be made of this island, as follows: Every male over the age of ten will be rendered permanently sterile. You have a population problem anyway. The choice is yours. If that is what you want, continue the killings and test me."

If there was anything the macho types who were killing in Haiti did not want, it was sterility. Free elections were held and the remaining candidates were allowed to live.

In the meantime, Xan-Tu's threat against Haiti sent shock waves of horror around the world. Could he do this? Could he do as he suggested selectively on one island? A cartoon in a Miami paper, widely reproduced, showed a male with a world for its head, looking down, examining to see if his gonads were gone. Gone from the whole planet.

The possibility of sterility reminded me of how Xan-Tu had originally talked to me about watching our X-Rated movies on television as he flew toward our planet. I don't suppose we humans thought much about how we were letting the whole universe see our way of procreation. Things are pretty unplanned on our world.

The situation on Haiti was only one example of a thousand unfolding events worldwide. Everywhere there were efforts made by those in power to thwart the will of the people. In dozens of instances Xan-Tu appeared suddenly on local television, explaining the situation to the people in their own language. This happened so often that a few clever reporters, who followed the events with care, discovered that Xan-Tu was often in more than one place at the same time. In several countries there were government planned riots on election days. Every government on earth thought about the elections, and all took some actions to try to solve real or imagined problems. In the end many people voted for candidates already in power as a protest against Xan-Tu.

American President Hamilton was easily elected again in the United States as a kind of slap at Xan-Tu for forcing us to go through the process. The rivals were perfunctory and often said they would run again in three years when the next "real" election according to the American Constitution required it. In Britain, France, and Germany the same people were returned to office.

When it came time for the elections on creating new nations, the United States had a number of issues. Statehood was offered to Puerto Rico but the island refused this offer because then they would have to pay federal income taxes as did the people in other states. Some American Southern states talked of secession without a Civil War. A dozen little areas such as Michigan's Upper Peninsula and the Conch Republic of Key West demanded concessions or a vote on secession. These votes failed to produce succession from the United States. Some people in Guam wanted their own republic and the island was deemed too small to offer statehood. Guam finally stayed on in its present provincial status.

For many people around the world the elections appeared to be an opportunity for a small group to establish their own nations. South Africa gerrymandered its country in all directions. Israel lost some Arab lands it had once conquered. There was a successful vote to place Jerusalem under the United Nations. A section of Northern Ireland voted for independence. Quebec eventually stayed with Canada, but not without a vote.

Tibet, Mongolia, and Hong Kong all voted successfully to be independent states. Tamil and Punjab in India were only the beginning in that region; many new nations were going to divide up India. Separatist movements everywhere had their day. Andorra became a larger nation and Catalonia in Spain and France became independent of both countries.

I was not personally involved in very much of this and became aware that Xan-Tu was talking to dozens of advisors in lands around the world. I began to wonder why I was even being kept around.

A reporter wanted to interview me again and I accepted. He was a young man. I felt he was the kind of person who would stand at the coal mine entrance after the explosion and thrust a microphone in a young widow's face to ask how she felt right now. His main aim was apparently to extract an admission from me that Xan-Tu was mistreating mankind and forcing us to do things that destroyed our will.

"Not at all," I finally interrupted the young reporter's tirade. "Think of how badly Xan-Tu could have really treated mankind if he had been a conqueror, evil, or mad? We have been extremely fortunate."

"But we don't know if he will still do those things. And surely our liberty to choose, our freedoms, our rights, our sovereignty, still hang in the balance," the reporter persisted.

I cut him off again. "For most of the earth's people economic freedom is more important than liberty, which is why Communism was so often successful at snaring its victims. We must first have liberty to eat, freedom to work, the right to a good life, the sovereignty of no nuclear weapons."

I was seriously misquoted as saying that I thought Xan-Tu was a Communist.

And the interview did set me to wondering. As a Science-Fiction fan I thought of Star Trek and their directive against interference in the progress of backward civilizations. And I thought also of Isaac Asimov and his prime directive which robots were to follow that they could do human life no harm. I wondered if Xan-Tu was at all controlled by rules that he must obey. Did our situation cause him to interfere to save us? Then I decided Xan-Tu was probably right; I was not at all sure humanity had the wit to survive without outside help. Humans might well reinvent nuclear weapons after Xan-Tu left. Humanity might be one of his failures.

Somehow the common man felt that there were experts around the world who would not let nuclear disaster happen. Yet all the experts I met were scared.

Then the great disaster in my personal life occurred and even Xan-Tu was not able to prevent what happened.

UL

"I have stayed on earth a year and a day and made with all of you people one full rotation of your planet around its star. I have obtained the feel of your life in all its phases and seasons." Xan-Tu

For Xan-Tu I am sure a lot of the time was a waiting game, while mankind sorted itself out. "Time changes everything," Xan-Tu said once. But what can you ever do to alter events ahead?

The waiting period provided quite a series of exploring adventures for me.

Xan-Tu told me: "Man and his world have become one. Earth is your home. If you burn down your home, dirty it up, make it less livable, you will have no good base from which to explore the broad universe."

On several occasions during the waiting, I was privileged to join Xan-Tu in an exploration of mother earth. I *have not spoken of this before, but it was the most interesting thing that ever happened in my life.* With force shields on Xan-Tu and I traveled independently of the space ship, all about the planet. I was sometimes aware of others around us, but they were flying so fast on other time planes as to be almost spirits.

No doubt the alien had advisors from various countries, but this was a mere impression. I think Xan-Tu wanted to keep the illusion, when we traveled, that we were alone and he was talking only to me.

We flew over Antarctica and I felt nothing of the bitter cold outside as we explored. The force field around me kept the air a constant temperature. We flew high above the earth and looked down upon our small water planet, seventy per cent of the surface covered with liquid. We submerged ourselves in the Pacific Ocean depths and descended several miles in the deep to look at life growing without any sunlight it was so far beneath the surface. I had never snorkeled or tried scuba diving, so the undersea world was especially fascinating to me. The number of growing things, especially at great depths, was really incredible.

"Here are your last earthly frontiers," Xan-Tu declared, "Antarctica and the depths of the oceans. After that there is only what you call outer space."

Later a reporter, to whom I spoke of these adventures, asked me how much air the force screened area around me contained and wondered how I continued to be able to breathe under those conditions. I did not know the answer to that. I trusted Xan-Tu and had reached the point that I was ready to follow wherever he led.

I felt really lucky to have discovered Xan-Tu, to have been summoned by Jose Herrera to the desert. Somehow after events occur, they all seem inevitable.

There were new nations on earth now, new governments, and some countries even began to change their minds and asked to rejoin existing states to which they had belonged before. Then a remarkable thing happened. Other countries in the world, especially in South and Central America, began to ask if they could become states that were a part of the United States while retaining their own language. Instead we began working on a regional organization with close economic ties and one currency, akin to the European Union.

I remembered that some American presidents had believed that one day the United States might spread throughout much of the Americas. Now I began to see possibilities for the "idea of America" spreading in the world. It would not be manifest destiny, colonies, imperialism, but unity among equals. I suppose it would be a Confederation.

Xan-Tu made a speech to the world again. He spoke of trillions of dollars each year being spent on arms worldwide much by America, Russia, and China. If some of that money could be spent on progress of another kind, it would be wonderful.

*　　*　　*

During the year Helen and I spent at Duncan House, all of our children came to visit us in Washington D.C. at some point. They all came again together that Christmas. This was quite a reversal, since before Helen and I were dividing holidays among our children. I was sure it would be our last time all together, but I did not know how true that was to be.

Usually at Christmas my wife Helen and I visited one of our oldest two children, Don in California, who had four children, all boys, or Betty who lived mostly in Manhattan and had three girls, one by each of her now former lawyer husbands. Helen and I would visit Betty on the occasions she was between divorces and was stable. Susan, our youngest, who was in her fifth year of college, in a four year program, would usually come to whichever place Helen and I went that Christmas.

Traditionally in childhood Christmas is a time of great expectations, impossible desires, and so enormous disappointments. It is a joyous, hopeless time, so sacred.

Xan-Tu hovered over our Christmas, a silent presence, graciously thanking me for allowing him to intrude on our festivities. I explained my own joy, telling the alien I ought to thank him for bringing my whole family together.

Here I am putting the story on hold and taking a bit to discuss my family.

Our daughter Betty, finalizing her third divorce, actually arrived with her daughters at Thanksgiving and just stayed on for some months. Soon she met another lawyer in Washington.

Betty specialized in marrying lawyers. She spoke jokingly of disposable husbands. She would always be my daughter no matter what she did. I had given her away three times, and none of the givings had taken. Perhaps Duncan House offered her something secure in the wreckage of her life or maybe she discovered that Washington D.C. had more lawyers per capita than any other city.

I talked to Betty most, trying to untangle her life. She was such a pretty girl, slim and pale as my wife Helen once had been. I realized she was going to take more straightening out than I could manage.

"Do you think Xan-Tu has any solution for me?" Betty asked me when we were alone having lunch in the kitchen of Duncan House.

"Don't bother him, Betty," I requested.

"Oh, I just thought perhaps, being neither male nor female, he could look upon our world as no one else could. I have been to the counselors and the psychiatrists, and you know something Father, they are all either male or female."

I laughed, uneasily. "What are you looking for, Betty?" I asked.

"There must be some men out there who are in charge of their lives, in control of themselves, deciding calmly what they will do, not slaves to each passing breeze."

"You're not going to find a man who is a robot as Xan-Tu. You have to decide what you want and then stick to it," I told her. Then I took a deep breath and continued: "When you have three divorces, it may be because you are picking the same man each time, someone who ultimately you can't stand." My words sounded hollow even as I spoke. Why do we parents always feel we must give advice?

"I've known forever that there was something out there watching us, Father," Betty mused, on her own track, not listening to me.

"Something is looking at our silly, small lives, our absurd efforts to do something, our pompous, petty, and presumptuous posing, posturing, and pretending at being something. It has watched us forever and is laughing at us. We are the greatest show on earth as we fumble along."

"Be careful the paranoids don't get you," I suggested, laughing. "Man has always had the fear that something smarter than he was around in the universe. Even the pre-Christians, the Greeks and Romans, saw gods watching us and interfering in our lives."

Then I asked: "But what of you? Will you marry this new man you have met here in D.C. and have one more child by him?"

"We all marry to please the most important person in the world, ourselves," Betty declared. "As to children, there are people who at any given moment aren't born yet."

"You have a great mental attitude about it all," I told her in some surprise. "You're a happy person, and that's important. You might as well laugh at life rather than cry. In some ways it is all an enormous joke."

"I'm the philosopher's daughter," she replied simply, squeezing my hand. "Always remember, Father, it's better to be a young, rich, happy, healthy winner than an old, poor, miserable, sick loser."

I let that one go. "But when you marry these lawyers and have a child, how come you always get custody of the children?" I asked.

"My lawyer was always better than their lawyer." Betty chortled.

"Tell me about your life?" I was trying to lead her on.

Betty settled in on the stuffed kitchen chair opposite me and spoke confidentially: "I've had a separate life with each of the men I've known. They aren't all alike, Father, and I've known and lived with many more men than I have married. I hope that doesn't shock you. You should have seen some of the ones who got away. Do you want to hear more?"

I nodded in the best tradition of the psychiatrists and Betty went on: "All right, this is True Confessions time. We turn to others when we can no longer stand ourselves. It is better to talk to others than yourself."

"How did you feel when you broke up with them?"

"Often I've died a little when we broke up. There was always interwoven the mysterious special jokes and stories, the speech, food, and love. I'm spoiled, Father."

I laughed a little to show I understood and meant no harm. How do you warn a thrice married daughter?

Betty laughed too. "Sometimes you can't stand them even one night. I remember one worst case scenario. He had a coupon book for restaurants that offered one dinner free with each purchase. He used it for our first date. We looked through the book together and selected a restaurant. After dinner, he suggested we start our relationship right by going Dutch Treat that very night. He said that women were pressing for equality and equal pay for equal work, yet they wished to be treated when they were taken out to dinner. So I agreed to the Dutch Treat. Then, after dinner, he declared that since he had the coupon book for his meal, I should pay for mine!"

"That's not quite women's lib," I ventured, laughing with her.

"Some of my men have thought I spend too much. But I like shopping. Do you know, Father, that stores all over the world are having their greatest sales ever, today, this very day?"

"How come?" I asked becoming the willing straight man.

"Well, they always are."

It was a joke, I guess. Betty went right on: "Sometimes I feel I should attach a sign: 'Stop me before I buy more.' Some things make me laugh, as when the stores have a sign in the window: 'Inventory reduction sale.' As if they did not want to reduce inventory all the time."

She was all over the map. I felt I needed a butterfly net to talk to her. My daughter the flake. "Forget the shopping, Betty," I demanded. "Tell me, why so many men? Why not make it work with one?"

Betty paused, reflecting, frowning, and I wished I could have put a finger on her lovely forehead and wiped the sudden wrinkles away. We age fast enough.

"Father," Betty finally answered, "why do people read stories of love affairs and go to see movies and plays that have as their theme, boy meets girl, boy loves girl, boy marries girl?"

"Well we're all sympathetic to such stories, Betty. They are romantic, a dream, and evoke strong emotion."

"Exactly, and this is because the readers or viewers themselves want to do it again and again, consciously or unconsciously. They live the fullest part of life once more through such stories. They would like multiple lives of falling in love. The courtship and honeymoon are the best part. The classic line of Shakespeare: 'Wherefore art thou, Romeo?' is the epitome of woman."

"And I don't understand you."

"That's what all my husbands have kept saying." She smiled and patted my hand.

"But the children," I began and paused."

"The most wonderful thing about raising children is that you have a ready receptacle for all your prejudices," Betty divulged, reflecting. "Washington D.C. breathes politics. Everyone I meet here is trying to turn being a lawyer into being a politician."

"Well Betty, George Bernard Shaw said 'Those who can, do, and those who can't, teach.' That always used to bother me when I taught at the University. But I believe those who can't teach, administrate. And those who can't even administrate, run for office. But I was asking you about your children."

"So I have three children. Father do you think that the natural enemy of the environmentalists should be the 'Right to Lifers,' because overpopulation is the main environmental problem? Over- population is the root cause of many of our problems from wiping out whole species of animals and plants, too much garbage, too many factories and cars polluting the air, water going bad, quality of life in trouble, shortages of raw materials." Her voice trailed off.

I told Betty "I'm on your side."

"So, If you're on my side get off my back," she replied. "You know all of my husbands were smart, but possessed galloping immaturity. They hadn't learned yet that when you married a woman, you didn't own her nor was she an extension of your personality."

Betty got up and walked around a little, putting things away in the kitchen and I watched her. Then she continued: "An Englishman I dated recently told me that the modern preachment that women are equal spoils them all. He said, and I quote: 'The liberals and do-gooders run around and tell the ladies that their brains are as good as ours. How much better in the old days when we ordered the women about,' he said, 'and we expected a dowry before we married them, took over their estates and money, demanded they wait at home while we went out to our clubs. We anticipated good sex relations as our right, and even were allowed to beat the women a bit if they misbehaved without some social worker making a lot of noise about poor battered women.' I didn't have to marry him to know it wouldn't work."

I nodded in the best counselor's tradition of urging her on and Betty did continue: "Sometimes I do think I'm living in the wrong age. I think to be young and living in the 1960's might have been really fun."

I smiled now. "Your mother and I used to say that we missed the sexual revolution, but we missed it together."

Betty stood up, framed in the doorway. "Father, I'm really all right. I've finally become the person I want to be." She left the room and I sat quietly wondering what it all meant.

*　　*　　*

I was beyond Christmas, but loved it anyway. When I could, I engaged in child study among my grandchildren. Now I had a new role, grandfather. The old are another race, removed from reality, and perceived as never having been young.

Betty's three girls were all different, Cathy dark, Amy a golden, honey blond, Paula a bright redhead. Yet they were all the same too, thin, delicate, energetic, loving. I took Betty's three girls, aged seven, four, and two out to the stores to see Santa all by myself.

The middle girl, Amy, struggling to get dressed for this adventure told me: "I could put on these shoes, if I could," which was true enough.

Later I watched Amy snuggle up to the Santa in the store and say: "Bring me some goodies." And I felt rewarded.

Children finally fly from the nest. Yet our hopes and fears, all our warnings and tears, all our praise and cheers, everything we have put into raising them through the years, goes with them when they leave.

My daughter Betty seemed to be using the parties and social events in D.C. to which I was invited, to find another lawyer. Our situation gave her entry into a whole new circle in Washington.

For my part, I must say I have never seen such a bunch of total parasites as attended the parties in Washington. I met so many people whose function as a part of our government I thought had no purpose. Further, a massive circle of minor agents of foreign powers lived in Washington, not really caring for their own home governments, but they were here in America having a good time. If you asked this group to do any work you were interrupting them.

"What are you really looking for out there?" I asked Betty again, directly, one spring day when we were alone in the living room of Duncan House.

She laughed her self-deprecating tinkle. "I am sure she used that laugh a lot when playing her game. "Merely the perfect man, father," she replied. "Why is life in the movies so easy?"

"In the movies they can remake the scene. They show the hero getting on the train and getting off. The audience doesn't have to take the whole ride with him." Abruptly I threw up my hands. "Betty, you keep looking for the same thing and finding it. And it isn't what you want."

"But what do I want, father?" she asked.

In the end Betty's affair with the latest Washington lawyer ended and she returned to New York City.

Our oldest son, Don, had already gone back to California to continue working with his music group. He too capitalized on my friendship with our alien visitor, writing a successful song about Xan-Tu the robot, which reached diamond status on the charts.

In the spring our youngest daughter, Susan, finally graduated from college. She moved to Washington, living at Duncan House for several months. Sue began dating here, but soon returned to Florida where she had gone to school. She was going to try for an MBA. It seemed to me that it was a way of extending childhood. I asked Sue why she had broken up with her boyfriend and she replied: "I didn't want to make the same mistake once." I almost understood her.

My wife, Helen, was settling in at Duncan House. She requested an exercise machine for our bedroom which was installed in front of the television. I commended her on rebuilding herself, but instead it seemed to cut her television watching.

*   *   *

I returned once that Spring to check on our home in Arizona. The small city of Las Palmas had become a tourist town. Sadly, Jose Herrera had quit high school and become a tour guide, escorting the curious visitors to the site of the alien ship's landing. That was not what I wanted to see happen to Jose Herrera.

Back at Duncan House and alone with Xan-Tu I asked a question that had been troubling me for some time. "Xan-Tu," I said, "you have twenty-four arms, feelers, appendages. Yet I never see you do more than wave a couple of these about. You seem to be able to move things and accomplish your desires by something close to pure thought. So what is the purpose of your many appendages? Excuse me If I overstep the boundaries of our friendship."

"None of your questions have ever bothered me, Jerry West. On some of the worlds I visited I have encountered intelligent creatures you might see as beetles, giant or tiny, whose conversation is entirely managed by antennas. Speech is not the normal communication of the universe. This is one reason why your scientists have not heard from intelligent life forms earlier. Without these appendages I would not be able to communicate on some worlds."

*   *   *

For months there had been a growing group of protestors parading around Duncan House carrying signs that declared quite plainly: "Xan-Tu go home." As the weather warmed in the spring the number of protestors grew.

As a former historian I was reminded of the time in ancient Greece when some of the leading citizens of various Greek cities were banished. "Ostracizing" was what the Greeks called the expelling of citizens from a community. One man in Greece was sent away from his home city by the citizens who got tired of hearing him called "the Good."

When my personal disaster occurred it all happened too fast for even Xan-Tu to intercede. Did he know something violent was coming and want to allow the world's people to see what it might be like after he left unless stringent measures were taken?

It was at another party in Washington D.C., which is a center for continual parties. The affair was at a huge home of one of the powerful leaders of the Quadrilateral Commission. There was a great banquet table set up and people milling about. Xan-Tu had learned the trick of toasting. He would extend a tentacle through his force shield and hold a wine glass high. Then, without his drinking any, the liquid would slowly disappear, apparently running down into the stem of the glass.

Now a bearded man in a tuxedo extended his hand to shake mine and I let him in to my personal force shielded area. He had a small gun concealed in his palm.

I had heard that great pain produces automatic bodily cutoffs and I now found out how true that was. I felt nothing as I lay bleeding and dying on the floor. Then there was more shooting. Several waiters were blasting away at the crowd with automatic weapons from the balcony. I saw all of this as if in a dream, as I lay on the floor.

Xan-Tu paralyzed the attackers with one sweep of his light ray, but it was too late, though I did not know that at the time. Xan-Tu patched up my heart from across the room right on the spot, sending out a bolt of light from one of his tentacles. It was probably some process akin to laser technology. Still I had lost a lot of blood and was brought by ambulance to the hospital.

It was later when I found out. The attackers, posing as a catering service had killed the American President, Reed Hamilton. Others had been murdered at the same time but among these killed was my wife, Helen, shot several times in the head.

There I was at the hospital, the doctors remarking on how well my heart and arteries had been repaired. They gave me a blood transfusion and bed rest. Several hours later Xan-Tu came floating in.

"I am so sorry, Jerry," he began, and since I knew nothing about what had happened since my only view was from the floor of the banquet, it all came as a surprise. Xan-Tu told me of President Reed Hamilton's death and then about Helen.

"They could not reach me and wanted to hurt me in some way," Xan-Tu suggested. "And I can not prevent all the mad things men may do. You humans are a violent people."

I lay there with the tubes up my nose, in my arm, and even in my penis to remove fluid, all drugged up, almost unable to comprehend. I felt guilty for I had been on an ego trip from the beginning, loving the experience of being at the center of events. My wife Helen had always been on the outside, even here in Washington, wanting nothing more than to watch her television. And now she had been killed.

"I must say, Jerry," Xan-Tu continued after a bit, "that even after what you humans call death, I could have used the cells to restore life, to Reed Hamilton, to Helen, and to others. But it would not have been the same life. If so many people had not been shot in the head from above, including your Helen and President Hamilton, it would not have been a problem. But serious head injuries in humans bring brain death to the images that mean memory. Restoration is impossible."

Xan-Tu paused so I could absorb that much. "I could do something akin to what you call cloning," the alien continued, "but the American people would not want a look-alike man who could not remember his past. You would not want Helen without her past memories. They would apparently be the same person, but without memory. There was no use my trying to fool anyone."

I nodded as best I could, feeling desolate. There was one more pause and then Xan-Tu concluded: "As to yourself, your heart and arteries are stronger, for having been repaired. Jerry, if I were to genetically redesign humans, the first thing I would do would be give you several small hearts down the middle of the chest instead of one. Each heart would have cut-offs so the others could function if something went wrong."

*   *   *

I was in the hospital for a week and on an exercise schedule after I got back to Duncan House. Our children were all back for Helen's funeral. It was after this, when I was told that Xan-Tu was leaving shortly, that he offered to take me along.

"I have been thinking about it Jerry and I am concerned that you will be a target again once I leave. I cannot allow you to keep the force shield. Think it over."

I accepted the offer. I was still feeling depressed, but I had done by best for my children and Helen was gone.

"Once we leave the planet it will be journey of several earth years before we reach our next destination," Xan-Tu told me. "I will have to alter your form so that you continue to live as we proceed with our trip. It is not exactly immortality, but close. You will appear to be a man and think as one." Xan-Tu told me a bit more about the process, which I will not relate here. In any case, I agreed.

When the word got out that I was leaving with Xan-Tu one Washington newspaper, who hated the visitor, suggested I had sold myself to the alien and had no other recourse but to flee. I felt quite the opposite about my decision. Xan-Tu could kidnap whom he wished and he had asked my permission. As it turned out there were many who began to appeal to Xan-Tu to go along, all of whom he refused. I was going off to see the universe.

VLL

"To one thing do all men agree and that is there is no general agreement among men on anything. And yet in all societies survival depends upon agreements." Xan-Tu

In the end many people said this whole year with Xan-Tu meant nothing. Humans could have done everything that Xan-Tu did all by themselves. We needed no outside help. Perhaps. Or perhaps it would have been the end of mankind. If we could only see beyond the curtain of time, how differently we might all act at any given moment.

True, there was no new knowledge imparted to mankind by our alien guest except that we were not alone in the universe. And even the messenger from beyond had been unable to prevent the shooting deaths in the final days of his stay.

The human race was still on its own. Mankind could yet choose to change or to destroy itself.

I have here written up an account of what I have experienced. I won't be around to see how the game is played out.

*   *   *

Editor's note: As the spaceship with Xan-Tu and Jerry West departed for the stars, many of us watching wished we could have gone too. And we never will forget the last words of Xan-Tu as he left:

"We shall be in touch," he said.

What if you were crazy?

The Madness Within

I rolled over fitfully and the bright sunlight hit me flush in the face. Sunlight! Hadn't I closed the blinds? I looked up, blinking into the blazing open sky. Then I felt hastily for my bed and came up with a handful of sand. Now I jerked abruptly upright. What does the brain do in a case like this? How do you sort out the impossible? I was lying on sand, in the midst of what appeared to be a wide beach. There was roaring surf a little ways down. My eyes swept the horizon. I was alone right out in the open.

I'm Joe Daniels, one time a very minor league football player, now a scientist who had just lost his job at the age of 28. Normally I'm an early riser who doesn't like early rising. In the morning I follow a hateful awakening ritual of hitting the snooze button on the clock and rolling over. Gradually life comes to my fingers and toes. Finally I manage to stumble into the bathroom and wash my face.

Now I noted with real surprise how quickly I moved, how fast I came awake. In an emergency the old survival instinct still came into play. I fairly leaped up and then crouching I ran a little ways bare-footed down the beach. I had not even started to ask where I was or how I happened to get here. The only things that worried me were that I was in my pajamas and out on an open beach. I saw nothing familiar. Ten-foot high black rocks jutted out ahead and I slid behind them.

I rubbed the last cobwebs of sleep from my eyes, managing to get some sand in. Now I rubbed my eyes carefully till tears cleared the sand. Desperately I tried to remember last night. Although it was hard to recall all the events of last evening, I was increasingly sure that I had made it home.

Yesterday there was the final argument with Peter Quinn, the last battle in a long-term disagreement. He had told me I was crazy one time too many and I quit. I am sure he was trying to goad me into leaving. Two years of work and I was out. We were working on multi- dimensional propulsion, an increasingly advanced program right out of string theory and quantum physics. I wanted to report to the Foundation that was sponsoring the project.

After I walked out I planned to write the Foundation about my reasons for resigning. Then Chuck Jax, the little engineer who worked with us, suggested we have a few drinks. Chuck seemed genuinely sorry over my trouble with Quinn. Since he had not heard the inside story, I felt glad to unload my version of truth. Chuck was sympathetic but in no position to help.

And drinking is never the answer to a problem. At last we both sat there teetering on bar stools, saying inane things that meant something at the time, but were soon forgotten. Even now my head still throbbed from the liquor I had consumed and my throat was dry with a thirst I felt an ocean could not satisfy. I could feel that pizza, a greasy undigested lump.

But now the important question was: how had I gotten here? Yes, I had made it to my apartment last night. I remember getting out of the cab, climbing the steep stairs, and fumbling with the door key. That was close enough. So, how come I was here?

I looked down at my green stripped pajamas, certainly mine, and reflected that surely I had not gone outside like this. It had been cold last night, November, a prelude to winter. Here it was hot under the white brilliance of the sun. This was too expensive for a joke. Maybe I was dead and this beach was the prelude to Heaven. Or Peter Quinn was right and I was crazy. At work I kept attempting new things with our experiment and wanted further funds to try more.

I tried to think further. Yes, I had reached my apartment. My pajamas proved I had arrived in the bedroom. It was too hot in my bedroom as usual and I opened a window. Was there anything more? I felt thirsty, as I always did after drinking. That is curious, but true. Drinking made you thirsty. And the open bedroom window made it too cold quite soon. Had I gotten up to close the window or left the apartment for some reason? No. I had been very tired. I searched my mind for more and there was no more.

I peered around the edge of the rocks. There was nothing but sand, jutting black pointed rocks, and high waves splashing. Suddenly a thought struck me and I acted upon it. Odd, isn't it, how civilized men will try to observe the proprieties in any situation or circumstance. Anyway I removed my pajama tops, and then rolled the bottoms up as far as they would go. Now with my pajamas rolled up it might appear I was wearing bathing trunks.

This was probably the ocean, and I was no doubt wasting my time for the surf was rushing in too turbulently for it to be lake water. Still I had heard a person could drink small quantities of seawater, and I was thirsty enough to try. I folded my pajama tops and left them neatly on some rocks. Then I walked down to the surf. The water was cold, rushing over my feet and then receding so rapidly that I had to wade out a distance before I could bend down and obtain a handful of water.

It was fresh water, effervescent, delicious, and clear as a mountain stream. After several drinks I felt contented in spite of my predicament. I stretched lazily. There was no one else on the beach as far as I could see around the curve of the land in either direction. Inland there were only more rocks. And then the second sun arose on the opposite side of the sky!

This second sun came on slowly, a red orb perched overlong on the horizon. Then it was an orange bright circle, climbing skyward. Eventually it became a massive yellow globe of flame moving toward zenith. For perhaps an hour I stood, the waves slapping my feet, while I watched these two opposing suns, staring, fearing, and wondering. Then, feeling the beginning of sunburn, I returned to the shade of the rocks and put on my pajama tops and sat down frightened.

Before it could have been a joke or a trick, but there was no simulating an artificial sun. And it was no illusion, unless I was mad. There were two enormous suns in the sky traveling toward each other. Before my problem had been explaining how I got from a cold climate to a warm one, from my bed to a sandy beach? Now the problem was quite different by several orders of magnitude. I stood on that beach for hours, numb with fear until I decided to look around further. For long bits of that time my mind was essentially blank. I had been working hard lately, twelve, fourteen, sixteen hours a day, going over equations, feeding data into computers, designing and redesigning.

The present situation resolved itself into three possibilities: One, someone was playing an elaborate trick on me; two, I was insane; three I was suddenly on another planet in another solar system. This certainly was not a dream.

The second possibility seemed the most likely. Yes, drunk as I was last night someone could have slipped me a knock out potion and then brought me south to a warm beach. But two suns! I checked my vision. I carefully winked and closed one eye at a time. The suns were still there, larger than I remembered our sun being, rising toward the sky's center, toward each other. Would they crash? Ridiculous! I was thinking like a madman.

Was I insane? Peter Quinn had been telling me that for several weeks, saying it too often. That was the most likely answer, although naturally my mind rejected this solution. All insane minds would! But if I remembered my psychology aright, then the insane never questioned their insanity. Still if I questioned my sanity, to prove I was sane, because crazy people didn't do that, then what? My mind did a sudden flip flop and for a moment I clutched tight at the sharp rocks.

The rock was very hot. The temperature must have been over a hundred degrees. Yet, now, at the heat of the day I made my decision to explore. I called out first, a hearty "hello" that seemed lost in the waves of surf. There was no answer. My feet burned on the hot sand as I left the shade of the rocks. I hurried to the water's edge, walking in the moist sand, the water still happily cool. I paused to drink. Then I splashed water on my pajama tops, my face, my hair, and continued to walk.

I continued up the beach, walking in surf. It was difficult to guess at the temperature and time seemed irrelevant. There were no clouds in the sky, no shells on the sand, and no birds in the air. Ahead around the curve of the beach there was just more sand and jutting rocks. The two blazing hot suns had passed each other now and were probably very far apart. Ahead there was cold, clear water stretching out from the beach to infinity. I walked on endlessly, thinking again and I did not like my thoughts. Sometimes when men go mad it must be like this, in a world all their own.

And then abruptly I stopped as a sudden clutch of fear gripped me. There were footprints in the sand ahead, naked human footprints.

Human! There was a big toe and four little ones. I rushed up to the footprints and examined them. They came down from the shadow of the rocks and disappeared into the waves. I looked more carefully. No! The footprints came down to the beach and then traveled along the water's edge, wiped out in places, but not always completely. They continued further ahead, entering and leaving the edge of the water, as I did.

I stood very still realizing the truth. They were my footprints. Ahead were the two sets of prints I had made going to the rocks and back. I was on an island and had walked clear around it.

I wet my feet well so I would not burn them and returned to the shade of the rocks. It was cooling off. The one sun had set and the other would be setting soon. I was very tired, very hungry, and very afraid. Tomorrow I would have to explore the interior of the island and if it was all only rocks and sand, as it appeared, then I would have to resign myself to death by starvation.

After resting a bit I felt renewed strength. The temperature was a bit cooler. I would find out right now. Carefully I walked inland up around the rocks, staying on the sand. The rock outcroppings were in clumps, sharp at the top, mostly black but sometimes speckled. I am not a geologist and could learn nothing by examining the rocks. Going inland took me increasingly uphill. Now the second sun was setting and it was growing dark. I felt the need to return to the safety of the shore. Safety?

On sudden impulse I called out loudly: "All right. The game is over. I give up. Get me out of here. Please." The last word was a shout that hung on the night air like a thing with a life of its own.

Instantly I was sorry I had called out. There could be nocturnal creatures that would now know my location, beasts that avoided the blazing suns, but came forth in the darkness.

I raced back to the shore, but I cut my foot on a rock and this slowed me down. The last sun had set. The darkness swept in decisively. I glanced skyward; the stars were out in surprising number. There was no moon. I looked for the moon, longed for the moon, but there was none.

I wished for more knowledge of astronomy. There seemed to be many more stars visible than I had ever seen before. I couldn't find the Big Dipper, which was the only star group I had ever been able to locate. I cursed my ignorance. Mine was the ignorance of the educated, knowing a great deal about one small branch of knowledge and no more than a fifth grade child about everything else.

There seemed to be no lights inland. I heard no sounds aside from the roaring surf. How far had I walked today? Perhaps I had gone fifteen miles along an irregular beach. The island could not be more than three or four miles across, in that case. I should be able to see any lights in the interior.

I lay down at last on the warm sand. That was it. I was crazy. I belonged in an asylum. Thoughts kept sliding through my mind, each more hideous than the last.

*   *   *

I heard the bell and sat up groggily, reaching to turn off the alarm which was not anywhere. I was in a top bunk. I hit my head on the ceiling as the bell stopped. Then I leaned forward and sat up, the events of yesterday and the day before ricocheting back and forth in my numb mind. Two men confronted me, both seemingly bewildered, uncertain as to my presence.

We three men were in a cell with three bunks along one wall. There was a wooden table and three stools in the middle of the room. The one high window that allowed in light was barred and there were likewise bars on the huge door. I was in a cell, a jail, or an asylum. I was crazy! Huge segments of my memory must be disappearing. Yesterday there was the desert and today here. How much time had really elapsed? I was still in my pajamas. Suddenly I looked at my leg. The place I had cut my foot on the rock last night was still not healed. Well, better to be here in this cell then dying on a deserted island. Maybe!

Again a bell rang. My two companions in this cell wore gray and white striped coats and loose trousers. The tall young man was slack jawed. Most of his teeth were missing. He had a pale, thin battered face, as if he had been beaten. His head was topped by an untidy mop of uncombed hair. The other man was old, white haired, wiry. Both men possessed facial hair that had been trimmed carelessly all around, leaving almost an inch of stubble. They regarded me with open stupefaction until the clanging bell caused the old man to react.

"Quick, put on Jock's clothes," he ordered, handing me a dirty gray and white stripped top and trousers such as they were each wearing. What appeared to be some slippers were handed to me next. When in the asylum do as the inmates do. I put the clothes on over my pajamas, not really wanting them to touch my body. The old man seemed to feel dressing was urgent while the younger person continued to look at me stupidly.

Just as I finished dressing the older man seemed to hesitate, as if changing his plans for me, and then abruptly ordered: "You must hide. If they find you here there's no telling." His voice trailed off as if he were uncertain what would happen if I were found here. Then he decided: "Lie still in your bunk."

I did as I was told. Scarcely had I assumed the prone position requested when the cell door next to ours was opened with a clang. Would they take my companions away? I did not want to spend another whole day alone. I raised my head, surveying the two men. "Where am I?" I whispered. "What is this place?"

"Shah," the old man responded, making a silence signal with a finger to his lips.

"I want to know now," I demanded.

The old man only shook his head at me in displeasure. Then I heard a sound and lowered my head, holding my breath. The door opened with a harsh grating of metal. Someone entered and then left. The door shut. I waited a moment and then raised my head. The two men below turned to the solitary table that now held a tray with two steaming plates of food or slop. There were two metal cups of water as well.

The two men sat down at opposite ends of the table on the stools, apparently having forgotten about me already. They ate with big wooden spoons, blowing and swallowing mechanically.

"Horrible food," I grumbled, sitting up. "Why don't you complain?"

The old man shrugged but the young man eyed me proudly. "I eat to please them," he related scornfully in a hoarse voice. "It is the best they have. I do not have to eat, you understand? I am above all that."

"No," I answered frankly. "What do you mean?"

The young man looked at me oddly as if I should know, as if everyone should know: "I am really not even here," he answered. With that he went back to eating, which he had said he did not have to do.

Neither man offered me any, but the brown lumpy stuff looked so unappetizing that I had no desire for it, though I had eaten nothing yesterday, if yesterday had existed. But there were some things I had to know.

"We are in an asylum?" I asked.

"The walls are protection, to keep the sane people out," the old man answered, chuckling.

I was shaken by this and lay some minutes considering my plight. Then I tried again: "What is your name, old fellow?"

"Aaron of York." The old man was finished eating now and turned toward me. "I am the greatest poet the world has ever produced."

I thought of inquiring why he was here in that case, but instead asked the younger man: "And you sir, what is your name?"

"Chester. Chester Giddings. It is a name I use because no one must know I am the rightful king."

I let that one go also. "How did I get here?" I inquired

The old man looked at me curiously: "You came in the night, appearing in Jock's bed." The old man shook his head sadly. "He was a good companion these many years. He died yesterday. They left his clothes for you." The old man bowed his head.

I shuddered at wearing a dead man's clothes. Then I clenched my teeth and continued:" But who brought me here?"

Aaron of York looked at me strangely: "You do not know either? Then it was indeed witchcraft. You were here in the morning in Jock's bunk."

"But I don't belong here," I insisted.

"They all say that," Aaron of York replied. "Many strange things happen and one could go mad with questioning."

The cell next to ours opened with a clang. I slid back in the bunk and then decided I wanted to know. I had to find out. The guards could at least check. Then I'd get out of this bedlam.

At that instant a creature came into view. It was about nine feet tall and blue in color. Aside from the glistening scales it looked much like a crocodile standing up on two enormous back legs. It opened our cell door with two small front arms. Perhaps it was more like a kangaroo without a pouch, but still reptilian in appearance. How we try to turn the grotesque into the familiar. The head was small with two rows of tiny teeth, for now its mouth opened in what I considered surprise as it looked at me.

I screamed out in fright in spite of myself. I was insane. Then the creature spoke, using English with an accent: "We arise here and dress when the first bell rings. That is why you received no food. Next time you will know better." The blue being paused, reflecting: "This is odd, however. I was not told this cell had been filled again. I shall have to check." The creature seized the empty food tray and took it away. The door clanged shut.

I sat for a while in the upper bunk, shaking slightly. "What are these creatures?" I demanded at last.

The young man continued to look at me strangely. Aaron of York replied softly: "They are the Conquerors."

"Then you saw what I saw?"

"I do not have your eyes."

"No. I mean the blue creatures?"

"Azure. They are azure in coloring."

I sat for a long time just staring into space after that. Then abruptly a slender pole thrust into the cell struck me on the side and I fell from the bunk. A loud laugh greeted my fall. Several human men stood outside of the bars with long sticks. They slashed at us.

"Jump fools, jump," one man on the outside shouted. The poles slid along the ground under the bars. I was hit in the shins several times. I jumped after that.

"I'm not crazy," I called out loudly. "Get me out of here and I'll make it worth your while." I got a blow in the stomach for that and two quick thrusts at my ribs.

Tickling the insane, I thought. This was medieval torture. The outsiders were picking on me now and aiming at my head. Abruptly I was saved when the tall young man stopped jumping entirely. He waved his arms widely: "Away, all of you," he demanded. "I will jump no more. I am not really here."

They really hit him for these words, until a heavy blow to the head sent him spinning to the ground. His head struck the corner of the bunk.

The men with the poles moved on to the next cell. Aaron of York lifted the young man in his arms, deposited him on the lowest bunk, and then sat down quietly. I returned to my bunk and lay there, silent, watchful, afraid, fondling my bruises. I wondered what would happen when the blue jailer-creatures did check the records and found that I had not been placed here? Or would there be a record of me? That would be even worse!

Hours passed. The old man was sitting quietly, mumbling to himself, apparently counting his fingers. I climbed up to the top bunk and looked through the upper barred window. There was grass, trees, and a high wall beyond that. The sky was filled with gray clouds and it was hard to see the sun.

Abruptly I asked: "How many suns do you have?"

The old man turned as if he had forgotten about me again. "None here. Only in the sky," he answered.

"In the sky then," I added hastily, almost adding: "You fool."

"One. One sun. How many would you have?"

I made a face and turned away. If this was an asylum, they would think I was crazy after I asked that question. The thing I felt most right now was hunger. "How often are we fed?" I asked.

"Twice. Twice a day."

I turned away again. After a while the young man in the lower bunk came awake moaning. Finally I turned to Aaron of York again and asked: "How long have you been here?"

"Time is irrelevant," he replied, adding solemnly: "All is not all."

I winced. There was no use talking to him. But he was all there was. The young man was useless. Hours passed. At one point I saw three of the blue creatures walking in the courtyard below. Then the single blue jailer came clanging down the corridor, opening cell doors. When he reached our cell he entered and took three trays with food and water from a huge cart and deposited them on the table. As the blue being left I clamored down from my perch and clutched the bars tightly, peering after it. "Have you checked?" I inquired. "I don't belong here."

The creature laughed. "Where do you belong, then?"

My confusion showed on my face. The creature laughed again, a snorting "Ho ho." Then the creature added: "I cannot check until tomorrow. This is Tollsday, you know."

His words left me feeling ill. Still I persisted and called again: "And if you do check tomorrow and I do not belong here, what then?" I inquired.

"You will no doubt be executed as a Yermanite spy," the creature responded laughing again.

I turned to the table with a sick feeling and the food slop made me feel worse. Still there were three plates and cups now.

The old man motioned for me to sit down. "You sit over there, Jock," he instructed.

"I'm not Jock," I told him.

He frowned looking puzzled over this news. "Who are you then?"

"My name's Joe Daniels."

"An odd name," Aaron of York replied.

"I'm from the Bronx. You ever hear of the Bronx?"

"No. That must be beyond the meridian."

I plunged right on, heedless of the madness, unconcerned now. "It's part of New York City. That's in the eastern United States. It is part of America. You know, it was discovered by Columbus in 1492."

"New York," the old man pondered. He had finished eating and gave the problem his full attention. "I am Aaron of the city of York, but I do not think there is a New York. Still I have been here many years; but it seems to me that 1492 is some years away." He scratched his white head.

I turned to the slop in my bowl. After my long fast anything might have done, but this tasted worse than my low expectations. It seemed to be on a par with greasy dog food, though I have never tried that dish. Perhaps the blue creatures were running this planet and treating all men like this. But some men were out, poking sticks at us.

"The Conquerors," I inquired. "No, let's start with the men. Who are those men who poked us with the sticks?"

The old man shrugged. "They pay to see us. They come every Tollsday. It is part of the Great Bargain of 1227."

I pushed the rest of my food away, climbing back into the top bunk to look at the fading light. The creature returned for the plates. "You have not eaten much yet," it remarked. "You will get hungry and eat tomorrow no doubt." Then he examined the young man who was sitting in his chair and holding his injured head. "You will jump better next time," the creature predicted.

We were left alone again. I thought of hunger and reflected that a primitive man might kill an animal and gorge himself and then not eat for several days. But a civilized man, accustomed to a routine of eating three times daily weather hungry or not, that was a different story.

At last it was completely dark. I was in the top bunk so I could look out of the lone high window, but there were no lights anywhere. The other two in this cell had settled into their bunks without questioning.

"Are there no electric lights here?" I inquired.

Aaron of York answered sleepily: "What is that?"

"Do you have artificial light?" I asked again.

I could almost feel him frown in the darkness below. "You mean candles, lanterns. The Conquerors have such things. They have more. They brought them out of the sky when they came in their great sailing ships. That was before my time."

"Then they were not always here," I continued.

"No one is always here." Aaron of York concluded.

I let it go at that, lying back on the bed. I was thinking of food that was edible, piled high, huge roasts, sliced thick with the center still pink, heaping plates of vegetables, goblets of fine liquors, white tablecloths, and a comfortable bed.

What was similar about the last two days? In both there had been danger. Yesterday no people at all and today people imprisoned. On neither day had there been any women I had seen. This was as hopeless as the island yesterday. In both cases I was trapped. Give me the wide open spaces, I thought. If only there was something I could do, someplace where I could fight and win. Blood, carnage, slaughter, kill or be killed, I cared not. But give me a chance to strike a blow. No, I wanted more. I wanted to win. The blue creatures came from the sky in space ships. No women, no food, and no way out. Where was the pattern? There must be hope. And my mind wandered until the darkness closed about me.

* * *

I awoke, remembering in a flash my predicament, feeling for the bunk or the sand and instead I felt the downy softness of a lace-edged sheet. While I was still lying in an upper berth, far off the floor, even in the semi-darkness I could see this oval room was vastly different than the one I occupied yesterday. Slightly hysterical laughter convulsed me. Existence always seemed unreal, even on earth in previous times; my senses did not seem to apprehend reality sufficiently.

Now, at least, I was in a well-appointed room. But suppose I was not really here, as the inmate Chester believed in my last incarnation? This could be a great dream, encapsulated in a smaller dream, infinite receding realities as mirrors within mirrors. Madness loomed close in around me again. Purposely I hit my head hard on the bedpost and enjoyed the pain of reality. But even that did not prove reality. Perhaps only the absence of reality proved reality! No, no. I was beginning to think like the weird men in that asylum yesterday.

And then as I sat up, my feet dangling, I became aware that I was not alone here either. A yawn came from below and a thin white arm protruded from the lower bunk striking my dangling feet. A soft white hand extended out with pointed fingers. Then suddenly the clenched hand pulled back. A feminine scream issued from below. I pulled my offending feet back up onto my bunk, wondering what to do.

It was a new situation each day.

The powers that be,
Were trying to see,
How much I could take,
Before I would break.

Soon my thoughts would be coming in heroic verse, iambic pentameter, dactylic hexameter, sonnets of thought, and cantos by the hour perhaps as created by the great poet Aaron of York.

The arm from below reached out again and pulled a long silken cord beside the bed. I sat waiting fearing the worst.

The door opened softly and a portly man in a splendid green uniform stood outlined in the entrance. "You rang, Lady Jean?" he inquired.

"Yes," replied the feminine voice below. "I believe there's someone else in here. Turn on the light please."

A button was pushed and the room flooded with lights from wall panels. I shut my eyes involuntarily and I heard the man in uniform gasp. I actually recovered before he did, being acquainted with confusion now. I jumped from the bed, colliding with the woman below who was about to get up. She was scantily clad in a flimsy gown that tore easily as I slid into her and we both tumbled. She was a pretty, leggy young thing, but this didn't look like a lasting relationship.

I dashed for the open door. I had enough of this. At last I had a chance to act. This was neither an asylum nor an uninhabited island. The portly man tried to block my exit, but I was out and into a corridor. Somehow I had to get out of this building and away. Then I could figure out where I was and what to do next. I bolted to the left just as an alarm bell rang sharply down the corridor.

The corridor turned ahead and I rounded it on a dead run. I heard the sound of pursuit behind. Three men in green uniforms were ahead standing in a little alcove looking through a huge window. I caught my breath as I reached them, trying to orient myself fast. The window was a vast screen showing stars in the distance, moving stars. I was moving. The whole place was moving. I was on some sort of a space ship!

My pursuers rounded the corridor. "There he is," the portly man exclaimed. I dashed on, hopelessly now. If I was in space, then this ship was a closed unit, just as the island or the asylum. I couldn't just go outside to the next building. Peace would have to be made with the authorities and I had already offended them.

Again it all seemed without pattern, purposeless, mad. None of this could be happening. As I rounded another turn two men wearing the same green uniforms blocked my path. I was trapped. Unless! I opened the first door I reached by pushing on a button. Once I was inside the door shut automatically behind me.

"How dare you enter without knocking," a large bearded man grumped. The man looked at me oddly, squinting one eye. "Who are you, anyway?" he demanded. "I've never seen you before."

The door opened behind me and several men entered. Two of them quickly grabbed my arms. "A stowaway Captain Gilman, hiding in Lady Jean's room."

The Captain arose and walked closer to me. "Lady Jean's room! Did he lay a finger on her?"

"Knocked her down."

"Take him out and kill him, only slowly. Slowly, do you hear?"

"Wait, wait," I cried out. "I can explain."

The Captain's chin and pointed beard quivered with rage. "You have one minute. Make it short and good."

"I was transported here by accident. Somehow I am bouncing from one place to another. I don't know how or why. I can't control it. Give me until morning and I probably will have vanished from your ship in my sleep. Only give me that long, please. I really meant no harm."

"Absurd. Absurd. Take him out and kill him."

The men grabbed me, pulling me into the corridor. Just then the whole ship gave a lurch, so that we all tumbled to the hall floor. "It's the pirates," someone gasped.

"LeBloc here?" someone else asked. "How could he get through?"

I got up hastily and ran down the corridor.

"Stop him, he's probably a pirate spy," someone shouted.

Again the corridor pitched at a new angle and we all went down. "They've got grapples on us," one of the crew exclaimed. "They're alongside. They'll be burning through the airlocks next."

I decided not to run anymore. The Captain was out in the corridor too. His face looked cadaverous and his voice trembled. "Break out the small arms and defend the locks," he ordered.

The Captain turned toward me only for an instant. "Hanson, Branders, take this fellow out and kill him." Two men grabbed me. We went one way and the Captain and his crew went the other. I felt dazed. If they killed me that would prove this was real. I didn't want that proof.

Then Jean, the girl in whose cabin I had awakened rounded the corridor. "Hanson," she inquired. "What's going on?"

"I'm afraid it's LeBloc, the space pirate. He could be boarding any minute."

The girl's eyes widened with fear. She had long dark hair, held up by several sparkling silver combs. She was in a pantsuit now, also a silver outfit that clung tight to her upper body. "Can we escape?" she inquired.

"They have already shot away our stabilizers and resisters. We are coupled to their ship."

I spoke up out of sheer desperation: "Lady Jean I meant you no harm. I will help your Captain fight the space pirates."

She turned from me as another man came running up: "A message to you from the Captain, Lady Jean." He gave a paper to Lady Jean, saluting and waiting expectantly.

She snapped open the paper and read it aloud quickly. "I am to use the 'A Deck' escape pod. We are to leave on a signal when the pirates enter the ship."

"Right," the messenger explained, 'once many of pirates are on our liner, they will not be able to pull away and come after the escape pod. But we must hurry."

Lady Jean and her escort went off. I turned to Hanson and Branders, two rather large men. "What are you going to do with me? The Captain will need every man against the pirates."

"We have our orders," Hanson snarled. "We'll dump you out with the rest of the space garbage." He motioned for me to go through a rather narrow door. I went through the door. Hanson reached in to push a button and the wall at the end turned translucent. While Hanson was doing this I slammed the door back hard on his hand. He yelled out and threw open the door. I kicked him in the stomach. As he doubled over I kicked him in the face and he rolled back against Branders. Now I saw what appeared to be a big monkey wrench on hooks on the wall. I pulled it loose as Blanders came into the room after me. I swung and missed. We maneuvered a bit and I swung again. Blanders fell back against the wall. To my surprise he went right through. The garbage disposal I decided, which had been readied for me. I ran back into the corridor and found another door, shutting it behind me.

There was a confusion of voices in the corridor outside and then ominous silence. Whoever won I would be in trouble. I rushed into a huge room and paused, for at the other side was a beautiful sight. Here was a large banquet table covered with a white tablecloth and laden with food. Large roasts were partially cut on enormous platters. Disjointed fowl steamed from big bowls. Tossed salads of magnificent proportions lay crisply waiting to be eaten. And goblets of sparkling wine sat inviting before the empty plates. Somehow those goblets appeared almost familiar. Could I dream of goblets and convey them into being?

I rushed to the dinner table and crashed into a wall of firm nothing. An invisible screen held me back. It was a plot, I decided, a mad effort to finally drive me completely over the edge.

Then the door behind me opened. Five men entered, swaggering actually, wearing gaudy costumes and carrying large weapons that to me resembled toy store ray guns. "And what have we here?" their leader exclaimed. "We are just in time for lunch. And who are you?"

I confronted the new group so disoriented now that I really could see no hope. "Joe Daniels. You are LeBloc the pirate."

"My reputation precedes me." He laughed. "Are you a member of the crew or a passenger?"

"Neither. I'm a stowaway. Your coming saved my life, so far."

"Aha. Perhaps you would like to join us. I lost four men on this venture so far."

"Gladly," I replied, looking at the food.

"Fine. We will test the truth of your words later. Now let us enjoy the Captain's repast. Henry, tell the men to come in and get it. Find the suspension button, Jerry."

Someone pushed a button. "Wonderful things, suspension fields," the pirate chief remarked. "A piping hot feast for the Captain and his crew was prepared and we take it out of suspension and eat it for them."

LeBloc walked to the head of the table and sat down. I was motioned to a seat. But no one ate. I was desperately hungry, but surely did not want to offend my new companions by digging in. In a few minutes more men arrived bringing in Lady Jean and the crewman who had accompanied her.

"They were in an escape pod," one of the pirates explained to his chief.

LeBloc laughed loudly. "We always encompass every ship with a suspension field before we attach ourselves to the airlock." The pirate Captain pointed to Lady Jean. "Please sit down, lady." Then he asked the crewman who had been trying to escape with her: "And you, will you join our feast and our company later?"

The man was pale, trembling. "Never," he managed to stammer.

"Spoken like a true man," LeBloc replied. "And this fellow," the Captain pointed to me, "do you know him?"

"Probably a stowaway spy from the Imperial Fleet. We should have killed him at once."

LeBloc raised his eyebrows at this. He nodded at me: "Then perhaps you spoke the truth so far." He turned back to the other man. "Come. We will have to leave our feast for a moment and watch him walk the plank."

LeBlanc arose and his crew did likewise. They all watched Lady Jean closely as we went into the corridor again. How I hated to leave that food. I actually hoped they would dispose of the unfortunate fellow quickly so we could eat. Down the corridor was a large room still filled with the debris and the smoke of battle, wiring burning, bodies strewn about like the last act of Hamlet. I stepped over Captain Gilman's body and several others, unthinking. This was not my war.

We stopped before a solid appearing section of wall. A button was pressed. Then a twenty-foot plank was thrust half way through the now translucent wall, until it wavered half way out of the ship. Pirates lined the interior section of the board.

"Very well, brave lad. Let us see how you die," LeBloc demanded jovially.

"I will die, but they will catch you one day, Sir Pirate."

"Ah yes, we must all go someday. Only today is your day." And LeBloc gave a great Homeric laugh, prodding the crewman onto the plank. LeBloc lacked only the missing hand of Captain Hook, I decided.

"Only take care of Lady Jean," the crewman pleaded.

"I shall take personal care of her," LeBloc promised, laughing again.

The man on the plank turned, as if he might yet try to come back. "Heat pistols burn very badly," a pirate crewman warned.

The man on the plank winced at this, and then turned, walking forward, one step, two, and three. He hesitated and then jumped through the wall, actually taking another step beyond before his body exploded in outer space flying in all directions by the force of its own demolition.

I didn't feel quite as hungry then. He was brave, but there had been nothing I could do. Lady Jean was sobbing as we returned to the banquet hall. She sat through the meal, very straight, very pale, and not eating. Looking at the food was enough to bring my appetite back and I ate very well indeed, eating and then eating more. The wine made me rather giddy since I had been without nourishment for so long. The conversation of the pirate crew around me was reckless, filled with profanity, and loud laughter.

After a bit I began thinking again. I had come to accept things as they happened, and whatever took place next I felt ready to face. New experiences were actually good, pulling one from the rut of constant repetition. If people could have new experiences daily they would grow in intellect or perhaps indeed go mad. I was thinking about madness, living on nerve, on the point of a crackup, and beyond anything sane. There was no reality, no life, no me, no space ship, no asylum, no island, no people, only the great consciousness of being. Maybe this was all some test I was taking.

LeBloc arose, wiping his mouth with a flourish on a lace sleeve. The pirate chief and his crew dressed the part, weather from simple bravado or historical romanticism I did not know. I was still wearing my pajamas topped by the dirty-stripped uniform of the asylum. The pirate chief looked my way, and then motioning to two of his companions, he ordered: "Come, let us test this story of the stowaway. Henry bring the lady aboard our ship and then return to supervise the unloading of the stock of this future space derelict. We have dined well but now we must make our departure quickly."

LeBloc then led the way through the airlock to his own ship the crew and I following. We walked down a narrow hallway to a low-ceilinged laboratory. "Sit in that chair," LeBloc demanded.

I sat reluctantly and was strapped in. The Captain and his men watched the big dial on a connected panel hesitate and then stop at dead center.

"Have you told me the truth in all things so far?" LeBloc asked.

"Yes. I have told the truth." I paused watching as the needle moved to the white half of the dial. LeBloc nodded approvingly, though he seemed obviously surprised. I don't think he really believed me. Suddenly I was very afraid of the questions.

"Now, I do not want you to answer beyond a simple 'yes' or 'no', the pirate Captain ordered. "Have you any plans or even thoughts of harming me, my crew, or my ship?"

"No," I answered truthfully and again the needle moved to the far white side of the dial. LeBloc seemed quite shocked at that answer. But I had never even considered the matter. This was not my war. Actually the pirate's arrival had saved my life.

"Would you prefer to being left in one of our out-stations rather than continuing on with my crew and me?"

I didn't know what the out-stations might be. "I can't answer that 'yes' or 'no', but I believe I would prefer joining your crew."

Again the needle flipped to the white area, a little more uncertainly.

LeBloc smiled at this. "Afraid of something in the out stations maybe. Well, tell me Mr. Daniels, have you ever heard anything about me that would make it difficult for you to work for me?" He evidently felt this was the cincher.

"No," I replied truthfully. "I haven't." I had really heard nothing about him at all until today.

LeBloc looked pleased. "You're my man," he laughed. "And now,' and he took out a gun pointing it straight at my face. As I said before they had monstrously huge guns. "You will answer the next question 'Yes' or I will kill you."

"Yes," I responded, trembling.

"Not yet. The question is: Would you like for me to kill you now?"

I hoped I understood what he was doing, trying to see what the machine registered when I lied. "Yes," I replied, pulling back my head in the chair as far as it would go and waiting for death.

The needle slid all the way over to the black area. LeBloc laughed outrageously loud and suddenly I furiously hated him. Fortunately he asked no more questions, but ordered my straps removed.

Then the Captain asked me: "Are you just a stupid beggar in those clothes? What is the square root of three?"

"1.732," I replied without hesitation.

The Captain nodded. "You do know something. Jackson, get this man some suitable clothes."

Some crew members returned at that moment. "Both the cargo and provisions of the prize are unloaded sir. We are ready to cast loose and destroy the liner."

"Very well. We need to hurry. All crew will assume their positions and stand by."

Jackson gave me a pirate crewman's uniform to wear. Soon I was decked out in fresh underwear, a white shirt, dark pants, and a blue coat. Also I received a pair of what were described as space boots which seemed overly heavy. I was glad to discard my pajamas and dirty asylum clothes.

Later I was allowed in the control room, watching the navigator who was examining star charts. All the while I had a feeling of detached loneliness as if I were not here at all. I felt as a spectator in this drama rather than a participant.

I had avoided death on the island by being transferred to an asylum. I had escaped death in the asylum by being transferred to space. I had escaped death on the space ship by the arrival of the pirates. It was all too fortuitous. Was this a real world or was I in some mad unending dream?

Now that I had eaten and things had calmed down, I felt more able to analyze my plight. First, if there was no reality and had never been a reality, then there was no hope. So I must reject this idea.

I had been shifting to another world after I slept every time. If this were all real, would I be shifted again when I slept? Perhaps if I stayed awake tonight I could control the situation. I resolved to stay awake tonight and see.

I stood in the Control Room with many others of the crew, but had no assigned task. Indeed no one really talked to me, perhaps because they were all busy. I tried to understand the instruments without any luck. I did not dare to exhibit my ignorance, in case I was questioned further so I just stood there waiting.

LeBloc, the pirate Captain, entered and asked me: "Well, what do you think of our ship now?"

I had to say something. "Where are we going?" I asked.

"Our main base. The caves within an asteroid. There are men who would give much to know where." He paused, still judging me, looking me over. I was sorry I had asked the question now, since it probably made me appear suspicious all over again. Then Captain LeBloc added: "We return with our prize."

"And what might that be?" I inquired.

LeBloc looked surprised: "Why the Lady Jean of course. You saw her on board the ship, did you not?"

"Yes, of course." I did not ask more out of fear of giving myself away further.

"What greater prize in these strange years," LeBloc concluded, winking at me. "You stay here a bit. We will put you to work tomorrow." The Captain left the bridge or whatever they called the Control Room on a space ship.

I scratched my head in bewilderment. One of the crew was pressing little buttons on a wide instrument panel, perhaps a computer, and I observed him for a while uncomprehending. Finally I asked: "Have you ever visited a planet with two suns? Have you seen the blue or azure monsters?"

The crewman turned away from his work and looked at me as if I was mad. "What are you talking about?"

"In my travels about the universe, I began," and then I paused.

"There are no such things that I have heard about. Have you been to the out-regions beyond?"

"Yes, briefly," I replied. "The people there," I paused and stopped. I was saying too much.

"There are no people in the out-regions? What is it with you?"

I shook my head. "Sorry. It's all right."

The crewman returned to pushing buttons on his instruments. I was concerned he would tell the Captain about my strange questions. These men had traveled in nearby space. Probably in the last two days I had been on two completely different planes of existence. Multi-dimensional theory was what I had been working on back on earth.

I tried to understand my situation. Were co-existent universes possible? I had been working on multi-dimensional propulsion, but when we tried our small model on a monkey it simply disappeared. Well I had disappeared too. The asylum I was in yesterday had seemed like late medieval earth, only a different earth taken over by alien creatures. I had exposed myself to no rays or machinery, so how did I get there.

Then a new thought came my way. Suppose Peter Quinn and Chuck Jax had built a larger multi-dimensional mechanism and I had been exposed to it? In that case I might have been sent anywhere, without pattern, without hope of ever returning. They could get rid of me. Was I being shunted about at random? There was nothing in our theories and certainly nothing in the mechanism to control such traveling. But even that theory was better than being insane.

At last there was a call to dinner. We sat down to another sumptuous repast during which the wine flowed freely again. I drank very little, wanting a clear head. Afterwards Harry, who seemed to be First Officer and wore a uniform only slightly less splendid than the Captain, showed me to the bunk where I might sleep that night. The bunks were built right into the walls in a long narrow room. Here perhaps twenty men might sleep. When I asked, Harry explained the crew slept strapped in, in case the gravity simulators failed or something else went wrong. Harry seemed surprised at my inquiries and wanted to know if I had been to space before.

I replied "Not often," wondering how long I could keep up this deception.

It was obvious I would need a cover story of some kind to explain to the crew why I did not want to lie down in my assigned bunk. Of course I did not want to lie down for fear I would drift off to sleep and disappear again to someplace even stranger and more fantastic.

"Look," I asked of Harry, "is there anything I could do tonight to earn my way. I have not done anything to help our cause as yet. I do not feel tired and require very little sleep anyway."

"It is refreshing to hear someone volunteer for duty," Harry, the first officer, declared. "You don't seem to know much about space ships, but the Captain feels you are trustworthy. I will issue you a small stun gun and you will stand guard outside Lady Jean's room tonight. You are not to enter the room itself under penalty. An alarm will be set to make sure of that. You are to prevent anyone else from entering. The crew is well behaved, but she is a female after all. If someone tries to enter the room, warn them and then shoot. There will be enough problems with Lady Jean when we land. Come, I will show you to her room's door. Can you do this?"

"Yes," I agreed.

Harry led me down corridors to Lady Jean's door. "You may sit on one of these pull out seats or stand here," he advised. "And one final thing, I will have the cabin boy check on you each hour, in case you want food or drink. You will not budge from this post. Since you volunteered for this duty, let me state precisely that if you are found asleep by the cabin boy, you will be executed. Do you understand? This is important."

"Yes. I shall stay awake." Harry spoke further and then left. I actually chuckled aloud. Now I would have to stay awake. If I were transferred to another universe tonight I could watch it happen. Maybe! Anyway if I disappeared the pirates could not kill me. But was there such a thing as night in space? And if I became impossibly sleepy tomorrow and took a nap anyway, what then?

I heard a click behind me and turned about just in time to see Lady Jean peering at me through a tiny panel of the door that she had opened at the top. She shut the opening quickly when she saw me.

"You have nothing to fear from me," I whispered.

She opened the tiny aperture once more. "You are the stowaway," she declared, "the traitor in league with the pirates. You are the worst of the lot. You are in the pirate uniform now, showing your true colors."

I shrugged. "You may think of me as you like. I meant no harm to your ship or to you especially. I joined this crew only so my life would be spared."

Lady Jean's eyes opened wide: "But where did you come from then? How did you get past the guards at the door and in the bed above me? The door was locked and I am a light sleeper. The Captain questioned me. He thought you were my lover and I had managed to smuggle you on board."

"I do not know how I came to your cabin. I can tell you my story but it does not explain much."

"So tell me your story," she suggested, seeming to disbelieve me before I started.

So I told her a condensed version of my story. As I did so I began to see some possibilities I had not considered before. I concluded by saying: "Now you tell me. Is this existence real? Am I mad? What should I do?"

"Your story is incredible," Lady Jean replied at last. "Still it is the only explanation I have heard so far that would bring you to my cabin. No, I do not believe you are mad or dreaming, unless perhaps I too am mad and dreaming and our dreams have coincided."

"Why," I asked, "do the pirates consider you such a prize?" I stopped abruptly, realizing what I was saying, and added: "I mean you are very lovely, but surely there are other women. Are you an aristocrat, from a rich or noble family? It is not that you are just a woman." I stopped, realizing I was becoming more involved by the moment and not saying appropriate things.

"Now I almost believe your story," Lady Jean ventured to reply. She looked at me hard in silence through the small door opening before continuing: "You see it is just because I am a woman that I am considered a prize. There are not enough women. I do not understand the politics very well. I only know there have been interplanetary wars. In this absurd war, someone developed a gender specific plague which rendered most of the women on the larger home planets barren. Only a few women were plague-resistant. I am one of these."

"Good Heavens," I exclaimed. "But why then were you taken on a space ship?"

I could see Lady Jean flush through the door opening. "I am an article of trade. I am an export commodity."

"Yes, but," again I hesitated, but I had to ask: "how many pirates could you mate with?"

She flushed more brightly now. "You really don't know! My eggs will be taken. I will be harvested."

She went right on, desiring to change the subject: "But what the pirates do not know is that there were three ships in my convoy. There were two battle cruisers as escorts. We were attacked by a Larmathion flotilla, a poor group of fighters, but they were enough to separate us temporarily. The battle cruisers went off, but they will return soon to the original site. The escorts will pick up our trail. By now they will have found the space flotsam of the ship I was on."

"The pirates have a base in an asteroid cave somewhere," I said. "Once we reach that, they believe they won't be found." I motioned her to shut the door opening for I heard footsteps.

It was the cabin boy. I told him I wanted nothing and he departed. Lady Jean returned to the door opening. "I have been thinking," she suggested. "If a light wave signal could be sent, the ships of my escort could track us more quickly."

"I can't leave this post and I know nothing of the machinery of this ship," I told her.

She sighed.

"If you are indeed just an article of export, than I can't see what difference it makes whether you go with the pirates or not."

"It does. The pirates will sell me to the highest bidder and some of the methods employed are not pretty." She broke off suddenly sobbing.

I tried to comfort her, but she bid me goodnight and shut the door. I wished then that I had inquired if these people were originally from earth and what year this might be.

The cabin boy came by each hour and I asked for coffee to stay awake. The cabin boy was a thin, nervous, furtive adolescent who seemed to hope to catch me asleep so he could report me.

When I was alone I sat down in the corridor and toyed with the weapon, the stun gun I had been given, until after a bit I understood how to shoot it. At length I felt quite drowsy, so that I could easily have fallen asleep. I arose and began pacing to stay awake.

Finally I inquired of the cabin boy as he made his rounds, "When is breakfast? How soon will we arrive at our base?"

The lad replied: "Morning call for the crew is in an hour and you should be replaced then. Breakfast is in two hours. I don't know when we will reach anywhere."

I reflected again on my plight as I waited. In the next hour I might disappear or continue on this ship. Then I would know if I traveled only during my sleep. Was it my fate to remain a pirate?

A bell rang throughout the ship, probably announcing the morning had arrived as far as this ship was concerned. I had no watch and a watch would be useless anyway, for time must be entirely arbitrary in space.

The cabin boy was sauntering down the corridor in that peculiar gait which I might dub spaceman's wobble. There was another crewman with him. Again he seemed displeased to find me awake, so he could report me. "Anything more for you now, sir," he asked.

"No."

The other man was yawning, but informed me: "I'm Hank Wright, sent to relieve you."

Just then there was another bell, a sharp staccato alarm and Hank jumped. "We're under attack." He looked at the cabin boy and ordered: "You boy, stay here and if you leave, you know the penalty."

The lad nodded solemnly. "Come with me, Daniels," Hank ordered me.

We both raced down the corridor. Abruptly the ship began careening from side to side. "Quickly, the magnetics," Hank instructed. And he reached down to a button on the top of his boots. When I stood there stupidly he switched on my boots as well. Immediately my feet felt like they weighed fifty pounds apiece. But we both remained upright as the ships motion became worse. I followed Hank as best I could, a steady blundering pace lifting one foot after the other slowly.

"This is serious," Hank informed me. "We are so near our base that even if we escape, they may find our base."

Now we reached the open Control Room, a scene filled with action. There were crew men all over at various controls none of which I understood. LeBloc stood in the middle, his feet wide apart, giving orders. "They have a fix on us. If we can get beyond the rim of the asteroid then we have a chance," he said.

At that moment the ship pitched violently, sending me over backwards, although my feet felt glued to the floor. I just sat there. A rumbling explosion followed and the great ship computer screen before us cracked down the center. The lights dimmed and smoke filled the room smelling like burning wiring and overheated plastic.

"Keep those resisters up," LeBloc hollered above the din. He was still standing even in the pandemonium around him, but his sang-froid was fading.

I sat rubbing my knees, wondering if I should even try to get up. I decided I would just sit out this battle.

"Resistors at point twenty-seven," called a crewman's voice.

"No wonder. They slammed us around with that last blast," LeBloc moaned. "Get the power back up."

"We're four units from the asteroid rim," Harry, the first officer, declared.

"Losing air fast," a crewman managing the controls announced. "We'll have to put on space suits."

"No time for that," LeBloc countered firmly. "We'll have to make it now or we're lost. Give it more power."

"We're overloaded now," Harry replied. "We're only three units away from the rim."

"Five more robot bombs on the left screen coming in at nine o'clock," another voice declared.

"Resistors down to point nineteen," a crew man reported.

"Turn the fans on full," LeBloc ordered. "There are two Imperial ships out there, both bigger than we are. We can't turn and fight."

"The air's bad now, sir. We'll lose what's left."

"You heard me," LeBloc ordered. "Damn the air in here. We have to see. We're being destroyed."

The fans came on and the air did clear, but the oxygen felt very thin.

"Two units from the asteroid rim," Harry declared at last.

"Resistors at point twelve."

Sweat stood out on LeBloc's forehead. "We have to keep the force screen resisters above point ten. Can we switch to direct power?"

"We'll blow the main controls. We're functioning beyond ship limits now."

"Hand me that communicator," LeBloc ordered. Suddenly he seemed to notice me for the first time as I sat uselessly on the floor. "Go get Lady Jean," he told me, flinging a key that I caught.

I arose unsteadily, moving as quickly as possible with the magnetic boots. Suddenly I wished I had slept last night and been transported elsewhere. Where was elsewhere? Well, why not back home?

The ship was convulsed with a series of shocks.

Ahead the cabin boy was standing outside Lady Jean's room. He was frightened. "What's happening?" he pleaded. "We're going to get away aren't we? We always do."

"I'm to bring Lady Jean to the Captain," I told him. I unlocked the door. "Come with me, please," I prompted Lady Jean.

She looked to see who it was in the dim corridor and then came out. I guessed the battle was diverting most of the power in the ship to the resistors, whatever they were. "Oh, it's you Joe," she said. "What's happening? Is it the ships of my people?"

"I don't know. I am to bring you to the Control Room and the Captain."

She shrank back now. "Oh, if you could help me, you would be rewarded."

"How would I be rewarded? You said yourself you are an export commodity."

"On this colony I would be treated like a queen," she declared.

"A queen bee," I hazarded.

She winced at this. The ship gave another massive shudder. "Hurry," I told her, lightly taking her wrist. "Let us see what is happening?"

She was perhaps as curious of the outcome as I, so she followed along, both our magnetic boots clanging. The cabin boy came behind us mechanically. The air was thin and cold enough for my breath to show white.

"Resistors are at point eight. Their next blasts will come right through," a terrified voice greeted us before we rounded the final corner.

"We're so close: right at the rim of the asteroid now. One more minute and we're there." I recognized Harry's voice, the first officer.

"We'll have that minute," growled LeBloc. "There's Lady Jean." Immediately I wished I had not hurried so.

We were standing at the alcove entrance to the Control Room, LeBloc still firmly in the middle. I understood his intentions even before he spoke: "This is Captain LeBloc speaking to the Imperial fleet," he bellowed, microphone in hand.

"Come in LeBloc. It is time you answered our signal. Halt your ship and surrender or we will use our torpedoes."

"Switch to internal screen so they can see us," the pirate Captain demanded. "There. Lady Jean is standing right here. If you fire again I will personally blast her down."

I still had Lady Jean by the wrist, and I felt her tense. Out of the thoughts swirling in my mind, I remembered that I still had the stun gun under my belt.

There was a moment of silence from the attacking ships. Harry's voice came in a whisper. "Thirty seconds and we'll be in the clear."

"Let Lady Jean speak to us," a voice replied from the other ship.

LeBloc motioned to me: "Bring her here, Daniels."

And then abruptly I decided. I pulled out the stun gun and fired at LeBloc who fell over. Next I fired at the men at the controls. One of them pitched into the computer and there was a puff of explosion. The ship reeled, seeming out of control.

"Get him," Harry shouted, but I cut Harry down next. Then I pulled Lady Jean out of the room. She followed willingly. Blast guns fired at us. We were around the corner now, snaking through the winding corridor on magnetic boots. Then there was a great crash and the lights went out entirely. We both fell forward, which was fortunate, for blasters arced above our heads down the corridor.

The ship had hit the asteroid. The air was being sucked out everywhere. I took one last great breath and tried to hold it.

Ahead of me I saw three men in space suits, powerful flashlights on their headgear lighting the way. They were coming toward us and fired at the pirate crew. We had been boarded.

The air was so thin and I was so tired that it was best to just lie there. The lowest area would have the most air. But above all I must not fall asleep.

Now oxygen masks were being given to us. Lady Jean got her mask first. The invading party seemed uncertain about me until Lady Jean declared: "He saved me."

"Is this where you wanted to go?" I asked Lady Jean.

"Yes," she replied. "I did not want to be the pirate's prisoner. Thank you."

I did not pass out, but the next hour was almost a dream. I was conducted to the Imperial ship, thanked, fed, given a sedative, and then put to bed. At this last crucial moment I wondered if I would again be transported to some unlikely location when I went to sleep. Perhaps if I thought hard about returning to my own earth, my own city, my own time, maybe the morning of that fateful last day, somehow I could make everything right. And then everything seemed to come together for me.

On that fateful night in New York I had been out drinking with Chuck Jax. Then I went home, found my apartment hot, opened a window, and during the night I was very cold. I dreamt of a warm beach, water to drink, warm sunlight, and then I awakened on this island. Why two suns? Was I thinking double due to drinking?

Anyway after I spent a day on that island thinking I was crazy and believing I belonged in an asylum, wondering about alien worlds and about what creatures might inhabit the interior of the island I was on, then I awoke in an asylum run by hideous monsters. I found the blue monsters came from outer space. I went to sleep that night thinking of space ships, women, and food, wishing I were in an environment where I could fight with a chance to win and change things, rather than an island or an asylum where there was no hope to change anything. No wonder those wine goblets on the banquet table had looked familiar. I had really pictured them in my dream of food and drink. Then I awoke on a space ship, inside a woman's quarters, with plenty of food nearby and an opportunity to fight and change things all right. I had enough of adventure now.

Sometimes it takes a while for the facts to add up. At first I had been in a state of shock. Then gradually as I was shunted from one universe or dimension to another, I began to realize there was a pattern after all. Now under the calming effect of the sedative it all seemed to fall into place. But how had it all started?

Somehow I had been the guinea pig in an experiment. I had been exposed to a multi-dimensional propulsion unit of the kind I had helped design. And the triggering mechanism was simply my last thoughts on falling asleep. I not only had to go back to my own time, but earlier in the day to see what had happened. I had to think of a time, a day, and a place. It is difficult to hold onto specific thoughts as you fall asleep, but the sedative I had been given actually calmed me and helped.

*　　*　　*

And I awoke in my own bed. The clock was pointed directly at noon. I hadn't believed it really would work. I used my telephone to check the time and exact date. I took off the uniform of the space pirates and hid it carefully. Next I spent some time looking for my best suit. Then I realized that I was wearing that suit at work right now. Yes, it was just after noon on the day I would have my final argument with Peter Quinn and quit. That would be in about two hours. Then I would say goodbye to everybody. Afterwards I would pack my things from the lab and my desk in the trunk of my car. Then as I left Chuck Jax would suggest I meet him at a bar we both frequented and have a talk.

It was fantastic, but I had to be correct now.

So I put on another suit and then took a taxi down to my former office. I watched an hour later from across the street when I made the first of several trips to my car. It is odd watching yourself. Looking at yourself in the mirror is not the same as actually seeing yourself.

For a moment I thought of going over and talking to myself. But what would that do to the timeline, if such things as timelines existed? Instead I used my cell phone and called Mr. Al Larabee, one of the Foundation directors who had given us the original grant for this work. Larabee was a thin, gray, older man, but he had been a friend of my father. I am particularly fond of him and I think he liked and trusted me. I asked to see him right away and took a taxi to his huge office.

He naturally thought I was crazy, "finally cracked under the strain," he phrased it.

"Only hear me out this one time, and if this does not come off as I predict, then you can have me committed or whatever."

Larabee agreed rather reluctantly and we picked up a police detective he knew. The detective was even more skeptical, but I am sure he thought it would be amusing to see this through one way or the other. So we took a taxi out near my apartment to the bar I would be in with Chuck Jax right now. Larabee and the detective went into the bar and ascertained from a little distance that the earlier me was actually there. Now both Larabee and the detective were more nearly convinced that this was worth investigating. We waited outside in the taxi until Chuck Jax and the earlier me left the bar. Then the three of us followed to my apartment from a distance and watched in the tree shadows across the street.

When Chuck Jax left my place Peter Quinn drove up and met Jax. They waited in front and we investigators watched down the street. After a while the lights in my bedroom went off. Quinn unloaded two large suitcases from his car, which were carried into my apartment. Jax must have taken my keys as he departed. My keys were always left hanging on a hook at the door.

I explained what I surmised, that Peter Quinn wanted to get rid of me so he could market the multi-dimensional propulsion unit as his own.

They would probably search my apartment and leave with the design drawings I had. I was to just disappear.

We waited an hour, and when the two men did not come out, we three went in. According to our plan Larabee and the police detective went in first. Jax and Quinn denied they were burglars or had harmed me. Their story was that I had quit and disappeared. They added they were searching my apartment because I had made off with some of their property. The apartment was a mess and had certainly been ransacked.

About then I came in the door. Jax and Quinn changed their story at once, saying contradictory and amusing things while trying to laugh it all off as a joke. "Joe Daniels is all right," Quinn declared, "for since he is here, no harm had been done."

When I suggested we set up the apparatus again and use it as an experiment on them instead, they broke down and confessed.